# Samantha Moon Rising

Including Books 5, 6, and 7 in the Vampire for Hire Series:
VAMPIRE DAWN, VAMPIRE GAMES, MOON ISLAND

*Plus the Short Story "Teeth"*

## J.R. RAIN

BENBELLA BOOKS | DALLAS, TEXAS

Vampire Dawn © 2012 by J.R. Rain
Vampire Games © 2012 by J.R. Rain
Moon Island © 2012 by J.R. Rain
Teeth © 2010 by J.R. Rain

BenBella Books, Inc.
10300 N. Central Expressway, Suite #530
Dallas, TX 75231
www.benbellabooks.com
Send feedback to feedback@benbellabooks.com

Printed in the United States of America
10 9 8 7 6 5 4 3 2 1

Library of Congress Cataloging-in-Publication Data

Rain, J. R.
  [Novels. Selections]
  Samantha Moon Rising / J.R. Rain.
       pages cm. — (Vampire for Hire Series)
  "Including Books 5, 6, and 7 in the Vampire for Hire series: Vampire Dawn, Vampire Games, Moon Island, plus the short story Teeth."
  ISBN 978-1-937856-82-3 (pbk.)
  1. Vampires—Fiction.  I. Rain, J. R. Vampire dawn.  II. Rain, J. R. Vampire games.  III. Rain, J. R. Moon island.  IV. Title.
  PS3618.A389A6 2013
  813'.6—dc23
                                                    2012051816

Proofreading by Brittany Dowdle and Laura Cherkas
Cover design by Sarah Dombrowsky
Text design and composition by Integra Software Services Pvt. Ltd.
Printed by Berryville Graphics

Distributed by Perseus Distribution
www.perseusdistribution.com
To place orders through Perseus Distribution:
Tel: 800-343-4499
Fax: 800-351-5073
E-mail: orderentry@perseusbooks.com

Significant discounts for bulk sales are available. Please contact Glenn Yeffeth at glenn@benbellabooks.com or (214) 750-3628.

# CONTENTS

BOOK 5

# Vampire Dawn

*Vampire for Hire #5*

DEDICATION

*To Scott Nicholson and Aiden James.*
*Great friends, great writers.*


ACKNOWLEDGMENTS

*A special thank-you to the following readers: Beth*
*Lidiak, Kathy Woodard, Leslie Whitaker, Lori Lilja, Holly*
*Sanders, Rhonda Plumhoff, Sandy Gillberg, Andrea*
*DaSilva, Amanda Winger-Stabley, Carmen Vazquez-*
*Rodriguez, Mary Adam-Dussel, Vicki Dussel and Michelle*
*Craig Sanders. Thank you all for your help!*

They had forgotten the first lesson, that we are to be powerful, beautiful, and without regret.

—*Interview with the Vampire*

I can smell the sunlight on your skin.

—*True Blood*

# Vampire Dawn

# 1.

It was early afternoon and I was vacuuming.

Others like me were, undoubtedly, sleeping contentedly in crypts or coffins or castle keeps. Me, I was vacuuming up bits of pretzels and popcorn. Last night was movie night, and the kids had picked *Captain America*, and I did my best not to drool over the bowl of popcorn I pretended to eat. Yes, I have to *pretend* to eat around my children. Since I'm unable to eat any real food, I'd become a master of hiding my food in napkins, in the bottom of sodas, and even on others' plates. More than once little Anthony had turned to look at something that I pointed at, only to discover that he had, remarkably, even *more* fries in his Happy Meal. Miracles do happen.

As I vacuumed, I caught snatches of Judge Judy wagging her finger at a cheating young man who looked like he was on the verge of tears, but then again, that could have just been wishful thinking. After all, there's something special about watching a strong woman reduce a dirtbag to tears.

Maybe it's the devil in me.

Or the cheated-on wife in me.

At any rate, I had just put away the vacuum and straightened the pillows on the couch when the doorbell rang. I flipped down my sunglasses and, after mentally preparing myself for the short blast of sunlight that I was about to experience, I opened the door.

I always gasp when I'm exposed to sunlight, and now was no exception. Even with the shades on. Even with the sunscreen I wear indoors. Even with all the layers of clothing I presently had on. I always gasp. Every time.

Standing in the doorway was a big man. Not as big as Kingsley or even my new detective friend, Jim Knighthorse, but certainly big enough. Detective Sherbet of the Fullerton Police Department was one of the few people who knew my super-secret identity. I hadn't planned on telling him what I was, but the detective was no dummy.

So I had decided to come clean, and he had proven to be a true friend. Not only had he maintained my secret, he sought my assistance.

Like now, apparently.

I absently adjusted my hair. For someone who was insecure at best, not having full use of a mirror was a major setback. Although I could make out the general shape of my face in a mirror if I was wearing enough make-up, my hair, strangely, didn't reflect.

I mean, what the hell is that all about?

I knew the answer, but that didn't make it any easier to accept. On that accursed night seven years ago when I was forever changed, my body had somehow crossed from the natural world into the supernatural world. A world where mirrors were no longer relevant.

"You look fine, Samantha," said Detective Sherbet. "Quit worrying."

I stepped aside as he moved past me. He was carrying a greasy bag that looked suspiciously like donuts. I quickly shut the door behind him.

I turned and faced him, recovering from the shock of sunlight. "Why did you say that?" I asked.

"Say what?" he asked, easing his considerable bulk down onto my new couch. The couch was one of those L-shaped deals that a mother and her two kids could get comfy in. At least, that was the theory. In practice, getting comfy with Anthony invariably meant dealing with a steady onslaught of gas.

"That thing you said about not worrying."

Sherbet was already rooting around for his first donut. "Because you sounded worried."

I leaned a shoulder against the door. "Except I didn't say anything, Detective."

Sherbet plucked a pink cake donut from the depths of the bag and, looking imminently pleased, was just bringing it to his mouth when he paused. He didn't look happy pausing. "Yes you did, Sam."

"No, I didn't."

"You were talking about make-up and not seeing your hair in the mirror—and I gotta tell you, kid, you nearly bored me to tears." Now he happily resumed consuming the donut. Watching such a big man, such a distinguished man, eat a little pink donut was, well, cute.

I moved away from the door and crossed the living room, noticing for the first time a pair of Anthony's dirty skivvies jammed into the corner of the couch, maybe two feet away from Sherbet. How and why they got there would be an interesting conversation between Anthony and me later.

For now, though, I sat next to the toxic undies, so close to Sherbet that I was nearly in his lap. The big detective looked at me curiously but didn't say anything. I casually felt for the dirty skivvies, found them, wadded them up, and stood. I was certain Sherbet hadn't seen me, although he was watching me curiously. Then he looked at the unfinished pink donut, turned a little green, and dropped it back into the bag, which he promptly set on the floor between his feet.

He said, "Geez, Sam. Talk about your donut buzz kill."

"What do you mean?"

"The dirty underwear talk. Look, kid, I've got a boy, too, and I've seen my fair share of skid marks. But you sure as hell don't need to go on and on about them while a guy's trying to enjoy a donut, especially after the day I've had."

"But I didn't say anything, Detective."

"Of course you did."

"No, I didn't. Just like I didn't say anything about my hair."

"I heard it plain as day."

"No, Detective, you didn't."

He looked up at me from the new couch. There was a bit of pink frosting already caught in his thick, cop mustache. He looked at me, frowned, and then slowly wiped his mustache clean.

He said, "Your lips never moved."

"No, they didn't."

"But I heard that bit about the frosting in my mustache."

"Apparently."

"What's going on, Sam?"

"I think," I said, sitting next to him and patting him on the knee, "that you're reading my mind."

"Your mind?"

"Yes."

"Ah, hell."

# 2.

After a moment, Sherbet said, "What, exactly, does that mean, Samantha?"

"It means exactly that, Detective. You're reading my mind."

The detective didn't look so good. He sat forward, rubbed his eyes with a hand that was bigger than even Kingsley's. I noticed scarring on his knuckles that I had missed before. He looked down at his own knuckles, and said, "I used to be a fighter. A brawler, really. A real hothead back in the day."

"You're doing it again, Detective."

"But you said—"

"I didn't say anything."

Some of the color drained from his face. "I feel sick."

"Hang on, Detective."

I left him alone for a moment while I tossed Anthony's undies in the laundry room. When I returned, the big detective was apparently over his initial shock. He was not only holding the greasy bag of donuts, but had just consumed the last of the pink donut. All was right in the world.

"Not quite," said Sherbet, licking his fingers, but then suddenly stopped. He looked up at me. "I'm doing it again, ain't I?"

"Yes, you are."

"What's happening to me, Sam?"

I sat next to him and gave him my "penny for your thoughts" face. He smelled of Old Spice and donut grease.

I said, "You're not losing your mind, Detective. Sometimes those closest to me have access to my thoughts. I also suspect it's because you're one of the few who know what I really am. I've put a lot of trust in you. And you in me. It has something to do with that." I smiled brightly at him. "So, as you can see, having access to my thoughts is a rare privilege."

He snorted. "I feel honored." He was about to turn back to his bag of donuts when a thought occurred to him. "So does that mean you have access to my thoughts, too?"

"It does."

"I'm not sure how I feel about that."

"Don't worry, Detective. Your deep, dark secrets are safe with me. Besides, I won't access your thoughts unless you give me permission."

"Do you know how crazy that sounds, Sam?"

"I do."

"Are we both crazy?"

"Maybe."

Sherbet stared at me. He was an old-school homicide investigator. Strictly by the books. Just the facts, ma'am. Logical, rational, tough, fair, street smart. A skilled investigator. Then one day a vampire appeared in his life—granted, a cute and spunky vampire—and his neat little world came crashing down.

"I wouldn't say crashing down, Sam. Maybe turned upside down a little. And, yes, I know I'm reading your thoughts again."

I grinned. "Maybe we should get to why you're here."

He sat straighter. "Gladly. Which is an odd thing to say about a serial killer."

"He struck again," I said.

Sherbet nodded. "Corona this time."

"Drained of blood?"

He nodded. "Completely. Same M.O. Massive wound in the neck. Knife wound, we think. Bruising around the ankles. Found this one wrapped in a blanket in a ditch."

"Female?"

"Male."

"So he's alternating his kills," I said. "Male, female, male."

Sherbet thought about that. He also thought about another donut. A moment later he was pulling out a strawberry French cruller that looked all kinds of delicious.

"It will be," he said, reading my mind again without realizing it. "And I suppose the killer is. Three males, and two females. As you know, that doesn't fit the typical profile. Serial killers tend to stick to one gender."

"Unless they're after something besides kicks."

"They? You think there might be more than one killer?"

"Like you said, it doesn't fit the profile."

"Same pattern, though."

"All drained of blood," I said.

"The work of a vampire?" he said.

"The work of someone," I said. I found myself watching his every move as he worked on the cruller. Crullers had been my favorite. "Vampires don't need that much blood."

Sherbet stopped chewing. "And how much blood does a vampire need?"

"Sixteen ounces or so, every few days."

At least, that's how much were in the packets of animal blood I received monthly from the Norco butchery.

Sherbet stared at me openly, even forgetting to close his mouth as he chewed. Still, seeing the half-masticated cruller did not kill my brief donut craving. He asked, "And what happens if you don't get your blood?"

I shrugged. "I turn into a raving, blood-sucking maniac who prowls the streets looking for victims. Prostitutes mostly, but sometimes hipsters at Starbucks, or those young guys who dance around street corners holding signs pointing to furniture stores going out of business."

"Are you quite done, Sam?"

"Quite."

He reached inside his light jacket and removed some folded papers. "Here are my notes on the latest victim. Read through them, see what you can find."

"Will do, Detective."

Months ago, when the case had turned from weird to weirder, Sherbet had hired me to be an official consultant on the case.

His fellow detectives didn't like it; after all, why hire a private dick? Well, what they didn't know wouldn't kill them.

Sherbet eased his bulk off the couch and stood, knuckling his lower back. "You're one freaky chick, you know."

"Words every chick wants to hear."

He quit knuckling and looked at me with so much compassion that tears nearly came to my eyes. He reached out and pulled me in for the mother of all bear hugs. He said, "I'm sorry all this happened to you, Sam."

I hugged him back. "I know."

"You're going to be okay, kid."

"Thank you."

He stepped away. "Now, let's catch the son-of-a-bitch who's doing this to these people."

"We will, Detective."

He seemed about to do something, then nodded and left, gripping his bag of donuts like a lifeline.

# 3.

At 3:30 p.m. on an overcast Tuesday afternoon, lathered in Aveeno SPF 100 sunscreen, I dashed out my door and sprinted across my front yard as if my life depended on it.

And I'm pretty sure it did.

Despite the gray skies, the thick jacket, and the layer of greasy sunscreen, my skin still felt like it was on fire. My garage is not attached. Back in the day, my ex-husband didn't think we needed an attached garage. Houses with unattached garages were cheaper.

*Thanks, asshole.*

Of course, little did he know that one day the sun would be my enemy and I would have to endure daily torturous mid-afternoon sprints.

Anyway, at the garage, I fumbled with the Master Lock until I got the key in and opened the sucker. I noticed my hands were already shaking and reddening. Any longer and they would begin blistering.

*I'm such a freak.*

I yanked open the garage door far harder than I probably should have. The thing nearly tore off its rusty tracks. Once it was open, I dashed inside and breathed a small sigh of relief, even though there was never really any relief for me. Not during the day, at least. Not when I should be sleeping in a dark room with the blinds pulled shut and dead to the world.

I started the van, cranked up the AC, and let it cool my burning flesh. Finally, I backed out of the garage and headed for my kids' school.

Just another day in the neighborhood.

• • •

After picking up the kids and spending the evening helping them with their homework, I called up a new sitter I'd been using lately, a very responsible sixteen-year-old girl. Luckily, she was available, and when she arrived, I hugged my kids and kissed them and told them to be good. Mercifully, neither shuddered at my cold touch. Cold lips, cold fingers, and cold hugs were the norm in our family. Still, Anthony promptly wiped his kiss off.

"Gross, Mom," he said, never taking his eyes off his video game, giving it far more concentration than he ever did his homework. As an added precaution, he absently raised his shoulder, using it to wipe his cheek clean.

Now, with the sun mercifully far behind planet Earth, I found myself heading east on the 91 Freeway. Me, and nearly all of Southern California, too. I settled in for the long commute, tempted, as usual, to pull over and take flight.

Instead, I sat back and turned up the radio and tried to remember what life was like before I became what I currently am.

But I couldn't. At least, not really, and that scared the hell out of me. My new reality dominated all aspects of my life, all thoughts and all actions, and as I followed a sea of red taillights and bad drivers, I realized my humanity was slipping further and further away.

I hate when that happens.

# 4.

The crime scene wasn't much of a crime scene. It also wasn't too hard to find. At least, not for me.

Using Sherbet's notes, I soon found an area of road that had recently seen a lot of activity. The dirt was grooved deeply with tires, and there was even some crime scene tape left behind in one of the sage brushes.

I parked my minivan off the side of the winding road and got out. Yes, there are actually winding roads in Southern California. At least, up here in these mostly barren hills. Winter rain had given life to some of the dried-out seedlings that baked during the spring, summer, and fall seasons, which, out here in the high desert, was really just one long-ass summer. The stiff grass gave the hill some color, even at night. At least, to my eyes.

I shut the door and beeped it locked. Why I beeped it locked, I didn't know. I was alone up here on the hillside, parked inside a turnout, hidden in shadows and what few bushes there were.

Which made it even more remarkable that the body had even been found in the first place.

According to Sherbet's notes, a city worker making his routine rounds had come upon the body. He might not have found it, either, if not for the turkey vultures and the foul smell.

Predictably, it hadn't been a pretty sight.

Like the others, this one was rolled up in a dirty sheet and tied off on both ends. The same type of sheet, every time. A sheet commonly sold at Wal-Mart, of all places. The vultures had gotten through the sheet, using their powerful beaks. Apparently, they had made a meal of the intestines, but that's as far as they got before the worker showed up.

I had seen a handful of corpses back in my days as a federal agent. But, mercifully, I had never seen a human body eaten by vultures. I was glad Sherbet spared me the photos.

Yes, even vampires get queasy.

The air was cool and crisp. I was wearing jeans and a light jacket, although I really didn't need a jacket. I wore it because I thought it looked cute. Really, when you're as cold on the inside as the weather is on the outside, jackets are a moot point.

Unless they're cute.

The air was heavy with sage and juniper and smelled so fresh that it was easy to forget that bustling Orange County was just forty-five minutes away.

I studied the crime scene. It was a mess. What few plants there were had been trampled. Footprints everywhere. Tire prints. And deeper gouges into the earth that I knew were from the Corona mobile command. A trailer they hauled out to process evidence, or as much as they could, right there on the spot. I even found two deep ruts in the road that I seriously suspected were from a helicopter's skids. It was a wonder the rotor downdraft hadn't erased all the other tracks.

I scanned the area, looking deeper into the darkness than I had any right to see, seeing things that I probably shouldn't. I'm talking about energy. Spirit energy. Even in the desert I sense and see energy. Small explosions of light that appear and disappear. These are faint. Mere whispers.

What I wasn't seeing was perhaps more telling. There was no lost spirit here. No lost *human* spirit.

Which told me something. It told me that I was either completely insane and lost my mind years ago and was currently babbling away at some mental hospital, or that the victim had been killed elsewhere.

I was hoping it was the latter. Although, trust me, there were times I actually hoped it was the former.

Anyway, what I didn't see is the bright, static energy that often makes up a human spirit. That is, one who has once lived and passed on. The newer the spirit, the sharper they come into focus. I've gotten used to seeing such spirits these days. I'm a regular Sylvia Browne, although you won't find me on Montel Williams. At least, not yet. Maybe if he asks nicely.

Then again, I had a tendency to not show up in photographs or video.

*So much for my talk show circuit,* I thought, as I circled the area where the body had been found. As I did so, the wind picked up, lifting my hair, flapping my jacket.

I tried to get a feel for the land, for what had been here. For *who* had been here, but these psychic gifts of mine were relatively new and I was only getting fleeting images. One of those fleeting images was that of the body still lying undisturbed on the ground, wrapped in the dirty sheet.

I went back to the spot where the body had been found and knelt to examine the ground. There was nothing left of the crime scene, of course. The investigators had been all over it.

Most telling, there hadn't been any blood. As I knelt in this spot with my eyes closed, feeling the wind, hearing the rustle of dried leaves, I heard something else.

A voice. No, a memory of a voice. A hauntingly familiar voice. Deep and rich. Telling someone to dump the body here. Good, good. Let's go.

And that's all the psychic hits I got.

No, not quite. Another memory came to me. Another image. A snapshot, really. I saw a bag. Lying in a deep ravine.

Except there were damn ravines everywhere. Hell, there were ravines within ravines. I only had to think about it for a second or two before I started stripping out of my clothes.

Right there at the crime scene.

# 5.

There's nothing like being naked in the desert.

Seriously. With my clothing folded on the hood of my van, I stepped across the cool dirt, picked my way through a tangle of elderberry and carefully stepped around a patch of beavertail cactus. I moved past the general area where the body had been found and headed deeper into the empty hills.

The desert scents were heady and intoxicating. Sage and juniper and creosote. Pungent, sharp and whispery. The desert sand itself seemed to have a scent all its own, too. Something ancient that hinted at death, at life, of survival and of distant memories. This place, so close to civilization, yet so far removed, too, smelled as it had for eons, for millenniums. The sand, I knew, was sprinkled with the bones of the dead. Dead vermin, dead coyotes, dead anything and everything that ever ventured into these bleak hills.

I continued through the empty landscape. I was alone. I could sense it, see it, feel it.

I moved over springy, green grass that stood little chance once the brief winter rains ended, once the heat set in again. Southern California is mostly desert, and never is it more apparent than in these barren hills.

The moon was nearly full. *Uh oh.* That meant Kingsley would be, ah, *indisposed* for a few days.

My body felt strong. As strong as the wind that had now whipped my hair into a frenzy. Sometimes I felt elemental, too. Tied to the days and nights, to the sun and earth. Tied to blood.

Elemental.

Like a dark fairy. A dark fairy with bat wings.

I headed deeper into the desert, following a natural path that might have been a stream bed in wetter times. The rock underfoot was loose, although I rarely lost my balance. Down I went, down the slope, following the rock-strewn path, until before me a deep blackness opened up. A ravine.

I stopped, breathing in the cool, desert air, although these days I no longer needed much air. I opened and closed my hands, feeling stronger than I ever had. Then again, I always feel like that, each and every night. Stronger than I ever had.

I continued on, skirting a copse of stunted milkwoods along the edge of the ravine. I felt a pair of eyes watching me. I turned my head, looked up. There, a coyote sitting high atop a nearby boulder, eyes glowing yellow in the night. Its eyes, amazingly, like Kingsley's. Now I saw more movement from around the boulder. Heard claws clicking, scratching. More coyotes. I could smell them, too. Intoxicatingly fresh blood wafted from their musky coats. They had just feasted on a recent kill.

My stomach growled.

I cursed and moved on as the pack watched me silently, warily, keeping their distance. Soon, I reached what I had been searching for: the cliff's edge. Here, light particles swirled frenetically, seemingly caught in the updraft of wind gusts that moaned over crevasses and caves and outcroppings of rock.

My toes curled over the edge. Loose sand and rock tumbled into the ravine. Behind me, I heard the coyotes turn and leave.

I listened to the wind moving over the land, to the insects scurrying and buzzing, to my own growling stomach. I inhaled the last of the lingering, haunting scent of blood before the coyotes were too far off for even my enhanced senses.

I looked out over the ledge. The cliff dropped straight down, disappearing into blackness, although I could see an outcropping of rock about halfway down. I would have to avoid that.

I closed my eyes and exhaled slowly. If my life hadn't been so weird over these past seven years, I might have been surprised to find myself standing naked at the edge of a cliff, in the high deserts outside of Orange County.

But now weirdness was the norm, and so I just stood there, head tilted back a little, hair whipping in the wind, hands slightly outstretched, until the flame appeared in my thoughts.

Within the flame appeared something hideous . . . and beautiful. The creature I would become.

With that thought planted firmly in mind, I leaped from the cliff's edge and out into the night.

# 6.

I arched up and out.

I hovered briefly in mid-air at the apex of the arch, my arms spread wide, my hair drifting above my shoulders in a state of suspended animation.

From here, as I briefly hovered, I could see Lake Mathews sparkling under the nearly full moon. I could also see the barb wire fence, too. Only in Southern California do they surround a lake with barb wire. Beyond, the cities of Corona and Riverside sparkled like so many jewels. Flawed jewels.

And then I was falling, head first, like an inverted cross. The bleak canyon walls sped past me, just feet away. Dried grass swept past me, too. Lizards scuttled for cover, no doubt confused as hell. Dry desert air blasted me, thundered over my ears.

I knew the protrusion of rock was coming up fast.

I closed my eyes, and the creature in the flame regarded me curiously, cocking its head to one side.

Faster, I sped. My outstretched arms fought the wind.

The creature in the flame, the creature in my mind, seemed somehow closer now. And now I was rushing toward it—or it was rushing toward me. I never knew which it was.

I gasped, contorted, expanded.

And now my arms, instead of fighting the air, caught the air, used the air, manipulated the air, and now I wasn't so much falling as angling away from the cliff, angling just over the rocky protrusion. In fact, my right foot—no, the claws of my right foot—just grazed the rock. Lizards, soaking up what little heat they could from the rock, scurried wildly, and I didn't blame them.

Here be monsters.

I continued angling down, speeding so fast that by all rights I should be out of control. Wings or no wings, I should have tumbled down into the ravine below, disappearing into a forest of beavertail cactus so thick that my ass hurt just looking at them.

But I didn't crash.

Instead, I was in total control of this massive, winged body, knowing innately how to fly, how to command, how to maneuver. I knew, for instance, that angling my wings minutely would slow me enough to soar just above the beavertail, as I did now, their spiky paddles just missing my flat underside.

Yes, completely flat. In this form, I was no longer female. I was, if anything, asexual. I existed for flight only. For great distances, and great strength, too.

Now, as the far side of the canyon wall appeared before me, I instinctively veered my outstretched arms—wings—and shot up the corrugated wall, following its contours easily, avoiding boulders and roots and anything that might snag my wings or disembowel me.

Up I went, flapping hard. And with each downward thrust, my body surged faster and faster, rocketing out of the canyon like a winged missile.

In the open air, I was immediately buffeted by a strong wind blowing through the hills, but my body easily adjusted for it, and I rose higher still. I leveled off and the thick hide that composed my wings snapped taut like twin sails.

Twin black sails. With claws and teeth.

Below, I saw dozens of yellow eyes watching me silently. I wondered just how much these coyotes knew . . . and whether or not they were really coyotes.

The wind was cold and strong. I was about two hundred feet up, high enough to scan dozens of acres at once, as my eyes in this form were even better, even sharper.

I was looking for the ravine that I had seen in my vision. Only a brief flash of a vision, of course, but one that remained with me, seared into my memory. In particular, I was looking for what had been tossed *into* the ravine.

No doubt, whoever had tossed it had thought the package was as good as gone. After all, even a team of policemen and state troopers couldn't cover every inch of this vast wasteland.

I flew over hills and canyons, over Lake Mathews and its barbed wire fence. High above me came the faint sound of a jet engine, and in the near distance, a Cessna was flying south. I wondered idly if I showed up on their radar, but I doubted it. After all, if I didn't show up in mirrors, why would I show up on radars?

The wind tossed me a little, but I went with it, enjoying the experience. Everything about this form was enjoyable. The land spread before me in an eternity of undulating hills and dark ravines, marching onward to the mountain chains that criss-crossed Southern California. Yes, even Southern California has mountain chains.

I flapped my wings casually, without effort or thought, moving my body as confidently and innately as one would when reaching for a coffee mug. I circled some more, looking for a match to the snapshot image in my head. I continued like this for another half hour or so, soaring and flapping, turning and searching. And then I came upon a hill that looked promising.

Very promising.

I descended toward it, dipping my wing, feeling the rush of wind in my face . . . a rush that I would never truly get used to. Or, rather, never wanted to get used to. How does one ever get used to flying? I didn't know, and I didn't want to know. I wanted the experience to always remain fresh, always new.

The hill kept looking promising, and now there was the same stunted tree that I'd seen in my vision.

I swooped lower.

There, resting next to the tree trunk and nearly impossible to see with the naked eye, was a small package. No, not quite. A bulging plastic bag.

I dropped down, circling once, twice, then landed on a smooth rock near the tree, tucking in my wings. Feeling like a monster in a horror movie, I used my left talon to snag the bag, then leaped as high as I could, stretched out my wings, caught the wind nicely, and lifted off the ground.

A few minutes later, back at my minivan and naked as the day I was born, I opened the bag and looked inside.

"Bingo," I said.

# 7.

I was alone in my office with the dead man's bag.

The drive back from the hills outside of Corona had been excruciatingly long, despite the fact there had been no traffic. Excruciating, because I was itching to get a better look inside the bag. The bag, I knew, was key evidence. I also knew that I should hand it over to Detective Sherbet ASAP. And I would. Eventually.

After I had a little looksee.

With the kids asleep and the babysitter forty bucks richer, I sat in my office and studied the still-closed bag. It was just a white plastic trash bag with red tie handles. The handles were presently tied tight. The bag itself was half full, which, on second thought, said more about my outlook on life these days than about anything in the bag.

I was wearing latex gloves since I didn't want to ruin perfectly good evidence. To date, there had been five bodies located. Five bodies drained of blood. Sherbet had brought me on board after the fourth. Unfortunately, I hadn't been given much access to the actual evidence, despite Sherbet's high praise for me and my background as a federal investigator. Ultimately, homicide investigators still saw me as a rent-a-cop, someone not to take seriously, a private dick without a dick, as someone had once said.

Anyway, Sherbet had mostly gotten me caught up via reports and taped witness statements. Sadly, the witnesses hadn't witnessed much, and the four previous bodies had yielded little in the way of clues. And what clues the police had, they weren't giving me access to.

So, this little bag sitting in front of me represented my first—and only—direct evidence to the case.

And I wasn't about to just turn it over. At least, not yet.

So I photographed the bag from all angles, noting any smudges and marks. Once done, I carefully used a pair of scissors and clipped open the red plastic ties. I parted the bag slowly, and once fully open, I took more photos directly into the bag, carefully documenting the layout of the items within. Then I painstakingly removed each item, setting each before me and photographing them as they emerged.

All in all, there were fifteen items in the bag.

Most of the items were clothing: jeans, tee shirt, socks, shoes, underwear. There was jewelry, too, a class ring and a gold necklace. The necklace had some dried blood in it. There was blood splatter on the tee shirt, too, and the running shoes.

But, most important, there was a wallet, complete with a driver's license, credit cards, folded receipts and even a hide-a-key tucked behind the license.

"Well, well, well," I said.

In a slot behind one of the credit cards was a private investigator's wet dream: his social security number. With that, he would have no secrets from me.

His name, for starters, was Brian Meeks. He was twenty-seven years old and even kind of cute.

But most important, the moment I began extracting items from the bag and then from the wallet, I began receiving powerful hits. Psychic hits. Haunting, disturbing, horrific hits.

I saw his life. I saw his death.

I saw his killer.

And when I finally put the items away, back into the wallet and back into the bag, I sat back in my chair and pulled my knees up to my chest and buried my face between my knees and sat like that for a long, long time.

# 8.

*You there, Fang?*

When I had caught my breath and my hands had quit shaking enough to type, I had grabbed my laptop and curled up on my new couch. The new, L-shaped couch was nearly as big as the living room itself, and that's just the way I liked it. There was enough room for some serious cuddling on here, and luckily my kids were still young enough to want to cuddle with their mommy. Even if Mommy had perpetual cold feet. Hey, if I had to put up with Anthony's farts, then they could put up with Mommy's cold feet.

A moment later, the little circular icon next to Fang's name turned green, which meant he had just signed on. Next, I saw him typing a message, as indicated by a wiggling pencil in the corner of the screen.

*You are upset, Moon Dance.*

Fang, like Detective Sherbet, was psychically connected to me. He would know how I felt, and what I was thinking, especially if I opened myself up to him.

*Very upset.*

*Tell me about it.*

I did. Fang, like many in Orange County, knew about the drained bodies and about the serial killer. The papers were having a field day with this story, as were late-night talk-show hosts. With the world currently in the grip of *Twilight* mania, a real story about real bodies being drained of blood was making some national headlines. As Fang knew, I had been hired as a special consultant to the case, I simply caught him up to date on tonight's adventures. I also caught him up on the psychic hits I'd received.

*He was hanging upside down?*

*Yes.*

*And he never got a good look at his killer?*

*No. I think he had been rendered unconscious. I only got a sensation of him returning to consciousness.*

*And when he did, he was hanging upside down?*

*Yes.*

Fang wrote: *What else did he see before he was, you know . . .*
*Killed?*

*Yes.*

I rubbed my head as the images, now forever imprinted into my brain, appeared in my thoughts again. I wrote: *He didn't get a good look. He was swinging wildly upside down, trying to break free.*

*His hands were tied?*

*I think so, yes.*

*And he saw only one man?*

*Maybe two. Hard to know. That's when he started screaming.*

*And that's when the knife appeared,* wrote Fang.

*Yes,* I wrote, feeling drained, despite this being the middle of the night.

*And they cut his throat,* wrote Fang.

*Yes.*

*This doesn't sound like a vampire.*

*No,* I wrote.

*It sounds like a sick son-of-a-bitch.*

I waited before replying. Finally, I wrote: *There's more, Fang. I saw . . . other bodies. At least two more. Both hanging upside down.*

*Jesus, Sam.*

*They were suspended over a tub of some sort.*

*A tub?*

*Yes.*

*They were collecting the blood,* Fang wrote.

*That's what I think, too.*

*But why?*

I thought about it for only a moment before I wrote: *If I had to guess, I would say that he supplies blood for vampires.*

# 9.

Kingsley was waiting for me outside Mulberry Street Café in downtown Fullerton.

He looked dashing and massive, and I think my whole body sighed when he smiled at me. A big, toothy smile. Confident smile. Deep dimples in his cheeks. His ears even moved a little. The way a dog's might. He was wearing a scarf that matched his eyes and I think I might have mewed a little. Like a kitten.

"Hello, beautiful," he said, smiling even bigger.

"Hello, Mr. Observant," I said, grinning, and came to him. He wrapped a strong arm around my lower waist and pulled me into him, lifting me a little off my feet. I wasn't entirely sure he knew he had lifted me off my feet. One moment I was standing there, the next my heels were free of any gravitational pull.

He set me down again. "God, you smell good."

"For a dead girl?"

"You're very much alive."

"Well, that's good news."

He planted a big, wet kiss on my lips that I didn't want to end. At least, not for the next two or three hours. When we separated, I noticed an old man watching us. Hell, I would have watched us, too.

"You hungry?" asked Kingsley. I noticed his five o'clock shadow was looking more like a three-day growth. The surest indicator that a full moon was rising.

"Hungry enough to suck you dry," I said.

Now he shivered. "With talk like that, we might just skip dinner."

We were seated immediately at our favorite table near the front window. The waiters here knew my preferences and, after giving us one of their finest white wines—one of the few non-hemoglobic beverages I can enjoy—they brought us our meals. Salmon for Kingsley. Steak for me. Rare.

Very, very rare.

Rather than use a knife and fork, I used a spoon, and, as casually as I could, I dipped it into the warm blood that had pooled around the meat and brought it to my lips. I tried not to feel like the ghoul that I was.

Just a girl with her man, I told myself. A man, of course, who just so happened to be bigger than most men. And far hairier. Especially at this time of the month.

Kingsley, suffering from no such eating restrictions, went to work on the salmon. Although the defense attorney dressed immaculately, he ate like a pig. And, yeah, I was jealous as hell.

The waiter came by and filled my wine glass. Since I had taken precisely three sips, the filling part didn't take long. Kingsley ordered another beer, and when the waiter was gone, I said to him, "I found another medallion."

"Another what?" he mumbled around his salmon. Or, rather, I *think* he said.

"Medallion. You know, like the one before. But this one is inlaid with amethyst roses, rather than ruby."

Kingsley's lips were shiny with grease. His impossibly full lips. His longish hair hung just below his collar. He was the picture of the maverick attorney, who just so happened to look like a ravenous wolf, too. "Tell me about it," he said.

And I did. I told him about the case I had taken on around Christmas, a case in which I had helped a sweet man find a family heirloom, of sorts. A sweet man who just so happened to be a hoarder, too. For payment, I was permitted to pick anything I wanted from his piles of junk. I had cheated. I had used my intuition to hone in on something particularly valuable, something that had lain hidden and mostly forgotten under piles of crap.

A box. With a medallion.

A medallion that was a near-exact replica of the one I had owned six months ago. And that medallion had contained powerful magicks. So powerful, in fact, that it had reversed vampirism.

"So the question is," I said. "Can this medallion do the same?"

During my recounting, Kingsley had finished his salmon and was now working on his cubed rosemary potatoes. The fork in his hand looked miniature. "Do you have the medallion with you now?" he asked.

I did. I showed it to him. Kingsley immediately frowned. A frown for Kingsley meant his bushy eyebrows came together to form one long incredibly bushy eyebrow. "You should have left it at home," he said, glancing around.

"And miss seeing your bushy eyebrows come together?"

"I'm serious, Sam. Stuff like this . . ." he lowered his voice. "You, of all people, know the lengths some people—"

"Or vampires."

His long eyebrow quivered. "Yes, Sam. Vampires. Some vampires will kill—"

"And kidnap."

"Yes, and kidnap for these things."

I set it on the table and mostly covered it with my hand. "And what is this thing? Another immortality reverser?"

Kingsley shook his head sharply. "No. There was only one of those made."

"And you know this how?"

"I know some things," he said.

"Because you've been around longer than me."

"A lot longer than you, Sam."

"Fine. So only one of those were made. Then what's this?" I moved my hand aside, revealing the shining medallion again. It caught the overhead chandelier light and returned a thousandfold, and the three amethysts within twinkled like powder blue stars.

Kingsley glanced briefly at the medallion before reaching across the table and covering my hand with his own. Hell, he covered most of my wrist, too. And some of my napkin and plate. Big hands.

"I don't know yet," he said. "But I can tell you one thing."

"And what's that?"

"It's valuable as hell. Which means . . ." And his voice trailed off.

Unfortunately, I knew the ending to this sentence all too well. "Which means some people will kill for it."

"Some people," said Kingsley, "or some vampires."

# 10.

"You tampered with evidence. What were you thinking, Sam?" scolded Detective Sherbet.

"I was thinking about finding our killer."

We were in his glass office. Some of the officers on duty were watching us from outside the office. One or two were shaking their heads in a way that suggested they did not approve of me or of the department using my inferior services.

"Your men don't like me," I said.

"They see it as a slap in the face, a blow to their ego," said Sherbet, sitting back in his chair. He laced his thick fingers over his rotund belly. The rotund belly was looking a little more rotund these days. This time, however, I shielded my thoughts from him. He didn't need to know what I thought of his belly. He went on, "They don't understand why I brought you in, so they see you as a sort of indictment on their own abilities."

"If they only knew," I said.

"Truth is, sometimes I wish I didn't know, Sam. I mean, isn't this kind of stuff supposed to just be in books and movies?"

I said, "Someone told me recently that if enough people believe in something, put their attention on something, then that something becomes a reality."

Sherbet immediately shook his head. "That doesn't make sense," he said, which didn't surprise me much. Detectives lived and died by things that made sense. Cold hard facts. "Who told you this?"

"My guardian angel. Actually, my ex-guardian angel."

Sherbet blinked. "Please tell me you're kidding."

"Sadly, no. He visited me over Christmas. Expressed his undying love for me, in fact."

"Please stop. There's only so much I can handle." Sherbet massaged his temples. "We sound crazy, you know."

"Maybe we are," I said.

"Crazy, I can accept. Guardian angels, not so much. Can I really read your mind, Sam?"

"Yes."

"And you can read my mind?" he asked.

"If I wanted to."

"My head hurts, Sam."

"I imagine it does."

He looked at me some more. As he did so, his jowls quivered a little. His nose was faintly red. "How do you do it?" he finally asked.

I didn't have to be a mind reader to know what *it* was. I said, "One day at a time. One minute at a time."

"If it were me, I would go bugfuck crazy."

We were quiet some more. The smell of coffee seemed to permanently hang suspended in the air of his office, although I could see no coffee cups. Outside his glass office wall, I could hear phones ringing, phones being answered, the rapid typing on keyboards.

"Back to you tampering with evidence," said Sherbet. "Officially, I have to ask you to never do that again."

"And unofficially?"

"Unofficially, I have to ask you what you learned."

"He's not a vampire," I said. "At least, I don't think he is."

"Then what is he? Why does he drain the bodies of blood?"

"Think of him as a supplier."

"A supplier? Of what? Blood?"

"Yes."

"For who?"

I didn't say anything. I let the detective think this through. As he studied me, I glanced around his small office. There was a picture of his wife next to his keyboard, a lovely woman I'd met just this past Christmas, a woman who was easily twenty years younger than Sherbet.

*You go, Detective.*

Finally, he said, "Are you implying he supplies blood to . . . vampires?"

"Maybe. I don't know for sure."

"Which begs the question: where do vampires get their blood?"

"We get it from all over, Detective. I get mine, as you know, from a local butchery."

"Animal blood."

"Right."

"So, this guy supplies human blood."

"Right."

"Have you ever heard anything like that, Sam?"

"Not quite like that."

"What have you heard?"

"That some people act as donors."

"Willing donors?"

"Some of them," I said.

"And some not so willingly?"

"Would be my guess," I said.

Sherbet started shaking his head, and he didn't quit shaking it until he spoke again. Finally, he said, "So, what else do you know about our killer?"

"He's got blue eyes."

"That's it?"

"That's it."

"No other psychic hits?"

"He hangs the bodies upside down to drain."

"Like a butcher."

"Yes," I said.

"Which makes sense if he's a blood supplier; after all, he wouldn't want to waste a single drop."

"Blood is money," I said.

"Jesus. Where did he kill his victims?"

I shook my head. "Hard to know. Brian Meeks regained consciousness while hanging upside down."

"Jesus," he said again. "And you saw this, what, through his eyes? From touching his stuff?"

"That's how it seems to work."

"Do you have any fucking idea how crazy we sound?"

"Some idea," I said.

Sherbet shook his head. "Did he—or you—see anything else while he was hanging upside down?"

"Yes."

"Don't say it, Sam," said Sherbet, and I think he caught a glimpse of my thoughts.

"More bodies," I said.

"I asked you not to say it."

# 11.

With the body now identified and most of the Fullerton Police Department looking deeply into Brian Meeks's personal and professional life, Detective Sherbet had asked me to lay low for a while and let his boys think they were doing some actual work.

I told him no problem, smiled warmly, and promptly looked into Brian Meeks's personal and professional life.

Since I knew the cops were currently turning his small apartment upside down, looking for anything and everything that
could help identify the killer, that left his professional life.

Which is why I found myself outside the Fullerton Playhouse. Turns out that Brian Meeks had been an actor here in
Fullerton, working primarily with local theater and community
colleges. Which might explain why he lived in a one-bedroom
apartment.

The Fullerton Playhouse is located on Commonwealth,
near the Amtrak train station, and near what had been one
of my favorite restaurants, back when my diet wasn't so one-
dimensional. The Olde Spaghetti House will always have a
special place in my heart. The fact that I would never again
eat mizithra cheese spaghetti was a crime in and of itself.

I parked in the mostly empty parking lot next to the wooden
playhouse. A marquee sign out front read, "Elvis Has *Not* Left
the Building: The Musical." Under the sign were the words:
"The King Is Back!"

Boy, was he ever. Last year, while searching for a missing
little girl, I had teamed up with, among others, an investigator
from Los Angeles. An investigator from whom I had received a
very strange psychic hit. An investigator who vaguely looked and
sounded like the King himself.

Turned out, the old guy had secrets of his own, secrets I would
take with me to my grave, whenever the hell that might be.

Now as I sat in the parking lot in my minivan, shrinking away
from the daylight, I closed my eyes and cleared my mind and
cast my thoughts out and directed them toward the theater. Yes,
I was getting good at this sort of thing.

Now, as my thoughts moved through the theater, I could see
various people working together in small groups or individually.
Actors and stage hands and set designers, anyone and everyone
needed to put on a show.

So far, no hit. Nothing that made me take notice.

I pushed past the main stage to the backstage. Still nothing. I
meandered down a side hallway and into a storage room. Props
were everywhere. Rows upon rows of costumes hung from racks
and hangers. Still nothing. I was about to snap back into my
body when something appeared at the back of the theater.

A shadow.

It appeared suddenly from the far wall, scurried up to the ceiling, then down a side wall, then huddled in a dark corner, where it waited. I sensed that it always waited, that it was always afraid.

I shivered. Jesus, what the hell was that thing? I'd seen my fair share of ghosts and spirits, but never a shadow. Never this.

And it came from the mirror hanging from the back wall. No, not the mirror. Behind the mirror. There was a doorway there. A hidden doorway.

I tried to push through the secret door, but I was just too far away. My range is limited, and I was at the far end of it.

I snapped back into my body and, briefly disoriented, gave myself a few moments to get used to seeing through my physical eyes again. The sun was still out, which meant that the next few moments were not going to be very fun. When I had mentally prepared myself, I took a deep breath and threw open my minivan door. I dashed across the parking lot, keeping my head down, leaping over cement parking curbs like a horse at a steeplechase.

When I finally ducked under the marquee and into the blessed shade, I was gasping and clutching my chest and maybe even whimpering a little. The sun was truly not my friend. And that was a damn shame.

When the burning subsided enough for me to think straight, I pushed my way into the theater's main entrance.

# 12.

The theater looked much the same as it had in my thoughts, except for the details.

The same crew was on stage, hammering and sawing away on a wooden cut-out of a pink Cadillac. The same group of actors were going over lines off to the left of the stage.

No one noticed me. No one cared. And why should they? They were all busy putting on a stage show about Elvis, and what could be cooler than that?

With murder cases, you always interviewed those closest to the victims, then worked your way out. I would let the police interview any family members, although precious few showed up in my preliminary research. Still, most people tended to open up to an official murder investigation. Not everyone opened up to private eyes.

Go figure.

So as I stood there and surveyed the darkened theater, watching workers carry props and pull cables, actors read and re-read lines, and various stage hands in group meetings, I realized why I was here. Why I had jumped the gun and come here on my own. Against Sherbet's wishes, no less.

*He's here,* I thought. *The killer is here.*

Before me, the stadium seating sloped downward. The Fullerton Playhouse wasn't huge. I would guess that it could seat maybe one thousand. The seating itself was arranged into four quadrants, with two aisles leading down and aisles on each side. I was standing on a platform near a metal railing. Wheelchair seating, if my guess was correct. Various lights were on throughout the theater, but certainly not all of them, as much of the seating was in shadows.

A quick count netted me twenty-four people. And one of them was the killer. I was sure of it.

How I knew this, I no longer questioned or doubted, and as I stood there scanning the theater, I felt that something was off. And I was pretty sure I knew why.

There was more than one killer.

It takes a certain kind of personality to be an actor, or even hang around the theater. You had to love masks, the ability to pretend to be something other than what you were. Which was a pretty useful trait for a killer, too.

As I stepped forward, a small man appeared out of the shadows to my left. Holding a clipboard and mumbling to himself, he nearly ran into me before looking up. He was exactly an inch taller than me.

I held out one of my business cards. "Hi. My name's Samantha Moon, and I'm looking into the murder of Brian Meeks."

He looked at the card and blinked twice. "Are you with the police?"

"I'm a private investigator." One of the stipulations with Sherbet was that I was never, ever, to state that I was working with the police. It was a gray area he wanted to avoid. My official employer was the City of Fullerton. In fact, my checks had been issued by the city clerk's office.

"Working for whom?"

"An interested party."

He finally took my card. "What are they interested in?"

"Finding the killer." I tried not to be sarcastic, because that never helps. What did he think, the cops wanted to know his favorite picks to win the Oscars? "Can I ask you a few questions about Brian Meeks?"

He looked at my card, looked at me, looked over at the stage. I sensed his hesitation, his pain, and finally his resolve. "Okay, but only for a few minutes. We're putting on a show in a few days. Opening night. Crazy as Lady Macbeth here."

"Gotcha. We'll hurry this along. Did Brian Meeks work here as an actor?"

"For a few years now."

"Did you know him personally?"

"Not necessarily personally, but professionally. Then again, in the world of theater, personal and professional lines tend to get blurred. We're all so close."

"I bet. Are you an actor?"

"Director only."

"Gotcha. Did you direct anything Brian was in?"

He nodded. "Our last show, *Twelfth Night*. Brian was supposed to be in this new show, but . . ."

"He's been missing."

The little director rubbed his face. "Right. Missing. Until we heard the news this morning that he was found dead. Murdered."

"Did Brian have many friends?"

"Funny you should ask . . . I was just trying to think who his close friends were. I was thinking of doing some sort of memorial for him. Something either before or after our opening show this weekend . . ."

"And?"

"And I couldn't think of anyone who had been close to him."

"Is that common for an actor?" I asked.

"Actually, no. We don't get many loners in this business. Extroverts, yes."

I skipped the questions of whether or not Brian had any enemies. Whoever had done this to him was doing the same thing to many people. I doubted a personal vendetta had anything to do with his death. I asked, "Had there been any other strange occurrences in this theater?"

"Strange, how?"

"Has anyone reported seeing anything . . . odd or unusual?"

"Not that I can think of. But a theater is a pretty odd place anyway."

"How long have you worked here?"

He looked again at the stage. I could see that a few people were waiting for him. "Five years. Worked my way up as a lighting guy out of college."

"Good for you. Who owns the theater?"

He pointed to a man sitting on a foldout chair on stage. The only man, apparently, not doing anything. "Robert Mason."

"The actor?"

"The one-time actor. His soap opera days are over. This is where he spends most of his time."

"May I have your name?" I asked.

"Tad Biggs."

I nodded and somehow kept a straight face. I said, "May I ask what's in your back room?"

"Back room?"

"Yes, the storage room at the far end of the hallway."

He blinked. Twice. No, three times. "How do you know about the storage room?"

"I'm a heck of an investigator."

"That room is strictly off limits."

"Why?"

This time he didn't blink. This time, he just stared at me. "Because Robert Mason says it is. Look, I gotta go. We have a show to put on. I hope you guys catch the sick son-of-a-bitch who did this to Brian."

I nodded and watched him hurry off. Then I flicked my eyes over to where Robert Mason was sitting in the foldout chair on stage—and gasped when I saw him staring back at me.

He was still as handsome as ever. Older, granted, but one hell of a handsome man. He stared at me some more, then looked away.

I shivered, and exited stage left.

# 13.

I was watching them from the parking lot.

Not exactly the best seat in town, granted, but it would have to do. Lately, I seemed to be almost completely intolerant to the sun. Brief sojourns were excruciating, even when I was fully clothed and lathered.

And so, while my son played soccer, I sat alone in my van, huddled in the center of my seat, thankful for the surrounding tinted glass. Of course, from where I sat, I couldn't see the entire playing field, but beggars can't be choosers.

It was a crisp late winter day, warm for this time of year, perfect for anyone who wasn't me. Before me were some bleachers filled with moms and dads and relatives and friends. The mothers all seemed to know each other and they laughed and pointed and cupped their hands and shouted encouragement. They shared stories and drinks and sandwiches and chips.

I sat alone and watched them and tried not to feel sorry for myself. Easier said than done.

From where I sat, I couldn't tell who was winning, so I just watched Anthony as he ran up and down the field, disappearing and reappearing from around poles and bleachers and hedges.

From what I could tell, he had real talent, but what did I know? These days, he almost always scored a goal—sometimes even two or three. He seemed to have the strongest leg—kicking leg, that is—and a real nose for the action; at least, he was always right in the thick of things. Mostly I cringed and winced when I watched him, praying he would be careful. My overprotectiveness wasn't a surprise, especially when you consider what I went through seven months ago.

Presently, the action was coming toward my end of the field, and I sat forward in my seat. Anthony was leading the charge, elbowing his way through a crowd of kids who clearly didn't seem as athletic. And now Anthony was mostly free, pursued by opponents on either side. Amazingly, Anthony pulled away from them. Not only running faster than them, but running faster while kicking a soccer ball.

Then he reared back and kicked a laser shot into the far corner of the net, blowing it past the outmatched goalie.

Anthony's teammates high-fived him. Parents stood and cheered. I shouted and stamped my feet in the minivan. No one heard me cheer, of course. Especially not Anthony.

Still, I cheered alone from inside the minivan, rocking it all the way down to its axles. And when I was done cheering, done clapping, I buried my face in my hands and tried to forget just what a freak I was.

After the game, as parents and grandparents hugged their excited and dirty kids, I saw Anthony coming toward me. Alone, and perhaps dirtiest of all. One of the other mothers saw him and asked him something. He pointed to me sitting in the minivan. She nodded and smiled and waved to me. I waved back. She then gave Anthony a big hug and congratulated him, no doubt on playing a great game. By my count, Anthony had scored three goals. She gave him another hug and set him free.

*That should be me hugging him,* I thought. *That should be me walking him off the field.*

There was blood along his knees and elbows. The kid had taken a beating scoring those three goals. But he didn't limp; in fact, he didn't seem fazed by the injuries at all.

*Tough kid.*

He flashed me a gap-toothed smile, and my heart swelled with all kinds of love. Now he was running toward me, his cleats clickity-clacking over the asphalt. He looked like an athlete. A natural athlete. His movements fluid and easy, covering the ground effortlessly, cutting through cars and people with precision. On a dime. By the time he reached the minivan he was sprinting. He skidded to a halt and yanked open the door.

"Mom!" he shouted. "I scored three goals today!"

"Incredible!"

He jumped in and lunged across the console and gave me a big hug. The strength in his arms was real. He nearly tore me out of my seat. "Did you see them?"

"Some of them," I said. Two, in fact. Both scored on this side of the field. "So when did you get so darn good?"

He shrugged. "I dunno. Lucky, I guess."

But something suddenly occurred to me. Anthony hadn't been very good just a year ago. In fact, I distinctly recall him coming back to the van crying, wanting to quit his team. Now he was coming back to the van as the hero of the game.

And not just a hero, but clearly the best athlete on the field.

I was about to say that luck had nothing to do with it when I looked down at his legs. The cuts I had seen just a minute earlier were . . . gone. Only dried blood remained. And only a little bit of dried blood.

I think my heart might have stopped.

"Anthony, how do you feel?"

"Great! We won!"

"Yes, I know, but do you feel . . . sunburned at all?"

"Sunburned?" Distracted, he waved to a friend passing by the van.

"Yes, sunburned or sick?"

"I feel good, Mom. I promise. Stop worrying about me."

I bit my lip and somehow managed to hide my concern. "Are you hungry, baby?"

"Duh. Of course I'm hungry."

"Of course. What do you want?"

"Duh, hamburgers!"

"Of course," I said, backing the minivan up. "Duh."


# 14.


*You there, Fang?*

*I'm always here for you, Moon Dance.*

*Except when you're not.*

*Hey, a man's gotta work. What's on your mind, sweet cheeks?*

*Sweet cheeks?*

*Oops, did I write that out loud?*

*You did.*

*My bad. So what's on your mind, sugar butt?*

*Oh brother.* I grinned, shook my head, then quickly turned somber. *There's something going on with my son.*

*Is everything okay?!*

*Yes. I mean, I don't know.*

*He's not sick again, is he?*

*No. In fact, quite the opposite.*

I told him about the healing in Anthony's leg, and my son's seemingly increased athletic ability. There was a long pause before Fang wrote back.

*Maybe you are mistaken, Moon Dance. Is it possible that his blood had already dried?*

I shook my head, aware that I was alone in my living room and no one could see me shaking my head.

*No. I saw the fresh wounds. My eyes happen to be very, very good.*

I projected the image I had in my mind. My own memory, in fact.

A moment later, Fang wrote: *We used to call those strawberries. Probably got them sliding over the grass and maybe on some dirt.*

*Right,* I wrote. *And even if it had been dried blood, where was the wound?*

*There was no wound?*

*None.*

*Just dried blood?*

*Yes.*

There was another long pause, followed by: *And the dried blood was recent?*

*Of course. It wasn't there when I dropped him off.*

*Is there a chance it wasn't his blood?*

*No. I saw the abrasions.*

*In the image you projected to me,* wrote Fang, *I'm pretty sure I see them, too.*

*We're weird,* I wrote.

*Yes we are, Moon Dance. A very good kind of weird.*

*So what does this mean with my son?*

*I don't know, Moon Dance.* There was another pause. *And you say he's getting better in sports, too?*

*Much, much better.*

*Supernaturally better?*

*Last year about this time he was benched for picking his nose. Now he's the leading scorer. I wouldn't have thought anything about this, except . . .*

*Except when you combine it with the disappearing wound . . .*

*Right,* I wrote. *There's something weird going on with my son. Fang, could you . . .*

*I'll look into it, Moon Dance.*

*Thank you, Fang.*

And as we were about to sign off, I caught a fleeting glimpse into Fang's mind, a thought that I was certain I wasn't supposed to see or hear. Except it wasn't so much a thought as a feeling.

Fang was hoping that if he helped me, I would help him in return. To do what, I didn't know.

But I could guess.

# 15.

I was in bed with Kingsley.

Not a bad place to be. Ever. It was the day after his "change" and he was feeling particularly, ah, ravenous. And not just for food. Yes, he had prepared a delicious meal for himself, and supplied me with a particularly fresh goblet of hemoglobin.

We had spent the evening in his kitchen, drinking and eating over his counter, while he looked at me with yellowish eyes that suggested that he was not only going to tear my clothing off my back, but he was going to do so in a particularly inspired way.

He didn't tear off my clothes. But they did come off quick enough, and we spent the next few hours putting our immortal bodies to good use. Very good use.

Now, we were both lying on our sides, naked and talking quietly. The lights were off but I could see every square inch of Kingsley's epic body, which I never really got used to. It was like lying next to a small land mass, a living peninsula. Hard, corrugated, with peaks and valleys and forests and plains. Epic, immovable, sexy as hell.

I knew he could see every curve of mine, too, being a fellow creature of the night. That he could see every curve of mine gave me some degree of anxiety. I might be immortal, but I was insecure as hell about my naked body.

Kingsley, not so much. He liked to be naked. Lucky for him, I liked when he was naked, too. Presently, his shaggy hair hung down to the bed sheet, a bed sheet that was still soaked with our sweat. His relaxed bicep still looked bigger than my waist. His chest hair was thicker than normal thanks to his beastly visitor from the night before.

Yes, the big oaf was shedding all over the place. Additionally, his eyes were glowing more yellow than normal, also a residue of his recent transformation.

"Kingsley," I said.

He was presently running a thick finger over my hip. "Yeah, babe?"

"Are there really . . . things living inside us?"

His finger stopped on my waist. "That's not exactly bedroom talk, Sam."

"Sorry, but it's been bugging me."

"Since you met your guardian angel?"

I nodded, which looked more like a shake since my head was propped up on my hand. The lights were out in the room, and only the silver glow from the still-mostly full moon bathed our naked bodies. "He kind of freaked me out."

"He was trying to freak you out, Sam. And he's certainly not a guardian angel. Not anymore."

"A fallen angel," I said.

"Right," said Kingsley. "Something like that."

"I spoke to whatever's in you," I said. "He said you were his vehicle to gain entrance into the mortal world again."

"So you said before. Remind me to kick his ass if I ever meet him."

I tried to smile. Mostly, I was successful. I said, "Do you feel him inside you?"

"Not really, Sam. Then again, I don't necessarily feel much when I change."

"Do you feel anything?"

"I feel anger and hate and blind rage."

"But you didn't attack me in my room last year."

"No."

"Why not?"

"Because I knew it was you."

"But did you want to attack me?"

"A part of me did. Very badly."

"But you resisted," I said.

"With all my strength and will."

"What would have happened if you attacked me?" I asked.

"We wouldn't be here now."

"Because I would be dead."

"No . . . you would have survived. And I would have survived, too. Vampires are as strong or stronger than even a full-blown werewolf. I'm not sure our relationship would have survived."

I shrugged. I hadn't thought of that. I said, "So, I'm as strong as you?"

"Don't sound so pleased, but yes. Although my size factors into things, I would say you are particularly strong, even for a vampire."

"Why is that?"

"I don't know. There's something going on with you that I haven't quite put a finger on."

"Oh, you put a finger on it."

He laughed. A sharp bark that startled me. "Anyway, even your everyday vampire at full power is nearly unstoppable."

"But you stopped Dominique," I said, referring to the events of seven months ago, when my son had been dying and I had faced down a particularly old and desperate vampire.

"I said nearly," said Kingsley. "That night could have quickly gone south for me."

I patted his hearty chest. I could have been slapping a side of beef. "Then it's a good thing you're such a big boy."

"Big has its benefits."

I rolled my eyes. "Please not another penis reference."

"Fine. I won't refer to my big penis."

"Oh, God. *Annnny*way, I still can't imagine anyone—vampires or otherwise—being able to stop you."

He chuckled lightly, then studied me for a few seconds. "Actually, you could, Sam."

I snorted. "I doubt it."

"You are stronger than you realize. In fact, rumor has it that a Mr. Captain Jack was perhaps the strongest vampire of them all. That is, until you came around."

Kingsley was referring to a missing-child case that had led me to an Indian casino in Simi Valley, where a young girl's blood was being siphoned by a particularly sick son-of-a-bitch.

Kingsley went on, "From what I understand, most others in the vampire world steered clear of Captain Jack. And look what you did to him."

"I was lucky. I had help."

"But who's alive, Sam? You vanquished a powerful vampire. You are not one to mess with."

The talk was getting a little serious, especially since we were both naked in bed. I ran a finger through his tangle of chest hair. "Then what were you doing just a few moments ago?"

He reached over and pulled me close to his superheated body. "Oh, I wasn't messing with you, Sam." And now he flipped me over onto my back and climbed on top of me. "I was making love to you."

I blinked. Hard. This was news to me. "Love?"

"Oh, yeah, Sam." He lowered his face to my skin. "Love."

At least, that's what I think he said. His words might have been a little muffled.

# 16.

It was early afternoon and I was at the Cal State Fullerton library.

I waved to my cute friend working behind the help desk. He smiled brightly and rose from his chair, but I breezed past, blew him a kiss, and hurried into one of the elevators going up. At the third floor, I wound my way through a maze of book aisles until I came upon the special collections room.

Cal State Fullerton had many special collections. In the science fiction wing, there was a room devoted solely to local science fiction authors. One could find original *Dune* manuscripts by Frank Herbert along with his personal notes. My favorite was the Philip K. Dick room. The world at large thought the man had a screw loose, and maybe he did. But I happened to think he was onto something. Or something was onto him.

Anyway, this was the Occult Reading Room, which consisted of extremely rare manuscripts. Like with the science fiction room, these books couldn't be checked out. Only admired. Or feared. And, yes, there were one or two books in here that definitely aroused some fear. Okay, a lot of fear.

Except today I wasn't here to read books, or even to peruse the shelves. I was here to meet a young man. A young man who, I suspected, wasn't so young.

I hung a right into the Occult Reading Room and wasn't too surprised to see that it was empty. Well, empty of anything living, that is. A very old man in spirit form sat in one of the chairs and appeared to be deep in thought. Then again, most ghosts appeared to be in deep thought. As I came in, he looked up at me, startled, frowned grumpily, and promptly disappeared into the nether-sphere.

*Well, excuse me.*

The reading room was really a library unto itself. It had its own shelves, its own filing system, its own desks and reading chairs. Even its own help desk, where I rang the little bell.

As I waited, I could hear something scratching from deeper within the reading room, followed by some whispering and even the occasional moan. I shivered. Creepy as hell.

A young man soon appeared from the back offices. What he did back there, I didn't know. Who he was, exactly, I didn't know that either. For all the world, he appeared as just another handsome college student with a bright smile.

His name was Archibald Maximus, and I suspected that Cal State Fullerton, unbeknownst to the students and faculty, housed perhaps one of the world's most dangerous collections of arcane and rare books, books full of dark power. Books that could do great harm in the hands of the wrong person.

I suspected young Archibald Maximus, or Max, was a gatekeeper of sorts. A watcher. A protector.

His particularly bright aura suggested I might be onto something. Although not as bright as the angel I'd met last month, Max's aura was damn bright. So much so, that it suggested he wasn't entirely of this world.

*Or I could be as crazy as a loon.*

"Hello, Samantha," he said, smiling, reaching across the counter and taking both of my hands in his, as a grandfather might do with his grandchild.

"You remembered my name," I said, looking from his slightly pale, but quite warm, hands. I briefly reveled in the warmth.

His eyes twinkled. "How could I forget?"

Archibald Maximus. Yes, he sounded more like a Greek god than a young librarian. Somehow, I suspected it was closer to the former than the latter.

Anyway, this was one of the rare times that I didn't worry about my cold flesh. Archibald, after all, was very aware of who I really was.

When I was done acting like a bashful schoolgirl, I opened the box I'd been carrying with me and presented the contents to Archibald. He silently held up my newest medallion and let some of the muted light play off its golden surface. The three amethyst roses sparkled with what I was certain was supernatural intensity. As he studied it, I heard something call my name from deeper within the reading room, near where I knew some of the darker books were shelved. I gasped.

"*Ssssister,*" the voices whispered, melding into one slithering, slippery sound.

"Ignore them," said Maximus, as he continued to study the medallion.

"*Ssssister Moon . . . come to us.*"

The hair on my arms stood on end. "They know my name," I said.

"Yes."

"Who are they?"

"Bound spirits."

"Bound in the books?"

He nodded without looking at me. "Yes. Waiting for someone to release them."

I shivered again. "They sound . . . evil."

He looked at me sharply and the merriment in his bright eyes briefly faded. Then he gave me a lopsided grin. "It's why I'm here, Sister Moon," he said. But before I could respond to that, he plunged forward, somewhat excitedly, waving the medallion. "You seem to have a penchant for attracting rare artifacts."

"How rare?"

"The rarest. Hang on . . ."

He moved lithely around the center help desk, swept past me, and headed deeper into the reading room. I noted that the whisperings stopped in his presence. While I watched from the help desk, he used a step stool to fetch a thick book along the upper shelves. No, not the upper shelves . . . it was resting *on top* of the shelf. No one would have known it was there. No one but him.

He came back a moment later, blowing dust off what appeared to be leather skin, but with an odd yellow tint to it. "Is that leather?" I asked.

He set the heavy book down in front of me and, as more dust billowed up, looked deep into me. "Not quite, Samantha. This is human skin."

"Eww."

"Eww is right," he said, but that didn't stop him from eagerly cracking open the oversized book. "Human skin makes a surprisingly suitable book cover, as you can see. Pliable without breaking."

"Eww again."

Fighting back a dry heave or two, I did my best to ignore the yellowish edges of the book and watched as Max carefully turned what I knew to be a different kind of skin. Vellum, or lamb skin. I had, after all, read *The Historian*. You can't help but come out of that book a minor expert on ancient bookbinding.

Anyway, Max was working his way slowly through what appeared to be a very old book filled with wonderfully ornate and colorful drawings. Page after page of strange-looking creatures, symbols, and coded drawings. Finally, he stopped at a page containing four drawings, two of which looked very familiar.

"My medallions," I said.

"Yes," he said. "Two of them."

Indeed, there were the medallions with the ruby and amethyst inlaid roses. Also pictured were medallions inlaid with opal and diamond roses.

"Who wrote this book?" I asked.

He looked up at me and a very strange grin appeared on his handsome face. "Me."

"But it's centuries old."

"I do good work."

"But . . . who are you?"

He held my gaze for a heartbeat longer, and his bright green eyes, I knew, somehow looked deeply into my soul. What it found there—or *who* it found there—I may never know. But after a moment, he said simply, "Hey, I'm just a simple librarian."

"Bullshit. That's like saying I'm just another mom."

"But isn't that also true, Samantha? Do not many things define you?"

"So, you really are a librarian?"

"In part." He reached over and patted my hand warmly, then turned his attention back to the ancient text. I noted that his nail, unlike mine, was round and smooth and very human-looking. He said, "There are four known medallions in the world, Sam. You have now possessed two."

"Who made the medallions?"

"We're not sure, but we suspect whoever *initiated* your race."

"You mean whoever created vampires."

"Yes."

"And who's *we*?"

Archibald Maximus smiled at me from behind the counter. Our faces, I noted, were a mere eight inches apart as we both hovered over the old book. He could have been just another college student working his way through school. Could have been. But wasn't.

"Others like me, Samantha."

"Other . . . librarians?"

He dipped his head a little. "Yes, something like that."

I suddenly had an impression in my thoughts of various old souls positioned around the world, fighting a fight that few knew existed, and fewer still would ever believe in. I relayed my impression to Maximus.

He dipped his head. "Your impression is correct, Sam."

I next had an impression of the Asian philosophical yin and yang symbol, the white and black teardrops interconnected, and

I understood that Archibald Maximus, and others like him, were here to balance a darkness that had taken root.

He said, "Do you understand, Samantha?"

"I think so, yes, but—"

"Good, good. Now, the medallions were created for specific purposes."

I blinked, got the hint. He didn't want to talk about it. At least, not now. I said, "And why's that?"

"The reason, Samantha, is hidden even from me."

"But why?"

"The same reason why all the secrets of the universe are hidden from all humans, Samantha. Life on earth is our chance to grow, to learn, to observe, to interact, to trust, to give and to receive." He smiled sweetly at me. For someone who was centuries old, he was sure a cute little bugger. He said, "Now, much of what I just described would not be possible if we had all the answers."

"So, you're as much in the dark as me."

Now he gave me a slightly crooked smile. "Well, perhaps a little more in the light, Sam. Remember, I've been at this a lot longer than you."

"And you are an immortal, too?"

"In my own way."

"And what way is that?"

"One does not need to be a vampire, Samantha, or even a werewolf, to be immortal."

In that moment, I saw a man working feverishly in an old-style laboratory. Something Benjamin Franklin might have worked in. Or even Leonardo da Vinci. I saw many concoctions being attempted. Many concoctions being tossed out. And one concoction in particular that gave eternal life.

"Alchemy," I said, breathing the word.

He grinned again . . . and tapped the book again. "Shall we get back to your medallion, Sam?"

I nodded.

"Good," he said. "Because I've some very good news for you."

# 17.

After my meeting with Max—and after a mad dash through the parking lot—I was back in my minivan, gasping.

Now, as I sat there shaking violently, watching college students strolling past with their backpacks and cell phones and serious faces, I knew that I was losing my humanity.

I hate when that happens.

I sucked in air because sucking in air seemed to help me fight off the excruciating pain caused by the sun. I had to fight off the pain because I had to pick my kids up from school. But I couldn't get my hands to stop shaking. Couldn't get them to form around the key and insert it into the ignition.

So I breathed and shook and tried to calm down.

And as I sat there, I recalled Max's words spoken to me just a few minutes earlier: "I have some very good news for you, Samantha," he'd said. "The amethyst medallion is reputed to reverse the effects of . . . the sun."

"What, exactly, does that mean?" I had asked, not daring to believe what I thought it might mean.

"Once you unlock the medallion, Samantha Moon, the sun will no longer have power over you."

But his words were just not sinking in. It was just too much to hope for. Too much to believe. "I . . . I don't understand."

He had reached across the counter and gently took my hand. "It means, Sam, that you will be able to live in daylight again."

"But . . . how?"

He smiled mischievously. A mischievous smile in this situation was, in fact, maddening. He said, "Unlocking the secret to the medallion is easy enough, Sam, for those of great faith."

"Great faith? What does that mean?"

"You will know what to do, Sam."

Except I didn't know what to do. And, hell, when did I ever know what to do?

Now, as I continued to shake and breathe and burn in my van, I whispered his words again: "To live in daylight again."

I nearly wept at the thought.

Nearly. After all, I had my kids to pick up, and I wasn't going to be late again, dammit.

So, when the shaking had subsided enough to control the smaller movements of my fingers, I started the minivan, and as I drove, I saw myself at the beach with my kids, swimming with my kids, hiking with my kids. And watching my son play soccer in the bleachers with all the other parents.

Okay, now the tears found me.

And in my mind's eye, I saw myself sitting quietly high upon a faraway mountain and watching the sun rise for the first time in nearly seven years.

At the next red light, I buried my face in my hands and wept until the light turned green.

• • •

Damn.

I was a little late picking up the kids, which netted me a scowling look from the principal, who I'm sure didn't like me much. I knew he saw me as an unfit mother, especially after the bogus ideas Danny had planted last year.

Bastard.

Bogus or not, I was now on the principal's radar. I hate being on anyone's radar, let alone a principal's. Sigh.

On the way home, we stopped for some burgers at Burger King. Anthony had branched out a little and discovered that he now liked mayonnaise. But just a little mayonnaise. My little boy was growing up.

At home, while the kids ate and I made yet another excuse for why I wasn't hungry, I found myself in my office and working when my cell phone rang. I glanced at the faceplate, saw that it was a local number.

"Moon Investigations," I said cheerily enough, although I was hearing the grumblings of a fight brewing in the living room.

"Ms. Moon?" said an oddly familiar voice.

"Go for Moon," I said. I've always wanted to say that.

"Ms. Moon, my name's Robert Mason. I own the Fullerton Playhouse."

"And starred in *One Life to Live*."

"I wouldn't say 'starred,' but, yes, I had a recurring role until a few years ago."

"When they killed you off with a brain tumor."

"It saddens the heart. Were you a fan?"

"It happened to come on after *Judge Judy*."

He laughed a little. A deep, rich laugh. A deep, rich, fake laugh. "Judge Judy was a great lead-in."

It was at that moment that a full-fledged fight broke out in the next room. I even heard something break. Something glass. Shit.

"Hang on, Rob," I said.

I left the phone on the desk, dashed into the living room, and saw Anthony sitting on Tammy. Now that was a first. Tammy was always the bigger and stronger one. Granted, she was still bigger, but clearly not stronger. Her struggling seemed to be in vain. Indeed, she was looking at her brother oddly. No doubt marveling at what I was seeing, too.

I plucked him off his sister and deposited him on the new couch. I spent the next thirty-three seconds listening to "He said and she said and did that she started," and decided I'd heard enough. I turned the TV off and banished them both to their bedrooms. As they moped off, I couldn't help but notice the red mark around Tammy's arms where Anthony had pinned her to the floor.

*Jesus.*

Back in my office, I wasn't very surprised that Robert Mason hadn't hung up. After all, I suspected there was a very good reason why Robert Mason had called me.

After I apologized for the disruption, he said that was quite all right and that he wanted to meet me ASAP.

Yeah, that was the reason.

# 18.

I was waiting at Starbucks.

It was evening and the sun still had not set. By my internal vampire clock, I knew it was about twenty minutes away. My internal vampire clock also told me that I should be asleep, to awaken just as the sun set. I think, maybe, that's happened only two or three times. And that was when the whole family was sick.

Now, of course, only I was sick. Eternally sick.

The Starbucks was near the junior college, which meant there were a lot of young people inside with longish hair, random tattoos, squarish glasses, fuzzy beards, and cut-off jean shorts, all working importantly on their laptops. These were hipsters feeding and drinking in their natural habitat.

As I sat with my bottle of water, keenly aware that the two young men sitting at the table next to me were not only barefoot but one of them had tattoos of sandals on his feet, a handsome older gentleman stepped through the door, blinked, and scanned the coffee shop.

I waved. He spotted me and nodded. I think my stomach might have done a backflip. Someone might have gasped. Actually, that someone was me, never mind. The closer he got, the bluer his eyes got and the deeper the cleft in his chin seemed to get, too.

Not to mention, the darker his aura got.

I'm familiar with dark auras. The aura of the fallen angel who had visited me last Christmas had progressively gotten darker. Robert Mason's aura wasn't quite as foul, but the thick black cords that wove around and through him were disconcerting at best. What it meant, I didn't really know, but it couldn't be good.

Especially since my inner alarm began ringing.

He stood over me and reached out a hand, but now my warning bells were ringing so damn loud that I automatically recoiled. Women stared. Men stared. Hipsters glanced ironically. It was surely an odd scene. A renowned soap actor and a skittish woman afraid to make contact with him.

After another second or two, he retracted his hand and sat without me saying a word. As he made himself comfortable, I noted that the black snakes now moved over and under the table, slithering like living things. I shivered. No, *shuddered*.

He watched me closely. "Some would be insulted that you didn't shake my hand."

"And you?" I asked, noting that my voice sounded higher than normal. I verified the mental wall around my thoughts was impenetrable.

He tilted his head slightly, studying me. "I find it curious. You seem to be having a sort of . . . reaction to my presence. Why is that?"

"Well, you are the great Robert Mason, famous for playing the evil Dr. Conch on *One Life to Live*."

He continued studying me as he adjusted the drape of his slacks. He was, I noted, the only man in Starbucks wearing slacks. Maybe the only man ever. His jawline, I noticed, was impossibly straight. The women all checked him out, but he paid them no mind. Indeed, he only looked at me. No, stared at me. So intently that he was giving me the willies.

After a moment, he said, "Or perhaps you didn't want me to touch you, Ms. Moon. Is there something about me that repels you?"

"Your jawline," I said.

"What about my jawline?"

"It's impossibly straight."

His right hand, which was laying flat on the smooth table, twitched slightly. The black snakes that wove through his aura seemed to pick up their pace a little. The jawline in question rippled a little as he unconsciously bit down. He said, "I think you see things, Ms. Moon. Perhaps things around me. Tell me what you see."

"I thought we were here to discuss Brian Meeks."

His lips thinned into a weak smile. "Of course, Ms. Moon. What would you like to ask?"

Except that before I could open my mouth to speak, I felt something push against my mind, against the protective mental wall, and it kept on pushing, searching, feeling.

It was Robert Mason, who was staring at me intently. The man was extremely psychic.

My thoughts were not closed to those who were psychic. Only to other immortals and often to my own family members. Someone like Robert Mason could gain entry . . . if I wasn't vigilant.

I knew this wasn't really a meeting, but a feeling out of sorts. He wanted to know who he was up against. By not gaining entry into my thoughts, he might have gotten his answer. What that answer was, or how close to the truth he got, I didn't know.

So, I decided to ask him the only question that mattered. "Did you kill Brian Meeks?"

The coiling, smoky black snakes that wove in and out of his aura seemed to pick up in intensity. They appeared and disappeared. Robert Mason didn't react to my question. He sat calmly, hands resting on the table, blue eyes shining. Although I think the dimple in his chin might have quivered a little.

After a moment, he said, "Ah, but that wouldn't be any fun, would it? Taking away all the mystery?"

His own thoughts, of course, were closed to me, which I was eternally thankful for. I was honestly afraid to know what was lurking inside that handsome head of his. Hard to believe that one of America's favorite daytime soap opera stars was so damn . . . creepy.

"There's a door in the prop room," I said. "A door behind the big mirror. Where does it lead to?"

I probably shouldn't have asked him about the door. I probably should have left well enough alone and directed Sherbet to the door later. But I wanted to see Robert Mason's reaction now, and I got the one I was looking for. His eyes widened briefly, just enough for me to know that I was onto something.

He said, "How do you know about the door, Ms. Moon?"

"We all have our secrets. And taking away the mystery wouldn't be any fun, right?"

He looked at me. I looked at him. We did this for a few seconds, then he said, "I suppose. Very well, Ms. Moon. The door leads to another prop room. A long-forgotten prop room."

"Why did you call this meeting?"

"I saw you in the theater the other day. You looked interesting."

"Interesting how?"

He suddenly leaned over the small, wobbly table and whispered, "I know what you are, Ms. Moon. Mystery solved."

And with that, he got up, winked at me, and walked out.

# 19.

We were in Tammy's bedroom.

She was sitting on the floor in front of me while I brushed her long, dark hair. Tammy loved having her hair brushed, even when my cold fingers sometimes grazed her neck, inadvertently causing her to shudder. She used to hold my hands, back in the days when my hands were warm. These days, however, she almost never held my hands, and I didn't blame her. Who'd want to hold hands with a living corpse?

I cherished these quiet moments when I brushed her hair, listening to her stories about school and boys, teachers and boys, and movies and boys. She often asked me what it was like to kiss a boy or to be in love. She sometimes asked why Daddy and I were no longer together. Mostly we laughed and giggled, and if we were being too loud, Anthony would sometimes stick his head in the door and tell us we were being lame.

Tonight, Anthony was in the living room watching cartoons. Something on Nick at Night. He laughed, slapping his hand on the carpet the way he does when he sits on the floor. The vibration reached even us.

"Cartoons are so juvenile," said Tammy.

"Totally," I said.

"I haven't watched them in, like, a year."

"Same here."

"Well, I guess there are one or two that are okay, but mostly they're lame."

"Mostly," I said, nodding.

Anthony erupted in laughter again, hitting the floor even harder. The thuds reverberated up through our butts.

"God, he's so annoying," said Tammy. She didn't sound annoyed. She sounded impressed that she knew the word "annoying."

"He's eight years old," I said, as if that explained everything.

She shrugged and I continued brushing her long hair. Warm air from the heater vent washed over us. The TV blared from the living room. Yes, I truly cherished these small moments.

"Mommy?"

"Yes, baby?"

"There's something different about Anthony."

I stopped brushing. I think my heart might have stopped altogether. I resumed brushing and kept my voice as calm as possible. "Different how?" I asked.

"Well, yesterday I saw him wrestling with some other boys."

"Boys like to wrestle. It's what makes them boys."

"No, not that. He was wrestling the other boys."

"What do you mean, honey?"

She turned and looked back at me, her big round eyes looking at me like I was the world's biggest dolt. And maybe I was. "It was him against like seven other boys."

"They ganged up on him? That's not fair—"

"No, Mommy. They didn't gang up on him. They couldn't do anything to him. He was throwing them around like they were, you know . . ."

"Rag dolls?"

"What's a rag doll?"

"Never mind."

She went on to tell me that Anthony Moon, aged eight, was probably the strongest kid in their school.

I processed that information as I continued to brush. Somehow the subject turned to zits and I was telling her about the big one I got on my right nostril when I was in the tenth grade, and soon Tammy was doubled over on her side with laughter. From in the next room, I was vaguely aware of the TV being turned off and the trudging of footsteps.

Anthony stuck his head in his sister's room, looked at us on the floor, and said, "Lame."

And walked on.

# 20.

*Hi, Moon Dance.*

*Hey, big guy.*

*Big guy?*

*It's a term of affection,* I wrote.

*So you feel affection for me?*

*Of course I do, Fang.*

I felt him probing my mind a little, small, shivery touches that let me know he was there.

He wrote: *I think you love me, Moon Dance.*

*Friendly love, Fang.*

*I'll take friendly love. For now.*

*Good. Now, what's up?*

*I've got news about your son.*

*Talk to me.*

*First of all, is he still becoming stronger?*

*More so than ever. Tammy said he now routinely wrestles seven boys at once.*

*So, you could say he's seven times stronger.*

Put that way, and I nearly went into a panic. I wrote: *Yes, I guess. What does it mean?*

*I can feel you panicking, Moon Dance. Don't panic.*

*Please just tell me what's going on, Fang. I can't handle this. I'm seriously freaking out.*

*Okay, okay, hang in there. According to my sources, the vampire blood that briefly flowed through him hasn't entirely left him.*

"Oh my God," I said out loud to the empty room. More panic gripped me. Nearly overwhelmed me. I wrote: *But the vampirism has been reversed, Fang. The medallion . . .*

*Yes, the vampirism has been reversed. No, your son isn't a vampire. Not technically.*

I found myself on my feet, reeling, staggering, pacing. Jesus, what had I done to my son?

The IM window pinged with a new message. I sat back down. Fang had written: *Hang on, Moon Dance. It's not all bad. In fact, it's kind of good news, if you ask me.*

*Kind of? What the hell is going on, Fang? Please tell me.*

*Sam, your son will have all the strength of a vampire, but none of the weaknesses.*

I read his words, blinking through tears. *Are you sure?*

*Pretty sure.*

*He won't need to consume blood?*

*We don't think so.*

*Who's we?*

*My sources.*

*Fine,* I wrote. I didn't care about Fang's sources. Not now. I wrote: *What about the sunlight?*

*It should not affect him, Moon Dance.*

*And immortality?*

There was a small delay, followed by: *Perhaps.*

*Perhaps what?*

*There's a good chance your son might be immortal.*

*I don't understand. Why?*

*I don't think anyone really understands, Sam. The system was flawed somewhere, broke down. But, yes, we think he will retain the good qualities but none of the bad.*

*And being immortal is a good quality?*

*For some, the very best, Moon Dance.*

*But why did this happen?*

*Whoever created your kind, and whoever created the medallion, was not perfect. In essence, a mistake was made somewhere along the line. The reverse was not complete.*

*What do I do, Fang?*

*It is up to you to make the most of this, Moon Dance, and to help your son make the most of this, too. Think of this as an opportunity, Moon Dance. Not a curse. For both you and your son.*

I hung my head for a minute or two, then typed: *Thanks for your help, Fang.*

*So what will you do, Moon Dance?*

*I'm going to have a talk with him.*

*When?*

*I don't know. Goodnight, Fang.*

*Goodnight, Moon Dance.*

# 21.

Celebrities can hide their electronic footprints a little easier than the average citizen. This is because they can hide behind accountants and handlers. Because of this, my background search on Robert Mason took a little more digging than usual.

And what came up wasn't much.

I had his current residence. Or, rather, his last known residence. He was living in the hills above Fullerton. Nice area. Big homes. Lots of space. Perfect place to secretly drain someone dry. Or maybe many someones.

Interestingly, I knew of two people who also lived in the hills. Detective Hanner and a very old and very creepy Kabbalistic grandmaster. One was a vampire, and one was a kind of vampire.

Anyway, Robert Mason had no criminal record. An ex-wife of his accused him of abuse. He was never arrested, although a restraining order had been placed on him. I'd only met the guy once, and I wanted to put a restraining order on him, too. He had no kids, only the one marriage—divorced now fifteen years.

His last known professional acting job had been on *One Life to Live*, five years ago. And, according to the various reports I'd dug up, he'd been fired from his job. The reasons were conflicting, but more than one article suggested substance abuse.

Why he was fired or why he was divorced didn't seem to be of importance presently. That he was a full-blown psychopath now was obvious to me. That he harbored a deep evil was also obvious to me.

As I sat in my office, with my kids asleep down the hallway, I called Kingsley. He picked up on the second ring.

"Hi, baby," he said.

I didn't respond. At least, not with words.

"What's that sound?" he asked.

"I'm panting," I said. "You know, like a dog."

"Oh, brother. But, please, Sam. Say no more over the phone."

"Oh, I'm not saying anything," I said, and panted some more.

"Cute, Sam. Do you actually have something on your mind, or did you just call to make those ridiculous sounds?"

"Both," I said, and stopped panting long enough to catch him up to date on my investigation—in particular, my meeting with Robert Mason.

"Like he said," said Kingsley. "He knows what you are, Sam."

"In so short a time?"

"He must have suspected you were something more, which is why he scheduled the meeting. No doubt his suspicions were confirmed at the meeting." Kingsley paused. I knew he was choosing his words carefully over the open phone line. "We can hide from the majority of the world, Sam, but not from the truly psychic. They tend to see through us. Thankfully, there's not many of them."

"And those who do see us?"

"Well, those who are vocal about it are silenced."

I thought about his words. "I think Robert Mason saw an opportunity."

"To supply blood?"

"Yes," I said.

"No doubt a very lucrative gig."

I asked, "What do you know about blood suppliers?"

"Not much, but I know someone who undoubtedly would."

"Detective Hanner," I said.

"Boy, Sam. It's almost as if you could read my mind."

"I'll never say."

He laughed and we set up a dinner date later in the week, and when we had hung up, I made another call.

To the only other creature of the night that I knew.

# 22.

We were on her wide, wraparound patio deck.

The deck overlooked the same Fullerton Hills that Robert Mason lived in. And a famous Dodgers manager. And a very creepy old man who bartered in human life.

Detective Hanner was a beautiful woman. She was also a vampire. Perhaps a very old vampire.

We talked a little about the case as we sat back in wicker chairs, drinking from glasses just like regular people. My ankles were crossed and my pink New Balance running shoes couldn't have looked cuter. Detective Hanner was barefoot. Her talon-like toenails came to sharp points. Almost enough for one to lose one's appetite.

Almost.

But not quite. After all, we were both drinking from massive goblets of blood. We were sipping casually. Or trying to sip casually. Generally, there were long beats of silence as we each glugged heartily, since drinking blood is really a race against time and coagulation. It was all I could do to not make yummy smacking sounds. The blood was human, that much was obvious. It was also fresh. So very, very fresh.

Straight-from-the-vein fresh.

*So who am I drinking?* I wondered.

But I didn't ask. Not at the moment. At the moment, I was consumed by the blood, the taste, the high, the joy, the pleasure, the satisfaction.

Detective Hanner and Kingsley had slowly introduced me to the decadent pleasure of human blood. I hadn't liked it, not at first, and each time felt like a depraved journey into ecstasy.

*That's a lie. You always liked it. A little too much.*

And here I was again, indulging all my cravings with a vampire far older and more experienced than I was. It felt natural, probably the way any addict feels when they tap the needle or pop a cork. Like this was what I was made to do.

But I didn't have to enjoy its thick, sweet texture so much, did I?

Finally, I managed to pull away. I knew some blood was running down the corners of my mouth. Now, as I wiped my chin and licked my fingers, I could only imagine what I looked like.

*Like a monster,* I thought.

Hanner watched me from over her own goblet, her wild eyes shining with supernatural intensity. I noticed that she rarely blinked, and when she did, it almost seemed an afterthought. A reminder to look human.

I said, "I think our killer is a blood supplier."

She nodded. "It's easy to assume that."

"What do you know of blood suppliers?"

"Mortal or immortal?"

"What do you mean?" I asked.

"Vampires supply blood to other vampires. Like I just did you."

"Mortal," I said.

She held my gaze for many seconds. I couldn't read her mind, or even get a feel for what she was thinking, but I suspected she was debating how much to tell me. Finally, she said, "Yes, some are killers, although many get their supply from hospitals or mortuaries."

"Mortuaries?"

She nodded. "Of course. Why let all that valuable blood drain away when it could be put to good use?" She held up her nearly-finished goblet. "But fresh human blood is always preferable."

"How fresh?"

"Straight from a living source, even if that living source dies shortly thereafter."

I shuddered. Even though I knew most of this already, it always chilled me to think about it. And a cold-blooded vampire like me is hard to chill. "Why a living source?"

"Because blood is suffused with life force, Sam. Energies that vibrate at the cellular level. The residual energy left behind in animal blood—or that from a human corpse that's been deceased for an extended period—doesn't vibrate at the same frequency. Such blood is not in tune with who you are, Sam."

"So the fresher the blood . . . "

"The stronger we are. The healthier we are. The more extraordinary we are."

"How many mortal blood dealers are there?"

"Not many."

"Do you know of any?"

She stared at me for an uncomfortable amount of time. "I have found having a living donor in my house to be more ideal. A ready source, as they say." She grinned. "Sometimes, many ready sources."

I wondered if she used her looks to lure her living donors. Some guys would do anything to be with a woman as beautiful as her. Anything.

As we sat back in the wicker chairs, aglow with fresh blood, I realized that Detective Hanner hadn't really answered my question.

Now, why was that?

# 23.

My alarm clock blared.

It did this for a full five minutes before I emerged from whatever black abyss I descend into when asleep. Another five minutes before I could move my legs enough to sit up in bed. Truly, I was the waking dead.

As I sat there on the edge of the bed, wishing like hell I was back in that abyss, my cell phone chimed with a text message. I flopped my hand onto the night stand, felt around until I found my phone, brought it over to my half-open eyes.

A text from Danny, my dear old ex-husband, only not so dear anymore. It was simple and to the point and aggravated me to no end: *Coming over. Need help.*

"Shit."

And just as I deleted his message—as I do all his messages—there was a loud knocking sound on the front door.

"Shit," I said again. Definitely not how I wanted to start my day.

Ever.

I hauled my ass out of bed, stumbled through my room, then plodded barefoot to the front door. Along the way, I grabbed my sunglasses from the kitchen table, put them on, and opened the front door.

It was, of course, Danny. In all his pitiful glory, silhouetted against the glare from the afternoon sunlight. Too much sunlight, especially after just awakening. I backed up, shielding my eyes, feeling like something out of a Bela Lugosi movie.

"Sam, can we talk?"

"Do I have a choice?"

He came in, shutting the door quickly. Danny knew the routine. He'd lived long enough with my condition to know what to do. I felt my way over to the dining room chair and sank down.

"Geez, Sam. You don't look too well."

"Ya think."

Now that he was inside, I took in his unshaven face, wrinkled suit, disheveled hair, and couldn't find the energy to say something about the pot calling the kettle black. Instead, I said, "What do you want, Danny?"

"I need to hire you, Sam."

I nearly laughed. Hell, I wanted to laugh. Except laughing was for people who hadn't just emerged from the blackest depths. "You're kidding."

"I'm serious, Sam. I need to hire you."

"You, who hasn't paid me a dime of child support in seven months?"

He shifted in his seat. As he did so, I saw that his upper lip was swollen. "I know, Sam, and I'm sorry. This hasn't been easy on me, either."

I didn't want to get into it with Danny. At least not now. Hell, I had a whole lifetime to get into it with him.

"Fine," I said. "What kind of help?"

"Protection."

"What kind of protection?"

"From men."

"What kind of men?"

He looked away, adjusted his tie, giving his Adam's apple more wiggle room. "They're a gang, of sorts."

"Of sorts? What does that mean?"

Now I saw the sweat on his brow and along his upper lip. I also saw the fear in his eye. He waved his hands weakly. "Thugs. A local street gang, I dunno. They sort of run the area I do business in."

"They beat you up?"

He shrugged, too prideful to admit to being smacked around, but not enough to come to his ex-wife for help.

I said, "And by doing business, you mean that shithole where you charge lonely men to look at lonelier women's boobs?"

"Yes, Sam. My strip club."

I shook my head sadly.

"What, Sam?"

"You used to be ashamed of your club."

He was pacing now, running his hand through his thinning hair. "Well, I'm too afraid to be ashamed."

"Sit down," I said. "You're making me nervous."

He sat, although his knee still bounced up and down. I said, "They're extorting money from you."

He nodded. "A grand a week. For protection, of course."

"Of course," I said. "So what do you want me to do?"

He frowned a little. He hadn't really thought this through. "I'm not sure."

"Do you want them to stop picking on you?"

"Sam . . ."

"What?"

"Fine. Yes."

"The price for keeping these boys from picking on you is . . ." I did some quick math, which, in my groggy state, took a little longer than it should have. I said, "The price is four thousand, two hundred and sixty-two dollars."

"Jesus, Sam. You can't be serious."

"Oh, but I am. Seven months of child support, plus my usual fee. Have the cash here on my table in one hour and you just hired yourself a bodyguard."

He looked down at his hands. His knee continued to bounce. Loose change in his pocket clanged. Finally, he nodded and stood.

"I'll be back," he said.

"We'll see."

He did come back. Funny what a little fear will do to a man. He handed me a white envelope full of money, which I counted in front of him. Once done, I grinned and held out my hand. He looked at it reluctantly, then finally shook it, wincing as he did so.

After all, I might have squeezed a little too hard.

# 24.

I was sitting cross-legged on a large boulder, on a rock-strewn hill, high above the deserts outside Corona.

I was, in fact, not too far from where Brian Meeks had been found. Or dumped. It was a quiet spot, miles from any major roads. Just me, the lizards, and the coyotes. And maybe a rattle-snake or two.

In the far distance I could hear the steady drone of the 15 Freeway. In the near distance, all I could hear was the wind, moaning gently over the boulder and, subsequently, me. Rocking me a little. I let the wind rock me, as I felt the latent heat from the boulder rise up through my jeans.

My minivan was parked on a dirt service road not too far from here. The service road had been closed off by a locked gate. Amazingly, the lock just happened to fall apart in my hands as I innocently examined it. Shoddy workmanship.

So, what the hell, I let myself in.

Now my jeans were dusty and my cute shoes were officially dirty. But I didn't care. I needed to be out here. Craving the solace, the peace, the oneness.

I closed my eyes and rested my hands on my knees. My children were at home with the sitter, and so I let all worry for them disappear. I took a deep breath, not because I needed the oxygen, but because I wanted to center myself. Years ago, I had done yoga. I knew something about centering myself.

Months ago, I had learned the art of automatic writing, in which one channels another entity to receive messages from angels, or the spirit world, or from Jim Morrison.

Either way, the results were interesting, but now I was determined to go beyond automatic writing. To go deeper, straight to the source. And what was the source? I didn't know. Not entirely. But I was determined to find out.

With my eyes still shut, I tilted my face up toward the heavens, and was met immediately by a mostly cool breeze laced with some tendrils of heat. I always welcomed heat, no matter how small or fleeting.

I focused on my breathing, releasing my thoughts to the wind, where I imagined them being snatched up and escorted far away. To meditate—to do it right—I had to have my mind blank. As blank as I could make it.

Breathing was the key. No, the act of focusing on my breathing was the key. Focusing on something simple. Mindless. It settles the mind. Relaxes it. Bypasses the ego. The ego, the foremind, that thing we use to calculate and imagine and worry and ponder, didn't like to be bypassed. The ego liked to remain in control.

So I continued concentrating on the fresh air flowing into my lungs. Despite my best efforts, my mind drifted to my son and soon worry gripped me, but I released that thought, too. To the wind.

Breathing.

Flowing in and out.

In and out.

Over lips and teeth and tongue . . . deep into my lungs.

I thought of blood dealers and corpses hanging upside down.

I shivered and released that thought, too. Into the wind.

My mind felt blank, although fleeting images sometimes crossed it. Kingsley. Fang. Sherbet. Strong men. Strange men. Sexy men.

I released those thoughts, too.

I felt myself relaxing as I did more deep breathing. I didn't need to breathe, granted, but oxygen in this case wasn't the purpose here. The purpose here was to relax my mind. To calm it. To calm it so completely that I could access . . . what?

I didn't know.

But I was about to find out.

Breathe in, breathe out.

Breathe in, Samantha.

Just breathe.

*It's easy. Yes, so easy. Do you see how easy it is, Sam? Focus, child. There now. Good, good. Just focus on your breathing. You're almost there. Good, good.*

*Good . . .*

It took a moment for me to realize that the thoughts in my head were no longer my own.

*Welcome back, Samantha Moon,* said the voice.

# 25.

I knew I was still sitting on the boulder overlooking the desert, but I also knew that something very, very strange was happening to me.

The strangeness boiled down to a feeling. I felt unhinged, disconnected from my body. I knew I was sitting cross-legged on the hard surface, but I felt as if I were somewhere else, too. Not necessarily above my body. Somewhere else. Where, exactly, I didn't know. As I thought about this, I suddenly felt a jolting wave of dizziness.

*Ground yourself, Sam,* said the voice.

I knew something about grounding, having done it back when I was doing the automatic writing. Quickly, I imagined three silver ropes, attached to my ankles and lower spine, reaching all the way down into the earth—down, down— all the way to the center of the earth, where they fastened themselves around three massive boulders. Grounded. To the very earth itself.

*Very good, Sam.*

Instantly, the feeling of separateness ceased. I was back in my body. Although my eyes were still closed, I began seeing light appear at the peripherals of my vision. The light continued filling my head, growing steadily brighter, so bright that I was suddenly sure it wasn't coming from inside my mind after all. Surely it was coming from somewhere beyond me. Above me. Around me. Within me. From everywhere.

And from within that light I saw a vague shape materialize. A woman. A glowing woman. Her face and body remained indistinct.

*Baby steps, Samantha. I'll reveal more later. Once you've gotten the hang of this.*

*Hang of what?*

*Speaking to me.*

*Who are you?*

*Everything and nothing.*

*I don't understand.*

*You will. In time.*

The light coalesced into a room made of crystal. Now the burning white light shone brightly beyond, refracting through the crystal, exploding, washing over me. For the first time in a long, long time, I didn't shrink from the light.

*Where am I?*

The woman stepped closer to me. She was, in fact, a lovely older woman. Roundish. Happy, smiling face. Pink cheeks. She looked like anyone's kind grandmother. Serenity surrounded her, radiated from her.

*You are in a safe place, Samantha.*

*What's happening to me?*

*You've bypassed the physical world and entered into the spiritual.*

*But I'm still sitting here on the ledge.*

*Yes, Sam. The spiritual is never very far away. In fact, it's closer than most people think.*

*I don't understand.*

*You will. In time.*

*You keep saying that.*

*Because it keeps being true.*

*So I'm in the physical, but also in the spiritual? I'm in both places?*

*You are more than your physical body, Sam. The body is the physical receptacle of the soul.*

*Except my body can't die.*

*Not anymore. Not in the traditional sense.*

*Then I'm a freak.*

*You are the result of entities long ago attempting a shortcut, entities who lived in fear.*

*Lived in fear of what?*

*Dying. Their creation—the vampire—lives on to this day, as do similar creations.*

*I never asked for this.*

*Not overtly, Sam.*

*What does that mean?*

*It means that, on some level, you did ask for this. On some level you did ask to become more than you were, stronger than you were, faster than you were, braver than you were.*

*And this is the answer? To turn me into a ghoul?*

*It was an answer. An answer that you would accept.*

*But I'm living a nightmare.*

*You are choosing to live a nightmare, Samantha Moon. Choose differently.*

I grew silent, fully aware that I was still sitting on the boulder overlooking the desert, but also aware that my mind—or spirit—was in this crystal room. I'm certain the sensation would have disoriented me, if not for the grounding done earlier. The woman moved a little closer, her hands clasped before her. She seemed content to watch me sweetly, lovingly.

*Who are you?* I asked, thinking the words. *And please, no cryptic answers.*

Now the woman in front of me disappeared. So did the crystal room. I was given a view of the universe, which spread before me in every direction. I sensed everything, saw everything, felt everything. I also sensed a glorious presence that infused everything, a presence from which all things were born.

*Is that you? The thing that is in all things? Everywhere and nowhere?*

*A good way of looking at things, Sam.*

*But, then, why are you talking to me?*

As I thought those words, I was once again back in the crystal room. I sensed that if I would open my physical eyes, all of this would disappear and I would be back on the boulder, alone in the desert, and no doubt wondering if I had dreamed all of this. So, I kept my eyes closed. Yes, tightly closed.

*Because you are seeking answers, child. I have the answers.*

*To everything?*

*In a word: Yes.*

I let that sink in. Beyond the crystal walls, the shining white light seemed to grow in intensity, its radiance reaching through the walls and through me, too. My body felt cleansed. My body felt light. There was no judgment in this light. It just was. Pure and perfect and eternal.

The smiling woman before me cocked her head to one side. *You are here for a specific reason, Sam.*

*I am.*

*Tell me what's on your heart.*

I thought of my son, of his increasing strength. What would happen to him? What other vampiric attributes would he take on? I thought of this and more, as fear and uncertainty coursed through me. As these thoughts filled my head, the light wavered along the peripheral of my vision. The woman in front of me faded, too. She nodded, and I knew she knew my thoughts.

*Release the fear, Sam.*

*But I . . . can't. He's my son. I'm so scared.*

More darkness encroached and the light beyond dimmed.

She gripped my hands even tighter. *What do you want, Sam?*

*I want my son to have a normal life.*

*Then proclaim it. State it. Feel it. Believe it. Do not grovel for it. Do not beg for it. Instead . . . be it.*

*But something's happening to him.*

*Yes.*

*Something that I did to him.*

She nodded and held my hands, and for now, the darkness that had been encroaching along the edge of my vision seemed to pause, although it was still there. Seemingly waiting.

*Find the good in all things, Sam. Find the beauty. And you will find peace and joy.*

*But my son . . . he's so different now.*

*We are all different, Sam. And we are all the same. Love who he is. Teach him who he is. Believe in who he is.*

*And who is he?*

*A magnificent being, as are you.*

I held back the tears. I held back a strong urge to let out a choking cry. It had been so long since someone had spoken to me in such kind, loving words. Since someone had given me such pure, unconditional love.

*But will he be okay?*

*With his mother's love, he can be anything. Show him love and strength, Sam. Not fear and worry.*

I nodded. The darkness began retreating, and as I lifted my head and opened my heart, the darkness disappeared completely. The woman came toward me and took my hands. She smiled at me comfortingly and lovingly.

*Open your eyes now, Sam.*

I did, and I was back on the boulder, with the wind blowing in my hair and dust covering my clothes. I sat like that for a few moments, coming back to my senses, back to my body. Shortly, I checked my cell. I had been sitting there for three hours. I stared disbelievingly at my phone. Three hours. It had felt like ten minutes.

Something squeezed my hands, something unseen, and electricity surged through me. No, not electricity.

Love.

The feeling rippled through me again and again, then slowly disappeared, and I was left alone.

# 26.

It was late.

I was perched on the ridge of a high gable next door to Robert Mason's opulent home. Granted, the home I was perched upon wasn't too shabby, either. The entire tract was filled with mini-mansions, all nestled in the hills high above Fullerton.

The community was gated. In fact, there were even two sets of gates. Twice I spotted security guards rolling quietly through the streets in their electric golf carts. Never once did they think to look up at me. If so, they might have been in for the shock of their lives.

I had spent the past two days reviewing missing-person files with Sherbet. In particular, looking for a connection to Robert Mason. Sherbet knew about my strange meeting with the ex-soap opera star. The detective agreed that if we could connect another victim to Robert Mason, then we might convince a judge to give us a search warrant.

But so far, nothing.

This was my second night of surveillance, too. Or, more accurately, my second night perched up here like a living gargoyle. The first night had been uneventful. Robert Mason had come home around 2 a.m., pulling into his garage in a slick new Jaguar. His windows were tinted, too dark for even my eyes. The lights had remained on inside the house for about an hour after that, in which I'd seen only one figure moving through the house. I had waited another two hours, then leaped from the perch, flapped my wings hard, and somehow managed to elude the two guards in their electric golf cart.

Now I was back for a second night. What, exactly, was I looking for? I didn't know. A pattern perhaps. Something that stood out. Who he was meeting with. Who was coming and going? Anything that I could follow up on.

Tonight, the house was empty and dark. It was also well past the time he'd returned last night. Instinctively, I knew the sun was about two hours away, about the time I had abandoned my post last night.

So, where was Robert Mason?

I knew he lived alone. I knew he was divorced. I knew his ex-wife had a restraining order on him. I also knew that everything was leading to one thing: the secret door behind the mirror.

So far, his house was proving uneventful, although I now knew the freaky bastard was prone to staying out all night. Whatever was happening, it wasn't happening here, in this ultra-exclusive and highly-secured community. Poke fun at them all I want, the guards here kept strict schedules. Nothing much was coming or going without their knowledge. If Robert Mason was the killer, he was taking a phenomenal risk bringing any victims here.

Unlike his theater.

Which he owned and had total access to at all hours of the night.

The golf cart came again. Two guards, sitting next to each other, huddled against the cold. I didn't huddle against the cold. I sat like a demon, high above the housing tract.

Waiting and watching.

# 27.

I parked across the street from my ex-husband's strip club. Remarkably, a tear of shattered pride did not come to my eye.

Danny and his partners of sleazeballs had cleaned up the place a little. The ugly cinder block building had been painted white. The dirt parking lot had been paved over. And a flashing neon sign now indicated that here be nude women. I shook my head sadly. Men slouched in and out of the club. Single men. Most didn't appear happy. A big black guy stood at the front entrance checking IDs. Music pumped enthusiastically from the open door.

I sat and watched, my heart heavy. Above, the moon was half-full. The stars were out. No clouds. No wind. A perfect night to see desperate women exploited for dollar bills.

I was feeling sick, and not because I was parked outside Danny's house of flesh. Earlier, I had consumed a packet of animal blood. Pig blood, this time. The impurities in the blood always made me sick. My digestive system was designed for blood only. Not the bits of bone, hair, and meat floating around in the stuff they sold me. I probably should filter the blood myself, but I honestly didn't want to see what I was drinking. Better to tear the packet open, close my eyes, down the stuff as fast as possible, and will myself not to gag.

Impurities or not, the animal blood never truly revitalized me. It satisfied a hunger, a craving. It kept me alive and functioning. But it did not energize me. Not the way human blood did. And that scared the shit out of me.

There was really no comparison. My kind was obviously designed to consume human blood. And there was such a ready supply of the stuff.

Mercifully, the animal blood kept my hunger in check, but I wondered for how long. Would there come a day when animal blood would no longer suffice? I didn't know, but that thought alone was enough to get me rocking in my front seat, holding my aching stomach.

A few minutes later, with my stomach still doing somersaults, I pulled away from the curb, drove past the strip club, and was soon trawling through some pretty rough-looking neighborhoods. Most homes here were surrounded with low, wrought-iron fences. Most windows were barred. More wrought iron. Clearly, iron work was alive and well here in Colton.

Five minutes later, while waiting for a light at a mostly empty corner, I watched a boy on a bike ride up to three young men lounging near a liquor store. The boy gave a tall black guy an envelope. The black guy gave the boy a baggie.

Bingo.

I pulled up next to them in a no-parking zone. I parked there anyway and got out. They stared at me. I was wearing jeans and a light sweater. They were wearing jeans and heavy jackets. The heavy jackets reminded me of the Michelin Man, or maybe something astronauts might wear in deep space. This wasn't deep space. This was a hood in Colton and I knew what was inside their jackets. Drugs and guns. I had to act quickly.

"Hey pretty lady—" one of them said, turning to me.

But that was as far as he got. I punched him hard enough to lift him off his feet and into the liquor store wall behind him. While he was busy passing out, I turned and punched the lone Hispanic guy square in the nose. His head snapped back so violently that I thought I might have broken his neck. One moment he was standing there. The next, he was on his back and bleeding.

The third guy was making a move to reach inside his too-thick jacket when I slapped him hard enough to get his attention, but not so hard as to knock him out cold. A few encouraging smacks later, followed by a knee to the groin, and I had the information I was looking for.

Their boss was a guy named Johnny. And he was here. At the liquor store.

I smacked the third guy again, this time for selling drugs to kids, and sent him spinning into my minivan's front fender, which he promptly bounced off of, leaving a skull-sized dent. He lay unmoving on the sidewalk.

Now, how the hell was I going to explain that to my insurance agent?

I headed into the liquor store.

# 28.

It was empty, except for an old black man sitting behind the counter. Apparently, he hadn't heard the ruckus outside. He was casually flipping through a newspaper, safe behind his bullet-proof glass which sported two deep fractures. Bullet impacts.

I scanned the store. There was a back room, from which I heard voices. I headed toward it, passing a glass cooler and a Red Bull display along the way. The smell of weed grew steadily stronger as I approached the back door, which I promptly kicked in.

There were two of them, both smoking and drinking and playing cards. Rap music played in the background. The room was just big enough for the two goons to sit comfortably. On the far wall, an open door led down a short hallway. Two big hand-guns were sitting on the table. They reached for them. I did, too. Unfortunately for them, I was faster.

I pointed both weapons at them. "Don't move," I said.

They didn't move. I left the room and headed down the short hallway. There was a shut door at the far end. Yellow light under the door. I heard frantic shuffling inside.

I picked up my speed, and threw a shoulder into the door and spilled into the room, rolling, coming to my knees and holding both handguns out before me as the only man came up from behind his desk holding a shotgun.

He saw the weapons pointed at his face and made a very smart move. He set the weapon down on the desk and held his hands up. He was a handsome black man. Young, maybe twenty-five, maybe a little older. His teeth were perfect and he was wearing a nice suit. He looked, if anything, like a young man trying to be taken seriously. Trying to be something he wasn't.

"Sit down," I said.

He sat, watching me closely, curiously. Since there was no-where for me to sit, I went around and sat on the corner of his desk, next to him. Our knees were almost touching. I heard some noise down the hallway, but I wasn't worried about the noise down the hall. My inner alarm was not ringing. There was no real danger here. At least, not yet. The smell of weed was not so prevalent in the back room.

"We have a problem, Johnny," I said.

"What problem?" he asked easily, smoothly, confidently.

Johnny didn't sound like a kid from the streets. He was well-spoken. Enunciated his words crisply. He also watched me carefully. No doubt his brain was having a hard time processing what he was seeing. A woman. A white woman. A lone white woman. Here in my office. I'm sure it wasn't adding up. No doubt it wasn't computing. And so he stared and waited and processed.

"You've been threatening local businesses," I said. "Extorting money from hard-working people."

His eyes narrowed. "You a cop?"

I swung my feet a little. My sneakers just missed hitting the ratty carpet. "Nope."

"You with the feds?"

I smiled. "Just little ol' me."

"Who are you?"

"Now, if I told you that I'd have to kill you."

He stared at me. I smiled sweetly. Sweat rolled down from inside his hairline and made its way into his collar. This wasn't looking good to him, and he knew it. In fact, I could almost see the moment where he went from thinking this was surreal, to thinking his own life might actually be in jeopardy.

"What do you want?"

"You're going to stop extorting from local business. Got it?"

He sat back in his chair and relaxed a little. He said, "You're kind of a badass, huh?"

"Kind of."

He was handsome and he knew it. He gave me a bright smile and did something with his eyes that made them sparkle even more somehow. As if he could flip a switch.

He chuckled. "You come in here, kick in my door, and tell me how to run my business."

"That about sums it up."

"You might be the craziest bitch I've ever met."

"Maybe."

"Now, why is that?"

"Let's just say I've got mad skills."

Now he laughed, a deep, hearty laugh, and showed a lot of teeth. Nice laugh. Nice smile.

"Mad skills," he said. "That's good. Who are you working for, baby?"

"An interested party. But I don't say 'goo goo gah gah' and I'm not wearing diapers, so I'm not a baby."

"Okay, I get it. Now, if I don't suspend operations?"

"You'll be seeing me again."

He held my gaze. I think I swallowed a little harder than I intended to.

"Maybe that ain't such a bad thing," he said.

"Just ask your boys outside."

He laughed again, shook his head. "You're one freaky lady. Okay, you win. No collections. For now."

"Smart move."

I got up, headed for the door. As I was about to exit, he said, "Can I have my guns back? I do, after all, have a business to run."

I paused at the door and thought about it, then turned and set the pistols next to the shotgun. I said, "I'm watching you."

His eyes flashed. "I hope so, pretty lady."

I turned and left.

# 29.

"Your son was in a fight today, Ms. Moon," said Principal West.

I was in his office with Anthony, who was sitting next to me. Anthony smelled of fresh grass, sweat, and blood. His clothing was torn, and there were grass stains along his shoulders and knees. There was a small spot of blood on his shirt. He breathed easily, calmly, staring straight ahead. He didn't appear the least bit upset. This coming from a boy who used to cry if his sister gave him a noogie.

"What happened?" I asked.

"Your son, Ms. Moon, beat up a young man so severely we had to call an ambulance."

I gasped and faced Anthony. Now I could see the tears forming in his eyes. I didn't have much access to my son's thoughts, but I could read auras and body language, not to mention I just knew my son. Knew him better than anyone. And he was scared. Perhaps for what he had done. Perhaps for the harm he had caused. Perhaps for who he was becoming.

The principal continued, "From what I understand—and this has been confirmed by nearly a dozen other students and teachers who witnessed the fight—the school bully, a kid nearly twice the size of your son, and two of his friends were picking on a girl. Grabbing her. Apparently one tried to kiss her. And that's when your son stepped in."

Now my son looked at me for the first time. Tears were in his eyes and there was some dirt in his hairline, but what I saw most was the defiant look in his eyes.

"She was crying, Mommy. She kept asking them to stop. But they wouldn't. They kept picking on her. And no one would help her." He looked forward again, clenching his little fists in his lap. "Everyone's afraid of them, but I'm not."

No one said anything. The principal stared at my son. In complete disbelief, judging by the look on his face. A moment later, the principal continued the story.

Anthony stepped in, pulled the main bully off the girl. And not just *pulled*. Threw, apparently. The other boys jumped my son. The fight was chaotic. Fists swinging, bodies rolling. No one would help. No one would jump in. It was a third grader against three sixth graders. And then something miraculous started happening. One by one, the sixth graders started falling by the wayside, rolling out of the melee, bleeding and groaning and hurt, until finally my son had ended up on top, leveling punch after punch into the older boy's face. It had taken three teachers to pull him off.

The principal's voice trailed off and he looked again at my son with complete awe. Myself, I had never been prouder.

"The leader is in the hospital. Apparently they're stitching his mouth and replacing some teeth."

Outside, I heard some excited voices in the various offices. The principal rubbed his face and kept staring at Anthony. Finally, he sat back in his chair.

"I've never seen or heard anything like this in my twenty years in teaching, Ms. Moon. What your son did . . . was very brave, very selfless, very admirable. But I have to suspend him."

"For protecting a girl?"

He smiled gently. "For fighting, Ms. Moon. We have a strict policy on that. The other boys will be severely dealt with, trust me. But let's let things cool off for a few days. Your son has caused quite an uproar. And, of course, there could be legal consequences."

A few minutes later, as Anthony and I exited the administration offices, I couldn't help but notice everyone staring after us. The principal, secretaries, students and teachers.

Staring at the freaks.

# 30.

We were at Cold Stone Creamery.

The place was empty. No real surprise there since it was the end of January, still cold even for Southern California. Of course, the cold weather didn't stop the sun from searing my skin as I dashed across the parking lot. Now, as Anthony hungrily ate his bowl of ice cream, I sat huddled as far away from the windows as possible.

"I'm sorry, Mommy," said Anthony, in between mouthfuls of ice cream, a masterful concoction of chocolate ice cream, brownies, and Snickers bars, all prepared on a cold stone which, apparently, made the ice cream magical. I wouldn't know, but I think the brownie and Snickers bar had something to do with it.

"Sorry for what?" I asked.

"For fighting."

"Are you sorry for helping the girl?"

"No. She was crying."

"Are you sorry for hurting the boy?"

He thought about that. There was ice cream on his nose. "Well, yes. I didn't mean to hurted him so bad."

"Maybe you can apologize to him someday for hurting him so bad then."

"Okay, Mommy."

He went back to his ice cream, which was nearly gone. How he could eat ice cream so fast, I hadn't a clue. I distinctly recalled a little something called brain freeze. Anthony, apparently, powered through it.

"Tammy tells me that you can wrestle seven boys at once."

"Sometimes ten."

I think my eyes bulged a little, but Anthony was too busy dragging his plastic spoon along the inside edge of the bowl to see my reaction. His little face was the picture of concentration. Ice cream was serious business.

"That's a lot of boys against just one boy, don't you think?"

He shrugged. "I guess. I dunno. Maybe I'm just stronger. Can I have another ice cream?"

"One's enough. I'm making dinner soon."

He stuck out his lower lip the way he does when he wants something. He hardly looked like a kid who just sent the school bully to the hospital.

I said, "Do you like being so strong?"

He gave me a half-assed shrug, since he was still officially in pouting mode. "It's kinda cool, I guess." Then he began poking his fingers through the Styrofoam bowl and wiggling them at himself, then at me. "Ice cream worms!"

I took the bowl from him. His fingers, I saw, were now covered in chocolate ice cream. He pouted some more.

I said, "Do you wonder why you're so strong?"

He shrugged, though some of his pouting steam was dissipating. "Not really."

I looked at my son. He was still quite little for his age. Too little to be beating up three school punks. Too little to be wrestling a whole group of kids. His dark hair was thick and still a little mussed, no doubt from the fight. He showed no signs of having fought three older boys, although he had put one in the hospital. I suspected a legend was being born about him as we sat here at Cold Stone, whispered throughout school. His life, I suspected, was about to forever change.

*No, it changed seven months ago,* I thought. *When you changed him.*

*When I saved him, goddammit!*

I took a deep, shuddering breath. Presently, Anthony was using his fingertip and a few chocolate drips to make shapes on the table. Circles. Happy faces. Sad faces. Such an innocent boy.

*What have I done?*

"Anthony," I said. "I need to talk to you about something very important."

He looked up, terrified. "But you said you weren't mad, Mommy."

"I'm not mad, baby. This is about something else."

"About Tammy?"

"What about Tammy?"

"Because she smells so bad?"

And he started giggling, so much so that he passed gas, too. This led to more giggling and a scowl from the Cold Stone manager. And when a wave of gassy foulness hit me, I leaped up from the table, grabbed his hand, and we made a mad dash to the minivan, where Anthony continued giggling. Myself included.

Laughing and burning alive.

# 31.

Anthony knew the drill.

He knew that Mommy had to have the shades drawn in the car. He also knew that Mommy tended to shriek when sunlight hit her directly, so as I faced him in the front seat, as I pulled my knees up and kept my arms out of any direct sunlight, he didn't think much of it. Mommy, after all, was sick.

Or so he thought.

*It's time,* I thought. *Time to tell him the truth.*

Easier said than done. At least eight different times I opened my mouth to speak, and at least eight different times nothing came out. While I sat there opening and closing my mouth, Anthony played his Gameboy. There was still chocolate on his nose.

I pushed through the nerves and fear and got my mouth working. "Anthony, baby, I need to talk to you about something important—and, no, it's *not* about Tammy's B.O."

He giggled a little, then looked over at me, suddenly serious. "I'm sorry about those boys, Mommy."

"I know you are, honey. Put the Gameboy down. I want to talk to you about something serious, something related to what happened today."

"Related?" he asked, scrunching up his little face.

"It means 'connected.'"

"Like how relatives are connected."

"Yes, that's right. You see, Mommy is . . ." Except I couldn't finish the sentence. I paused and thought long and hard about the wisdom of continuing it. I paused so long that Anthony looked up at me, squinting with just one eye the way he does sometimes.

*He needs to know. He has to know. It's only fair. He can't grow up not knowing. But he's so young. So young . . .*

"Are you okay, Mommy? Is the sun hurting you bad?"

"I'm okay, baby." I took in some air to calm myself, then plunged forward. "Anthony, I'm not like other mommies."

He nodded. "I know. Because you can't go in the sun."

"That's part of it, honey. You see, I'm different in other ways, too. I'm stronger than other mommies."

"Stronger?"

I raised my arm and flexed my bicep, although I don't think much of anything flexed. "Yes, stronger. In fact, I'm stronger than most men, too."

"You mean strong like me," he said.

"Yes."

"Well, duh, Mom. I'm only your kid. Kids have the same stuff their mommies have. But only half of the daddy's."

Now I was confused. "Only half of their daddy's?"

"Duh, Mom. Kids *come* from their mommies, not their daddies."

"I see," I said. "Very logical."

Anthony nodded as if he'd spoken the truth. Then he turned to me, squinting with one eye again. "Is Tammy strong, too?"

"No. She's not like us."

"Why not?"

I shifted in my seat. I wanted to look away. I wanted to avoid his innocent stare. How do you look a little boy in the eye and tell him what I was about to tell him? I didn't know. I didn't know anything. He had to know. He had to. I believed that with all my heart and soul. My dead heart and damned soul.

I said, "Do you remember when you were sick last year?"

My son nodded absently. Mercifully, he looked away and was now playing with the zipper to his jacket.

"Well, last year you were very, very sick, so sick that Mommy had to make you stronger."

"Why?"

"So that you could fight the sickness."

"Oh, cool." He stopped playing with the zipper. He stared at it for a few seconds, then his little face scrunched up the way it does just before he asks a question. "But how did you make me stronger?"

The question I knew he would inevitably ask. Baby steps, I reminded myself. He needed only to be made aware that he was different . . . and why he was different. Baby steps for now. More later, when he's older.

"I gave you a part of me."

"What part?"

Looking into those round eyes, those red lips, those chubby cheeks . . . cheeks that were rapidly turning sharper and sharper . . . I just couldn't do it. I couldn't tell him that he fed from my wrist.

*Not yet,* I thought. Someday. Perhaps someday soon. Not now. Baby steps.

Instead, I tapped my heart. "I gave you love, baby. All the love I had in the world."

"And it made me stronger?"

"It made you strong like me."

"Wow."

"But this is our secret, okay?"

"Why?"

"Because we're a little different than other people."

"Can I still go in the sun?"

"Yes," I said.

"But how are we different?"

"Well, we are stronger than most people."

"Oh, cool."

"But it's our secret, okay? The way Superman keeps his identity secret."

"And Batman and Spider-Man!"

"Yes, exactly."

"Oh, my gosh! Are we like . . . superheroes?"

I thought about that. I thought of my son taking care of the school bullies. I thought of myself taking care of Johnny and his gang.

I nodded. "Yeah, a little bit."

"Oh, cool!" He paused and cocked his head a little. "But will I ever be normal again?"

His question hit me by surprise. Maybe I was dreading hearing it. Maybe I had hoped he would never ask it. I looked at him, then looked away. I rubbed my hands together, then ran my fingers through my hair. My son, I knew, would never be normal again. Ever. I was suddenly overwhelmed with what I had done to him.

"Why are you crying, Mommy?"

"I'm sorry, baby."

"Sorry for what?"

So innocent. So sweet. He didn't deserve this. Shit. I started rocking in my seat as my son watched me with wide, concerned eyes. He started patting me on the arm the way he does when he's nervous.

"I'm sorry, Mommy. I'm sorry I made you cry. I didn't mean to."

I covered my face and did my best to hide my tears, the deep pain that seemed to want to burst from my chest. I held it in. Or tried to.

"I'm so sorry, baby."

"It's okay, Mommy."

And he kept telling me it would be okay, over and over, as I rocked in my seat, weeping into my hands.

# 32.

On the way home from Cold Stone Creamery, I was certain we had picked up a tail.

It was a white cargo van with tinted windows. It had pulled out behind us as we exited the Cold Stone parking lot, then had dropped back four or five car lengths.

Where it held steady.

Until we were about halfway to my house, when it peeled away suddenly. I wouldn't have thought anything of it, except that my inner alarm system had begun buzzing steadily.

A block later, another van appeared behind me. A blue cargo van. Tinted windows. Again five car lengths behind. They were using a tag-team system. I was sure of it. If done right, it's a system that's nearly impossible to detect by the mark.

Except when your mark is a vampire with a highly sensitive inner alarm system. Except when your mark is an ex-federal agent trained to pick up tails.

I made a few random turns, and it kept pace. Anthony turned and looked at me curiously but didn't say anything. Mommy was weird, after all.

I led the van to a quieter street, one with only a single lane, and soon it was directly behind me. I didn't recognize the guy behind the wheel.

Soon, we stopped at a stop sign. Another thing I'd learned to do: reading license plates in my rearview mirror.

Backward.

. . .

At home, I ran the plate.

The owner was *A-1 Retro Services* out of New Jersey. No address. I did a Google search on A-1 Retro Services and got nothing.

This might seem like a dead end, but it wasn't. It was proof that I had indeed been followed. In particular, by someone who knew how to stay anonymous. Not hard to do, actually, but it did take some creative accounting.

I stared down at my screen, drummed my fingers, let the information soak in. Ultimately, the question remained: Why was I being followed?

I thought about that as I sat back in my office chair and listened to Anthony playing something called Skylanders on his Xbox. Tammy was still at school. I'd arranged with her best friend's mom to pick her up as well. These days, there were only so many times I could dash out the door and into the sunlight.

Either my condition was getting progressively worse, or I was becoming more monstrous.

Or maybe they were one and the same.

My inner alarm hadn't stopped jangling since we'd gotten home; now, it was just one long, continuous buzz inside my inner ear. Enough to rattle me and keep me on edge.

It's not uncommon for a P.I. to be followed. Granted, it certainly doesn't happen as much as it might in movies or books, but it can happen. The last time I'd been followed was seven months ago, by a handsome, blond-haired vampire hunter with issues. He was last seen heading west on a Carnival cruise ship to Hawaii, courtesy of yours truly.

So who was out there now? Who was watching me? And why?

The two vans had been driven by experienced surveillance drivers, working in tandem with each other. Now, private eyes piss a lot of people off. Especially cheating husbands and wives.

Except cheating husbands and wives did not use an advanced tag-team surveillance technique.

Down the hallway, in his bedroom, my son laughed loudly. Maybe I shouldn't let him play video games. Maybe a good mother would have punished her son for being suspended from school.

But I just couldn't justify punishing him for helping a girl. Punishing him for doing something *right*.

The inner alarm continued to buzz, so much so that I nearly yelled, "Stop!"

Instead, I got up and paced.

After a few laps, I realized the warning bells were only getting louder.

*Jesus, what was happening? What was going to happen?*

I didn't know.

Although my psychic abilities had grown, I still could not predict the future. And as I paced my living room, I paused twice to glance out the big living room window that overlooked the front lawn and the cul-de-sac leading up to my house. The cul-de-sac was empty. The street beyond was empty, other than two teenagers sitting on a neighbor's fence, talking and texting.

Random cars were parked here and there.

No sign of any cargo vans.

The buzzing between my ears sounded like a swarm of gnats circling my head. I nearly swatted at them, like King Kong swatting at airplanes on top of the Empire State Building.

I forced myself to sit on my couch, forced myself to take deep breaths, to calm down. I focused on my breathing.

*There. Easy now. Calm down.*

And from this state of semi-tranquility, I closed my eyes and was able to cast my thoughts out like a net. An ever-widening net that trawled through my house, through the different rooms, and out into the backyard—

Where I saw two men creeping through my backyard.

They were both armed with crossbows.

I gasped and snapped back into my body, just as glass broke from down the hallway.

Anthony's room.

# 33.

I stumbled off the couch, disoriented and dizzy, braced myself on a wall, then hurtled through my small house.

"Anthony!" I screamed.

I was in my son's room in a blink, and what I saw took a second or two to absorb. The bedroom window was broken. The sound of running feet. My son standing there in the center of his room, breathing hard, fists clenched.

"It's okay, Mommy. They're gone now."

I looked my son over wildly, then hurried over to the broken window. Our house abuts the Pep Boys parking lot, separated by our backyard fence. From inside the house, I could just see a white van peeling away from the fence, zigzagging briefly.

*Sweet Jesus.*

I considered pursuing, but there was no way in hell I was leaving my son. I noted the broken glass wasn't inside the bedroom, as I had expected. The glass was outside, littering the dry grass, sparkling there under the last of the setting sun. A sun that was even now burning me alive.

I fought through it, grimacing, trying to piece together what had happened. The glass was broken out, which meant . . .

And then I saw it, a few feet away. Anthony's Xbox controller was lying in the grass, too, broken into two or three pieces.

He had thrown it. Through the window. I looked back at my son. But he wasn't looking at me. He simply stood in the center of the room, fists clenched, looking out through the broken window.

"What happened, Anthony?"

"There were two of them," he said calmly. He did not sound like my little boy. He sounded years older. "I saw them climb over the wall. One of them looked in the window."

"And you threw your controller at him." My voice, still shocked, was now full of something close to awe. "Through the window?"

He nodded. "It hit him in the face. He screamed and fell down. When he got up, he was bleeding bad. I think some glass was in his face. Maybe his nose was broken."

*Holy shit.*

"Then both of them ran off again. They jumped the wall, and that's when you came in."

*My God.*

"You need to get out of the sun, Mommy."

My son took my hand and led me away, out of his room and into the hallway. I could smell my own burning flesh. If I looked hard enough, I might even see steam rising off my skin.

I said, gasping, "Are you okay, honey?"

"Of course, Mommy."

I pulled my son in close and held him tight. Two men with crossbows. Vampire hunters. Here at my house. Following me.

"Who were those men, Mommy?"

"Bad men."

"Were they robbers?"

I nodded but didn't say anything. I pulled him in closer, and we stood like that in the hallway, holding each other tight, while the cool wind came in through the broken window, rattled the blinds, and eventually found us huddling together in the hallway.

# 34.

*Have you pissed anyone off lately, Moon Dance?*

It was nearly midnight, and, after working with a 24-hour glass service, I had contacted Fang and gotten him up to speed.

*No more than usual*, I wrote.

*And you're sure one of them wasn't our vampire hunter from last year?*

I shook my head, although I was alone in the room. *I'm fairly certain. Randolf the vampire hunter worked alone, and this was a two-man crew. Besides, Randolf and I are on good terms.*

*Meaning what?*

*Meaning, I'm not very high on his kill list.*

*Randolf the vampire hunter doesn't sound very catchy.*

*Maybe not, but he's effective.*

*I still say you shoulda dropped his ass in the ocean. Why leave it to chance that he might return?*

*A judgment call.*

*A judgment call you might regret*, he wrote, paused, then added: *Sorry, Moon Dance. I'm just very, very protective of you, and two creeps showing up at your house with fucking crossbows scares the shit out of me. I mean, what if they had gotten a shot off at you, or your son?*

It was nearly too horrible to contemplate, so I didn't. Fang sensed this and changed the subject a little.

*Have you talked to Anthony about, well, everything?*

*Mostly. I told him that we were different. I told him that we were stronger than most people. He said something about being superheroes, and I went with that for now.*

*Except that might do more damage than good, Moon Dance.*

*For now, it's enough that he knows he's different and needs to keep it secret.*

*Baby steps*, wrote Fang, obviously reading my mind.

*Yes, baby steps. Also . . .*

But I couldn't finish the thought. I stopped writing, but Fang, privy to my thoughts, had picked up on it. He finished it for me, writing: *Also, you're tired of hiding who you are.*

*Yes.*

*Will you tell your daughter?*

*I think so. Yes.*

*How do you think they will take it?*

*I don't know, Fang. I only hope they don't hate me.*

*Well, I, for one, would think you were the coolest mom ever.*

*Yeah, well, you're also a freak.*

I could almost hear Fang chuckling lightly on his end. On my end, I could hear Anthony snoring lightly and faint music issuing from Tammy's room. The house creaked from somewhere and I nearly bolted to my feet.

*Just the house settling. Calm down, Sam.*

Easier said than done.

Earlier, Kingsley had offered to come over, but the big guy had an important court hearing in the morning, and I assured him I would be fine. Fang had offered, too, but I politely declined. Truth was, I doubted they would be back. Whoever they were, the element of surprise was gone. If they were going to attack, they were going to do it somewhere else.

And just who were they?

That was the question of the hour.

A minute or two passed before the pencil icon appeared again in the chatbox window, indicating Fang was typing a message, followed by: *I've been doing some research into blood dealers, Moon Dance.*

*Oh?*

He shielded his thoughts while he typed out his response. He didn't want me to know his sources, which was fine by me. We all had our secrets.

*Apparently, there's a sort of hierarchy to blood.*

*What do you mean?*

*Degrees of desirability. For instance, animal blood is the lowest. Deceased human blood is next.*

I recalled Detective Hanner's comment about gathering blood from morgues and hospitals. I shuddered.

I wrote, *And fresh human blood is the most desirable.*

*Not quite, Moon Dance.*

*What do you mean?*

*There's another source of blood that's even more desirable than human blood. Vampire blood. Apparently, Moon Dance, your blood fetches a pretty penny on the open market.*

*Jesus.*

*I suspect Robert Mason is far more dangerous than you realize.*

# 35.

We were cuddling in front of an 80-inch Sharp flat screen TV, which was a little like cuddling in front of a portal into the fourth dimension.

The room was also equipped with surround sound speakers which made the sound seem to magically appear as if from no-where. To this day, I haven't a clue where those speakers are embedded. Most important, the room came equipped, at least part time, with a beast of a man who, despite his size, was a helluva cuddler.

We were cuddling and watching Matt Damon's latest spy thriller when Kingsley turned to me and asked, "Would you like a drink?"

If he was offering wine or water, he would have said wine or water. *Drink* was Kingsley-speak for a very different kind of red stuff: blood.

I sat up, reached for the remote, and paused the movie.

"It's really a simple yes-or-no question, Sam," he said good-naturedly. Kingsley was wearing a tee shirt and workout pants, and both were filled to capacity. It took a lot of man to fill out an oversized pair of workout pants, but somehow Kingsley managed to do it. He also smelled of Old Spice. Simple. Manly. Yummy.

I turned to him. "May I first ask where you got your *drink*?"

He rolled his eyes. "Jesus, Sam. I thought we discussed that."

"No. You gave me a song and dance about vampires using var-ious willing and unwilling donors. So, tell me, was this a willing donor? I think I have a right to know who I'm consuming, don't you think?"

He turned and looked at me, his thick hair flowing over one shoulder. "Boy, I didn't see this coming."

Truth was, I didn't either. I knew there was a killer out there supplying blood, and I knew my current boyfriend purchased blood from . . . someone.

"I need to know," I said.

On the wall before us, Matt Damon used some impressive fight moves—and a lot of editing—to kick the unholy crap out of a spy that looked remarkably like a popular Hollywood star. In the kitchen nearby, I heard Franklin the butler humming to himself. Kingsley's resident freak had a surprisingly sweet voice.

Kingsley said, "I buy the blood from a trusted supplier."

I couldn't read the mind of another immortal, but I didn't need to be a mind-reader to know who he was talking about. I said, "Detective Hanner."

His lower jaw dropped a little. For a man who was legendary for keeping his cool, this statement caught him by surprise. And it was all the admission I needed.

"How long has she been supplying you?" I asked.

He cracked his neck a little. Clearly uncomfortable. So much for openness in a relationship. "A number of years, Sam. I normally keep only a small amount on hand."

"And here's the million-dollar question, babe," I said. "Where does Hanner get her blood?"

"Donors."

"Willing donors?"

"Jesus, Sam. You're closer friends with her than I am these days. You tell me."

I shook my head. "You've known her a lot longer. Hell, you're even a *customer*."

Kingsley stood in one motion, so quickly that it boggled the mind. One smooth motion. Like a spring being sprung. "Look, Sam. I'm not keeping anything from you. It's just that your kind and my kind don't generally discuss this topic."

"The topic of blood?"

"Right."

"It's taboo," I said.

"Sam, we all have skeletons in our closets. Especially us."
By "us," I knew he was talking about creatures of the night. "I
have them, you have them. We all have them. We couldn't exist
without collecting them."

"So, what's your point?"

"We don't dig too deeply into each other's lives, Sam. Dig
deep enough into mine and you might not like what you find.
And if I dig deep enough into yours, even in the short time
you've been a vampire, I might not like what I find, either."

"So you just stick your head in the sand?"

"Sometimes, it's best not to know, Sam."

I shook my head. "Real people are getting killed out there.
Real people with lives and families and hopes and dreams.
Slaughtered for blood. It's not right."

"Of course it's not right." He put his hand on my knee. "Let it
go, Sam, okay? She's not a killer. She's one of us."

I did not let it go. Could not let it go. The rest of the Matt
Damon movie was lost on me, and as I absently watched the
fight scenes, the chase scenes, and the bevy of cute buns, all I
could think about was one person.

Detective Hanner.

# 36.

It was just after 9 p.m., and I was going through the missing
person list again.

A sad list, to be sure.

The files were, of course, peppered with photos of the
missing. Driver's license pictures, family pictures, Christmas
pictures. Pictures of couples holding hands. Pictures with co-
workers. Only a small fraction of the missing were children.
Three, in fact. Most of the missing were adults, and most were
in their twenties.

In all, there were fifty-three missing-person cases in Orange
County over a five-year span. Higher than even Los Angeles
County, which, by my calculations, only had forty-one in the
same period. And Los Angeles was nearly three times the size of
Orange County.

That, in and of itself, was startling evidence.

There was an epidemic of missing people in Orange County, and so far, nothing had been made of it.

I studied the many pictures, trying to get a feel for them. Sometimes, I got blurry flashes, but the pictures and the files were too cold, too copied, too informal. Too old.

Over the past seven months, I'd enjoyed many goblets of fresh hemoglobin at Kingsley's and Hanner's. Looking at these files now, seeing these pictures now, spread before me in my living room, I was beginning to suspect with mounting horror that the blood I had consumed, the blood that had nourished my body, the blood that I had *relished*, belonged to these people.

*Sweet Jesus.*

Of course, I didn't know that for sure. Truth was, I didn't know what the hell was going on. Hanner had told me repeatedly the blood was from willing donors. But some of it was and maybe some of it wasn't. Maybe that was enough for her to lie to my face.

I was sitting cross-legged in the center of my living room, immersed in the missing. Having these files was highly illegal, which is why I had discreetly copied them while Sherbet had been on a curiously long coffee break. Just long enough, interestingly, for me to copy all the files.

So here I was now, late in the evening, scouring the files like my life depended on it. And maybe it did. Two men with crossbows suggested it did. Fang's recent revelation of the high desirability of vampire blood suggested it did.

Which was why my kids were presently staying with my sister, Mary Lou—which is where they would stay until I felt it was safe to bring them home again.

That Robert Mason was connected to all of this, I had no doubt. Sherbet agreed. For a case like this, a search warrant would do wonders. A suspect's home was thoroughly searched, and such searches usually turned up something, especially if the suspect was guilty.

Unless, of course, the suspect was an ex-soap opera star with a small amount of fame. A judge was going to be extremely careful handing out a search warrant.

Unless I could find something connecting Robert Mason to another victim.

Or, in this case, to a missing person.

I looked down at the dozens of files spread before me. Somewhere in this mosaic of the missing, this patchwork of faces and files, was the evidence I needed.

I was sure of it.

So, I closed my eyes and took a deep breath, exhaled, and expanded my consciousness out, touching down on each file. In my mind's eye, I saw a ball of light. I then slowly, carefully, opened my eyes and the ball of light remained, floating above the files.

This was weird. A damn new experience for me. Anything psychic before was generally done with my eyes closed.

I had created that light somehow. Could others see it? I didn't know, but I doubted it.

Either way, I watched as this ball of light moved over the floor methodically, like a slow-moving unmanned spy drone.

I kept breathing calmly, easily.

The ball of light neared the outer edge of the files. Maybe this was a lame idea. This psychic stuff was still so new to me. Or maybe I was barking up the wrong tree. Maybe the missing in California had nothing to do with Robert Mason.

Maybe. Calm. Relax.

The fiery ball in my mind's eye had begun to break up as my own thoughts grew more and more scattered. But I focused them again, and watched. And waited.

The light paused over a file. As it did so, a very strong knowing came over me. *That's the one.* As if on cue, the ball of light began descending, until it finally rested on the file.

And then the light disappeared.

I gasped and reached for the file.

# 37.

At first blush, there wasn't much here.

A twenty-two-year-old male. Missing since last year. No evidence that he'd ever worked for the Fullerton Playhouse, or that he was involved in acting in any way. In fact, he was a computer salesman at Best Buy in Fullerton. His name was Gabriel Friday, and he was last seen going to work.

Except he never made it.

That was sixteen months ago.

Again, not much there. Of course, I didn't need much. I just needed a connection to Robert Mason. As I flipped through the file, there was no surprise that Sherbet and I didn't see one here. There was nothing obvious here. Nothing that would indicate a connection of any kind.

Maybe I was wrong. After all, who trusts random balls of light?

I did.

I shoved the file into a folder, checked the time on my cell, then headed out to Best Buy. In the least, I could finally see what the hell a Nook was.

•  •  •

The Best Buy night manager in Fullerton was a black woman named Shelley, who was shorter than me and looked far tougher. She led me to a small office behind the help desk and showed me to a seat in front of a metal desk.

"So you're a private investigator?" she asked, easing around the desk.

"That's what it says on my tax returns."

She smiled easily. I suspected her easy smile could turn serious fast. "I've always wanted to be a private investigator. In a way, part of my job involves in-house investigations. Missing money. Missing shipments. Missing merchandise. Last month, I caught two employees loading up a minivan with Dyson vacuums."

"They're nice vacuums," I said. "Almost worth going to jail over."

She laughed. "And that's exactly where they are now."

"You're kind of a badass."

She leveled her considerable stare at me. "I'm a lot of badass, honey," she said. "Maybe we should team up someday and fight crime together."

I grinned. I liked her. A lot. "Our first order of business could be to take down an international vacuum syndicate."

"With stakeouts?"

"Of course."

"You've got yourself a deal." She smiled. "Now, how can I help you, Ms. Moon?"

"I'm here about Gabriel Friday."

"Gabriel. Was he found?"

I shook my head. "Not yet. I'm sorry."

She was about to say something, then closed her mouth again. She nodded once, and I saw that she was, in fact, trying to control herself.

"Were you close to him?" I asked.

"I try to be close to all my workers, Ms. Moon."

"Please, call me Samantha."

She nodded. "Very well, Samantha. Yes, as close as a manager and computer geek could be. We talked as much as time would allow, which might only be a few minutes a week, but I always make the effort."

"You said 'geek'? A term of endearment?"

"A job title. He was part of the Geek Squad, our mobile support techs."

"I see," I said, and now my mind was racing.

She dried her eyes and looked at me directly. "Why do you ask about him, Samantha?"

I shifted in my seat. "I have reason to believe that his disappearance might be related to another case."

I liked Shelley. She deserved the truth, no matter how hard it was for me to tell her. When I was finished, she ran both hands through her thick hair, then just kept them there, holding her head. She seemed instantly lost.

"I'm sorry," I said.

"Oh, sweet Jesus. He was such a good kid, such a good kid. He didn't deserve this. I got to know his mother through all of this. They weren't close, and had a falling out, but she loved him so much. Missed him so much. We were all looking for answers. This can't be the answer."

As she buried her face in her hands, I moved over to her side and put my arm around her shoulder as she wept quietly for a few moments. I gently patted her shoulder and thought to myself that everyone should be so lucky to have a boss who cared so much.

When she had gotten control of herself, blowing her nose on a tissue and sitting a little straighter, I moved back around the desk and asked if she still had records of Gabriel's clients.

She nodded. "I kept everything after his disappearance. Wasn't sure what would be important or not."

She had good instincts. I said, "Did the police go through the records?"

She nodded. "Cursory at best. They looked at them, but as far as I know, that's all they did."

"And what's in the files?"

"Just routine stuff. Records of various house calls. Sometimes to businesses, too."

"Businesses?"

"Yes."

"May I see his file?"

"Of course, honey."

She spun her chair around and rolled over to a big filing cabinet in the far corner of the office. There, she dug through the first drawer until she came out with a thickish folder.

"Everything's in here," she said, rolling back, setting it in front of me. "The service orders and final receipts. Not to mention his evaluations and anything else we had on him."

"Thank you," I said.

"If you need any help, Samantha Moon, you let me know. I would personally like to bring this piece of shit down, whoever he is."

"I'll keep you in mind."

She held my gaze a moment longer, and I think the two of us might have bonded. When she was gone, I cracked the file open. It took me precisely two minutes to find a service order for the Fullerton Playhouse.

Called in by Robert Mason himself.

# 38.

Sherbet answered on the first ring.

"First-ring relationships are serious business," I said.

"Don't get used to it, kid. I just kinda, you know, *sensed* you were going to call me. Or something like that."

I laughed. "Why, Detective, you sound kind of freaky."

He growled under his breath, which nearly made my phone vibrate against my ear. This was all new to Sherbet. After all, homicide detectives don't sense things. They operate on facts and evidence. At best, they might get an informed hunch.

"So what's the news, Sam? Out with it."

I told him about the file, about my trip to Best Buy, and about the missing tech guy. Although I still wasn't sure what the hell a Nook was, I had discovered that Robert Mason had hired the missing tech.

"Good work, and what's this Nook thing you're talking about?"

"I haven't said anything about a Nook. You're reading my thoughts again, Detective."

More growling. "What's this tech's name again?"

"Gabriel Friday."

"Hang on. I've got his file somewhere . . . okay, here it is."

I had no doubt that Sherbet's home office looked similar to mine, stacked with files and reports. I soon heard him flipping through pages. He paused in his flipping—reading, no doubt—then said, "Okay, so it says the kid disappeared on his way to work."

"Yes."

"And phone records indicate he received an unknown call just prior to coming in to work."

"Says the same thing in my file," I said.

"Probably because you illegally copied the file," said Sherbet. "So, what are you thinking, Sam?"

"I'm thinking Robert Mason gave Gabriel a call."

"Maybe asked him to swing by the theater early one morning, perhaps to fix a bug in the computer."

"Something like that," I said. "Sort of a follow-up call."

"Gabriel's car—a VW bug—was found burned out in Corona," said Sherbet.

"Near where Brian Meeks's body was found."

Sherbet paused, no doubt reading the same information I was reading. "Within a few miles, actually."

"Yup."

"So Gabriel Friday shows up to give Robert Mason a helping hand . . . maybe do some pro bono work to help out the local theater . . . and Mason offs him," said Sherbet.

"And drains him of blood."

"Jesus," said the detective. "I'll call you back in a few minutes."

He called me back, in fact, in fifteen minutes.

"I got it," he said.

"Got what?"

"The search warrant. We're going in tonight."

"Going in where?"

"His house."

"What about the theater?"

"The warrant only covers the house and any outbuildings on the property. The theater isn't on the property."

"But he owns it."

"Let's take it one property at a time, Sam."

"Fine. I want to go with you tonight."

"You can't, Sam. You know that. Official police business and all that."

"Then do me one favor," I said.

"This have anything to do with Hanner? Why did I just say that?"

"Because I gave you a peek into my thoughts."

I gave him another peek. In particular, I gave him access to my suspicions about Hanner.

"I don't understand, Sam," said Sherbet. "What's this got to do with Hanner?"

I next showed him an image—my own memory, really—of Hanner and myself on the deck of her house. Drinking blood. Together.

Sherbet didn't say anything for a long time. So long that I wondered if the old geezer had fallen asleep. But I knew he was working this through.

Finally, in a voice so deep that it nearly rattled my teeth, he said, "How did I not know, Sam? I feel like an idiot."

"It's a gift of hers, Detective. She can plant thoughts and, I think, alter thoughts. In the least, divert thoughts."

"Can you do this, too?"

"I . . . I don't know."

"So, as far as I know, this whole damn city could be full of vampires, and I wouldn't know. No one would know. Because

anytime one of us gets a whiff of a vampire, they put a sublimi-
nal thought in our head to order a Starbucks instead."

"Sounds like a valid conspiracy."

"This isn't funny, Sam. I'm seriously freaked out here. I mean,
a bloody fucking vampire has been working under my nose for,
what, five or six years, and I hadn't a clue."

"Don't be too hard on yourself, Detective. Remember, you
sniffed me out pretty quick."

"Not really. I just thought you were damn weird."

"Something every girl wants to hear."

"You know what I mean, Sam. You had my radar pinging. Detective Hanner . . . nothing. Not even a suspicion. And she even
works the goddamn night shift."

"She's an old vampire, Detective. Old enough, I think, to
know a few tricks."

"Worse," said Sherbet, "is that I like her. Legitimately like
her."

"So do I."

"Fine," he said. "I'll conduct this tonight without her. I'll
round up a few of our boys and hit this house hard. I'll call you
when it's over."

And he disconnected the line.

# 39.

I had just set aside my cell phone when there came a loud knock
at my front door. Loud and obnoxious.

And since my inner alarm was not ringing, I relaxed a little
as I moved through the hallway. Still, if there was a vampire
hunter on the other side of that door, he was in for one hella-
cious fight.

It wasn't.

As I glanced through the peep hole, I saw a wildly warped
and misshapen, yet familiarly handsome, face.

Fang.

His face, if possible, appeared even more misshapen due
to what he was holding in his right hand: a bottle of hooch. I
opened the door and he veritably spilled into my living room.

"Hope I'm not disturbing you or anything, Moon Dance," he said, catching himself on the center post that divided the foyer from the living room. His speech was nearly incoherent.

"You're drunk, Fang."

"Oh, am I? I thought I was just shit-faced."

I shut the door and double locked it behind me. As I did so, Fang began whistling for a dog. "Here, wolfie. Here, boy."

"Kingsley's not here," I said, irritated.

"Oh, that's a shame . . . I had brought him some bones from work. Ribs, I think." He briefly held up a greasy bag, which he shoved back into his coat pocket.

"You're being a jerk, Fang."

He stood before me, swaying slightly. "You'll have to forgive me, Moon Dance. I've kind of been dealing with a broken heart."

Fang wasn't looking too well. His hair looked dirty. His clothing was wrinkled. His hygiene was questionable. He also looked like he'd lost about ten pounds since I'd last seen him.

He held up his bottle of booze. Vodka. A big bottle, too, and it was nearly empty. "Would you like a drink, Moon Dance?"

"What are you doing here, Fang?"

"Oh, that's right. Vampires can't drink the hard stuff. Only the red stuff." He laughed a little too hard at his own joke, then pushed away from the center post and stumbled into the adjoining living room. Like I said, I live in a small house. With two or three steps, a person could go from the foyer, to the dining room, to the living room.

"You mind if I sit, Moon Dance? I'm not feeling too well."

As he stumbled across the floor, I ran to his side and helped him down onto my beautiful new couch. Once there, I positioned him so that his boots hung off the edge. I also relieved him of the vodka bottle.

As I positioned a pillow under him, he watched me with big, wet eyes. They were beautiful eyes. Knowing eyes. Drunk eyes. "Ah, Moon Dance. It almost feels as if you care about me."

"Of course I care about you, Fang."

I went into the kitchen, poured the booze down the drain, and deposited the bottle in my recycle bag. When I came back, Fang was trying to remove his boots. I knew that the drunk bastard would have to sleep it off here. Sighing, I helped him with his boots. Once again, he watched me. This time with a big, stupid, drunk grin.

"I like when you help me, Moon Dance. It feels good."

"Yeah, well, you smell like greasy ribs and vodka and it's turning my stomach."

"Words every man wants to hear." He patted the area next to him on the couch. "Lay next to me, Moon Dance."

"No."

"Why not?"

"Because it's not right."

"Hey, if you're not going to turn me into a blood-sucking fiend, then at least throw me a few crumbs here, Sam. Something, anything."

"If you're going to talk like this, Fang, then I'm calling you a cab."

"Talk like what, Moon Dance? Affectionately? Lustfully? I loved you long before your shaggy wolf friend came sniffing around. I poured my heart out to you. Gave you all my attention. All my love, even if it was from afar. How many times did I drop everything to help you? How many times did I forgo my own needs to help you, to talk to you, to be there for you?"

"You stalked me, Fang."

"It was the only way, Moon Dance. The only way. You would not have come out into the light. Literally."

"I would have. Someday."

"But not soon enough, obviously. I waited too long, and look what happened. *Aroooooo*."

"You're drunk, Fang."

"But that makes my pain no less real, Samantha Moon. I loved you like no other, and you tossed me aside for your doggie toy. The least you could do was turn me, to make me like you, to help ease the pain."

"You're trying to manipulate me, to make me feel guilty, Fang, and that's a shitty thing to do."

"It's nothing but the truth, Moon Dance."

"Get some sleep, Fang."

Indeed, his eyes were dropping fast. He turned on his side and wrapped an arm around himself and I saw something disturbing at his wrists. Fresh wounds. Bite marks. Had he been biting himself again? I didn't know.

I stared down at Fang, a man I legitimately cared for and loved on some level. A man for whom I had no answers. That he was miserable, there was no doubt. That he loved me in his own way, I had no doubt either.

What I should do about it all, I still didn't know.

Soon after he was snoring loudly into one of the couch cushions, I decided to follow up on a hunch.

I grabbed my stuff and headed out the door.

# 40.

I was looking down from a roof top, watching the Fullerton Playhouse below.

It was windy up here, and my light jacket flapped wildly. Too wildly. I think I was losing weight. A steady diet of blood will do that to you.

I was kneeling on the roof's corner, four stories up. Directly below me was a bank. Why a bank needed four floors, I hadn't a clue. Sure as hell wasn't to store my money. So far there was no movement below, although I had spotted something very interesting in the alley behind the theater.

A blue cargo van.

I waited and watched. Other than the van, the theater looked empty. There was no movement. No lights. It was well past time for any rehearsals and any cleaning crews.

I decided not to make a move, unless something prompted me to. I was here for one reason only: to keep an eye on the theater, should the shit hit the fan. Or should someone get tipped off about the police raid.

So far, all was quiet.

My cell phone chimed. A text message. I glanced at the screen. A text message from Danny.

*Thanks, Sam! They didn't come back to collect from me. Whatever you did, I owe you one.*

"You owe me two, loser," I whispered, and erased his message.

I was dressed in jeans and the aforementioned light jacket. There had been an old fire escape that I had managed to grab onto. Now, I waited and watched. Just another mom with two kids, waiting on the roof of a bank building for a serial killer to emerge from his creepy theater.

Perhaps an hour later my cell vibrated.

I picked up on the first vibration, which, I think, was the equivalent to a single ring. It was, of course, Detective Sherbet.

"Mason wasn't there," he said.

"Go figure," I said. "Anything turn up?"

"Nothing yet, but my guys are working on it. If there's a blood stain anywhere, they'll find it."

"Except if he's as good at killing as I suspect, then there's not going to be any evidence at his home."

"What are you saying, Sam?"

"He kills at the theater, Detective. You know that, I know that. He kills and drains and bottles his victims' blood all at the theater."

"A blood factory."

"Or a slaughtering house. A human slaughtering house."

"Jesus, Sam." Sherbet paused. "Then why not destroy the bodies there?"

"Maybe he does. Or maybe he *usually* does. Maybe he ran out of room. Or maybe he's decided to make it a bit of a game."

"Jesus, Sam. I'm too old for this shit."

"We have to stop him, Detective."

Sherbet paused again, said, "We've got another missing person reported tonight. A female. Twenty-three. Last seen leaving class at Fullerton College two nights ago."

"She's there," I said, with a surety that wasn't psychic. It was my gut. My investigator's instincts. "The son-of-a-bitch has her. And my bet is she's somewhere behind that door."

"We can't just go in there, Sam."

"Perhaps you can't, but I can."

"Sam, wait."

"What?"

He exhaled loudly and if I truly wanted to I could have followed his entire train of thought. Instead, I gave him his privacy, let him work this out on his own. Finally, after exhaling again, he said, "I'm coming with you."

"Welcome aboard, Detective."

# 41.

We met behind the theater.

Sherbet was wearing jeans and a leather jacket that barely covered his roundish mid-section. He was also sporting dark-leather shoes that looked like a cross between running shoes and hiking shoes. I knew he was packing heat, and the truth was, I felt better having him here. Sherbet exuded an aura of control and security. More so than any man I'd ever met, even Kingsley.

I might be a creature of the night who has faced my share of monsters, but sneaking into the dragon's lair alone just sounded like one hell of a shitty way to spend an evening.

The alley parking lot was empty, with only a single spotlight shining down on the back door. A sticker claimed that there was an alarm system in use, but we were about to see. I doubted there was. If this place was what I thought it was, then I doubted Mr. Robert Mason ever wanted the police anywhere near the premises. If anything, he would handle the intruders himself.

Not to mention, Mason had help. Two goons had shown up at my house and neither had been Mason, I was sure of it. Three against two. I liked our chances.

I doubted Hanner was directly involved in the production of the blood. She seemed more refined than that. She seemed . . . better than that. What her connection was, exactly, I didn't know.

But I was going to find out.

I was the first to try the door. Locked, of course. I turned the lever a little harder, and it broke free in my hand. "It's not really breaking in," I said, holding up the broken handle, "if the door is broken, right?"

Sherbet shook his head and eased his bulk around me. As he did so, I had a momentary whiff of Old Spice and sweat, which, for me, was one hell of a heady mixture. "We're not breaking in," he growled, as he broke in. "This is an emergency search. There's a young woman missing, and he's our only suspect. I'm sticking to that story until the day I die."

"Sounds good to me."

He removed his Smith & Wesson from his shoulder holster. "C'mon."

The hallway was pitch black to anyone but me. To me, it was alive and alight. Sherbet reached into a pocket and removed a small flashlight that had a lot of *umph* to it, revealing a narrow hallway with a door to either side.

"Lights?" I asked.

Sherbet shook his head and continued sweeping the powerful beam over walls and floors and ceilings. "I don't want anyone running; at least, not yet. We'll catch the bastards by surprise."

"Sounds like my last date."

Sherbet grinned. "Sure it does. So what are we looking for?"

"A storage room. Or a props room. We're close to it, I think."

"Then what?"

"We look for a mirror."

"A mirror?"

"Yes."

"And you know this how?"

"I'm a freaky chick."

He rolled his eyes. "Fine. Then what?"

"There should be an opening behind it."

"Thank God you didn't say *through it*. Dealing with vampires is bad enough. I don't think I can handle Harry Potter, too." Sherbet took another step, then paused. "Hey, do that crazy thing you do with your mind."

"My mind?"

"You know, one of those mental scouting jobs you do, or whatever you call it."

"'Mental scouting job' sounds good to me," I said. "Give me a moment."

"I'll give you two."

I closed my eyes, exhaled, and cast my thoughts out like a net. The net scattered throughout the theater, through rooms and offices, across the stage and theater seating, and even up into the lighting booth.

"We're alone up here," I said, reporting back, opening my eyes. "Except for the ghosts."

"What ghosts?"

"The ghosts that have been following us since we stepped foot in here."

"I didn't need to know that."

Lots of old places have spirits hanging around them, and this theater, which was decades old, if not a century, was no exception. Still, there seemed to be a lot of spirit energy here, more than to be expected, energy which flitted past quickly, energy which appeared and disappeared next to us, energy which watched us from the shadows. Some of the energy fully manifested into lightly glowing human forms. These watched us from doorways and rafters, from behind curtains and in windows. I decided not to tell Sherbet about the entity standing next to him. For a tough guy, he sure got the willies over ghosts.

"You said alone up here," said Sherbet. "You think this creep works below ground?"

"Would be my guess."

"And your radar whatchamacallit doesn't pick up Mason?"

"Not yet."

"Which means?"

"We're still probably too far from him."

"Or that the place is empty."

"We'll see," I said.

"Fine. C'mon."

We soon found ourselves somewhere backstage, where backdrops hung from flies and where trap doors were cleverly placed in the floor. Clothing racks filled with costumes lined both sides of the wall, and a catwalk ran along the upper levels. There were many, many ghosts moving back and forth along these metal walkways.

Lots of death here.

And, judging by the many gashes in their necks, lots of victims here, too. I kept this last assessment to myself. I suspected Sherbet was about to see for himself just what was going on here.

We found a hallway leading off to one side of the stage, which we followed to the props room. The door was ajar.

"This is it," I said.

Sherbet nodded and slipped inside first, holding the gun out in front of him even though we were alone in the theater. I think it made him feel manly. Not to mention, he was still a cop, and cops did these kinds of things.

I paused at the doorway, taking in the room despite the darkness. The room was, of course, exactly as I had seen it in my mind days earlier. Props of all shapes and sizes, everything from dinner tables and jukeboxes to plastic trees and park benches. Like a small town all crammed into one room.

I pointed to the far wall. "There."

Sherbet followed my finger, aiming his light, and illuminated a massive mirror that was apparently attached to the wall.

"The mirror. Just like you said."

"Yep."

"And you've never been here before?"

"Nope. At least, not physically."

"This is crazy."

"Welcome to my life."

He shook his head and I heard his thoughts, despite my best attempts to stay out of them. Rather clearly, Sherbet thought: *I'm going insane.*

The scent of blood suddenly wafted over me, coming from the far wall—from behind the mirror, no doubt. My traitorous stomach growled instantly. So loudly that Sherbet turned and looked at me. I shrugged innocently.

As we moved around a four-poster bed covered in cobwebs, Sherbet said, "I swear to God that if a guy in a hockey mask and a chainsaw starts singing about the music, I'm going to start shooting."

"You're mixing, I think, like three movies together."

"Well, they've been warned."

We found ourselves at the big mirror. The smell of blood was most definitely coming from somewhere behind the mirror. I said as much to Sherbet, even as my stomach growled again.

Sherbet looked at me, looked at the mirror, then looked at my stomach. He put two and two together and grimaced unconsciously. Finally, he said, "Help me with the mirror."

He holstered his gun and we each took one side of the mirror and lifted it off the hook. Once done, we set it to one side, and returned to the spot where the mirror had hung.

There was, of course, a door there.

A hidden door.

# 42.

The scent of blood was nearly overwhelming.

*So much blood.*

Sherbet and I had the same thought simultaneously: to scan the room beyond. So I did so, and saw that it was empty of anything living. I reported my findings to Sherbet.

He nodded and pointed at the doorknob. "Any chance this lock is broken as well?"

I reached for the doorknob and a moment later dropped the twisted metal to the floor. "I would say a good chance."

He shook his head. "I'm just glad you're on our side. C'mon."

He eased the door open, which promptly groaned loudly on rusted hinges. He flashed his light on the ancient, rusted hinges. He said, "My guess is there's another way down here. Probably accessible from the alley."

"Would make it easier bringing bodies in and out."

Sherbet nodded grimly. He next swept his light around the small room. "Another storage room."

I was suddenly having difficulty focusing on the detective's words. After all, the scent of blood was much stronger in here. Much, much stronger. And intoxicating.

Doing my best to ignore it, I stepped in behind Sherbet and saw that the room was filled to overflowing with even more theater junk. Moldy props. Moldy clothing. Hats that were badly destroyed by rats or moths. Boxes and crates and old furniture. And the moment I stepped inside, my inner alarm began buzzing.

"What's that sound?" asked Sherbet, pausing, listening.

"What sound?"

"You can't hear it? It's a steady buzzing. Like electricity crackling."

Stunned that the detective could pick up on my own inner alarm, and stunned at the depth of our connection, I told him what he was hearing.

"Thank God. Thought I was going crazy all over again. C'mon, let's check this out, and be careful. It's buzzing for a reason."

The air was alive with frenetic energy, which lit the way for me. Not so much for Sherbet. His flashlight would have to do. Tiny claws scrabbled in the far corner of the small room. A mouse or a rat.

By all appearances this was just a forgotten storage room. A storage room hidden purposely by a massive mirror. If I had to guess, I would say the crap in here hadn't seen the light of day—or the light of the stage—for over fifty years.

Most important: it appeared to have no exit.

We moved deeper into the room. Sherbet's breathing filled the small space. Mine, not so much. The wooden floorboards groaned under the big detective's weight. Me, not so much. The smell of blood was heady and distracting and reminding me all over again just what a monster I had become. Sherbet gave no indication of being able to smell the blood.

The metallic scent wafted through the far wall of the room, that much was clear. I moved toward the wall, toward the smell. Once there, I reached out a hand and placed it on the cool wood paneling. With Sherbet easing up behind me, I closed my eyes and cast my thoughts outward again. This time my trawling consciousness returned images of a short corridor and wooden stairs that descended down. At the base of the stairs, I saw another door. I tried to push through that . . . but the images beyond were vague and distorted. Too far to see. I snapped back into my body.

I reported my findings to Sherbet. He said something about me being handy to have around. I agreed enthusiastically. Next, we both felt around the wooden wall until we simultaneously found a seam. We kept feeling until we found a small notch in the wall. Sherbet stood back and I hooked a finger and pulled.

The wall instantly opened, rumbling along tracks hidden in the ceiling and floor. Dust sifted down. Cold air met us. Darkness lay beyond.

Darkness lit by supernatural light and infused with the scent of even more blood.

*So much blood.*

Stomach rumbling and hating myself, I led the way through into the passageway.

# 43.

I counted seven ghosts.

Some drifted along the dark corridor. Others simply appeared and disappeared, popping in and out of existence. Still others approached us, curious. Most were in their fuzzy energetic state and composed of tens of thousands of shimmering particles of light. Some spirits were brighter than others, and still others were more fully formed. Most, however, were just faint blobs of light drifting down the dark passageway.

Sherbet said, "I keep seeing movement out of the corner of my eye."

"You're catching sight of them, Detective."

"Them?"

"Spirits."

"We're still on that subject?"

"They're still here, Detective."

He aimed his flashlight down the long corridor. The light disappeared without hitting anything. A lesser man might have been scared shitless. Sherbet only said, "Again, I don't think I needed to know that. Which way?"

The tunnel led in both directions. I followed the scent of blood and pointed to the left.

"To the left it is, then," he said, and led the way, sweeping his light before him.

The corridor was composed of dank wooden panels. I had no doubt that we were following something built a century or more ago, walled off and hidden, and used by only those with secrets to hide.

As we walked along, I slid a hand along the rough paneled walls, risking splinters. I did this not for balance, but rather to receive psychic hits. I'd discovered that energy is stored in a location—in its walls, for instance. For me, all I had to do was touch such a wall to unlock a location's memory. Weird stuff, I know, but it works.

And what I was seeing now wasn't pretty.

Men and women being forcibly dragged along this very hall-way. Kicking and screaming and fighting. Horrific scenes and sounds forever recorded—embedded—within these very walls.

I shivered and, with a procession of ghosts trailing behind us, continued down the narrow corridor.

• • •

In the hallway before us, a partially materialized ghost—a fragment that looked barely humanoid—drifted toward me, unbeknownst to Sherbet.

It swept through Sherbet, who was leading the way and shivered noticeably, and headed straight for me. As it did so, it took on a little more shape and soon I could see that it was a young woman. Or had been a young woman. Like the others, there was a massive gash along her neck.

As I attempted to step around her—stepping through just seemed a little rude—she drifted to one side and blocked my path. She raised a hand. I tried stepping around her again and again she blocked my path.

"Jesus, Sam. You dancing back there?" said Sherbet, turning and shining his flashlight over me. The light went straight through the girl and even caused some of her form to scatter like frightened fish.

"I'm being blocked by a spirit."

"Of course you are. I should have realized."

The wound in the girl's neck was ghastly. Faint but ghastly. She drifted before me, rising and falling on the supernatural currents.

I said, "She's warning us."

Sherbet was about to say something, then stopped himself. I was giving him a glimpse into my thoughts, allowing him to see what I was seeing, through my eyes. I heard him gasp a little. He backed into the wall behind him.

As the old detective was working through his issues, I reached out a hand and touched the girl's hand. A cold shiver rippled through me, followed by something akin to an electric jolt. I whispered to her, "We'll be careful, I promise."

She was weeping now, into her other hand, and as I held her ethereal hand, which glowed in mine, I closed my eyes and wished very hard for her to leave this dark place, to leave and never return. When I opened them again, she was gone.

"Jesus, Sam," said Sherbet, holding his heart. "You've got to warn a guy before you pull a stunt like that. I damn near wet myself."

"Sorry," I said absently. "Let's go."

He led the way forward and soon we came upon the same wooden stairs I had seen in my vision.

"I guess we go down," said Sherbet.

"Would be my guess," I said.

"And away we go," he said, and led the way down.

# 44.

At the bottom of the stairs there was another door.

A light shone from underneath. More spirits were here. A lot more. I counted nine. Many were appearing and disappearing through the door. A few looked back at me.

"This is it," I said, whispering.

"How do you know?" said Sherbet.

"Trust me."

It was all I could do to control myself. Yes, I've had cravings in my life. Sugar cravings. Food cravings. When I was pregnant with Tammy, I had ice cravings.

This . . . this was no craving.

This was a hunger. A yearning. A need. I shielded my thoughts from Sherbet. No man should hear such thoughts, especially a man I liked and respected.

*So much blood, so much blood . . .*

*So fresh, fresh, fresh . . .*

Truth was, I had never been so close to so much blood. So much fresh blood. So much fresh human blood.

I heard Sherbet's thoughts as clear as day. He was wondering why they would dump the bodies when the bodies could be disposed of down here. He had just decided that perhaps the killers enjoyed playing a cat-and-mouse game with the police when we both heard a noise from behind the door. The sound of a man grunting. Perhaps lifting something. Sherbet cocked his head, listening.

And that's when a girl screamed.

Sherbet jumped backward, startled. I didn't jump. I kicked. I lifted my sneaker and kicked in the door as hard as I could.

# 45.

*Oh, sweet Jesus.*

The sight, although overwhelming, was not unexpected. Two human corpses hung upside down from the ceiling, suspended by ropes. Both were naked. Both had their throats cut open.

Both had been completely drained of blood. The gashes in their necks had been cut all the way to the bone, nearly decapitating both men. They were heavily bearded. One had a lot of tattoos. Both were likely homeless men.

*Oh, sweet Jesus.*

My knees threatened to give. Hell, my whole world threatened to give. If I had needed to breathe, I would have been gasping. I probably would have fainted, too. Sherbet stumbled in behind me, making a strangled sound. But he kept it together.

We both spotted the men with the girl at the same time.

"Get the fuck down, motherfuckers," said Sherbet.

There were two of them—the same two I had seen creeping around in my backyard. One was holding a wicked-looking knife. They had begun to make a run for it, but thought better of it. The one guy dropped the knife and got down.

The girl was sitting in a chair and shivering violently. Shivering because she was completely naked. She was also maybe eighteen years old, and if I had to guess she was a runaway: bruises on her body, needle tracks along her inner arm. She was whimpering and rocking hysterically.

So that's how they did it. Prostitutes. Bums. Or those without family and homes. Anyone who wouldn't be missed.

From deeper in the room, I heard the sounds of running feet and someone cursing.

"Get him, Sam," said Sherbet, nodding toward the sounds. "Get that piece of shit."

Now I was moving, flashing quickly through the cold room, around the hanging corpses, around a corner, and down a short hallway—

Where, at the far end, Robert Mason was opening a door.

I picked up my speed. The walls swept by in a blur, and I slammed into the ex-soap opera actor so hard that I drove him through the partially open door and into the room beyond, tearing the door from its hinges. We landed in a heap, with me on top, and I didn't stop punching Robert Mason and that beautiful face of his until I felt his cheekbones shatter.

# 46.

It was late. Or early.

I was sitting in the theater seats, in the middle row about halfway up, watching the spectacle unfold before me. Medical examiners poured in and out of the theater. Detectives interviewed theater workers.

According to snatches of conversation I was hearing, many bodies had been dug up within an adjoining dirt tunnel.

People came and went. Witnesses came and went. Reporters came and went. Covered bodies came and went.

I sat in the row of seats alone, watching all of this unfold before me like a macabre play. A play just for me. Except there was no plot. No lead character. Just an endless procession of dead bodies.

I had considered calling Kingsley. And I would, soon enough. Once I had processed what was going on around me. But I was missing something here. Something wasn't jelling.

Everything seemed so matter-of-fact. So seamless. No hysterics. And why was no one interviewing me? Other than Sherbet giving me a quick update, he mostly ignored me, too.

It was almost as if I wasn't there.

As I sat and watched, cradling my jaw in my hand, seeing again and again the image of the drained bodies hanging in the air, someone sat next to me. I turned, startled. It wasn't easy to sneak up on me.

There was, of course, only one person that I knew who could pull it off.

Although Detective Hanner's eyes were looking at me, I sensed she was also aware of all the activity still going on before us, too. Her eyes were always a little too wide, always a little too alert, as if she herself were always in a mild state of surprise. Too wide, too wild. There was something close to a fire just behind her pupils, too. Something that seemed to burn with supernatural intensity. Maybe only myself and those like me could see it, I didn't know. But it was there. These were not human eyes. She stared at me and did not blink. Not for a long time, at least.

I waved my hand toward the action on the stage. "You are a part of this."

"As are you, Sam."

"I don't know what you're talking about."

"You have partaken of many who have been slain here, Sam. Do not deny that you knew otherwise."

"You told me the blood was from willing donors."

"Some more willing than others, Sam. You knew this. I told you this, often."

"You did not tell me you killed these people."

She tilted her head a little. It was not a human gesture. It was, if anything, something alien. "I did not kill these people, Sam. I was a buyer only. And, perhaps, an active supporter." She grinned and spread her hands. "Of the arts."

"You covered up his crimes."

"Of course, Sam. He was of value to me and our kind."

"Sherbet knows," I said. "I told him about you."

The fire in her eyes briefly flared. "I know, Sam. I've re-moved the memory of your conversation." She motioned to the others moving across the stage, the policemen, detectives, medical workers. "As I have done with all here tonight. None will suspect our involvement, or the involvement of our kind. In fact, most are not aware that we are sitting here, watching them."

"But how?"

"It's not very difficult to do, Sam. With a little training, you could do the same. Especially you."

"What does that mean, especially me?"

"You are particularly . . . gifted."

"I don't understand."

"You display a wide range of . . . abilities."

"I thought all vampires do what I do."

She shook her head. "You thought wrong, Sam. Very few can do what you do, although most of us possess typical gifts."

"Typical gifts?"

"The ability to influence thoughts and change minds, minor psychic sensitivity, although only a few of us can transform into something greater."

"Can you?"

"Sadly, no. You, my dear, are a rare breed."

"Why?"

She studied me for a long moment. Never once did she blink. "The reason is the person who changed you, of course."

"Who was he?"

"One of the oldest of our kind."

"Why did he change me?"

"I don't know," she said, but as she spoke, the fire in her eyes dimmed a little.

"You're lying," I said.

She laughed hollowly. "Do you see, Sam? Most of our kind would not have detected a lie. Tell me, how did you know?"

"Your eyes."

"What about my eyes?"

"The fire in them . . . it went out a little, dimmed."

"What fire?"

"Just behind your pupils."

"You can see a fire there?" she asked.

"Yes."

"Interesting."

"Why?" I asked.

"Because I see no fire in your eyes."

"Fine," I said, turning a little more in my seat. "So, I'm a fucking freak among freaks. That has little to do with the issue here."

"And what is the issue here, Sam?"

"The killing of innocent people."

"The killers will go to jail. Sherbet will be a hero. In fact, he thinks he came here alone, that he acted alone tonight, that he stumbled upon the secret door behind the mirror, alone, that he stopped both killers, alone." She paused and stared at me.

"He has no memory of you tonight, outside of your phone call to him."

"Jesus. Does Sherbet still know about me?"

"Yes, although it was very foolish of you to have told him. I can only go back so far to remove memories, as you will someday discover yourself. Already you are becoming more and more like us, and less and less like them."

"No," I said.

"Oh? Do you not feel the stronger effects of the sun? Are you not able to venture outside as long as you could before?" She paused and actually blinked. "Someday soon you will never be able to venture out into the light of day. Ever. And your hunger for blood—human blood—will become insatiable."

"Stop it, goddammit."

"I will stop, Sam. But then you and I will have this talk again soon, and you will curse the day that you stopped such a productive output of blood. You will curse the day that something so useful had been wiped out."

I shook, my head, and kept on shaking it.

"I was like you, Sam. A mother. Full of love and hope. Hope that I would someday be normal again. Hope that this would all turn out to be a bad dream. That was a long, long time ago. Now my son is long dead. The hope is long gone. And I am hungry. Very, very hungry."

Solemn voices filled the theater. Police personnel continued pouring across the stage. All looked shell-shocked. All looked numb. Sherbet was speaking to someone urgently. My detective friend never once looked my way.

"There has to be another way," I said.

Hanner reached out and touched my arm. Her fingers were ice cold. "Someday you will see that there is no other way." She paused, then leaned in and whispered into my ear. "Someday soon."

She stood and was about to leave when I said, "So, this is it. You walk away from this?"

"Yes," she said. "And so do you."

# 47.

I was in the desert again.

This time, a little further out. In fact, about eighty-five miles out. I was in the hills above a small town called Pioneertown. A fitting name if ever there was one. Pioneertown had street names like Annie Oakley Road, Rawhide Road, and Mane Street, as in a horse's mane. Rebellious.

In all, it featured a few dozen homes, a post office, and an inn, all of which I could see from my position high upon this cliffside ledge.

Sunrise was about an hour away. My minivan was parked about a thirty-minute hike away. I was sitting on an exposed ledge with no hope for shade. Doing the math, that meant I had thirty minutes to decide if I was going to do this.

And I was determined to do this.

Seven months ago, I had leaped from a hotel balcony. Truly a leap of faith. I was either going to fly or fall. At the time, I had been at wits' end. My kids were gone, my house was gone, and my cheating bastard of a husband was gone. I had nothing to lose. And so I had leaped . . . and the rest was history.

Now, my life was a little more stable. I had my kids, my house, and a boyfriend who seemed to care for me, a boyfriend who happened to be a fellow creature of the night, even if it was only one night of the month.

The desert birds were awakening, chirping in and around the magnificent Joshua trees which were scattered across the undulating hills below me.

Although my personal life had stabilized, something else was unraveling: my physical body. Perhaps "unraveling" was too strong a word. Perhaps even the wrong word. Perhaps the better word was progressing. Progressing inevitably to a full-blooded creature of the night, unable even to step out into the light of day.

But I had to step out into the light of day, dammit. I had to pick my kids up from school. I had to watch little Anthony's soccer practices, even if from afar, even if from the safety of my van.

I had to.

I had to, goddammit.

I couldn't lose that. I had lost so much already. Watching my son play soccer from my minivan was not too much to ask for, was it? It was shitty, yes, but I at least had that.

My feet hung over the ledge. Directly under the ledge was, I think, a small cave, because I could hear critters moving around inside. These days, I didn't fear critters, even the slithery ones with rattles on their tails. Unless their fangs were composed of silver spikes, or their poison of molten silver, I was good to go.

I checked my watch. Fifty minutes until sunrise. I could still turn around and head back to the relative safety of my minivan, which was parked under the shade of a rocky overhang.

So, why had I come out here? All the way out here? The same reason I had leaped from the balcony seven months ago.

No turning back. I was going to do it.

Or I was going to die.

I held in my hand the amethyst medallion. The golden disk was nearly as big as my palm. I absently ran my thumb over the embedded amethysts, which were arranged into three roses. A cracked leather strap was threaded through a small hoop in the medallion.

Behind me soared the San Bernardino Mountains. The east-facing San Bernardino Mountains. If I was going to see my first dawn in seven years, I was going to do it right. I was going to do it high upon a hill, facing east, with nothing—and I mean nothing—blocking my view.

*This is crazy.*

Already I was feeling the first stages of exhaustion. Already I was feeling a strong need to lie down somewhere comfortable and prepare for the comatose state that was sleep.

Instead, I sat here on the ledge, and, as the eastern sky turned from black to purple, as the brilliant flares of light that illuminated the night for me began to decrease, I knew that soon there would be no going back.

No going back.

Ever.

Forty minutes to sunrise. I had ten minutes to make my choice. I found that I was breathing fast. Filling my lungs and body and brain with oxygen. Except these days I didn't need much oxygen, if any. These days it was an old, nervous habit. A remnant of my humanity.

And what was so great about humanity?

My kids, for one. And daylight, for another.

Thirty minutes. I began rocking on the ledge, forward and backward. If I wanted to comfortably work my way back to my van, then I had to leave now.

Now.

Except I didn't leave. Instead, I continued rocking, continued holding the gold-and-amethyst medallion.

I suspected the sun would kill me. Perhaps not right off. But soon enough. I suspected it would quickly render me incapable of movement and, once unable to move, I would just burn alive. In complete agony. Right here where I was sitting.

In twenty-five minutes.

As the sky continued to brighten, my heart rate, generally sluggish at best, picked up considerably. The wind also picked up, sweeping over me, rocking me gently. My pink sweats flapped around my ankles. I breathed in sage and juniper and milkwood and dust and the bones of the long dead.

Twenty minutes till dawn. I knew this on a sub-atomic level, my version of the circadian rhythm, or body clock. I was deeply tied to the sun. I knew, at all times, the exact location of the sun. I knew without a doubt that I had twenty minutes before the sun would first appear on the far horizon.

Nineteen minutes.

I rocked some more.

Breathed a little faster.

If I jogged now, I could still make it to my van in time.

Never in my life had I felt so exposed, so vulnerable. I might as well be naked in a shopping mall.

No, worse. Naked in a furnace.

The coming pain would no doubt be excruciating.

*And all I had was this.*

I looked again at the medallion. The gold surface caught some of the lightening sky, reflecting it a little. I recalled Max's one instruction regarding the medallion:

*"Unlocking the secret of the medallion is easy enough for those of great faith."*

*"Great faith? What does that mean?"*

*"You will know what to do, Sam."*

Easy enough.

Great faith.

I will know what to do.

Truth was, I *still* didn't know what to do, and my time was running out fast.

Fifteen minutes. A strong need to sleep was coming over me.

I would have to sprint now. An all-out run to make it back to my van.

*Great faith,* he had said.

Faith in what?

I thought about that again, perhaps for the hundredth time, as the wind picked up. Two or three tumbleweeds appeared out of the semi-darkness to skitter and roll in front of me far below. The sky continued to brighten.

There was only one thing I could think of doing with the medallion—and that was to wear it.

*You will know what to do.*

I dipped my head a little and slipped the cracked leather thong over my head and pulled my long hair through. Thoughts of my kids were dominant now. I could not lose them. Not to the morning sun. My kids were with my sister. The long night at the theater had culminated with me coming out here after a shower and quick change of clothing.

*Jesus, what was I doing?*

The weight of the medallion was heavy on my chest. After a moment's thought, I slipped it inside my tee shirt, where it now lay against my bare chest.

The sky brightened. Birds sang. Lizards scuttled. Sand sprinkled.

And I was doing all I could to calm down.

If I leaped from the ledge and changed into the giant flying creature that I am, I could probably just make it to my minivan. But I would have to do it now. Stand now and leap.

Now.

But I didn't stand. And I most certainly didn't leap.

The word "faith" kept repeating itself in my mind. I held on to it like a lifeline.

*Faith . . . faith . . . faith . . .*

*You will know what to do, Sam.*

*Easy enough,* he had said.

Well, there was nothing easier than wearing the medallion, right? Nothing easier than sitting here now and watching the horizon.

I rocked and maybe even whimpered.

*It's coming,* I thought. *The sun is coming. Hurry now. Back to the minivan. Sure, you might burn a little, or even a lot, but at least you will be safe. At least you will not die. At least you will get to see your kids again.*

I rocked and rocked and rocked.

And as I rocked, as I felt the tears appear on my cheeks, as I accepted that everything that I knew and loved could be taken away from me in this moment, I felt something strange.

The need for sleep was dissipating.

I buried my hands over my face. The tears were coming fast and hard. I wasn't even sure what the tears were for. More than anything, I was afraid to look to the east, afraid to settle my eyes on the distant low hills that led on to forever. But I pushed past my fear, and I took a very different kind of leap of faith.

I lowered my hands.

And for the first time in seven years, I saw something that I didn't think I would ever see again:

The upper half of the morning sun appearing on the far horizon.

I felt no need for sleep. I felt no pain. In fact, I had never felt more alive in all my life. And as the sun continued to rise, I rose to my feet and stood on the ledge and shielded my eyes and never in my life had I ever seen something so beautiful.

Or perfect.

[THE END]

# Vampire Games

*Vampire for Hire #6*

DEDICATION

*To those who care for the animals of this world.*


ACKNOWLEDGMENTS

*A special thank-you to Eve Paludan,
Sandy Johnston, Elaine Babich, and P.J. Day.*

And what is a vampire? It is something that creeps but never crawls. It is something that drinks but never feasts. It is something unseen but never forgotten.

—*Diary of the Undead*

# Vampire Games

## 1.

Judge Judy was letting this online con artist know what a scumbag he was—and I was loving every minute of it—when my doorbell rang. I nearly ignored it. Nearly. I mean, she was so very close to having this guy in tears.

Except I knew this was a client at the door. And clients paid the bills.

I reluctantly clicked off the show, set aside the Windex bottle and rag I had forgotten I was holding, and headed for the front door. As I did so, I instinctively reached up for the pair of Oakley wraparound sunglasses that were no longer there. My next conditioned movement was to check my arms and face and hands for sunscreen—which wasn't there, either.

Wasn't there, and wasn't needed.

That is, not since I'd donned the amethyst medallion two weeks ago. A medallion that had literally changed my life. A medallion that, curiously, no longer existed.

Two weeks ago, shortly after watching my first sunrise in seven years, I had reached down for the medallion, only to discover it was missing. Left behind had been a disk-shaped burn in my skin and the empty leather strap that had been holding the medallion.

Fang had thought my body *absorbed* the medallion. I had thought that sounded crazy as hell. Fang had reminded me that a skin-absorbed medallion was actually one of the least crazy things to happen to me in seven years.

Now, two weeks later, there still remained a faint outline of the medallion on my upper chest, seared into my skin.

*I'm such a weirdo,* I thought, and settled for reaching up and checking on my hair. Since mirrors were still out of the question, I had become a master at feeling my way through a good hair day. At least, I hoped they were good hair days.

As I stood before the front door, a lingering trepidation remained. After all, sunlight had been my enemy for so many years.

*You can do this,* I thought.

And I did. I opened the front door wide as sunlight splashed in. Brilliant sunlight. Splashing over me, but my skin felt . . . nothing. I felt nothing, and that was the greatest feeling of all.

No searing pain. No gasping sounds. No stumbling around and covering my eyes. No shrinking like a monster from the light of the day.

*Such a weirdo.*

Maybe. But now, not so weird.

Thank God.

Today, I was wearing torn jeans and a cute blouse, a sleeveless blouse, no less. Most importantly, I wasn't wearing multiple layers of clothing or one of my epic sunhats. Or satellite dishes, as a client had once called them.

It was just me. And that felt good. Damned good.

The man standing in the doorway was smaller than I expected. He was wearing a Chicago Bulls tank top and basketball shorts and high-top sneakers. He looked like he might have just stepped off the courts or raided a Foot Locker. The detailed tattoos that ran up and down his arms—and even along his neck—seemed to tell a story about something, although I couldn't puzzle it out at first blush.

"Russell?" I said.

"That's me," he said softly. "You must be Ms. Moon."

He dipped his head in a way that I found adorable. The dip was part greeting, part submission, and partly to let me know that he came in peace. We shook hands and I led him to my office in the back of my house, passing Anthony's empty room along the way. Well, not entirely empty. A pair of his white briefs sat in the middle of the floor, briefs that had seen better—and whiter—days. I reached in and quickly shut the door before my client got a good look at the mother of all skid marks.

Superman had Lex Luthor. Batman had the Joker. I had Anthony's skid marks.

Once safe in my office, I showed Russell to one of my client chairs and took a seat behind my cluttered desk.

"So, what can I do for you, Russell?" I asked.

"Jacky says you might be able to help me."

"Jacky, the boxing trainer?"

"Yes," he said.

"Jacky say anything else?"

"Only that you are a freak of nature."

I grinned. "He's always thought highly of me. What kind of help do you need?"

He looked at me. Straight in the eye. He held my gaze for a heartbeat or two, then said, "Somebody died accidentally . . . except I don't think it was an accident."

I nodded and did a quick psychic scan of the young man sitting before me. I sensed a heavy heart. Pain. Confusion. I sensed a lot of things. Most important, I did not sense that he was a killer.

"Tell me about it," I said.

# 2.

Russell Baker was a boxer.

A damn good one, too, apparently. He was twenty-four, fought in the coveted welterweight division, had a record of 22-3, and was moving quickly up the rankings. There were whispers that he might fight Manny Pacquiao—or Floyd Mayweather, Jr. His management was presently negotiating a fight on HBO. He'd already fought around the world: Tokyo, Dubai, South Africa. He'd already beaten some of the top contenders in the world. Only the best remained. Only the champions remained. Russell

Baker was on top of the boxing world and nothing could slow him down.

That was, until his last fight.

When he had killed a man in the ring.

Russell paused in his narrative, and I waited. He was a good-looking guy, clearly roped with muscle under his thin tee shirt. His nose was wide and flat, which I suspected was perfect for boxing. A long, pointed nose probably got broken routinely. He was also small, perhaps just a few inches taller than me. Welterweights must be the little guys. If I had to guess, I would have said that he was exactly half the size of Kingsley.

After collecting himself, Russell continued. The fight had been last month, in Vegas. Russell had been working his way through the top ten fighters in his weight class. According to Russell, rankings were influenced by a boxer's win-loss record, the difficulty of one's opponents, and how convincing one's victories were. The ultimate goal was to challenge for a title.

Last month, he'd fought the #7 ranked contender. Russell himself had currently been ranked #8. The fight was aired live on ESPN. The crowd had been full of celebrities. Up through three rounds, it had been a routine-enough fight, with Russell feeling confident and strong.

That is, until the fourth round.

It had been a short, straight punch to the side of the face. A hard punch. One that, if landed squarely, would rock most opponents. And Russell had landed it squarely. His opponent's head snapped back nicely. Russell had moved in closer to land another punch, but his opponent, Caesar Marquez, was already on his way to the mat.

Russell had been confused. The punch had been solid, sure, but not a knockout punch. But there was Caesar Marquez, out cold, motionless. Russell had celebrated, but not for long, not when Caesar remained motionless and a crowd began swarming around his fallen opponent.

Russell stopped talking and looked away, tears in his eyes. He unconsciously rubbed his knuckles, which were, I noticed, puffy and scarred. An IM message box appeared on the computer screen before me. It was Fang.

*You there, Moon Dance?*

I leaned forward and tapped a few keys: *I am, but working. Talk soon, okay?*

*The butler did it, Moon Dance. Always the butler.*

I shook my head and closed the box. Admittedly, I was mildly surprised that the box appeared. Fang always seemed to know when I was working—and respected my time with my clients. I frowned at that as I turned my attention back to Russell.

"May I ask how your opponent died?" I asked, lowering my voice.

"That's a good question, Ms. Moon."

"Please call me Sam."

He nodded. "Officially, they called it brain damage. Unofficially, they found nothing."

"How do you know this?"

"The M.E. told me. He personally called me up and told me that he couldn't find anything other than some bleeding—enough to officially label it a brain hemorrhage, but not enough to cause death. At least, not in the opinion of the medical examiner."

"Yes."

"So, why are you here, Russ?" I asked, trying out a nickname to get him to spill more details.

He continued rubbing his knuckles. His foot, which was crossed over his knee, was jiggling and shaking. Now he rubbed the back of his neck. The bicep that bulged as he did so was . . . interesting.

"I don't know, Sam. I don't know why I'm here."

"Yes, you do," I said. "Why are you here, Russell?"

"Because I don't think I killed him."

"If you didn't kill him, then who—or what—did?"

"I don't know, Sam. I guess that's why I'm here. I want you to help me find out how he died."

I sat back and folded my hands over my flattish stomach. Flat enough for me, anyway. I sensed so many emotions coming from Russ that it was hard to get a handle on them. Sensing emotion and reading minds are two different things. I wasn't close enough to Russ to read his mind, but his emotions were fair game to anyone sensitive enough to understand them.

Mostly, I sensed guilt coming off him. Wave after wave of it. I sensed that Russell hadn't been able to move forward from this fight and had been unable to deal with what had happened last month.

He needed answers. Real answers. Not the suspicious whisperings of a medical examiner.

"And what if I discover that you really did kill him, Russell?" I asked.

"Then I can live with that, but I need to know," he said, wiping his eyes and looking away. "I need to know for sure."

"Knowing is good," I said.

"Knowing is everything," he said, and I didn't doubt it for a second.

I nodded. "I'll need names and contact info."

He said he would email me everything I needed. We next discussed my retainer fee and, once done, he handed over his credit card. I spent the next few minutes embarrassing myself until I finally figured out how to use my iPhone credit card swiper. If I could have turned red, I would have.

We next shook hands, and if he noticed my cold flesh, he didn't show it. Or was too polite to show it.

As he left my office, I couldn't help but notice the dark cloud that surrounded him. His aura.

Guilt, I knew, was eating him alive.

He needed answers.

Badly.

# 3.

When Russell had gone, I brought up Google and researched the hell out of him.

In particular, I found the fight in question. The fight with Caesar Marquez had been a big deal, apparently. Both fighters were considered front runners to eventually contend for the welterweight title. Both fighters were roughly the same age. Same height. Same records. Same everything.

Except, now one was dead.

And the other was living with punishing, crushing guilt. I knew this. I had felt it from Russell, coming off him in wave after wave.

The crushing guilt was the least of my concerns. The black halo that completely surrounded his body was a different matter. A very serious matter.

Perhaps it was not so serious to others, but I knew the implications. Russell needed help. He also needed protection. And, considering the vast amount of guilt he was dealing with . . . perhaps he needed protection from himself.

No, he hadn't appeared suicidal, but I was also no expert in psychological issues. And since I wasn't close enough to him to read his thoughts, all I had to go on were my gut impressions.

And my gut told me that he had a very heavy heart.

Baker vs. Marquez hadn't been a big pay-per-view event, but HBO had hyped it up pretty good. All in all, the fight had lasted four rounds. Up through three rounds, two judges had scored the fight in favor of Russell, but one had it in favor of Caesar. Pretty even.

That is, until "the punch."

I wanted to see the punch for myself. It turned out that You-Tube had some pretty grisly videos on their website. In fact, there were easily a half dozen such boxing death videos. I first watched Russell's fight, then forced myself to watch the other five, too, for comparison.

Most of the videos showed two guys hammering each other in the ring. Generally, one guy was doing a lot of hammering, and one guy was doing a lot of receiving. At least that was the trend. In five of the six fights, one opponent was clearly dominating the other opponent.

But not in Russell's fight.

Their fight, at least to my untrained eye—and the truth was, I was perhaps more trained than most—their fight seemed fairly even, as the judges' scorecards had indicated.

Both fighters were trading punches. Both fighters were backing away. Both fighters were circling. Russell jabbed. Marquez blocked. Marquez circled, Russell followed. Both had quick feet. Quick hands. No obvious blood. No one staggered like in the other five video clips. No one was obviously getting their brains beaten in.

And there it was.

*The punch.*

It was a short, straight punch, designed to be used when two opponents were close-in to each other. Not a lot of back swing. Just power the fist at about shoulder height and use your weight to drive the punch home. Jacky had taught it to me years ago, and it was a common punch to use when practicing with the heavy bag. Myself, I had probably delivered thousands of such punches. They weren't generally considered knockout punches, although, if delivered with enough force, could certainly stun an opponent.

Except Marquez didn't look stunned.

He looked dead.

Prior to the punch, they had both been fighting an inside game, heads ducked, juking, bobbing and weaving, each looking for an opening. Russell saw his and struck, cobra-fast.

Marquez's head snapped back.

HBO had been right there to capture the next image fairly close up. Marquez's eyes rolled up. I saw the whites of them clearly. His hands dropped to his sides.

Russell had been about to deliver another blow when he clearly saw that something wasn't right with his opponent.

As Marquez's hands went limp, so did his knees and legs, and now he was falling forward, landing hard on his chest and face, where he proceeded to lay, unmoving.

I saw that Russell's first instinct was to help him—and I admired him for that—but then his trainer bull-rushed him and lifted him up off his feet. And as his trainer ran him wildly around the ring, I saw Russell trying to look back to his fallen foe.

The longer Caesar Marquez lay unmoving, the more chaotic the ring became. People swarmed and buzzed around him. Russell fought to get close to him. A stretcher appeared through the crowd and soon Caesar was being threaded through the ropes, through the crowd, and down a side aisle into what I assumed were the locker rooms.

I stopped the video and studied the crowded ring. Dozens of faces. Some confused, some concerned, many excited. Men, mostly, but a few women.

I replayed the video again and again. Watching his trainers, watching the crowd, looking for anything that gave any indication that someone might have known what was about to go down.

But nothing stood out.

Nothing at all.

## 4.

"So, do you still need to sleep during the day?" Kingsley asked, or, at least, I think he asked. Words had a tendency to get muffled when spoken around a side of beef.

We were at Mulberry Street Café in downtown Fullerton, sitting by the window, drinking wine and eating steak. Just like regular people.

Of course, one of us wasn't so much eating their steak, as slurping the bloody juice pooling around it, and the other wasn't so much eating his steak, as wolfing it down.

I nodded. "I'm still a creature of the night, if that's what you're asking. And, yes, I still need to sleep during the day. I'm still weak during the day. I still feel like crap when I have to get up and pick up the kids during the day. The medallion only gives me the ability to *tolerate* the sun."

"No more burning?" he asked between bites.

"No more burning."

Mulberry's was busy tonight. It was busy every night, as far as I could tell. It was our restaurant of choice, especially since the cooks and waiters here were used to my orders of raw meat, extra bloody.

Now, as I watched Kingsley tear through his meat in record time, something occurred to me. "Now I have a question for you."

"Shoot."

"Were you always this big?"

"Big . . . how?"

"Big, as in I've actually seen you turn sideways to go through doorways."

"Only some doors, and, no, the big part came later."

"How much later?"

"Over time. Decades. Little by little, after each transformation."

"You mean, you grew after each transformation?"

"Yes. At least, as far as I could tell."

"But why?" I asked.

"Survival, I think."

"But you're already immortal," I said, lowering my voice.

"A weak immortal doesn't get very far, Sam. And remember, I can't turn into"—and now he lowered his voice to a low growl—"the thing I turn into, on cue. That happens only once a month, and generally in a locked room. And when it does happen, I'm often out of my mind. Gone to the world for the whole night."

"While something else takes over your body."

"Right," he said.

"So, being big in your daily life has its benefits."

"Of course. Stronger, faster, able to protect myself."

"So how big were you before?"

"Big enough, but not this big."

"Do all werewolves get as big as you?"

"Some bigger."

I said, "I haven't gotten bigger. If anything, I've gotten smaller."

"And you won't get bigger, because each night you're at full strength. And even during the day you're not completely incapacitated."

"No," I said. "Even though I feel weaker during the day, I'm still far stronger than I used to be."

I recalled my boxing match with the Marine last year, the match that had occurred just before sundown. Sure, I had felt like crap, but I was still strong enough to take down America's finest.

"Also," added Kingsley, reaching over and cutting off a chunk of my nearly raw steak, "it's just the nature of my kind."

"For the host to grow big," I said.

"Right. We all have our quirks."

"I think your quirks are better than my quirks," I said.

"And who among us can fly?" he asked.

I thought about that. "Good point."

As the waiter refilled our glasses of wine, Kingsley asked what I was working on these days. I told him about my latest case, and as I did so, Kingsley began nodding. Turns out he'd seen the fight live on HBO.

"Wasn't much of a punch," he said. "Not enough to kill a man."

"Or so we think," I said. After all, I had done some research on the subject. "We still don't know his condition prior to the fight, or the amount of punches he'd taken in practice and other fights."

Kingsley shrugged. "True. Either way, it wasn't much of a punch; in fact, I thought the fight was pretty even up to that point. What's your gut tell you?"

I shrugged too, but, unlike Kingsley, my shrug didn't look like two land masses heaving. I said, "Nothing yet, although I think Russell's grasping at straws."

Kingsley nodded. "Looking for a way to live with his guilt, perhaps."

"Perhaps," I said. "One thing is clear: It's eating him alive. Literally." I told Kingsley about the black halo I'd seen around the young boxer.

"The same halo you saw around your son?"

"The same."

"What's it mean?" asked Kingsley.

"It means he needs help. Lots of help."

# 5.

It was after hours and I was sitting in Jacky's office.

Jacky, if possible, looked even smaller than usual as he sat behind a dented metal desk. He was drinking an orange Gatorade, which, I think, was the classic Gatorade. Of course, if I drank Gatorade now, I would heave it up in a glorious orange fountain.

Jacky, of course, didn't need to know that, and since I only spent a few hours a week with the guy—and most of that was spent with him yelling at me to keep my hands up—I hadn't yet developed a telepathic rapport with him.

Which was just as well. I seriously suspected that the old man had suffered some brain damage himself. He'd been a champion back in the day. And in Jacky's case, "back in the day" meant the early fifties in Ireland.

Jacky had spent the past few decades here in Fullerton. At one point his gym had been a happening place for up-and-coming boxers, with Jacky himself training a handful of champions. That is, until downtown Fullerton had become so trendy that Jacky—perhaps a better businessman than I'd given him credit for—had decided to turn his gym into a women's self-defense studio.

Then again, if I was a spunky old man, I'd rather train cute women, too.

Anyway, when Jacky finished off the Gatorade, he wiped the back of his hand across his mouth, dropped the empty bottle into a nearby wastebasket, and sat back.

"What did you think of the kid?" he asked, speaking in an Irish accent so thick that you would think he was only now making his way through Ellis Island.

"I think the kid is deeply troubled," I said. "And I don't blame him."

Jacky nodded. He seemed uncomfortable in his office. He seemed less himself, somehow. Out there, in the gym, he was larger than life, even though he was only a few inches taller than me. In here, at day's end, he looked like a shell of himself. He looked tired. Old. But not weak. Never weak. Even in quiet repose, the man looked like he wanted to punch something.

"Russ isn't the first lad to kill somebody in the ring, and he won't be the last. And usually it plays with a fighter's head, so much so that they ain't ever much the same again."

"He feels guilt," I said.

"They all do. Except it's part of the risk we take. Each kid knows that his next fight might be his last."

"Then why did you send him to me?"

Jacky didn't answer immediately. Through his closed door, I could hear someone sweeping and whistling. A door slammed somewhere, and I heard two women giggling down a hallway that I knew led to the female locker rooms.

"It's part of the risk, yes, but something about this one doesn't smell right."

I waited. I wanted to hear it from Jacky, someone who had seen tens of thousands of punches thrown in his lifetime. Jacky rubbed his knuckles as he formulated his thoughts. I wondered how difficult it was for Jacky to formulate his thoughts. How much brain damage had the old Irishman suffered?

There had to be some. His aura, which was mostly light blue and ironically serene, appeared bright red around his head. The bright red, I knew, was the body fighting something, perhaps a disease. Or dealing with an injury.

The Irishman rubbed his face and seemed to have lost his train of thought. The reddish aura around his head flared briefly.

I said gently, "You were saying something about this fight not smelling right."

"Was I now?"

"Yes."

"Which fight?"

"Baker vs. Marquez."

He nodded and rubbed the back of his neck and gritted his teeth. "It's hell getting old, Sam."

"So I'm told."

"And this noggin of mine just ain't right sometimes."

"Mine either."

He nodded, but I wasn't sure he'd heard me. He said, "Routine fight. No one beating up no one. Judges had Baker up a few rounds, but the truth is, they were only just beginning to feel each other out. No one had taken control yet. It was even as hell."

"Were you there?" I asked.

"At the fight? Hell, no. The wife doesn't let me anywhere near Vegas these days. She's afraid I'll spend our retirement—and then I'll never get to leave this damn gym."

"You love this damn gym," I said.

He winked at me, and I saw that there were tears in his eyes. Where the tears came from and why, I didn't exactly know. "More than anything," he said.

"You watched the fight on TV?"

"Which fight?"

"Baker vs. Marquez."

"Yes, of course. Russ is a local boy. He trains here sometimes. I showed him my best moves, and he never forgot his roots. Got to love a kid like that."

"Yes."

"Damn shame what happened. He ain't no killer. They were just boxing. Trading jabs, the occasional straight shot or hook. Nothing landed yet. Nothing really. No reason a kid should be dead."

Jacky fell silent and absently wiped the tears from his eyes. His knuckles were crisscrossed with scar tissue. I imagined Jacky raising hell in the streets of Dublin.

"So, what are you saying, Jacky?"

"I'm saying, in one fell swoop, two top contenders have disappeared. One's dead, and the other might as well be dead. There's something to that, Sam, something worth looking into."

I nodded, thinking about that, as Jacky sat back and closed his eyes and rubbed the scar tissue along his knuckles.

# 6.

*You there, Moon Dance?*

The IM box appeared on my laptop screen as I was packing my bags in my room. I quickly tossed my unfolded sweater in my suitcase. It was only February. Even Vegas was cold in February.

*To what do I owe the pleasure, Fang?*

*I need to talk to you.*

*In person?*

*Maybe. No. I don't know.*

*What's going on, Fang?*

There was a pause, and I was suddenly alarmed to discover my normally dormant heart had picked up its pace. It thudded steadily against my ribs, rocking me slightly. Normally, my own beating heart went unnoticed, which wasn't too surprising since these days it generally only beat about five times a minute.

Something was wrong. Or something could *potentially* be wrong. Or something was just . . . *off*. For starters, Fang seemed unusually closed to me. Not to mention, he didn't seem to be picking up on my own increasingly worried thoughts. What the hell was going on?

The little pencil icon appeared in the IM box, which meant Fang was typing something. A moment later, his words appeared:

*I recently . . . met someone.*

*Would this someone happen to be a female?*

*Yes.*

This wasn't horrible news. At least, not for me. I liked Fang. I appreciated his friendship and help. But I had always felt he had an ulterior motive: he wanted something from me. And what he wanted, he had made clear a year ago.

He wanted me to *turn* him.

Although I didn't doubt that he loved me, I always wondered where the love originated. Was it for me, or for what I am? A thought suddenly occurred to me, and I voiced it. Or, rather, wrote it:

*Is this woman a . . . vampire?*

*Yes.*

*A real vampire?*

*A real vampire, Moon Dance.*

*May I ask her name?*

*You know her.*

Something inside me turned to ice, which, for me, is saying something. I exhaled a steady stream of cold air, and wrote: *Detective Rachel Hanner.*

*Yes.*

*How did you two meet?*

*She came in the other night, sat at the bar. Ordered a glass of white wine, same as you.*

I read his words and would have held my breath, except I was never sure when I held my breath these days. He went on:

*There was something about her. Something . . . otherworldly. The way she stared at me. Her small, precise movements. Her faint accent. It wasn't long before I suspected what she was.*

I waited, re-reading his words, thinking hard, puzzling through this. What did this mean? I didn't know yet.

*It wasn't until later, after her second glass of wine, that I realized she had been reading my mind. Her intrusion wasn't obvious. Not like the way I know when you're in there. I mean, I can always feel when you're in my mind, Moon Dance. Touching down here and there.*

He paused and I was truly feeling sick. Down the hallway, I heard Anthony snoring lightly. Music came from Tammy's room. The house was locked. I always kept it locked. What was Hanner up to? I didn't know, but I had that creepy-ass feeling of being watched. Of course, with me, it might be more than a feeling.

I stood and walked over to my main window and looked out into the cul-de-sac. No one was out there. At least, not that I could see. All the cars on the street I recognized. But with Hanner—the only other vampire that I knew personally—she could be anywhere. She could be sitting on my roof, for all I knew. I shivered.

*Jesus,* I thought.

I sat back down and Fang's next message appeared almost instantaneously: *I think within a few minutes, she knew all my secrets. All of them.*

I knew what Fang meant. The man had some killer secrets. Literally. The kind that would send him back to jail—or a mental institution—for the rest of his life.

*I see,* I wrote, mostly to let Fang know I was still here.

*She showed me her badge and told me she knew who I was. She called me by my name . . . my real name. She next gave me her home address and told me to meet her there after work.*

*When was this?*

*Last night.*

"Shit," I whispered.

*What happened next, Fang?*

I wondered if Fang knew what had happened. After all, I knew that Hanner had a . . . gift for removing memories. Indeed, I sensed a lot of vagueness from Fang, and it was clear that our personal connection had been broken, somehow. I thought Hanner had something to do with that.

*I'm . . . I'm not really sure,* he wrote, confirming my suspicions.

I had a vision of blood, a lot of blood. Fang might have been more closed off to me than normal and, although I wasn't sure what the hell was going on, we still seemed to have some sort of connection.

Enough for me to see the blood.

But most disturbing of all—

I wrote: *You drank blood.*

He paused only slightly before writing: *Yes, Moon Dance.*

I sensed his shame, but I also sensed his excitement. Fang had grown up with elongated canine teeth, a rare defect that had grown into an even rarer psychosis: as a youth, he began to actually believe he was a vampire. Crazy, but that was exactly what it was.

*Crazy.*

His psychosis had led to the death of his girlfriend, a teenage girl who had been partially bled to death . . . and partially consumed.

By Fang.

His escape from a high-security mental institution had been in all the papers, and his subsequent manhunt had been well documented. But he had slipped away.

And assumed a new identity.

Aaron Parker, aka Fang, now went by the official name of Eli Roberts—and how he landed in my life was one of coincidence and obsession. Although I doubted he still saw himself as a real vampire, I knew he retained a hunger for blood. I knew this because every now and then I would see it in his thoughts. His hunger. But over the years, he had controlled himself. Controlled *it*.

We were both silent. Or, rather, the IM message box remained silent. I wasn't sure what to say. I sensed that Hanner was working her way into his world, but for what reason, I didn't know. But one thing I did know: none of it was good.

*So, what will you do now, Fang?* I finally wrote, deciding on the direct path. What else could I say?

*I don't know, Moon Dance.*

*Did she threaten you?*

*She didn't have to. I understand the implications. I'm a fugitive. She's a cop. Things could go very badly for me.*

*Did she say what she wanted?*

*From me? Not yet.*

*She wants something from you, Fang.*

I sensed him nodding, and after a moment, he wrote: *I know.*

But I sensed he was holding something back, and finally wrote: *There's something else, isn't there, Fang?*

*Yes, Moon Dance.*

I waited, suddenly afraid of the answer.

After a moment, he wrote: *She wants to give me something, Moon Dance. The one thing you wouldn't do for me, the one thing you wouldn't give me.*

*Ah, Fang . . .*

*Yes, Moon Dance. Immortality.*

# 7.

The flight to Vegas was of the commercial airline type.

Although only forty-five minutes from John Wayne Airport in Santa Ana, I had plenty of time to think about Fang and Hanner. How she had found him, I didn't know. I suspected she had followed me or had someone watch me. That she had gone over my phone records wasn't out of the realm of possibility, either. Generally, the police needed a damn good reason to scour one's phone records. She could have made up a reason, or done so secretly, in a way that I wasn't aware of. Private investigators don't have such access to phone records. A homicide investigator would.

The plane hit some turbulence, which I ignored. Turbulence didn't bother me. Nor did the thought of the plane plummeting to earth in a fireball. I was fairly certain I would have been the one passenger on board to walk away from such a crash. Or fly away.

If Hanner had gone the phone record route, she would have seen the pathetic few times that Danny had called to speak to his own children—and the pathetic short amount of time he had spent talking to them, as well.

She would have also seen the occasional phone call from Eli Roberts, aka Aaron Parker, aka Fang.

Some minor research into Eli's background would have netted a curious result: his background didn't go very far back. A quick scan of his current background would have resulted in seeing his current employment. From there, all she would have had to do was swing by for a visit . . .

And scan his thoughts.

She would have known then who he was. No secrets would have been hidden from her. She would have known his murderous past, and his current desires.

But why?

Hanner had proven to be helpful in the past, but perhaps she was just covering for her own kind. After all, she had, on more than one occasion, successfully hidden my supernatural activity from the local police. More than helping me, we had drunk blood together. Discussed our kids together. Laughed together. I had found her insightful and knowledgeable, if not a little feral. Whereas I fought to hold onto my humanity—at least what I thought made me human—Hanner clearly embraced her vampiric nature. She was all vampire, through and through, and any vestiges of humanness were long, long gone.

As an immortal, her thoughts were closed to me, so I could only guess what her intentions were. Clearly, she was obsessed with me. If not obsessed, then overly *aware*. Perhaps she was this way with all local vampires. Or with any vampires with whom she crossed paths. Perhaps she considered all other vampires her enemies.

I shook my head at that thought and leaned back in my economy seat. No, if she considered all vampires her enemies, then she wouldn't have supported a local blood dealer—the actor, Robert Mason—who, in turn, provided blood for many other vampires.

Perhaps her interest in me had something more to do with our last conversation, when she had said that I was a rare breed.

That I had special gifts.

That I could do things other vampires couldn't.

Or perhaps her interest in me had something to do with the old vampire who had turned me seven years ago. The old vampire now dead thanks to Randolf the Vampire Hunter. He of the cute buns.

I thought about all of this as the plane landed. A jolting landing. I, myself, landed far smoother, of course. Which reminded me: According to Hanner, I was one of the few vampires who could transform.

When the plane finally came to a stop, I stood with the others, got my bags like the others, and waited in line to shuffle off the plane. Like the others.

But I was not like the others.

No, I was not like them at all.

# 8.

Dr. Herbert Sculler looked like a character out of a Tim Burton movie.

The short doctor wore round glasses and a lab coat that looked far too big for him. His face was whiter than my own and he smiled far too often, at least too often for a medical examiner who spent his days around corpses.

We were sitting in his office, which was next to his examining room. There was a man lying on one of the tables, under a sheet, waiting patiently for the doctor's return.

Sculler's office was small. I suspected it was so because he spent the majority of his time in the examining room. There, against the far wall, one, two, three corpses were lined up in plastic bags on shelves.

More interesting was the male spirit standing off to the side of the dead man in the examining room. The spirit crackled with energy, even when standing motionless. So far, it had not taken its eyes off the body under the blanket. From here, I could see two dark holes in the spirit's chest, which I knew to be bullet wounds. After many months of seeing the dead, I knew that spirits often mirrored their appearance at death.

*Welcome to my life.*

The spirit merely stood there and stared, wavering in and out of existence. Meaning one moment he was a fairly full-formed human-shape; the next, he was nothing more than static electricity. Upon closer inspection, I saw other spirits in the lab, too. In fact, dozens of them. But most were nothing more than faint balls of light.

"Ah, here we go," said Dr. Sculler, who was busy clicking away on his computer. "Caesar Marquez, boxer, age twenty-five, head injury."

"You examined him personally?" I asked.

Sculler nodded gravely. Cutting dead people open was, after all, serious business. "Yes, performed it myself."

"How long have you been a medical examiner, Dr. Sculler?"

"Twenty-two years."

"How many fatally injured boxers?"

"Just the one, although I've seen my share of brain injuries. Particularly football injuries."

"Was Caesar Marquez's brain similarly injured?"

"I'm scanning the autopsy images now, if you would like to look."

"I would."

"Then come around here."

I hadn't worked for the federal government long, but I had seen my share of medical examining rooms and corpses. And these days, death was something to analyze, not to fear. No, never again to fear.

There were dozens of images of a dead man in various stages of examination. The young man, from all appearances, was the same Caesar Marquez I had seen fighting in the YouTube clip.

As I leaned in behind Sculler, he clicked over to a cluster of photographs that focused on the man's head. A few clicks later and the top half of the skull had been removed. The skin itself had been peeled down over the face. The next image showed, from all appearances, a very healthy brain. Finally, the brain had been removed and was now sitting in a small metal tray.

Dr. Sculler zoomed in on the freshly-removed brain that had been housed in a perfectly functioning young adult male just a few hours earlier. Sculler pointed to the screen, in particular to a red discoloration along the left temporal lobe.

"Bleeding," he said. "The brain is susceptible to bleeding, especially after trauma. Unlike other body parts, however, when the brain bleeds, it's a major problem. Bleeding in the brain causes pressure. Pressure can shut down various functions of the brain . . . and can lead to death. Often quickly."

I said, "The official cause of death is epidural hematoma."

"Yes." He pointed to the screen. "Bleeding between the dura mater and the skull."

"A brain hemorrhage."

"Yes, but in this case the damage is technically classified as an extra-axial hemorrhage, or an intracranial hemorrhage."

I nodded, taking this in. More and more it was looking like Russell Baker didn't have much of a case. "Did you actually see the fight, doctor?"

"I did, yes. Later."

"And did you see enough to warrant a brain hemorrhage?"

The good doctor removed his glasses. As he did so, a spirit of an elderly woman materialized behind him in the far corner of the office. The skin on the doctor's forearms immediately cropped into goose bumps. He shivered slightly, oblivious to the sudden source of cold air. The old woman only partially manifested, hovering on legs that didn't exist. If the good doctor could see what I was seeing, he would undoubtedly run for the hills.

For now, he only shivered, blissfully unaware of the spirit energy around him. The woman faded just as quickly as she appeared. The hollow look in her eyes would have been haunting, if not so familiar. At least, familiar to me.

After shivering some more, he said, "Quite frankly, no."

I perked up. I just hate taking money from a client and then giving them nothing in return.

"No?"

"No. But that doesn't mean that any punch at any point in the fight couldn't have caused the injury. Very little is understood about brain injuries."

"I understand, but is it your professional opinion that you think nothing in the fight warranted death?"

"Not professional. Personal. Unofficial." He paused. "Officially, he died from a blunt force received during the fight."

"Officially, but not likely."

He stared at me, and then started nodding. "Not likely."

"How old was the wound?" I asked.

"It was within the correct time frame. I have no doubt that it happened in and around the time of the fight."

"Or possibly before?" I suggested.

The good doctor shrugged and rubbed his arms. After all, the old lady had reappeared in the far corner of the room.

"Possibly," he said.

# 9.

It took a few calls, a little waiting, a few more calls, and maybe a little begging to finally meet my next interview.

I met Ricardo Cortez at the Hard Rock Hotel's massive, central bar, where we sat across from each other and nursed our drinks. Mine was white wine. His was a beer. Both of our glasses were small. Around us were the sounds of money being won and lost. Mostly lost.

"You were the referee for the Baker/Marquez fight," I said.

He looked down into his beer. I suspected he often looked down into his beer for answers. That I quickly ascertained he was an alcoholic no longer surprised me. That I felt his over-whelming need and addiction to the stuff did surprise me.

It was almost as if I could reach inside his thoughts.

Almost.

Weeks ago, Hanner had told me that I could expect to start reading other minds—and not just those closest to me. And not just read.

Manipulate.

*Jesus.*

For now, I didn't want to think about manipulating another's mind—hell, it was all I could do to exist comfortably in my own.

Finally, Ricardo looked up from his beer. He said, "Yes."

"How long have you been a referee?"

"Eight years."

"Have you ever refereed a bout where a fighter was killed?"

Ricardo was a strong-looking Hispanic with what appeared to be the beginning of a tattoo under the right sleeve of his jacket. It looked like a snake tail. In fact, I was certain it was a rattle. We were mostly alone at the bar. Then again, the bar was so expansive that it was hard to tell where it ended and where it started. Nearby, a woman jumped up and down at the nickel slot machine. I think she'd just won a shitload of nickels.

Ricardo ignored the excited woman. Instead, he lifted his beer to his lips, and while he was guzzling he gestured for the waiter for another. Yeah, he was an alcoholic.

When he finally pulled away, he said, "That was my first death."

"Hard on you?"

"What do you think?"

"I'm thinking it was a shitty day for everyone."

"Yup."

The waitress set another beer before him, and Ricardo picked it up instantly.

I said, "Do you blame yourself for his death?"

"No one else to blame."

"What about the guy doing the punching?"

Ricardo shook his head. "It was my job to stop the fight before it gets to that point."

"Except it was a fluke punch. Everyone agrees. Most people think the fight was pretty even up to that point."

"No, it wasn't."

I blinked. This was new information. Investigators loved new information. New information meant that an investigator was onto something. I liked that.

"How so?" I asked.

Ricardo rubbed his face and I saw the scarring on his own knuckles. Ah, he had been a fighter himself. In fact, now I could see that his nose had undoubtedly been broken a few times. Probably not a very good fighter. Probably why he went into reffing fights instead of participating in them. Reffing was easier on the nose.

When he had collected his thoughts and had decided just how much to tell me—and how I knew this was beginning to trouble me—he said, "Caesar was not all there from the beginning."

"What do you mean?"

"Caesar looked, at least to me, that he'd already gone a round or two. Or maybe even three or four."

"Anyone else notice this?"

"Hard to say. I'm certain someone on his crew would have known."

"How could they miss it?"

"Easy to miss, unless you know what to look for."

"And you know what to look for?" I said.

"Of course. All good refs do. It's how we keep these guys from beating in each other's skulls."

"What do you look for?"

Ricardo was loosening up, forgiving himself, reminding himself that there might be more to this story than he knew. Again, how I knew this snippet of thought from him was seriously beginning to wig me out.

He said, "If you know a fighter, it's easier. Then you know their mannerisms. You also know how much punishment they can take."

"You ever work a fight with Caesar?"

"Yup. Two."

"And he was different from the get-go."

"Right. From the fucking get-go."

"What was he doing different?"

"Dazed. Slower than normal."

"Even though most judges scored it even?"

"I said slower than normal. Caesar Marquez was better than most. I even caught him staggering once or twice back to the corner. Not sure if anyone else had seen it."

"What did you think about that?"

"I thought that something was wrong."

"Enough to stop the fight?"

He shook his head and remembered the beer. He said, "I should have stopped it if I'd had any balls. I should have at least called one of the doctors over. But . . ."

"But you just weren't sure."

He looked at me funny, as if I had read his thoughts. "Right, I wasn't sure. There was no reason for his symptoms, after all. The fight had been fairly tame."

"But he was in trouble from the beginning."

Ricardo nodded. "Almost as if . . ."

He couldn't finish the sentence, and so I finished it for him. "Almost as if he'd been hurt before the fight."

Ricardo looked at me again. "Bingo."

"Hard to blame yourself for something like this."

"Hard not to, either. I should have stopped the fight."

"You did your best."

He shook his head, and kept on shaking his head even as he finished his second beer and held up his hand for a third.

# 10.

With Criss Angel in town, I figured something as mundane as a giant flying vampire bat would go unnoticed.

And so I stood on the ledge of my fifteenth-floor balcony at the MGM Grand, one of the few hotels in Vegas with open balconies. It was perfect for viewing the Vegas skyline from . . . or leaping from.

*Don't try this at home, kids.*

The hot desert wind buffeted my naked body. My longish hair snapped behind me horizontally. Standing naked on a balcony's edge was liberating. Despite being perpetually cold and despite the hot desert wind, I shivered slightly.

After all, the wind was blowing where, as they say, the sun don't shine.

I looked down at the city. An image of the young boxer collapsing in the ring came to me as I stood there. No surprise. This was the city where he'd died, where his autopsy had been conducted, and where I was beginning to suspect he had possibly been killed.

And not by Russell Baker.

Whether or not Caesar Marquez's death was an accident—or something else—remained to be seen.

I didn't need a psychic hit to know that something screwy was going on here. Something wasn't right. What exactly, I didn't know. Maybe I would never know.

I tilted my head back and spread my arms and deeply inhaled the heated desert air—air that was suffused with something that smelled suspiciously like all-you-can-eat $1.99 BBQ ribs.

I stood like that for some time, and the longer I did so, the more I was certain of one thing: I was becoming less and less human.

And more and more something else.

*One of them.*

I knew this because no human stood on the ledge of their hotel balcony, with arms spread, head tilted back, naked as the day they were born, reveling in their freedom, knowing that an even greater freedom was about to come. A freedom from gravity.

As I stood there, the wind whipping my hair into a frenzy, I wasn't thinking of my kids or Kingsley or Fang or anyone. In fact, I wasn't thinking at all. I was only *feeling*, only *sensing*.

The wind, the heat, the smells, the sounds.

I felt elemental. Animalistic.

I didn't feel like a mother or a friend or a lover. I didn't feel human. I felt, instead, deeply connected to the earth, a part of the earth, a part of its elements, its raw material.

I tilted my head forward, knowing that I had to either jump or go back inside. Sooner or later, the cops would be beating down my door. A naked woman on a balcony's ledge was bound to draw some attention.

And I sure as hell wasn't going back in.

The flame appeared in my thoughts. A single, unwavering flame, and within the flame was a creature that should have looked hideous to me, but didn't. It was a creature I felt an extreme fondness for. A love for.

It was, after all, me. In a different shape.

A very different shape.

I lowered my arms and looked down. There was nothing to hinder my drop. No buttresses or projecting balconies.

Just a straight drop.

And so I did just that, tilting forward away from the ledge.

Dropping.

# 11.

As I fell, as the warm desert wind thundered over me, the winged creature in the flame rushed toward me, filling my thoughts.

I shuddered violently—but kept my eyes closed as I continued to plummet.

I was bigger now, I could feel it, but I hadn't yet fully transformed. I didn't dare open my eyes, knowing the closing of my eyes, the flame, the image . . . and faith were all part of this process.

I continued to fall, knowing my body was changing rapidly. Metamorphosing. I also knew that the speed of my metamorphosis was contingent on the circumstance. A shorter drop would result in a faster transformation.

Now, I could feel my arms growing, elongating, feel my body becoming something greater than it was before. Denser, heavier. My awareness of my own body expanded instinctively, exponentially.

I was no longer what I was.

No, I was something much, much bigger.

Much greater.

My wings snapped taut, catching the air, manipulating the air, using the air, and now I wasn't so much falling as angling.

I opened my eyes.

Before me stretched the Vegas Strip, in all of its glittering, neon, sinful glory. I flapped my wings hard, instinctively, gaining altitude. Instinctively.

Keeping to the shadows in a city that never sleeps and never turns off was no easy task. And so I took it up another hundred feet or so, flapping my wings, catching hot drafts of sinful air. Yes, the wind was warm and dry and not very different from the air in Southern California. That would change in a few months. In a few months, Las Vegas would go from temperate to nuclear.

Too hot for even the undead.

I flapped my wings casually, cruising above the glittering city. I circled once around the superheated laser beam emitting from the Luxor. I continued on, moving north over a cluster of world-famous hotels. The Bellagio with its intricate fountains, the Paris and its Eiffel Tower replica, the Mirage and its gardens, Treasure Island with its pirate ship.

And one flying monster. I wondered idly if the Excalibur needed a real-life dragon. It could supplement my income.

So far, people weren't pointing into the sky and scattering like frightened rabbits before a hawk's shadow. That was a good thing, I guess.

I caught a warm updraft and spread my wings wide and hovered high above the city of sin, staring down, using my supernaturally-enhanced vision to see not only the multitudes crowding the sidewalks, but their actual expressions. Most looked tired. Most looked drunk. There were many groups of young people, no doubt celebrating twenty-first birthdays. A handful of older types wore shorts and tee shirts and sandals. One woman was walking through the crowd bare-chested, high as a kite, although not as high as *this* kite. People stopped and stared at her breasts, but for the most part, she was ignored.

*Welcome to Vegas.*

I saw young men handing out flyers to strip clubs. Most people tossed the flyers aside, which cluttered sidewalks and gutters, pushed along by the warm spring breeze.

I had seen enough of the lights, the gaudy hotels, the plaid tourist shorts, the filth, the degradation, the glitter—and beat my massive wings as hard as I could and shot up into the night sky. I continued flapping them, forcing the rapidly-cooling air down below me. I rose higher and higher, so high that Vegas itself was nothing more than a pinprick of light.

A *bright* pinprick of light, but a pinprick nonetheless.

Here, on the outer edges of the atmosphere, where little or no oxygen existed, I flapped idly, serenely, holding my position. My mind was mostly empty. Mostly. Images of Kingsley flitted through. Of my son with his growing strength. Of my daughter, who seemed to understand that something very strange was happening in the Moon household.

*I would have to tell her, too,* I thought. *Tell them both. Everything.*

Up here, far above the earth, it was easy to forget that I was a mother, that I had responsibilities. Up here, high above the earth, it was easy to forget who I was. Up here, drifting on jet-streams and updrafts, buoyed by winds unfelt and unknown by anything living, it was easy to forget I had once been human.

The wind was cold. But not so cold as to affect me in any way. I merely acknowledged the cold, like a scientist noting the cancerous effects of the latest sugar substitute in lab rats.

I spread my wings wide and rode the wind, rising and falling, listening to it thunder over my ears and flap the leathery membranes that were my wings. I did this for an unknowable amount of time, hovering high above the earth, correcting my altitude ever-so-slightly with minute adjustments to my wings, turning my wrists this way and that, angling my arms this way and that.

This way and that, adjusting, correcting, hovering.

Later, I tucked my wings in and shot down, aiming for the bright speck of light, perhaps the brightest speck of light ever.

Las Vegas.

# 12.

I alighted on the balcony.

There, I merged with the serious-looking, dark-haired woman in the flame and, after a moment of slight disorientation, found myself standing naked again on the balcony of the MGM Grand Hotel. I often wondered what the transformation process looked like to an outsider. Did I contort and jerk like they do in the movies? Or did I transform in a blink of an eye? I always sensed that my transformation took only a few seconds, but since my eyes were always closed and focused on the flame, I would probably never know. Maybe I would transform for Kingsley one night.

*Yeah, I'm a freak.*

I donned the white robe I had left draped over the railing and stepped back into my room. I was just tying the terrycloth belt when I paused. My inner alarm didn't necessarily go off, but it perked up. A slight buzzing just inside my ear.

*Someone's here,* I thought.

A shape appeared in my thoughts, something glowing—and it appeared, I was sure, directly behind me.

I was moving in an instant, turning, swooping low to the ground, and slammed into whoever was behind me so hard that I drove him into the drywall.

There, I held him up while plaster dust rained down over his shoulders and down onto my raised forearms.

A man. A very beautiful man.

Who gazed down at me with a bemused expression. He was, of course, not a man at all. He was an angel. My one-time guardian angel now turned rogue, so to speak.

I eased my grip and Ishmael dropped lightly to the floor. He shook his head and dust and smaller chunks of wall fell from his long, silver hair and broad shoulders. "Do you greet all your guests this way, Samantha?"

I dusted off my own arms. "Well, let's just say I haven't had a lot of luck in hotel rooms."

If not for a slight prickling of my inner alarm, I would have been completely off-guard. And these days, with my ever expanding extra-sensory perception, someone catching me off-guard was getting harder and harder to do. Unless, of course, that someone was a rogue angel, who seemed to be making a habit of catching me unaware.

"Not as unaware as you might think, Samantha," he said. Unlike other immortals, Ishmael had access to my thoughts. No surprise there, since he'd been my one-time guardian angel. He finished dusting himself off and looked at me. "For the first time, you sensed me nearby. That's quite an accomplishment, and a credit to your growing powers."

Still, I didn't like the implications of that statement. "So you're around me often?"

"What can I say, Samantha? Old habits die hard."

"So, you're often around me?" I repeated, digesting this news. He nodded. "Myself, and others."

"What others?"

"You know some of them."

"Sephora," I said, recalling the entity I had communicated with last year through automatic writing.

"Yes. Her and others like her."

"Spirit guides," I said, recalling one of my conversations with Sephora.

"Spirit guides, deceased relatives, angels. What some would call your soul group."

"And you."

"Not officially," he said. "Not anymore."

"Not since you fell."

His eyes flashed briefly. "Not since I *chose* a different path."

Although I couldn't read his thoughts—which seemed damned unfair to me—I could clearly see his aura. And it pulsated around, intermixed with rich color . . . and deep blackness.

What had once been pure white light—loving light—was now being slowly overrun with coils of blackness so deep that it gave even me the creeps. Even now, something dark and slithery wound around his narrow torso. I watched, fascinated, as it worked its way, around and around, to eventually plunge into his heart region. I was reminded of something monstrous rising up from the ocean depths, something that had no business seeing the light. I shuddered.

"I repulse you," he said. The sadness in his voice was obvious.

"What gave it away?" I said.

I suddenly wanted a cigarette. *Needed* a cigarette. I headed over to my purse, found the pack of Virginia Slims, and lit up.

Ishmael watched my every move closely. I sensed that he was used to watching me closely. That he had always watched me closely. From either afar, or nearby. He had been, after all, my guardian angel.

Of course, I use that term loosely.

That he failed his job miserably was an understatement. That he had done so purposefully was reprehensible.

"Reprehensible is such a strong word, Samantha," he said. "I needed you to be immortal. It was, after all, the only way we could be together."

"You put me in harm's way. You put my kids in harm's way. You put anyone who ever crosses paths with me in harm's way."

"Only if you do not learn to control who you are, Samantha."

"And I suppose you're just the one to teach me?"

"I can help you, Sam."

"Didn't you cause this mess?"

"I did it for love—"

"Shove it," I said, shaking my head.

His clothing, I noted, seemed to shift in color. One moment, his slacks were beige, then brown, then tan. Or maybe I was just going crazy.

"Not crazy, Sam. My clothing is an illusion, of course."

"Of course. That doesn't sound crazy at all."

I exhaled, and looked at him through the churning cigarette smoke. He was a beautiful man. Perhaps the most beautiful I'd ever seen. Too beautiful.

"And what about the rest of you?" I asked.

"Illusion, of course. But I see I have chosen a favorable form."

"Why are you here?"

He continued smiling, and the darkness that swarmed around him—the black snakes and worms and creepy-crawly things—seemed to grow in number. It was as if I was seeing evil multiplying before my very eyes. Deepening, propagating. I shivered.

"I'm here to give you news of your dog."

I looked at him sharply. He was, of course, referring to Kingsley. "What about him?"

"He's not a very loyal dog, now is he?" Ishmael smiled broadly. Wickedly.

"What the fuck do you mean?"

"When the vampire's away, the dog shall play."

I brought the cigarette up to my lips, but instead of inhaling, crumpled it in my hands. The temporary burn made me gasp, but the pain faded quickly. "You're lying."

He said nothing, only watched me from the deep shadows of my room, looking supremely pleased.

I looked at my hand. The red mark in the center of my palm was already fading. I threw the remnants of the cigarette over to the closest ashtray. It missed.

"You're trying to drive a wedge between us," I said.

"I didn't have to try very hard, Samantha."

I sensed the not-so-hidden meaning in his words. "You set him up," I said. "Planted someone."

"Call it what you want, Sam. But your doggie took the bait."

"Who is she?"

"Does it matter?"

A familiar sickness appeared in my stomach. Re-appeared. It was a sickness that had nothing to do with the supernatural, a sickness I had lived with for many, many years with Danny. I rubbed my temples and took lots of slow, deep breaths, and when I moved my hand away, I was alone in the hotel room, but I sensed the angel was near. Always near.

The son-of-a-bitch.

# 13.

It was early afternoon and something was wrong.

I'd been feeling it all day. The forty-five minute plane ride from Vegas to Ontario had seemed like an eternity. Now, driving home from the airport, an inexplicable fear gripped me. Something was seriously wrong.

Except I didn't know what.

*My kids,* I thought, pressing the gas harder. *Something with my kids.*

But what?

I didn't know. Not yet.

Having extrasensory perception had its benefits, but also its pitfalls. Being keenly aware that something was wrong, but not knowing what, was, if anything, torture.

A moment later, as the dread in me grew to a fever pitch, my cell phone rang. It was my sister, of course.

*My kids.*

A car blasted its horn next to me. I jumped, jerking my wheel. I had inadvertently swerved into its lane. It continued honking at me even as I snatched up the phone and made an inhuman sound. A squeak, of some sort.

My kids, of course, were staying with their Aunt Mary Lou.

"Mary Lou," I gasped, pressing the phone hard into my ear. "What's wrong?"

"How—never mind." She swallowed. "It's Tammy."

"What about Tammy? What's wrong?" My voice had reached a very loud, shrill note.

"She ran away, Sam."

I took in a lot of worthless air. I had expected worse, true. Running away wasn't the worst, granted, but it wasn't good either. Tammy was, after all, only ten years old.

"When did she leave?"

Mary Lou explained that Tammy had been grumpy all day, irritable. I nodded to myself as Mary Lou spoke. Yes, I'd been noticing this lately, too, although I had chalked it up to her going through some life changes. My sister had assumed Tammy was in her guest room all day, either reading or on the phone. Later, Anthony came out of the very same room and asked where Tammy was. They searched the house and called her cell phone. Her phone was turned off. And that's when Mary Lou called me.

"Did anyone see her leave?"

"No, but we're pretty sure she went out the back door, then through the side gates."

"Did she take a bike?"

"All the bikes are here."

"Did you hear a car pull up front?"

"No, but we weren't paying a lot of attention to the front of the house."

*Shit.*

Although I didn't have access to my own children's thoughts, that didn't mean they completely escaped my extra-sensory perception, which was why I had sensed something was wrong, and why I had seen the dark halo around Anthony last year, when he had been critically ill.

As my minivan's speedometer climbed past 110 mph, I told Mary Lou I would be there soon and hung up. I focused on keeping the minivan from flipping over.

And keeping myself together.

# 14.

On my way to my sister's house, I called three of Tammy's closest friends. No one had seen her or heard from her, although everyone pledged to do all they could to help me find her.

I also made another call, to an investigator who had a reputation for tracking down the missing, and as I pulled up to my sister's house in Fullerton, a nondescript Camry was pulling up just behind me.

Spinoza was a small man with a heavy aura. Not a dark aura. Just heavy. Something was eating away at him, making his life a living hell. I didn't need to be psychic to know that he'd lost something important to him.

Spinoza parked on the street behind me and got out. He was a small man. The complete opposite of Kingsley or the beast, Knighthorse. And as Spinoza came toward me, concern creasing his pleasantly handsome face, I suddenly had a whiff of something that made me nearly vomit.

The scent of burned flesh.

*Sweet Jesus*, I thought, as I saw in my mind's eye a burned hand and twisted metal and broken glass.

His son's hand. There had been an accident. Mixed with the smell of burnt flesh was alcohol. Spinoza, I was suddenly certain, had been driving. Drunk.

*Sweet Jesus*, I thought again.

Spinoza took my hand and as he did so, the psychic vision and smell of burning flesh disappeared. He next gave me a small, awkward hug. The look in his eyes was one of only concern. I suddenly suspected why Spinoza was known for finding the missing, especially missing children.

"How you holding up?" he asked.

"Been better. Thanks for coming out on short notice."

He nodded. "We'll find her, Sam. Don't worry." And his quiet strength and assuredness spoke volumes. It also calmed me down. Somewhat.

I led the way into my sister's house, where Detective Sherbet of the Fullerton Police Department was already inside. No, I wasn't too concerned that a homicide investigator was there since I had called him, too. Detective Sherbet had become a good friend. So good, in fact, that he and I now shared a deepening telepathic link. Granted, the good detective wasn't exactly thrilled by our telepathic link, but he seemed to be getting the hang of it.

*We'll find her, Sam,* he thought, nodding, his words appearing softly just inside my ears.

*Thank you, Detective.*

Mary Lou came over next with tears in her eyes, looking so distraught that I was the one doing the reassuring. "Not your fault," I said over and over as she completely broke down.

Once she'd gotten control of herself, I planned our course of action with the detectives. At ten years old, Tammy would have fewer choices available to her. She couldn't drive and she didn't have a lot of money. She wasn't addicted to drugs and didn't have a boyfriend. At least, as far as I knew.

Truth was, I had a hard time getting a psychic handle on my own kids. I could read their auras, but that was about it. It was the same with my sister and with her kids; and the same with my parents, although these days I didn't see them very often.

Mary Lou had confirmed that some toiletries were missing, along with her gym bag. We even confirmed that a jar of peanut butter and some saltines were gone, too. Tammy's favorite snack.

Still, a child walking the streets alone with a gym bag was trouble, and it was all I could do to stay calm. Running outside and screaming for my baby wouldn't help anything, although that's exactly what I felt like doing.

*Easy, Sam,* came Sherbet's words. *A child walking around with a gym bag would just as easily get the attention of police. And I have my best men out there looking for her.*

"Does she have a cell phone?" Spinoza asked. We were grouped around Mary Lou's living room.

"It's off," I said.

Spinoza and Sherbet winced. We all knew that a phone had to be on to be used as a tracking device.

"Laptop or tablet computer?" pressed Spinoza. "Anything with GPS?"

I shook my head. "No."

"Does she know anyone with a car?"

"She'd better not."

"Does she have access to a bike? Anything she can move quickly on?"

"The bikes are at home."

Spinoza glanced over at my sister. "And all bikes are accounted for here?"

"Yes. Bikes and skateboards."

I was having a hard time concentrating, focusing, and remembering what I should do in an investigation like this. *But it's not an investigation,* I thought. *It's my daughter—and she's gone.*

Sherbet glanced at me again and then looked over at my sister. "Do you have any recent pictures of Tammy?"

"I do, yes. On my cell phone."

"Can you print me out a half dozen?"

She nodded eagerly and dashed off to where I knew her husband had his own office at home.

While she was gone, we finalized our plan. Sherbet would work with the local beat cops and cruise the streets in a coordinated effort. Spinoza would hit every Starbucks, fast-food restaurant, and store within two square miles. I would contact all her friends and head straight to all her known hangouts.

Mary Lou came back with the color photos. Seeing her photo, with her happy, smiling face, made me almost lose it right there.

*Easy, Sam,* came Sherbet's soothing voice.

The detective next instructed Mary Lou to email the same image to his department. An APB had already been sent to all units with a description of my daughter, including her current, assumed clothing. Now they would have a corresponding photo.

*It's real,* I thought, listening to Sherbet instruct his department. *She's really missing.*

I fought to control my breathing. To control myself. Finally, Sherbet clicked off his phone.

"That's all we can do on this end," said Sherbet, turning to us. "Let's hit the streets."

# 15.

After we split up, I sat briefly in my minivan, searching for a psychic hit that wasn't there. Despite the many abilities I'd been given, a psychic connection to my own kids was not one of them.

For now, I was just a mom with a missing daughter.

I had just put the vehicle into gear, mentally going through a list of her friends and where they lived, when my cell phone rang. I gasped and swerved a little and reached for my cell.

Kingsley Fulcrum.

*Shit.*

I switched on my Bluetooth. "Hey."

"Sam! I just got your text. Have you found her?"

I had indeed sent him a text, but now I regretted doing so. Kingsley Fulcrum was the last person I wanted to think about now.

"Not yet," I said, as I turned right onto Commonwealth. My sister lived closer to downtown than I did. People were everywhere. I scanned the streets.

"I'm coming out now. Where are you?"

"No," I said. "Don't come."

"What—"

"I sent you that text an hour ago. Where were you?"

He paused only briefly, but tellingly. "I was with a client."

"I'm sure you were, big guy. And don't worry, we've got it handled."

"Sam—wait! Are you saying you don't want my help?"

"That's what I'm saying," I said.

"Sam—"

But I had already clicked off.

I sat back and gripped the wheel and wound slowly through downtown Fullerton, knowing that I could have used Kingsley's help, and knowing that I was allowing the hurt in my own heart to possibly get in the way of such help.

But I just couldn't see him. Or talk to him.

Not now. Perhaps not ever.

# 16.

I tried her cell phone for the tenth time.

And for the tenth time, it went straight to voicemail. Her voicemail message was the generic electronic one. I didn't even get the benefit of hearing her little voice.

I even checked once or twice to make sure I was calling the right number. Crazy, I know. It said "Tammy" right here in the "Contacts" list, the same Tammy I had called countless times since she had first gotten her cell last Christmas.

I set the phone in my lap, confirmed it was on, and realized that my brain was spinning, looping over the same things again and again. As soon as I set the phone in my lap, I wanted to pick it up again, and try her cell phone. Again.

Again and again.

*Deep breaths, Sam.*

Yes, I could have used Kingsley's help. Hell, I could use Fang's help, too. And Knighthorse's and Aaron King's and anyone else I'd ever come across.

*Deep breaths, Sam.*

*She's not far. Ten-year-old girls eventually get picked up by the police—*

*Or picked up by other people. Scumbags. Dirt bags. Killers. Child molesters.*

Now I was panicking all over again and stomping the gas and whipping through suburban Fullerton as if it was my own private race course.

I ended up at home, which was about three miles from my sister's home. I parked the van at an angle in front of the house, dashed out, hurdled the chain-link fence that surrounded the property, and plunged inside my house, calling her name.

No response.

I quickly scoured every room. My hope had been that she simply returned to her own home, her own room, her own bed. Still, I called her name repeatedly, searching everywhere and anywhere, even out in the garage. I moved quickly through the house. I sped around supernaturally quickly. The rooms and walls and carpet were a blur. Pictures were a blur. My head was spinning.

I caught myself on a wall.

I gasped, chest heaving. Having a full-blown panic attack wouldn't help anyone, least of all, my daughter. I knew this. I had cautioned parents of this very thing many times in the past, when searching for their own runaways.

*Deep breaths, Sam. Calm down.*

*Fuck calming down. I want my daughter.*

Shaking, I stood straight, hands on hips, thinking hard. Or trying to think hard. Truth was, my brain still hadn't entirely kicked into gear. Night was coming, but was not here yet.

I hated what I was sometimes. Hated it. Here I needed to find my daughter, and I needed to think *clearly,* but I couldn't push past the fog.

I paced and checked the time on my cell. One more hour until sundown. Then I would think clearly. Perhaps even get a psychic hit or two.

Except one hour might be too late.

My phone rang. I gasped, and nearly dropped it. Kingsley. Again. The asshole. The fucker. How dare he call me when he knew I was waiting to hear news about my daughter.

I ignored it. He tried one more time. I ignored that, too, hating him more and more.

I had tried her closest friends. Sherbet was cruising the streets with his patrol officers. Spinoza was hitting any and all shops within a reasonable radius.

How much money did she have?

I thought hard, forcing my mind to go back a few days, before my trip to Vegas. Yes, I had given her and Anthony $20 each. A twenty wasn't much.

I gripped my keys and turned for the door, nodding to myself. Twenty bucks was just enough for—

My phone rang again.

It was Spinoza.

I paused and clicked on, pressing the touch screen so hard I nearly cracked it. "Any news?" I asked. Or tried to ask. My voice cracked and sounded funny, even to my ears.

"Very good news, Sam," he said gently. "I've got someone here you might be interested in seeing."

"Oh, God," I said and sank to my knees.

"She's with me, Sam. Safe and sound. We're at the bus station in Buena Park. Do you know the one?"

I buried my face in my hands, pressing the phone against my ear. "Yes."

"We'll be here waiting."

I clicked off and let the tears flow, sitting there on my knees, my face in my hands.

# 17.

They were eating ice cream together on a bus bench.

Buena Park's Park and Ride was a big station, perhaps the biggest in north Orange County, too big for a little girl to be sitting alone.

I parked just behind the benches, where I could see Tammy and Spinoza, both happily munching on their ice creams. Tammy was swinging her legs. I could just make out Mary Lou's gym bag sitting next to her.

With the 5 Freeway roaring above, choked with rush hour traffic, and Orangethorpe Avenue opposite, nearly as busy, no one would have noticed a screaming girl being yanked into someone's car, never to be seen or heard from again.

I inhaled slowly, deeply.

But there she was, safely eating ice cream with Spinoza as if she knew the man. She didn't, of course. She had never met the investigator, and yet, there she was eating ice cream with him. So trusting. So innocent. He could have been anyone. Someone dangerous. Someone with not very good intentions. He wasn't dangerous, of course. He was a damn fine investigator. But she didn't know that.

Spinoza turned and saw me sitting in my van. Perhaps he was psychic himself. He waved, holding his ice cream. There was a vending machine nearby. No doubt it had been the source of the frozen dessert.

I sat in my car and waited for my heart to calm down, for my breathing to calm down, and, as I waited, never once did I take my eyes off my daughter.

• • •

Spinoza got up and pulled me aside as I approached.

"You know the drill," said Spinoza quietly. He was only a few inches taller than me. His height always surprised me. My memory of him was always as a bigger man.

I nodded, knowing where this was going.

The evening was giving way to dusk, and the lights in the bus stop were turning on. Tammy kicked her feet . . . and looked away. So far, she hadn't made eye contact with me. She was dressed in jeans and a tee shirt. She had on a pink belt. She was too damn cute to be alone at a bus station.

"She thinks you're going to be mad at her," he said.

I nodded. It's the same speech I gave parents myself, after finding their own runaways.

"She's also angry."

I snapped my head around. "Angry?"

Spinoza gave me a wry smile. "Life's unfair and all that. You know, typical girl stuff."

I nodded, relieved, although I wasn't sure about that "girl stuff" comment.

He continued, "Sherbet's on his way, too, so you'll have a few minutes alone with her. I tried to call him off, but he has to follow up, assess the situation, finalize a report, and call off the hounds, so to speak."

I nodded, looked at Spinoza. "How did you know she was here?"

"A hunch. I listen to them."

I suddenly gave him a hug which, I think, surprised the hell out of him, although it shouldn't have. He was lucky I didn't give him a smooch, too.

"I do, too," I said, releasing him. "Except this time I couldn't think straight."

"Hard to think straight when your kid's gone," he said, and now there was no mistaking the sorrow in his voice. I knew his own kid was gone. Long gone. He nodded toward Tammy. "Talk to her, Sam. Gently."

I said I would. He smiled and nodded and touched my elbow awkwardly, then slipped out into the night.

I turned to Tammy.

# 18.

"Hey, booger butt," I said, sliding next to her.

She turned her face away. "I'm not a booger butt."

The hems of her jeans were rolled up, exposing her pink socks and cute tennis shoes. She was wearing a pink Hello Kitty tee shirt. The purse sitting next to the gym bag was also Hello Kitty. The gym bag was my sister's. She continued kicking feet that didn't quite touch the gum-covered cement ground.

"Then what are you?" I asked, knowing it was a leading question.

"A young lady. A woman."

"A woman?" I said and it was all I could do to not laugh. She looked at me sharply and I literally swallowed my laughter as surely as if I'd swallowed food. *Liquid food*, of course.

"Yes, a woman," she said, sticking her chin out. A sharp chin. Danny's chin.

"I see. Well, I thought women were, in the very least, teenagers."

"No, Mom. That's why they're called teenagers."

It was all I could do not to point out that she herself was still three years shy of being a teenager. I said, "So, you're a young lady now."

"Yes."

"More mature than even teenagers."

She made a sort of "as if" noise. That my daughter considered herself superior to teenagers told me a lot about her. It also told me that she was a handful.

I said, "Mature enough to travel alone?"

She shrugged. She still hadn't looked at me. "It's just a bus. Kids take buses every day to school."

"A bus to where?" I asked. I was part amused, part horrified. Jesus, what if she had actually gotten on board the bus? Maybe nothing, actually. Bus drivers were trained not to let kids on board alone, unless Tammy came up with a really good story. She was, after all, a gifted storyteller. I often thought I might have a little writer on my hands.

After all, Tammy was the creator of Lady Tamtam, a crime-fighting superhero mom who could fly and shoot lasers from her eyes.

Lady Tamtam, I was certain, was based on me. And maybe a little bit of Lady Gaga, too. Except Lady Tamtam fought crime, while Lady Gaga, apparently, had sex with it.

Of course, Lady Tamtam shot lasers from her eyes, which I doubted I could. *Only one way to see.* I focused on an empty Cheetos bag sticking out from a nearby trash can. Nope, no lasers.

Tammy didn't know her mother's super-secret identity. Unless Anthony had spilled the beans. But I didn't think he had. He would have told me. Or I would have heard about it before this.

No, there was something else going on here.

"Tammy," I said, reaching out to her and taking her hand. She resisted at first, but then let me take it. She still wouldn't look at me. "Tammy. Why did you run away?"

I sat like that for a second or two, unmoving, holding her hand. She sat unmoving, too, although she bit her lower lip. A sure sign that she was thinking hard. Finally, she turned and looked at me for the first time, and there were tears in her eyes.

"Because I'm horrible, Mommy."

I squeezed her hand. "Why would you say that?"

Now her lower lip was trembling. "Because I hate Anthony."

"Why do you hate your little brother?"

She shrugged and lowered her head.

"Out with it, young lady."

"He's just such a jerk."

"A jerk, how?"

"I dunno."

"Yes, you do."

"I just hate him."

"Yeah, you said that. He's your little brother. You can't hate your little brother. I forbid it."

She stuck out her bottom lip. Anthony did the same thing, a habit he picked up from his older sister. A sister he idolized growing up. A sister he followed tirelessly.

I waited for her to sort out her thoughts and feelings. And since I couldn't dip into her thoughts, I had to wait just like any other mama.

"He's . . . different somehow," she finally said.

"So that's why you hate him? Because he's different?"

"No. Not really. Well, kind of."

"Tammy . . ."

"Everyone talks about him, Mommy. I mean everyone. I'm so damn tired of it."

"Watch your mouth, young lady."

"Sorry."

"Who talks about him, Tammy?"

"Everyone. Everyone at school. Everyone at home. You, Dad. Teachers, doctors. I'm just so sick of it."

"So you don't really hate your brother. You're just tired of people talking about him."

"No, I hate him."

"What did he do to you?"

"He's just a butthead."

Despite myself, I laughed, and shortly, Tammy started giggling. I reached out and tickled her and she laughed even harder, and as we both laughed I saw a pair of headlights appear in the parking lot, then another and another. Three cop cars closed in, with Sherbet in the lead.

I looked at Tammy. "Sweetie, someday we need to talk about something very important."

"I know, Mommy."

I opened my mouth to speak but stopped. I tried again, changing directions. "You know what, baby?"

"About you."

"You know *what* about me?"

"You're special, Mommy."

"Special how?"

She smiled sweetly and said, "You know, Mommy."

As Sherbet appeared, looking red-faced and relieved, I thought of Lady Tamtam and her supernatural powers. The mother who could fly. The mother who fought crime. The mother who shot lasers from her eyes.

Still, two out of three weren't bad.

# 19.

Russell Baker and I were at a Starbucks in Fullerton.

It was the same Starbucks where I'd met the very creepy Robert Mason, one-time soap opera star, one-time owner of the Fullerton Playhouse, who was now a full-time resident of a jail cell.

My time here with Russell Baker was decidedly more pleasant.

The young boxer was wearing a loose tank top and shorts. He had just finished working out with Jacky. Jacky wasn't his official trainer, but, like many young boxers, they sought his help and considered it an honor to work with the legendary Irishman.

More importantly, Russell looked good in a tank top. I suspected he would look good in just about anything. Of course, being in shape and looking good was expected from a professional boxer. Still, professional or not, sitting across from me was a very breathtaking man. Even for someone who doesn't need much breath.

I said, "I spoke with Dr. Sculler in Las Vegas."

"The medical examiner," said Russell, sounding very unboxer-like. He had a quick mind. I only hoped it wouldn't be beaten out of him by the end of his career.

"Right," I said. "The official cause of death is epidural hematoma."

"I know," he said. "I've read the report. A dozen or so times."

Russell was sipping from a bottle of water. Who goes to a Starbucks and orders a bottle of water? Then again, I looked down at my own bottle of water. Well, boxers in training and vampires, apparently. I wondered if we just might be the first two people in the history of Starbucks to only order two bottles of water.

*Big picture, Sam.*

I continued, "I'll admit it. I thought I was going to come back here and tell you that you don't have a case."

He glanced up at me, blinking. He cocked his head a little. "You *thought*? What does that mean?"

"It means that it's Dr. Sculler's *un*official opinion that you could not have caused the kind of brain damage he saw in the autopsy."

Russell sat up. I knew that this was the kind of news he was praying for. "I . . ." he paused, gathering his thoughts. "I don't understand."

"Officially, based on probable evidence, Caesar was killed in the ring. After all, he collapsed in front of the world."

Russell nodded.

I went on, "But Dr. Sculler didn't see enough evidence, based on what he saw of the fight, to warrant the scope of damage he saw in Caesar's brain tissue."

"Then why had he reported that it had?"

"Caesar was a boxer. He died of a brain hemorrhage. It's a slam-dunk case for everyone involved. The evidence is obvious. Unless—"

"Unless you look deeper," he finished.

Interesting. That was exactly how I was going to finish the sentence. I wondered again if I was somehow opening myself up to other people. How I was doing that, I didn't know, but I made a mental note to learn to stop it. At any rate, Russell seemed oblivious to the fact that he might have gotten a sneak peek into my thoughts. Into the mind of a vampire. Maybe his oblivion was a good thing.

"Right," I said. "Dr. Sculler also let it be known that he was by no means an expert in boxing-related brain trauma and could not, therefore, give me a true expert's opinion."

"So, a non-expert declared that Caesar's death was boxing related?"

"That's about the extent of it."

"Man, that shit ain't right." He turned away, swearing under his breath. He looked back at me. "I didn't kill him, Sam. Caesar and I were amateurs together. We practiced a few times, sparred together in the early days. That guy could take a punch. That last fight . . . we were only feeling each other out. I landed maybe one solid punch. One. And even that wasn't my best shot. Caesar could take dozens of those, maybe more."

And that was the crux. How much could one man take before his brain finally gave? How much was too much before a guy collapsed in the ring, dead?

"There's one other thing worth pointing out," I said. "The doctor does not dispute that Caesar suffered an injury that could cause death."

"Just that he didn't think I caused it in the ring."

"Right," I said.

"So, if I didn't hit him hard enough to kill him . . ."

"Then someone else did."

# 20.

I was on my way to L.A.

With me was a list of names provided by Russell Baker. On the list were three names: Caesar Marquez's trainer, cut-man, and manager, all three of which would have been in Caesar's locker room prior to the fight. And *prior* was key here.

After all, something had happened to Caesar before the fight, something that had directly led to his death. What it was remained to be seen.

As I followed behind an endless sea of red brake lights, my cell rang for perhaps the dozenth time that day. And for the dozenth time that day, I saw that it was Kingsley Fulcrum. This time, as the phone rang, a text message appeared. Virtually simultaneously. I guess the big oaf could multi-task.

The text message read: *Sam, please pick up.*

I thought about ignoring him again, until I realized the hairy bastard would just keep calling me . . . and since I wasn't in any kind of mood to see him face to face, I thought I might as well hear what he had to say.

The phone rang again and, when it was about to go to voice-mail, I picked up.

"It's your dime," I said flippantly.

"Oh, Sam! I was just about to hang up."

"That was valuable information to have. Thank you for sharing."

"Don't be this way, Sam."

"What way?" I asked. "Hurt? Betrayed? How would you suggest I be instead, Kingsley? Ecstatic that a man I was falling in love with fucked another woman?"

"Sam, we need to talk."

"Then talk."

"Not like this. Not over the phone."

"Perhaps in your bed where you fucked her?"

"Sam . . ."

I waited. I had broken out in a sweat. Many of my human functions had stopped altogether, but sweating was not one of them. I sweated with the best of them, especially in a warm minivan on a long drive to L.A., and dealing with *this*.

*Again.*

I shook my head, swearing silently. Kingsley and I had been dating over eight months now. I had just started feeling the love again. Had just started letting him in, had just started getting over the pain of my cheating ex.

"Sam," he tried again. "How did you know?"

"Does it matter?"

He must have thought hard about that because he paused good and long. "No. I guess not."

But I knew it was eating at him. Good.

We were silent some more. Traffic on the 5 Freeway was sick. It was midday and I had already made plans for Mary Lou to pick up the kids. I had made special plans to be with Tammy tonight. So had Mary Lou. We were going to have a girls' night out, so to speak. No boys allowed.

"Who was she?" I asked.

"I don't honestly know."

"What do you mean?"

"She just . . . appeared in the office. Wanted to make an appointment. Flirted with me endlessly. Caught me as I was leaving work for the day. Walked with me out to my car. Laughed at everything I said. Touched me, asked me questions. Then asked if I wanted to get a drink with her."

"And you said yes."

"Yes," said Kingsley. "I did."

"You didn't have to say yes."

"I know, Sam."

"But you did."

"Yes."

"Why?"

There was a lot of silence on his end. I could hear him breathing, each breath pouring over the receiver as if he were in a sporadic windstorm.

"I don't know why, Sam."

"Yes you do. Why?"

"She gave me a lot of attention."

"Lots of women give you attention."

"She was different."

"Prettier."

"Yeah, maybe."

"Prettier than me."

"I didn't say that."

"You didn't have to. So at what point did you fuck her?"

"Sam, how do you know this? Did you plant her?"

And that's when I hung up on him, nearly crushing my cell phone in the process. He cheats on me . . . and turns it around? The fucker. The piece of shit.

And as I drove into the afternoon sun, feeling eternally exhausted and too hurt for tears, I realized that Kingsley had been partially right.

He *had* been set up. Just not by me.

# 21.

Caesar Marquez was trained by his brother at the family gym in downtown Los Angeles, which is where I found myself now.

His brother's name was Romero and he and I were walking through the gym together. The gym was not unlike Jacky's gym in Fullerton. The difference, though, was that Jacky catered to teaching women to defend themselves. The Marquez Gym catered to extremely muscular young men who seemed to take delight in punching the crap out of each other.

"We've produced eleven number-one fighters," said Romero. Sounding remarkably like Jacky, he paused to tell a young Hispanic kid, who was working a heavy bag, to keep his gloves up. I thought trainers everywhere were entirely too concerned about gloves being up. Then again, what did I know?

I said, "Must be good for business."

He nodded and we continued on, weaving slowly through the gym. I was, I noted, the only female here. Once or twice I spotted a set of eyes watching me, but mostly, the young fighters kept their heads down and their gloves up.

As we circled a ring where a black guy and a white guy, both wearing head gear, were trading jabs, Romero said, "Caesar would have been the twelfth."

I said, "I'm sorry to hear about Caesar."

Romero nodded again and we watched the two fighters above us. Both fighters were slugging it out. Fists flew, sweat slung. Some of the sweat landed on my forearm. *Eew.*

"My family," began Romero, as I discreetly wiped the sweat off on my jeans, "are all fighters. I was good, but it turns out, I'm a better trainer than a fighter. Caesar, well, he was something else. He was on his way up. Moving fast, too. He was already ranked in the top ten in his weight class. Top ten and moving up."

"How many brothers do you have?"

"Three living, now one dead."

I blinked, astonished. "There were five of you?"

"Yes. Four now. All boxers. Caesar was the youngest and probably the best. Our father started things off by boxing in a few amateur fights back in the day. He was okay but didn't love it enough to pursue it. My oldest brother, Eduardo, loved it. Passionately. He was good. That's him over there." He pointed to a stockier version of himself, a guy who was maybe in his mid-forties and was working closely with a young black guy. They were practicing bobbing and weaving drills. I'd done a few of those with Jacky. "Anyway, his passion drove all of us. Especially Caesar."

Romero's voice was steady, his eyes dry. That he was discussing a brother who had passed not even three weeks ago, one would never guess. Then again, his voice was too steady, and he blinked too much. He was doing what he could to control himself. I suspected this was a very macho culture, and brothers who ran a world-class boxing gym were perhaps the most macho of all.

We continued through the gym and, without thinking, I threw a punch at an empty heavy bag. It was still daylight, and so I couldn't put much into the punch, but I think Jacky would have been proud. It had been a straight shot and I had gotten most of my weight behind my punch.

Romero, who had been leading me into his office, just about stumbled over himself. He looked at the bag moving violently back and forth, creaking along its chains. Then he looked at me.

"Do that again," he said.

"Lucky punch," I said, realizing my mistake. I really, really hated drawing attention to myself. What possessed me to punch the bag, I don't know.

Or, maybe a part of me envisioned it being Kingsley.

Or Ishmael.

"Humor me," he said in his thick Spanish accent. "Please."

I gave the bag a half-assed jab.

"No, *chica*. Hit it again. Like you did before. Please."

*Screw it,* I thought. The cat was already out of the bag, so to speak, and Jacky himself had been secretly spreading the word that he had on his hands a woman who could beat most men. Perhaps even Romero had heard about me through the boxing grapevine.

So, I took a breath, focused on the bag in front of me, bounced on my feet a little, positioned my shoulders the way Jacky had taught me, and punched the bag with all my strength, which, of course, was diminished, due to the time of day. And this time I really did think of Kingsley's face . . . and this time, the heavy bag did much more than swing and creak on the chain.

It flew forward and up—so hard and fast that it dislodged itself from the hook it was hanging on. Now it was tumbling end over end, to finally come to a rest halfway across the gym. A few boxers had jumped out of the way.

"*¡Ay Dios mio!*" said Romero and he made the sign of the cross.

Many others had turned to watch me. All looked startled. Or, in the very least, confused. Then they all went back to working out and keeping their hands up.

Romero continued to stare at me.

"Oops," I said.

# 22.

We were in his office, which had a view of most of the gym. Presently, two men were hoisting the heavy bag and repositioning it on the hook. They were using a stepladder and were sweating with effort.

Romero had yet to say anything. He was in his late thirties, extremely fit, and would have been good-looking if not for the fact that he seemed to have a permanent case of cauliflower ear. That was the condition many fighters got when the ear swelled up.

Ah, screw it, I decided. He was still damn good-looking, cauliflower ear and all.

He was leaning back in his office chair, lightly tapping the tips of his fingers together over his chest. The words on his tank top said: *Marquez Gym - Elite Training*.

"You gonna say something," I said, "or just sit there and look at me like I'm a freak."

"I'm sorry, *señorita*," he said, literally shaking his head. "I'm trying to understand what happened out there."

"Sometimes, there are no easy answers."

"I suppose not," he said, then his eyes sort of glazed over a little. I think he was re-living the moment, especially as he began voicing his thoughts. "Good form, good stance, a good punch. A straight shot."

He rubbed his face and looked at me.

I smiled sweetly. "What can I say," I said. "A lucky shot."

"A helluva shot. Or punch. Jacky's been talking about you."

"Jacky exaggerates."

Romero shook his head. I think—*think*—his cauliflower ears might have wobbled a little. "Actually, no, *señorita*. I would say

Jacky is not known to exaggerate. If he says a boxer is damn good, the boxer is damn good."

"I'm not a boxer," I said.

Romero raised his eyebrows. "Maybe not, but you can punch."

"I'm not looking for a trainer," I said. "I'm here about your brother."

That snapped him out of whatever reverie he was in. "My brother?"

I nodded. "I'm looking for answers, Romero."

He didn't want to let go of what he'd just seen outside the office—in his own gym, no less—something that defied logic and common sense. He finally looked at me, and he finally showed me his real self. Maybe my little display had broken through his machismo and affected him on a deeper level. I didn't know. But there was a change in him. His walls were coming down and as he looked at me, simply staring at me with an intensity I'd only seen a few times in my life—and perhaps only from Kingsley's hauntingly amber eyes—Romero broke down.

And he broke down hard.

He covered his face with his hand and wept into it, shuddering, his shoulder muscles and triceps rippling. I watched the tears appear through his fingers and cascade down over his knuckles, and watched as his aura rippled with hues of blues and greens.

After a few minutes of this, he rubbed his face with the backs of his hands. "I'm not sure what came over me."

"It's natural," I said. "And perfectly okay."

"It's not natural for me." He wiped his eyes some more. "I miss him so much, Ms. Moon."

"I understand."

"He should not be dead." Romero shook his head, rubbed his arms. "Caesar rarely absorbed punishment. He was good. Damn good. He was the one handing out the beatings. And when he wasn't punching, he was ducking and weaving."

"Tell me about the fight."

"The fight was no different than the rest. Russell Baker's good, but not that good. He must have landed a lucky shot or two, enough to do damage. Hard to say."

"Is it your professional opinion that your brother was hit hard enough to be killed?"

"From what I saw? No. From what I know about boxing? Anything can happen."

"Who's allowed in the locker room before a fight?"

He shrugged. "I guess anyone the fighter allows."

"And who did your brother allow?"

"Myself, my older brother, Eduardo, his manager, his girlfriend, and his promoter."

"That's a lot of people."

"Not really. Mostly Caesar was with me and Eduardo, discussing strategy, last-minute thoughts, and trying to calm him down. He is always so excited before a fight."

"But you were Caesar's official trainer, correct?"

"Yes. But that didn't stop my other brothers from coming in and giving us their two cents' worth."

He chuckled. I chuckled. I said, "Was there ever a problem having that many people in the locker room before a fight?"

"Rarely. Call it controlled mayhem."

"Tell me about the locker room on the night in question. Did anything happen that stands out? Anything unusual? Out of the norm?"

He was shaking his head and thinking hard, now running his fingers through his thick, black hair. I noticed some magazines near his computer keyboard. No, not magazines. Travel guides to the Bahamas. "No, sorry. Nothing that stands out."

"You said his girlfriend was in the locker room that night."

"Yes."

"What was his relationship like with his girlfriend?"

Romero shrugged. "Normal, I suppose."

"Define normal."

"They mostly got along."

"Mostly?"

He shrugged again. "They fought like anyone, I guess."

"They fight physically?"

Romero paused and cocked his head a little, giving me a better view of his cauliflower ear. I tried not to make a face. "I'm not sure what you're suggesting, Ms. Moon, but I can assure you that he did not have any altercations with his girlfriend before the fight. I was with him the entire time."

"Did your brother mention if he'd been fighting with his girlfriend earlier? Say at the hotel room?"

Romero looked away and shrugged. "He mentioned a small fight. Nothing big. But they had made up by the time of the fight."

"Prior to the Vegas fight, when was Caesar's last fight?"

Romero looked up, thinking. "Four months ago."

"So three months before his death?"

"Yes."

"How rigorous are his sparring sessions?"

"Rigorous?"

"Yes. Could he have suffered any punishment during practice?"

"We use headgear, Ms. Moon. We go light. Not too heavy. We break up anything that gets too physical."

"Is it your expert opinion that Caesar could not have suffered any real injury in his practices leading up to his last fight?"

"None."

"And he didn't have a history of brain trauma?"

"None. He was just a kid and a damn good fighter. Damn good. He could have been the best."

I nodded, and wondered why I was feeling like I wasn't getting the whole story. Romero was fighting back tears. Caesar was dead, and there was only one obvious lead. I said, "Can I have his girlfriend's information?"

# 23.

I somehow found a parking spot on the street near Allison Lopez's Beverly Hills apartment. By *near*, I meant three blocks away, all of which I hoofed under the last rays of the setting sun.

Normally I would have been sprinting . . . and my skin would have been burning and blistering. Even in the setting sun.

But now, all I felt was mildly uncomfortable. No sprinting needed. If anything, I felt like I was coming down with a cold. Or a feeling of weakness. Mild apprehension.

And so, I moved along the tree-lined sidewalk with as much energy as I could muster, knowing that in about twenty minutes, I would have all the energy in the world.

*Just twenty more minutes.*

I moved between opulent apartments and condo skyrises, some many dozens of stories high, and all boasting glass and steel and smooth plaster. All reflecting the setting sun. Some had limousines parked out front, waiting with doors open, chauffeurs standing ready. I saw no fewer than three Paris Hilton look-alikes, all texting while their dogs squatted on narrow strips of grass out front. The dogs each looked up at me in unison as I passed, baring their little white teeth. One of them even leaped at me, nearly causing its owner to drop her phone.

Whew!

Dogs didn't like me, which was annoying, since I was a dog lover. But I was especially a wolf lover. Except that thought, of course, depressed me instantly, so I let it go.

At Allison's apartment—one of the bigger and more opulent ones, no less—I followed the instructions as given to me by her during our brief phone conversation just a few minutes earlier.

I pressed the pound button on the caller box but nothing happened. I pressed it again. Nothing. No response. There was no sign that the damned thing was even working. Frustrated, I dialed Allison's cell number; it was busy. Unlike New York apartments, few L.A. apartments have doormen. This one didn't. The plush lobby, just beyond the glass entryway, was empty.

I stood there, frustrated.

I looked around. One of the Paris Hilton look-alikes was still texting, even though her dog had finished piddling minutes ago. I looked over another shoulder. No one.

I looked back at the locked glass door. There was no doorknob, just a handle. A heavy deadbolt fastened the door to a thick metal frame. No doubt, everyone within the building felt safe and secure in their posh apartments, as well they should. This bolt was serious business, released only by the occupants within. The sign above the handle said "Pull."

Two things happened simultaneously. The first was that the sun had finally set. I knew this because I suddenly felt more alive than I ever had before, which is saying something. The second was that the deadbolt tore through the metal door frame, ripping sideways through the metal.

The sound was god-awful loud. I looked casually back to the Paris look-alike. She was still texting, oblivious to life beyond her smart phone screen. I did, however, have the full attention of her little dog.

I wiped the handle clean of my prints, stepped through the doorway, waved to the security camera, and headed over to the elevators, knowing full well that I wasn't wearing enough makeup to even show up on camera.

Sometimes it was good to be me.

# 24.

Allison answered her door with her own cell phone pressed against her. She waved me in without a thought. I wondered if she was aware that she hadn't actually buzzed me in.

The apartment was smaller than I had expected, but the monthly rent was undoubtedly quadruple my own mortgage. The door opened into a small hallway that led first to a smallish kitchen. Shoe boxes were piled on the counter and spilled over onto some stools, as well. The shoe boxes were printed with Jimmy Choo and Manolo and Valentino, words that were foreign to a single, working mother who lived in the suburbs.

I continued following Allison into a smallish living room, where she motioned offhandedly for me to sit on an oversized couch. I was just figuring out how to offhandedly sit, when I saw something I probably shouldn't have seen.

A fresh cut along the inside of her finger.

Normally, the sight of blood does little for me. Yes, I drink blood. Yes, it nourishes this strange body of mine. But that's about the extent of it. I have a supply of the stuff at home. It was not generally a big deal to see blood.

Until now.

Now, the sight of her bloody finger did something to me that concerned me greatly. It stirred a hunger in me. Real hunger. My stomach growled and my mouth watered and I hated myself all over again. I forced myself to look away, gritting my teeth and grinding my jaw. I looked down at my own pale hands and was surprised to see I had balled them into fists. Purple veins criss-crossed just below the surface of my skin.

A bleeding finger should not arouse a hunger. A bleeding finger should not arouse a *need*. It was just a wound.

Unless, of course, you were a fiend.

My stomach growled and roiled. It seemed to turn in on itself. Jesus, my sudden hunger was unbearable, unrelenting.

"Jesus," I whispered, still looking down at my clenched fists.

"Are you okay?" asked Allison. She was standing nearby. I could hear her sucking on her finger now.

My stomach nearly did a somersault.

*Jesus.*

I looked up, despite knowing that doing so might be a mistake. It was. Allison was still alternately sucking her finger and looking at the wound—and wincing. I didn't wince. I stared. No doubt hungrily.

*It's just a wound,* a voice in my head said. The voice, I knew, was the last vestiges of my humanity. *Just a wound. An injured finger. Nothing more, nothing less.*

Except I knew that it was more. So much more. The wound, and the resultant blood, represented so much. It represented complete satiation. Unlimited life. Unlimited strength. Complete and utter superiority.

I blinked. Hard.

Since when did superiority matter to me? Since when did I ever care to be better than others, or control them?

I didn't know, but that train of thought alarmed me more than my hunger. That train of thought was dangerous. Violent. Scary as shit.

"Oh, does blood make you queasy?" asked Allison.

I blinked and might have nodded.

She went on, moving her hand out of my line of sight. I tracked her finger closely, the way a cheetah might a wounded warthog. "I'm sorry," she said. "I was cutting an apple when the phone rang. My mom. Always my mom. Especially with Caesar gone. Everyone calls me these days. Everyone feels sorry for me. Anyway, long story short, I cut my finger pretty deep."

"I see that," I said, the words coming out sounding guttural, and not my own. "And, yes, I have a . . . problem with blood."

"Oh, geez. I'm sorry," she said sympathetically enough, but she was looking at me oddly. I didn't blame her. I suspected I looked like a complete freak, staring pale-faced, my voice barely intelligible.

*Samantha Moon, ace detective at your service.*

She went to the bathroom and returned with a Band-Aid. She was watching me as she returned. I knew she was watching me, but I ignored her curious stare. Instead, I was openly staring at her finger like the hobgoblin that I am.

"I'm just going to put this Band-Aid on. Do you want me to do it in the other room?"

"No, here is fine," I said, perhaps a little too quickly. I leaned forward a little in the process to get a better view of her finger.

*God, help me,* I thought.

Allison continued watching me as she sat across from me on the coffee table. She was Hispanic. Very toned. Lean muscles undulated with each movement. She was wearing short white shorts and a tight tank top. She looked, if anything, like the girl-friend of a world-class boxer. I knew from Romero that she was a personal trainer and competitive body builder. I didn't doubt it.

Except I wasn't looking at the way her muscles rippled or flexed. I was closely watching the way she removed the Band-Aid from the wrapper. She next peeled away the protective backings, exposing the sticky underside. I noted the way her blood continued to fill the open wound. It really was a nasty cut.

I began sweating.

What the devil was wrong with me? But I suspected I knew. I hadn't had human blood in a few weeks, and I was missing it terribly. I didn't want to miss it. In fact, I had made it a point not to think about it.

But to see it now . . . right in front of me . . . triggered some-thing in me that I was having a terrible time controlling. Or dealing with.

I looked away, breathing hard.

"Boy, you really do have a problem with blood," said Allison.

I think I nodded. Who knows. Maybe I drooled like a ghoul. I kept looking away, breathing slowly through my nose, focusing on the thing that was in front of me, which was a magazine with Katie Holmes on the cover. She looked happy and unencum-bered. The words above her said: "Freedom."

"I can go in the bathroom if you want," said Allison.

I was about to tell her to please do so, but there was something in her tone. Something . . . challenging.

"No, don't," I said. "I'm okay."

"You don't look okay."

"I've been . . . sick," I said, using my old standby excuse.

"I'm sure you have," she said, her words surprising me. "I'm sure you've been very, very sick."

I looked at her sharply. She had quit playing with the Band-Aid, which now dangled from her finger and thumb. She was squinting her eyes a little. Squinting them at me.

"You're here to find out who killed my Caesar," she said. She lowered her wounded hand in front of me.

"Yes," I said. The word was barely understandable to my own ears. The significant wound along her finger had begun bubbling over again with fresh hemoglobin.

"You are here to help us find answers," she said.

I nodded again, this time unable to speak.

"And you're also a vampire," she said.

I looked at her sharply, and her eyes narrowed further still. I said nothing. She said nothing. Blood was now dribbling freely down her finger. I swallowed hard. It was all I could do to not lunge forward and seize her finger.

She leaned toward me and held her finger in front of me. Like a carrot. "And you're very, very hungry, aren't you?"

I flicked my gaze from her wound to her eyes and found myself nodding.

"Then drink, Samantha Moon."

# 25.

It was after.

I hadn't drank much, but it was enough to feel good. *No, great.* To feel that special surge of energy, strength, and vitality gained only by drinking human blood. *Fresh* human blood.

And never had the blood been as fresh as this.

It was straight from the source, so to speak.

I had also drank enough to be embarrassed, especially now as I sat back on the couch and wiped my mouth. I looked away.

*Had I really just drank from her? From her finger? Sucking on it like a newborn from a teat?*

I had . . . and I had loved every second, even when she looked away, clearly uncomfortable and perhaps even in pain. Still I drank from the open wound in her finger. I drank and I drank.

It wasn't until when I had stopped, until when I removed my lips from around her finger, when my eyes finally focused again, did the embarrassment set in.

Allison had immediately pulled her hand into herself, holding it close to her side, as if she were cradling a baby chick. And that's how we currently sat. She, sitting on the coffee table, holding her hand. Me, on the couch, embarrassed as hell and slightly confused over what had just happened.

*Lord, I don't even know her.*

"I'm . . . sorry," I said after a moment or two. Outside, through the open sliding glass door, laughter reached us from the street below. Car doors shut firmly, and I suspected one of the limos had just left the scene.

"For what, Samantha?" asked Allison. She seemed to recover from whatever it was she'd gone through. She looked at her finger. "For being what you are? And for that, there is no apology needed."

"How—" But my words stopped abruptly when I looked at her finger. The wound was gone.

She saw the surprise on my face. "Yes, Samantha. Your healing qualities extend to your victims." She turned her face toward me . . . and smiled deeply. "Even willing victims. It's why, I suspect, vampires have existed among us for so long. The victims' wounds almost always heal."

I opened my mouth to speak, but I still hadn't completely regained my voice and, quite frankly, I felt a little high. The fresh blood was intoxicating, to say the least.

*Her blood,* I thought. *I drank her blood.*

"How . . . how do you . . ."

"How do I know so much about vampires?" she asked, finishing the sentence for me. "How do I know so much about your kind?"

"Yes," I said finally.

I quickly got over the initial high—the contentment, the satiation—and focused on my surroundings. After all, it's not every day that someone so easily surmised my true nature. So then what the hell was going on here? Was this some kind of a set up?

I doubted it.

For one, my inner alarm hadn't sounded. Two, I had sensed nothing but mild curiosity radiating from Allison. Nothing hidden. Nothing darker. Nothing malicious. But I'd been wrong before.

Finally, she said, "I was a plaything to a vampire, Sam. There's no easy way to say it. He used me, abused, me, and drank from me."

"He?"

She smiled again, and now I did sense something else coming from her. Waves of sadness. "He's dead now, killed by a vampire hunter who very nearly killed me, too."

She reached for a packet of cigarettes that were on a shelf under the glass coffee table. She opened the box and tapped out a cigarette and offered me one. I took it without thinking as she produced a lighter from a pocket and we both lit up, exhaling together.

"I'm sorry," I said.

She shrugged and dragged deeply on her cigarette. "I loved him, but he was a bastard. I suppose he had it coming to him."

I didn't know what to say, and so I smoked quietly, which was something I actually enjoyed doing. The act was very human, very real, and had no ill effects to my body, which was a plus.

She flicked her gaze my way. She studied me for a beat or two. "He also got that very same look in his eye. The one you had earlier. When he was hungry. Or when he saw blood."

"What look?" I asked.

"It's a fire. I can see it. Not everyone can see it, but I can."

I saw it, too, but said nothing. After all, I had seen it in Hanner's eyes last month. The smoldering fire. Just behind her pupils.

"Your eyes actually lit up. Fired up. Literally." She laughed. "You were either a vampire . . . or one sick chick."

I laughed, too. Nervously. All of this talk made me feel uncomfortable. After all, I was discussing my closely guarded secrets with a complete stranger. Then again, I had drank from her, hadn't I? Didn't that make her a kind of blood sister?

*God, my life is weird.*

As we finished our cigarettes—along with two more—she told me her story. She had met the vampire at a nightclub, where she'd been a go-go dancer. She had always been attracted to bad boys. He was the baddest of bad boys. She could see it in his eyes. He was trouble. He was dangerous, and he was a killer. She sensed all this from him. She had always sensed things from people, her whole life. Her grandmother had always told her she was a sensitive.

Later, after a night of dancing, he had brought her home and made love to her, unlike any man she had ever been with before. His home had been in the Hollywood Hills, and there she learned just how deep pleasures could go. He next fed from her. Without asking. Without prompting or warning. He began drinking from her forearm. She had fought him at first, until she realized the feeling was . . . incredible.

"Incredible?" I said.

"Don't you know, Sam? May I call you Sam?"

"I just drank from you," I said. "You can call me whatever you want."

She laughed a little. "The pleasure I receive from a feasting is almost as much as you receive from the feeding."

I hadn't known this.

She nodded. "You must be new to all of this."

"Fairly," I said, and left it at that.

She nodded after a moment. "I get it. You don't want to talk about it. It's personal shit. Trust me, I know. Nothing more personal than being what you are." She snubbed out her third cigarette. "I was addicted from the get-go. Addicted to being feasted upon. To being drank from. To being sucked. I was his for as long as he wanted me. Turned out, it was only for a few months."

"Until he ended up dead."

Her eyes filled with tears. "Right, dead. The bastard broke into the house. Shot my man in his sleep. In his *sleep*."

"I'm sorry," I said again.

She shrugged again, something I was beginning to think she did a lot. "Well, like I said, my vampire was a bastard. According to the hunter, my guy had hurt many people."

Now she was silent for a long time. I could hear her heart beating, which surprised me. I wondered if it had to do with me drinking her blood. Maybe we really were blood sisters.

Finally, she looked sideways at me, and put on what I suspected was a brave smile. "But that's not why you're here, Sam. Is it? We're looking for another killer."

I nodded, briefly jolted back to the reality of the situation. "Yes," I said.

"That's good," she said. "Because I have a theory about Caesar's death."

"A theory?"

"Yes," she said. "And you're going to think I'm crazy."

She looked at me. I looked at her. And we both laughed. "Well," she added, "crazier than you already think I am."

I laughed again, and by the time she was done telling me her theory, I decided that she was right.

She was crazy.

# 26.

She and Caesar had been at a charity event six weeks ago, exactly two weeks before his death.

Caesar was always doing charity work for the Latino community, and this event had been no different. Well, except for one small occurrence, an occurrence that Allison didn't think was small at all. It was an occurrence, in fact, that she was quite certain had been very big indeed.

So big that it killed Caesar.

Or so she felt.

It had been a charity fight. A professional boxer against a martial artist. And he was not just any martial artist: the current, reigning karate champion. The match had gone well enough for the first few rounds. Lots of posing and light punches. Lots of ducking and juking and sliding and laughing. Good times. The crowd was loving it. And why wouldn't they? Two pros, at the tops of their respective worlds, were matching techniques, wits, and punches.

Until it happened.

*The Punch*, as Allison thinks of it.

One moment the two fighters were exchanging cushy punches. The karate champion was even doing a few kicks that Caesar easily avoided. After all, this was a charity event. The punches and kicks weren't meant to land. And if they did, there wasn't much force behind them.

Allison had been on the phone, talking to a friend, when the fight suddenly took a very strange turn.

"He punched him, and hard," said Allison now, lighting up another cigarette and sitting back on the couch.

"Who punched whom?" I asked, fairly certain I was using correct English. I was a vampire momma, after all. Not a grammarian. If that was even a word.

"The karate champion," said Allison, exhaling. "One moment they were exchanging light punches—most of which were glancing off each other's shoulders—and the next . . ." She paused, looked at me. "And the next, this guy, this asshole, punches Caesar hard. I mean, really fucking hard. Caesar wasn't expecting it. It was a charity event, for crissakes. The first few rounds were light and easy. In fact, it was only a three-round charity match. There was only like twenty or so seconds left in the third round. It was almost over."

I perked up. "And this happened two weeks before his death?"

"Yes."

"What happened to Caesar after the punch?"

"It laid him out. Remember, the karate champion was using his *bare fists*. Caesar had gloves on. The fight was just for laughs. A joke. Nothing serious. Just two guys lending their names to a charity event."

I nodded, thinking, mind racing. There was something here. I could feel it. Whether or not this something was my enhanced psychic abilities kicking in or my detective instincts, I didn't know. Sometimes it's impossible to know. Logic suggested that the punch had occurred far too early—two weeks, in fact—for it to have any ill effects on Caesar's health.

And yet . . . it just felt right.

"How was Caesar after the fight?" I asked.

"Woozy. The punch really rang his bell. Remember, the guy was like a five-time karate champion. The dude knows how to throw a punch. But there's more."

I waited. I considered lighting up another cigarette myself, but didn't want to smell too much like smoke around the kids. Tammy has a sensitive nose, and there was a good chance she was allergic to the smell of cigarettes.

*I can't buy a break,* I thought.

When Allison had gathered her thoughts, she said, "I haven't told anyone this, mind you."

"I understand," I said.

"I mean, no one would believe me."

I nodded encouragingly, waited.

"You're the first person who I think I can trust with this information . . . and perhaps the first person who wouldn't laugh me off immediately. Maybe you are a godsend."

I wondered what God thought of that, but said, "Well, drinking someone's blood has that effect." I didn't mention that she also knew my super-secret identity, which bonded us further. Or condemned her.

She took in some air and plunged forward, "Caesar was never the same after that punch."

"What do you mean?"

"He was different. Not entirely . . . there. He seemed to have suffered a concussion, of some sort, but the doctors who checked him out said he wasn't showing typical concussion symptoms—nausea, blurred vision, vomiting, stuff like that."

"So what was wrong?"

Allison thought about that, pursing her lips. "Well, everything, actually. He rarely talked. Rarely slept. I would often find him sitting in the dark alone. He spoke in a monotone. He rarely laughed, and when he did, it seemed forced. My last memories of him are not good ones. My last memories of him—namely the two weeks leading up to his fight in Vegas—were filled with constant worry and concern."

"The doctors couldn't pinpoint anything?"

"The doctor didn't think anything was wrong."

"And you think the punch had something to do with his death?" I asked.

Allison held my gaze. I suddenly felt as if I'd known her for a long time. As if this wasn't our first meeting. I shook off the feeling.

She said, "I know the punch had something to do with his death, Sam." She got up and moved over to her sliding glass window and looked down at the street below. "I just know it. And he should never have fought Russell Baker."

"What do you mean?"

"He wasn't ready for the fight. He was still out of it. I mean, Jesus, he was *sleeping* before the fight. Sleeping. He never sleeps before a fight. He was usually bouncing off the walls."

Her words triggered a memory. "Romero told me he had to calm Caesar down before the fight."

"Usually. Romero was always good at getting Caesar to focus, to channel his energy, so to speak."

"But not this last fight?"

"No. Caesar was already calm. So calm that he was sleeping."

I nodded and thought about all of this, and kept thinking about it all the way home.

# 27.

It was late.

I was at home, looking into Allison's allegations. Unfortunately, there was no video of the charity fight anywhere. That would have been nice to see. The karate champion in question was Andre Fine, and he was generally recognized as the best in his weight class, holding various titles and many degrees of black belt. Apparently, he was the baddest of the bad.

I found his website and studied his many pictures. I also found many YouTube video clips of his fights. He was, from all appearances, lightning fast, and tended to really hurt his opponents. More than one went down and stayed down.

I sat back and rubbed my eyes out of habit. Truth was, they didn't hurt. Truth was, they never hurt and I had perfect vision. Especially after a day like today.

When I had consumed fresh human blood.

Human blood from a more-than-willing donor.

The small amount that I had indeed consumed from Allison's finger was more than enough to sustain me for a day or two. Human blood has that effect: long-lasting and filling. Even small amounts of the stuff went a long way.

I thought of Allison again, a woman who loved to have her blood consumed. And I mean *loved* to have it consumed. And here I was, a woman and vampire who knew the benefits of human blood. The supernatural, unparalleled benefits. It was hard not to see that this could be a match made in Heaven.

Or, more accurately, in one of the outer rings of Hell.

Andre Fine. He looked like a tough dude. He knew how to punch. How to guard. He seemed to have an almost supernatural grasp of what his opponent would do next. From the footage I saw, no one had gotten close to him. No one had hurt him, and all were beaten—badly.

Except, he didn't strike me as something supernatural. He wasn't a particularly big man, and, according to Kingsley the Buttface, I now knew that werewolves actually grew in size as time went on. Kingsley himself had started out as a much smaller man, which made me wonder how big Kingsley would eventually get. Or, if there was a capping-off of size.

Then again, maybe I didn't care, at least, not about Kingsley.

But I did care. I did care that he had cheated on me, and it was all I could do to not drive over there, kick his door in, and then kick his face in.

But he had been set up.

So what?

Easy excuse.

Jerk-off.

Perhaps Andre Fine was a *new* werewolf, then, not yet old enough to achieve the bigger size. Kingsley, after all, possessed such quickness and strength. But Andre Fine was slight, even. He was, in fact, often smaller than his opponents . . . although clearly faster and stronger and more skilled.

I shifted gears, and within a few minutes, I had all his personal information in front of me, as well. I now knew his last three residences, including his current one in Malibu. He was single, no kids, and had an interesting rap sheet. He'd spent time in county jail for beating a man nearly to death in a barroom brawl. His hands were registered as lethal weapons, so the fight was considered a felony. He also seemed to like to beat up his various girlfriends. Three different complaints from three different women. No arrests, warnings only. I looked up his birth certificate, and confirmed that he was not an immortal who had lived hundreds of years, although he certainly fought like an immortal. He was thirty-four.

Still, how could a single punch have an effect two weeks later?

I didn't know. But I knew someone who might. I picked up my cell and called Chad Helling, my ex-partner with HUD. He answered on the second ring.

"Better?" he asked.

"I like being a second-ring kind of gal," I said.

"You do realize we're not partners anymore, Moon Shine," he said, using one of his trillions of nicknames he had for me. "I'm not obligated to pick up at all. In fact, my life would be a lot easier if I just let your calls go to voicemail."

"Then why don't you?"

"I said my life would be easier."

"So that means you still love me."

"No, I love Monica. I put up with you."

"Good enough," I said.

"So, how can I plunder the government's resources for you this time, Sunshine?"

"Not the government's resources. Your gray matter. I'm calling to pick your brain. I need your expertise."

"In beer?"

"Fighting," I said, knowing that Chad Helling was an amateur MMA fighter.

"Sometimes they're one and the same," he said.

I rolled my eyes. I told him about my case and about Allison's theory. And to my complete surprise, Chad didn't laugh immediately, which is what I had expected.

When I finished, he said, "Andre Fine is a bad dude."

"That's what I gathered."

"No, I mean a bad dude."

"Okay, you lost me," I said.

"I mean, the guy is legendary in the fighting community. Not only is he the reigning karate champion, but he has been for the last five years in a row."

"But why is he legendary?"

"Did you catch the part about being champion for five straight years?"

"I did," I said. "But I also noted something else in your voice."

"Geez, Moon River, I can't keep anything from you."

"Nope. Now, out with it."

"Okay, here's the dope."

"Dope?"

"It's like the new catch phrase these days."

"Fine. Give me the dope."

"Ugh."

"Ugh what?" I said.

"Doesn't sound right coming from you. Sounds too mom-ish."

"Well, I am a mom. Now tell me what you know or I'll shove my mommy sneaker up your ass."

"Now that's the Samantha Moon that I remember."

"Chad . . ."

"Right. Fine. Look, some of this isn't easy to talk about. I mean, it's kind of crazy, actually."

"Crazy, how?"

"You know about Bruce Lee, right?"

"Sure," I said. "Kung fu guy?"

"Well, he was much more than just a kung fu guy, but yeah, him. Anyway, he died of cerebral edema caused by pain medication. A bad reaction, you know? He died at age thirty-two."

"So what about him?" I asked.

"In 1985, *Black Belt Magazine* stirred up some controversy when it suggested that Bruce Lee had, in fact, been killed by a *dim mak*."

"*Dim mak*?"

"Death touch."

"Of course," I said.

"You might laugh but there are lots of fighters and martial artists out there who think the *dim mak* is real."

"And how might one die from a *dim mak*?"

"That part isn't so easy to explain. But it has something to do with stopping life flow or life force, or what some call *prana*."

"Did you just say *prana*?"

"I know. New Age-y, woo-woo stuff. But think of it as the opposite of acupuncture, which encourages the flow of energy through a body."

"And the *dim mak* discourages the flow of energy?"

"That's the theory."

"On Google, do I just type in *death touch*? Or *touch of death*?"

"Like I said, Moon Glow, you can laugh, but there are many who believe it's real—and a few who claim they've seen the *dim mak* in action. And those who are reputed to have the skill are given a wide berth."

"Let me guess . . ." I said.

I could almost see Chad nodding his squarish head over there on his side of the line. "Yes," he said. "Andre Fine is one of those who's reputed to know the *dim mak*."

"Lucky him," I said.

# 28.

I was sitting at my desk, drumming my fingers, listening to my children sleeping from down the hallway, thinking about damned "touches of death" when it happened.

It was a vision.

A powerful vision, so powerful that I knew it could have only come from Fang. It filled my waking thoughts completely, blurring my vision enough for me to believe that what was happening to *him* was happening to *me*.

This happened to us sometimes. If Fang was experiencing something powerful enough, emotional enough, or exciting enough, it nearly always flooded my thoughts.

As it did now.

Usually, I can switch off the image, and leave Fang to his privacy. But as I sat back in my desk chair, the image I saw in my mind made me gasp.

It was of Detective Hanner. And she was hovering over Fang, straddling him. She was wearing next to nothing. The light shifted. His eyes shifted. Correction. She was, in fact, wearing nothing. Standing over him, naked.

*I shouldn't be watching this,* I thought.

I could turn off the image. Block it, so to speak.

But I didn't. I continued watching, like a voyeur through a bedroom window. I watched because I suspected I knew what was going to happen. I knew it, but I wanted to be sure. I wanted to see it for myself.

Fang, I saw, was naked, too. He was sitting in a chair. I could see his chest heaving. His skin was gleaming slightly. I hadn't seen him naked before. This was a first . . . and it was impressive. All of it . . . and all of him.

But I was seeing what he was seeing, and now his gaze shifted as she slowly swung a leg over him and straddled him. I felt him shiver. Heard him moan and gasp. She adjusted herself on him, reaching down, and now he moaned low and long as she slid him inside her.

A powerful wave of pleasure swept through him and subsequently me, too. I felt him throbbing.

*Jesus, no wonder guys love those things so much.*

But this wasn't about sex. I knew that. Fang knew it, too. This was just preparing him for what was to come. He was waiting for it. I could sense his thoughts, even if they were a bit scrambled. He was willing her to do it, to do it, to do it.

*Please. Do it. Please. God, please.*

His thoughts briefly overcame mine, his line of thinking replacing mine.

I shook my head, and nearly pulled out of the scene, but I had to see what happened next. I had to see what was going to happen to my one-time friend, Fang.

*Do it, love. Do it, baby. Do it, do it. DO IT!!*

I shook my head, trying to clear it, trying to focus on what was happening, but Fang's thoughts were too intense, too powerful, too overwhelming. I had two choices only: block the vision completely . . . or give into it.

I debated only briefly.

And gave into it . . .

# 29.

They writhed.

I writhed, too, along with Fang, since I was living through him, experiencing through him, feeling through him. All while I sat here alone in my office, while he made love in another part of town, with a vampire.

A very dangerous vampire.

I did not feel jealous. I loved Fang, but for different reasons. He had been a friend first . . . and a stalker later. Knowing his past later did not wipe away the feelings of warmth I had developed for him. He had helped me through some very dark times in my life, and for that, I would always be grateful.

That he had had an agenda only came out later.

Agenda or not, he had always been my Fang, my friend, my confidant, my rock, my source of information and sometimes, even inspiration.

But I was losing him tonight.

I was losing him forever.

The sound of his panting filled my thoughts. I could also feel his heart racing. Nearly uncontrollably. Fang had the mother of all delusions. Early on in life, thanks to a rare defect, he had believed he was a vampire. And a part of me suspected he *still* believed he was a vampire.

At least, a vampire at heart.

Fang was the embodiment of the Law of Attraction. He believed it hard enough, wanted it bad enough, lived it, breathed it . . . and now he was about to become it.

The real deal.

A vampire.

His lifelong wish, his fondest desire, his burning passion was about to become real, and he could barely control himself. No, he couldn't control himself. I felt ghost tears pouring down my face. But they were his tears pouring steadily down his face. Our connection was still so strong, so powerful. In this moment, we were one.

I could stop the connection, but still I resisted.

I had to know what was happening to my friend . . . I had to know what was going through him, and what she would do to him.

She writhed on his lap, faster and faster. From his blurred vision, I saw his hand reaching up for her hair, pulling on it. She went with it and bared her teeth. Not unnaturally long canines, no. Normal teeth. I was the same. My teeth were always the same size. Nothing pointy. Nothing I ever had to hide.

Thank God. Going through this life was hard enough being what I was. At least I didn't have to keep my lips closed, too.

Her teeth were unnaturally white. Same with mine. No coffee stains. No yellowing. Apparently, a steady diet of blood whitened teeth, too. Go figure.

Her chest was small. Not a lot of bouncing or heaving there, but I saw that one of Fang's hands were groping them absently. Mostly he was concentrating on her face, her mouth. I saw what he saw—and he was laser-focused on her teeth.

Her pure white teeth, which she flashed once more.

*She was going to do it. She's doing it. Please do it. Please. I need this. I have to have this. I must have this.*

Fang's vision focused and unfocused, wavered, spun briefly. He was close to hyperventilating. Close to passing out. He wanted this so bad, was so excited, so turned on . . .

*Deep breaths, Aaron,* he told himself, his thoughts appearing in mine. *Deep breaths. There. There. She's doing it. Oh, God, she's doing it . . .*

His eyes unfocused and I saw that Hanner had indeed lowered her face . . . briefly to his lips, which she grazed with her own, now down along his chin and onto his neck, all of which she kissed and licked hungrily . . .

*Jesus, it's really happening.*

I wasn't sure if that had been Fang's thoughts or my own, until I realized it didn't matter.

One thing I did know was that Fang was close to orgasm.

*Jesus, I shouldn't be seeing this, feeling this,* I thought.

Her rhythm increased, her hips riding me—Fang—harder and faster. I felt her body thrust against me, her breasts grazing me. Her lips kissing me. Fang and I were one, truly one, and it was all I could do to not gasp. Something was rising in him, an incredible sensation. It was building powerfully. He gripped the chair he was sitting in. I gripped my own chair.

And just as I felt a sharp pain in my neck—no, an excruciating pain—Fang released powerfully into her, crying out, holding her tightly.

Even while she drank deeply from him.

# 30.

It was the next day, and I was with my daughter.

We were at the Brea Mall, which was next door to the same Embassy Suites where I had stayed for a few weeks last year, back when my ex-husband, Danny, had been trying to destroy me. He's cute like that.

I was holding Tammy's hand. These past few days, ironically, she had seemed inseparable from me. She had only run away for a few hours. It had been just long enough to miss her mommy.

The mall was surprisingly quiet for a Saturday evening, although there was the usual amount of squealing teenage girls. Trailing right behind the squealing girls was a group of giggling boys. This trend was repeated throughout the mall, on every level of every quadrant. From Macy's to Nordstrom, from Sbarro's Pizza to Wetzel's Pretzels: laughing girls were followed closely by giggling boys.

Of course, there were whole families here, too. And couples shopping, and security guards strolling, and glass elevators elevating, and escalators escalating.

But none were as loud as the squealing girls.

"You don't have a lot of friends," I said after we stopped for pretzels.

I ordered two out of habit. I wasted more money that way, and as we continued our slow stroll through the mall, I broke off a big chunk of pretzel and just held it. I waited until Tammy turned to look at a poster of the latest *Twilight* movie, this one called *Midnight Sun*, and dropped the chunk of pretzel into a trash can. That was a damn shame, since it smelled heavenly and there were hungry folk in the world.

Tammy glanced over at me and smiled. I smiled, too, and pretended to swallow the non-existent pretzel.

I hated my life sometimes.

We continued like this until we got to the downstairs court-yard near JCPenney. When Tammy conveniently turned to look at something that surely caught her eye, I quickly disposed of the last of the pretzel—

But not in time.

She quickly glanced back at me . . . and only then did I realize that I'd been set up.

"Mommy?" she said.

"Uh, yes?" I had looked away, feigning interest in some shoes in a nearby window.

"Mommy, why have you been throwing away your pretzel this whole time? I've been watching you do it in all the windows." She looked at her own reflection in the store window and stared at my hand-less sleeves. "Well, sort of watching you."

Caught. Dammit.

"Mommy has a stomachache," I said.

"But you always have a stomachache."

"I know, baby. Sometimes Mommy is very sick."

"But you're always sick. If you didn't want the pretzel, then why did you order it?"

"I wanted it, sweetie. Very badly."

She stopped walking and took my forearm. Long ago, she had quit asking me about my cold flesh. Cold flesh and Mommy were one and the same. "Enough double talk, Mom."

"Double talk?"

"Yes. Double talk. It means you are telling me one thing but mean another."

"Oh, it does, does it?"

"Yes, it does. Mrs. Marks explained it to us the other day. And I realize that you do that a lot. Double speak."

"You think so?"

"I know so, Mommy. For instance, if you wanted the pretzel so badly, then why not eat it? Then why *pretend* to eat it? And if you actually had a stomachache, then why order it at all?"

I crossed my arms under my chest and leaned a shoulder against the window. I glanced at the time on my cell. He should be here any moment now. For once, I wished that Danny was early.

I said to Tammy, "I don't know, honey. You tell me."

"I think you do know, Mommy. I know lots of things these days."

"What things?" I asked.

"Secrets."

"Whose secrets?"

"Everybody's secrets."

"How do you know their secrets, honey?"

"I see them."

"See them how?"

"I just see them. Like visions."

"I see," I said. "So, what secrets do you know about Mommy?"

"For one, you've been lying to me and Anthony for years."

I opened my mouth to speak but nothing came out. My lips and tongue worked to form words, to no avail. Mercifully, across the mall, Danny appeared through the crowd, looking grim-faced and handsome and moving quickly.

"There's another, slightly bigger secret," she continued, following my gaze and seeing her dad approaching.

"What?" I asked with sickening dread.

"You're a vampire."

I think my eyes just about bugged out of my head, not that I could see my reflection. I pushed off the window just as Danny appeared and hugged Tammy. She hugged him back, but kept her eyes on me.

"Where's Anthony?" he asked me gruffly.

"He's with his cousins this weekend."

"Fine. Tell him I miss him."

"Will do," I said. But I was looking at Tammy.

Danny nodded and was about to turn away with the palm of his hand on Tammy's lower back, when he suddenly stopped. He looked at me curiously, then his daughter. "Everything okay here?" he asked.

"I don't know," said Tammy. "Ask Mommy."

"Yes," I said. "Everything's fine."

"Fine, whatever," said Danny, and now he took Tammy's hand and led her off for his weekly visitation.

As she followed behind him, Tammy looked back once . . . and gave me a knowing smile.

# 31.

I was sitting in my minivan, admittedly shocked.

My innocent children were innocent no more. Gone were the days where they would blindly accept Mommy's complaints of a tummy ache or of a rare skin disease or my even vaguer explanation that "Mommy is just cold."

I started and tried to predict the significance of Tammy also knowing that her mother was the freak of all freaks. I wondered if there was any hope that my kids might still grow up to be normal . . . and that thought alone nearly overwhelmed me. I buried my face in my hands all over again. I sat like that until the tears stopped.

As I sat there, face in my hands, two things occurred to me: one, how deep my hate was for the angel, Ishmael; and, two, that my daughter was steadily growing more psychic.

And when, exactly, did that happen?

I didn't know or had been too busy to notice. And where did these gifts come from? I didn't know that either. My son's own great strength was far easier to explain away. That his sister would also have abilities was beyond me.

As I contemplated this, drying my eyes, a sudden and severe pain blasted through me, doubling me over, wracking my body. I doubled over, and knew immediately the source of the pain.

Fang.

Still doubled over in the driver's seat, hands gripping the steering wheel, I shielded my thoughts, throwing up a mental wall around me. Immediately, the pain subsided, and then passed completely. But I knew the pain.

Intimately.

I had gone through it myself seven years ago, after my own attack. Fang was going through what I now knew was the trans-formation from mortal.

To immortal.

And I knew he was alone in his apartment, and scared shit-less. I felt his fear, along with his pain. I took in a lot of air, drummed my fingers briefly on the steering wheel, and then headed out of the parking lot.

To Fang's apartment.

# 32.

*Fang.*

My best friend. Perhaps even more than a friend. My mentor. His advice had been crucial. His guidance had been invaluable. It was safe to say that I might have—just might have—gone batshit crazy without his help.

No pun intended.

That he had stalked me and fallen in love with me were different matters entirely. That he had been a friend when I needed a friend the most was what I would always remember.

I was sitting across from him now in his small, one-bedroom apartment located at the edge of Fullerton, in a shabby complex where the great Philip K. Dick had once lived. Fang was lying on his couch in the fetal position, shaking violently. I was certain that he was not aware of me.

I was certain, in fact, that he was dying.

According to Fang, this was the very complex where Dick—the author of the stories that inspired *Blade Runner, Total Recall,* and *Minority Report*, to name a few of his more popular titles—had his reality-shattering religious and visionary experiences.

Except now, as I watched Fang curl tighter into the fetal position, I knew there was nothing religious or visionary going on here. What I was seeing was a man suffering horribly.

I knew the feeling; it wasn't nice.

What was going on here, I knew, was death. His body wasn't just changing into something out-of-this world. It was dying, pure and simple. And Fang wasn't just dying, I knew. He was being . . .

Replaced.

Something else would inhabit him. Something dark and sinister—and looking for a foothold into this world.

*Jesus.*

The energy around Fang was interesting, to say the least. The deep black halo that surrounded him was infused with particles of light. I had never seen that before. I was witnessing something extraordinary.

I had only been to Fang's apartment once, months ago. Back then, I was still on the fence with Fang, still open to the possibility of romance. He had served drinks and we had sat on this very same couch. He had played music and I knew his intention was to seduce me. There were some benefits to reading the guy's thoughts, after all. But we never got very far. From the moment he put his arm around me, I had known that this was wrong. I had stood and told him that I was sorry but I had to leave.

Fang had looked mortally wounded, but had given me a sweet kiss on the cheek and told me to drive safely.

And now I was back, and watching him writhe and sweat and pant on the couch. That is, until I heard the sound at the door.

Detective Hanner of the Fullerton Police Department was standing in the entrance, watching me carefully. How she got in without me hearing her was disturbing. We stared at each other some more. My shoulders tensed. I was ready to move quickly if I had to.

But I didn't have to. She nodded to me after a moment, then turned and quietly shut the door. Once done, she tossed her coat over the back of a dining chair and walked toward me. Her eyes didn't exactly glow, not like Kingsley's, but I could see what appeared to be tiny flickers of flames just behind her pupils.

"Good evening, Samantha Moon," she said evenly. When she spoke to me alone, she always spoke differently, reverting to a slightly formal way of speech, tinged with a hint of an Eastern European accent. Perhaps it was her natural dialect from wherever it was she hailed.

My inner alarm began ringing. I watched her carefully, aware that there was also movement in the shadows to my right. The movement, I knew, was not from a physical form. Something had, I was certain, materialized *within* the shadows. A shadow within a shadow. My alarm grew louder. Now I saw it from the corner of my eye, creeping away from the far wall.

*A living shadow.*

Hanner, as far as I could tell, was unaware of the shadow. Or chose not to acknowledge it. "I would strongly advise you, sister," she said, "that you not disrupt the *changing*."

Outside of a creepy book that had once called out to me, I had never been referred to as "sister" before. I didn't like it. It made my skin crawl. It made me feel less than human.

*More than human,* hissed a voice in my head. *Always more than human.*

And now I did turn—in time to see something step away from the wall. No, *peel away* from the wall like a pitch-black sticker. Although still dark as night, the two-dimensional shadow fleshed out, so to speak, into something three-dimensional, into something with depth and substance.

The entity soon stood before me, in the center of Fang's living room, rising and falling gently on ethereal tides that I neither felt nor saw. It was tall, a foot or so taller than me. But narrow. Its shoulders were nearly non-existent. Shadowy hands ended in curved, shadowy claws that opened and closed below its narrow hips. It stopped before me and I knew it was regarding me.

*You spoke to me,* I thought.

*Yesss,* the entity hissed, and I saw that its head tilted slightly to one side. Black mist swirled around it, rising up from Fang's carpet. *You are a sssister of the night, Sssamantha Moon. You would do well to never forget that.*

I knew that most supernatural entities did not have access to my thoughts, unless said entity was old enough or powerful enough, as was the case with Captain Jack last year.

And now, of course, this entity.

*Can she see you?* I asked it, indicating Hanner in my mind.

The entity paused only briefly before words appeared in my thoughts. *No, child. Only you can.*

*Why?*

There was another pause, this one much longer. *That remains to be ssseen.*

*What do you mean?* I asked. I sensed the thing before me was eager to move forward, to join its new host.

*You are very, very sssensitive, Sssamantha Moon. Yesss, I am eager to claim my host.*

I had another psychic hit, one that came to me with crystal clarity. *You have been dead a long time.*

The creature rose and fell silently. *A very long time, Sssamantha Moon. Too long.*

*But you were once alive,* I thought, as the hits continued. *Once human.*

*Very astute, child. And now I will be alive again. Just as my brother isss alive again in you.*

*But why?* I thought. *I don't understand.*

*It isss the way,* came the reply. *The only way.*

With that, the shadow slipped past me. Hanner was stroking Fang's hair, unaware of the approaching shadow behind her.

"No!" I shouted.

But as I spoke those words and as Hanner whipped her head up to look at me, the shadow poured forth into Fang, into the region of his heart. Fang gasped, his chest arched up. His eyelids fluttered wildly, and the dark halo I had seen around him, the halo once speckled with light, winked out of existence.

And with it, something else.

Fang's presence in my mind.

He was gone.

Forever.

# 33.

Fang settled back down onto the couch. The shaking, I noted, had stopped. His panting, too, stopped.

I suspected, on some level, that his body had expired . . . that it was now being fueled supernaturally by the dark entity that had entered him. I also suspected his soul was now trapped in this supernaturally vivified body. Forever.

"His mortality ends," said Hanner next to me. "And his immortality begins. Everyone should be so lucky."

Fang was closed off to me. Our connection was forever severed. I had mixed feelings about that. My connection to Fang had been turbulent, at best. At times, it had been comforting. To know that I had instant access to someone who seemed to legitimately care for me—and perhaps even love me in his own way—was a rock I had relied on for many months now.

Except that Fang always had an ulterior motive. Considering how the man had grown up and issues he'd dealt with, his ulterior motive would surprise no one. That he stalked and befriended and ultimately loved a real vampire should be of no surprise either.

I had seen more than enough of Fang's mind to know the man was single-mindedly obsessed. His desire to be a real vampire trumped anything, perhaps even his love for me.

As I looked at him now, lying there quietly, I noted that the wound in his neck—the wound I, myself, had felt just the night before—had already healed.

Yes, his desire to be a vampire had trumped even his love for me.

"Why did you do it?" I said to Hanner, without looking at her.

"I saw his potential, Samantha."

"He's not stable," I said.

"I'm not looking for stability. I'm looking for potential."

I nodded, understanding. "His potential to kill."

"So much potential."

"That's why you turned him," I said, looking at her. "To kill for you."

She calmly looked up from Fang and at me. She held my gaze. The fire just behind her pupil flared brightly. "He is his own free man, Samantha. But I am sure he will show his appreciation when I am done revealing to him all that I know."

"You're doing this because I shut down your operation," I said. "You're punishing me. You're stealing my friend—"

"I'm giving him everything you wouldn't, Samantha."

"You'll create a killer."

"He will be tamed, Sam. Even the worst of our kind can be tamed."

"Or what?"

"Or they are removed."

"You mean killed."

"You cannot kill what's already dead, Sam. The entity within will simply withdraw, sacrificing its existence for the betterment of our kind."

"And when the entity withdraws?"

"The body will perish. Instantly."

"Jesus."

Hanner winced slightly at my involuntary utterance, which I noted. The name "Jesus" had no effect on me, but it appeared to on Hanner.

*Interesting*, I thought.

"And what happens to his soul?" I asked.

"His soul?" asked Hanner, looking at me and making an almost comical effort to blink. "But whatever do you mean?"

"His soul," I said, my voice rising. "Where is it?"

Hanner smiled and it was, perhaps, the most unpleasant smile I had ever seen on anyone. *Ever.* "Why, Samantha. His soul is long gone."

A wave of panic swept over me. I wrapped an arm around myself. Hanner's unpleasant smile remained frozen on her face. The smile was not human. She did not look human. She looked slightly misshapen, hunched. She looked like pure evil.

"You're not Hanner," I said. "You're the thing that lives in her."

"Very good, Samantha Moon," she said. Or *it* said.

"And you're trying to freak me out."

Hanner continued smiling that wicked smile. Or the thing within her did. "Is it working, child?"

"Go to hell," I said.

"Been there, done that," it said in a monotone, tilting its head slightly.

"Where's Hanner?"

"She's here. Next to me. Waiting. I've come for the big show."

"Big show?"

Hanner nodded toward Fang, who lay motionless on the couch. "I wouldn't miss his transformation for the world."

"Who's in me?" I asked.

Hanner grinned, except I knew it was not Hanner grinning. "One of us, child."

"Who?"

But Hanner shook her head. "Not now. Not now." And Hanner kept on shaking her head . . . and finally blinked. Hard.

She was back, looking slightly confused, and the thing within her—the thing that galvanized her dead body—had retreated, and was gone.

That such an entity was in me, watching over me, living through me, was almost enough to drive me insane.

Almost.

There had to be a way to fight back. To remove it.

And with that thought, I remembered the angel, Ishmael. He had told me he knew of a way for me to be free, to forever remove the thing within me. I thought about that, even while Fang continued to lay motionless, his chest unmoving. But alive. Supernaturally alive.

Fang had gotten his wish.

He was one of us now.

# 34.

I was flying.

It's what I did these days when I wanted to think—and apparently, I was one of the few who could.

*Lucky me.*

I was moving along the beaches, idly following the curving shore. It was hours before morning, hours before I would be exhausted enough to sleep . . . but not so exhausted that I had to sleep. The medallion had removed the effects of sunlight, but not my natural—or *un*natural—sleep patterns. My body still craved sleep during the day, happily doing so until sunset if I would let it. Two kids and a full-time job, unfortunately, wouldn't.

I flew five hundred feet above the crashing surf. The beaches were empty. Correction . . . mostly empty. There was a lone man jogging with a little squirt of a dog. A little red dog. Yes, my eyes are that good at night and in this form. The man looked vaguely familiar. Tall and muscular. As I flew overhead, the little dog stopped and barked. At me. The little shit. The man, stopped, too, and looked up, but I was already gone. I smiled to myself, now recognizing the cocky son-of-a-bitch.

The ocean rippled and sparkled, reflecting whatever ambient light was around. Fang would never be the same. Our relationship would never be the same. Hanner had plans for him, I was sure. But she could shove her plans up her pale ass.

*We'd see about her plans.*

Was Fang's and mine a true friendship? Perhaps, perhaps not. I liked to believe it was. I liked to believe he cared for me beyond what I was.

I had not yet made a decision about what to do about Fang's request. Truth be known, I was afraid of what would happen once I did. I was afraid for our relationship, for him, for the world. Of course, Detective Hanner had made the decision for me, thus forcing me and Fang's relationship to make that leap.

Fang was no puppet. Hanner was in for a surprise. Unless, somehow, the two of them had made a pact. Perhaps he had sold his soul, so to speak, to become that which he most wanted. Perhaps I had doomed him by delaying my own decision. Perhaps had I honored his request, he would not be bound to Hanner.

Was Hanner so bad? I didn't know. Not yet.

But one thing was sure: I would be there for Fang, for whatever reason, at any time. He had been there for me . . . and I suspected he was going to need my help.

Or perhaps not.

After all, he had Hanner now.

With a heavy heart, I turned to starboard, dipping one wing and raising the other, and headed over the million-dollar homes and back toward Fullerton.

# 35.

I was familiar with boxing gyms; not so much with dojos.

Andre Fine's Kenpo Karate Studio in Long Beach was about what I expected to see: lots of floor mats, lots of mirrors, two punching bags, a trophy case, and tons of newspaper and magazine clippings adorning the entrance/lobby room. A schedule next to the door indicated the next class would start in two hours.

Presently, there wasn't a soul around. I heard someone talking in a back office. On the phone, if I had to guess. Single voice speaking, pausing, then speaking, then yelling. More yelling. Then a slam.

*Oh, goodie,* I thought. *At least they'll be in a good mood.*

A man appeared a moment later, dressed in jeans and a tee shirt. He had a small beer gut and thick arms and a lot of muscle around his shoulders and neck. Probably, when he was in uniform and wore a karate robe, it bulged and opened around his mid-section. He probably *hee-yahed!* with the best of them. And I had no doubt that he had punched his way through many a wooden board in his time.

The man, who might have been talking to himself—and not very kindly—looked startled when he saw me. "Can I help you?"

"I'm here to see Andre Fine," I said, reaching in my purse and extracting a business card. I held it out to him. "I'd like to ask him a few questions regarding a case I'm working on."

He took the card, read it, and then handed it back. Most people don't hand my cards back. Most people hold them politely and talk to me civilly—then throw them away as soon as I leave. Handing my card back irritated me. Handing my card back made me hate his face. Handing my card back stirred a surprising amount of anger in me.

*Down girl,* I thought.

The anger subsided enough for me to reach out and take the card back and not break his fingers in the process. And as I took the card and slipped it back in my purse from whence it came, I had an image of me slamming this stranger up against the trophy case and . . .

Drinking from his neck.

*Jesus.*

This wasn't a normal reaction from me. This wasn't how I handled animosity. Not with anger. Not with violence. Maybe with a cute quip. Or to just brush it off. Not with images of violence.

*It's him,* I thought suddenly. *It's his thoughts. His anger. His violence. The thing inside me.*

"Hey, you okay?" asked the guy. To his credit, he looked a little nervous.

*He should be nervous.*

Again, that wasn't my thought. I wiped the sweat from my brow and nodded. "Yeah, I'm fine. Is Andre around?"

The guy looked at me some more, then got around to my question. "Sorry, but Andre doesn't actually work here. Sure, his name is on the sign outside and all the letterheads, but the truth is, he rarely shows up anymore. I thought you might want your card back because I would hate for you to waste it on me when he's never around."

I paused and collected my thoughts. "Thank you. Where . . . where can I find him?"

"These days? Pick any one of his many girlfriends. Sorry, I shouldn't say that about my boss, but he's a hard one to pin down lately."

"Why's that?"

"Hard to say. Too many distractions maybe. Too much success. Too many endorsements. Too many women."

"What would he say if he heard you say that?"

"I don't know. And I don't really care. This place is going to hell in a hand basket and he doesn't care. I just got off the phone with another parent who's pulling her kid. I don't blame her. It's hard to pitch a world-class studio when the head guy rarely, if ever, makes an appearance."

"Is it common for karate champions to own a studio?"

"Common and expected. And the ones who do at least make a courtesy appearance every now and then to keep everyone happy, maybe a demonstration here and there, something to keep the customers coming back."

"I've heard rumors that Andre Fine has been trained in," I paused, picking my words carefully, "other areas of martial arts."

The big guy crossed his hairy arms. "Oh? In what other areas of martial arts?"

I sensed that he knew immediately where I was going with this. I sensed that I wasn't the only one who had asked him this question. I also sensed that such accusations had been whispered about Andre Fine for many years now. But these were much more than just feelings. I had slipped briefly into the big guy's thoughts. I had done so effortlessly. All I had needed were a few moments with him. Now we were connected mentally. Only, he didn't know it.

"What do you know about *dim mak?*" I asked suddenly. "Or the *touch of death* as some call it?"

He chuckled lightly and blew air through his flat nose, air which ruffled his thick mustache. He waved his hand dismissively. "*Dim mak* is a bunch of hooey."

His thoughts gave him away. He didn't want to talk about it. In fact, he very much wanted me to leave and was thinking hard of an excuse to give me.

*No excuses,* I thought. I hadn't planned on directing his thoughts. I hadn't planned on anything of the sort when I arrived here just a few minutes earlier.

But seeing the direction he was going with his thoughts, sensing his intention to mislead and misdirect me, I instinctively stepped forward. I had not been aware that I could direct another's thought until speaking with Hanner last month—and watching her manipulate a theater of police officers.

I had thought I would never do it.

I had thought I would never resort to controlling another human being's thoughts.

But something within me *wanted* to control his thoughts. *Needed* to control him. *Needed* him to do my bidding. I suspected I knew what this something was.

I didn't want to control him. All I wanted was the truth. I wanted to know what he knew about Andre Fine. It was as simple as that.

*Tell me what you know about* dim mak, I thought.

He glanced at me, and as he did so I saw something disconcerting. His expression went blank. Dead. He opened his mouth to speak, faltered, then tried again. "*Dim mak* is not very well understood." He spoke in a flat monotone. "But it is real."

"Has Andre Fine been taught the *dim mak?*"

"Oh, yes. He's spent many years in Japan learning it from those who specialize in it."

"And what does the *dim mak* do?"

"It kills if struck correctly."

"And you believe this?"

"I have seen this."

"You have seen Andre Fine perform it?"

"No, another."

"And what was the result?"

He looked blankly. "Death."

"How long ago did this happen?"

"When I was in my twenties. I was a new fighter. We had all heard rumors that it was going to be performed in a fight."

"Tell me about the fight."

He did, speaking in his dead monotone. The fight had been an arranged fight. Both fighters were highly accomplished, and both were reputed to have mastered *dim mak*. The fight had occurred in a field, well away from the city. The fight itself had been a fairly long one, with both fighters evenly matched. That is, until one fighter struck the death blow. The *dim mak*.

"And what happened after that?"

The guy licked his lips and said, "The other fighter went down."

"Was he alive?"

"Yes."

"When did he die?"

"Two weeks later."

"And you believe it was because of the *dim mak*?"

He looked at me . . . and smiled emptily. "I know it was because of the *dim mak*."

Later, as I drove home, I realized that I hadn't even gotten the guy's name. I had controlled his thoughts, made him do my bidding, and I didn't even have the decency to know his name. Seemed rude.

*Yeah,* I thought. *I'm a monster.*

# 36.

"Well?" said Tammy.

We were in her bedroom. Anthony was in his room playing something called Nintendo 3DS. Whatever it was, it was little and expensive and if he ever lost it, I was going to play butt bongos on his backside until the cows came home. And since there weren't any cows in Fullerton, that might be a while.

"Well what?" I said. We were sitting on her floor in the space between her bed and dresser. Her back was to me and I was brushing her long hair.

"You know, Mom. Don't play cloy."

"Coy," I said.

She sighed. "Whatever, Mom. Cloy, coy. Either way, out with it."

"Since when did you get so demanding?"

"Since I realized that my mother has been lying to me my whole life."

"Not your whole life," I said, doing some quick math. She would have been about three when I was attacked. Anthony had been one. I had been a relatively new mom with one really freaky secret.

"So you've been lying for part of my life?"

"And since when did you get so smart?" I asked. She was skewering my words like an attorney. Like father, like daughter. That is, if you could call an ambulance chaser an attorney.

She waited, and not patiently. Down the hall, I heard Anthony groan and slap the floor, which sent minor shockwaves throughout the whole house.

*He's getting stronger,* I thought.

"I will tell you . . . more about me," I said. "But first, I want you to tell me why you think I have such a big . . . secret."

She held up her forefinger. "First, I don't think you have a secret. I know you have a secret." She raised another finger. "Two, you've always been weird."

"Thanks," I said.

"I mean, a person who can't go outside in the sunlight? A rare skin disease? I mean, c'mon!" She raised a third finger, and a fourth and fifth as she ticked off more points. "Three, you're always cold. Four, we have like *no* mirrors in the house. Five, you never eat." She lowered her hand and spun to face me. "Oh, you *pretend* to eat, but lately I've been secretly watching you sneak your food onto Anthony's plate. He's so dumb. He never notices it and just eats it. Such a doofus."

"Don't call your brother names."

"Sorry."

"Apology accepted," I said. "So tell me when you started having, you know, visions. When did they start?"

"Last month."

"When your period started," I said, nodding.

"Mom!"

Tammy hated talking about it, true. She thought it was gross, try as I might to convince her that it was the most natural thing in the world. Still, at ten, she was young to have started her period. She was young, but it was not unheard of. I had been ten, too, when mine started. Like mother, like daughter.

"Anyway," she said, rolling her eyes, "when *that* started, I also started seeing things."

"Seeing what?"

"I started seeing thoughts, I guess."

"Your own thoughts?"

"No, Mom," she said, nearly rolling her eyes full circle. "*Other* people's thoughts. I can already see my own thoughts. Duh."

"Be nice."

"Sorry."

"So, what did other people's thoughts look like, honey?" I asked.

She looked away, bit her lip. The aura around her was a light blue. Peaceful blue. There were flashes of greens and yellows, but she often had flashes of greens and yellows. Some colors were simply a part of someone. These were her colors. And, as always, I had no access to her thoughts. Other people's, sometimes. My own children, no.

Finally, she said, "They sort of appear as pictures. Fast pictures. They come and go quickly."

"How do you know they are not your own thoughts, honey?"

"Because they are things that I have never seen before. Things I had never *thought* about. Things I wouldn't . . ." She struggled for the right words.

"Things you wouldn't know," I offered.

"Yes, Mommy."

"So what did you think when you saw these strange images?"

She shrugged and reached down and cracked one of her excessively long toes. I cringed. I hated the sound, and asked her to stop. She rolled her eyes.

"Well, I was confused. But then I saw that the images seemed to come from people around me. I would see, for instance, Anthony's teacher in class, but from Anthony's eyes."

"So you concluded you were seeing his memories."

"Yes, Mommy."

"And the images only came to you when other people were nearby?"

"Yes!" she said excitedly. I think she figured I wouldn't believe her. Or that she was doing something wrong, somehow.

"So you weren't hearing their thoughts," I said. "But rather *seeing* their memories?"

She nodded and reached down for her toes, but then thought better of it. "I think so, yeah. Take Ricky Carpettle—he's the kid who always has boogers stuck to his forehead, 'cause, you know, he wipes his nose *up* instead of down. Anyway, I kept seeing him playing video games in his Batman underwear."

Despite myself, I laughed. I said, "How often do you see these images?"

"As often as I want."

"How do you stop them?" I asked.

She thought about that. "Well, I just sort of say 'Stop!' in my head real loud, and the images, you know, go away. At least, for a little while."

We were both silent. My daughter was a friggin' mind reader. How this came to be, I didn't know. Did her abilities have anything to do with me being a vampire? If so, how? My attack seven years ago should have no bearing on who or what she would become later in life.

My head hurt . . . briefly. I never had headaches for long. Still, I rubbed my temples, thinking hard. When I was done rubbing, I saw that Tammy was watching me closely. I didn't have to be a mind reader to know what she was going to say next.

"And when I'm around you, Mommy, I see things, too."

"Oh, God."

"You can fly, Mommy."

"Oh, God," I said again.

"It's you. I know it. But it's not you. You are something else, something huge. With wings, and you fly high above."

And now I really did have a headache, one that lasted a few seconds longer than normal. I buried my face in my hands and rubbed my head and wondered why the Universe was determined to utterly ruin my life and those of my kids.

"It's true, isn't it, Mommy? You can fly."

And the words I spoke next to my daughter should have sent me straight into an institution. Straight into a straitjacket. To be locked up forever. Words no sane person should ever, ever have to say. Especially not a mother to her daughter. And yet I heard them come from my mouth. I heard them from a distance. I heard the insanity of it all.

"Yes," I said, my face still buried in my hands. "I can fly."

# 37.

"What are you guys talking about in here?" asked Anthony, sticking his head in the doorway. I'd heard him coming and kept my face buried in my hands.

"About adult things, butthead," said Tammy angrily. "Now go away."

"You're the butthead. You go away."

"He can stay," I said. "And you both just lost TV and video games for the night."

"Can I still play computer games?" asked Anthony.

"Aren't those the same as video games?"

"No, Mom. Duh."

"Then those, too," I said. "And no one goes on the Internet, either. Oh, and both of you hand over your phones."

They did so grudgingly. We had a fairly wide-ranging Netflix account. Apparently, anything with a screen these days could access the TV. I thought of anything else I might have missed, going down my mental checklist: TV, Xbox, phones, computers, laptops. I snapped my fingers.

"Leave your iPads in my office, too."

"But Mom!" they both said in unison.

"That's what happens when you call each other names. We're a family. We don't call each other names."

"Since when?" asked Tammy.

"Since forever. And especially now. If you want to question me further, young lady, you can see what life is like without a DVR player."

"Sheesh. Sorry."

"That's better. iPads. Office. *Now*."

They stormed off. Tammy grabbed her iPad from her desk. I heard Anthony rummaging around his room for his own. I silently longed for the days when no TV had been enough. I also silently longed for the days when I could eat heaps of guacamole and chips. They returned a few moments later, both looking glum.

"Anthony, come in and shut the door. I'm going to talk to both of you."

Anthony's eyes widened a little. After all, he had done a darn good job of concealing our secret from his sister, although I suspected, with her newfound gifts, his secret wouldn't be concealed for long.

*Too many secrets, for too long.*

I patted the carpet in front of me and told them to sit. They sat. It was time for the truth, and so, I reached out and took their hands and told them everything. From my attack seven years ago, to my ability to fly, to their father's revulsion for me, to Kingsley Fulcrum being just as much a weirdo as me.

I told them everything.

Everything.

# 38.

We were at Cold Stone Creamery.

"Isn't it nice to know that you don't have to keep faking it all the time, Mom," said Tammy as we all sat in a booth in the far corner.

Although the weather was warming, the creamery was empty. I wasn't complaining. My kids couldn't keep their voices down even if I paid them to. Especially not now. Not with this much excitement in the air. After our talk a few hours ago, it had been Anthony who suggested we all go get ice cream. No surprise there. The kid was literally eating me out of house and home.

Interestingly, just in the past two hours, the kids were getting along better. And not just getting along but being—and get this—*friendly* toward each other. At one point, Anthony suggested to Tammy that she try the Snickers on her ice cream, and she actually did. She didn't tell him to mind his own business. She didn't ignore him. She didn't tell him he was stupid and looked funny. She said, "Sure."

I stood there in amazement, watching the scene play out. Tammy then nudged Anthony and pointed to a big stain on the worker's apron and they both giggled.

Together.

Granted, they were laughing at someone else, but at least they were getting along.

*Baby steps.*

I considered Tammy's question as I sat with the two of them. I was drinking from a water bottle and chewing gum. The gum was nice. It only gave me the smallest of stomach cramps—no doubt from the trace ingredients in the flavor—but it was nice to chew and drink and look like a real mom. I said to Tammy, "Yes. It is a relief, actually."

"You don't have to keep pretending to eat or to have stomach aches," said Anthony.

"At least, not around you two," I said.

"Or Daddy," said Anthony.

"I don't eat with Daddy anymore."

"Oh, right."

Tammy was eating her ice cream thoughtfully. "But when we are around other people . . ."

"Yes, I will still have to pretend to eat, or pretend that I'm full, or pretend that I have a tummy ache."

She nodded thoughtfully. Somewhere through all of this, my daughter had seriously grown up. Having access to others' minds might have something to do with that. Or maybe it was realizing that her mother was the mother of all freaks, too.

"Remember, what I am," I said to them again, "is a secret."

"We knoooooow," said Anthony, laying his head on the table. "You told us like a Brazilian times."

"Bazillion," Tammy corrected. "Brazil is a state."

"Country," I said.

"Whatever," she said. "The point is, we all have secrets now. We should make a pact."

"What's a pact?" asked Anthony.

I waited for his sister to ridicule his question, or, at least, to roll her eyes at his simplicity. She didn't. Instead, she surprised me again by turning to him and saying patiently, "It means we all agree to something forever."

"Forever?" said Anthony, blinking. "But Mom's a mimmortal."

"Immortal," said Tammy, only slightly losing her patience.

"That's what I said. Mimmortal. She lives forever. That's a long time to keep a secret."

I nearly fell out of my seat. Listening to my kids discussing something so casually that I had tried so hard to keep secret from them was just too surreal. I didn't know if I should smile, weep, or fear for the mental health of all of us.

"Okay," I said. "We'll make a pact to keep our secrets forever. Deal?"

"Deal," they said together.

We all looked at each other. Anthony voiced what was on all of our minds. "So, how do we make a pact?"

"I honestly don't know," I said.

"A blood pact!" said Tammy.

"I don't wanna make a blood pact!" screamed Anthony.

"No blood pacts," I said, shushing them. The Cold Stone worker had looked over at us.

"How about an ice cream pact!" said Anthony, although I was pretty sure no one knew what he was talking about, least of all himself.

I said, "How about a pinkie pact?"

"Yes! A pinkie pact," shouted Anthony.

Tammy nodded, too, and we all held our pinkies over the slightly sticky table. We interlocked them. Theirs were warm. Mine, not so much.

"Pinkie swear," I said.

"Pinkie swear," they said together.

"To keep our secrets to ourselves."

They both nodded solemnly, and we unhooked our pinkies and Anthony was about to go back to his ice cream when he paused and said, "Tammy can really read my thoughts?"

"Yup," she said.

"That is so weird."

"No weirder than you being half vampire."

"I'm not half vampire. I'm just strong like a vampire. Like Mom."

"That's the half part, buttface."

"You're the buttface, buttface."

"You can't say buttface twice, buttface."

"You just did!"

I rolled my eyes and checked my watch. They had gotten along for all of two hours.

*Better than nothing.*

# 39.

The Pacific Ocean at sunset.

It was beautiful. Expansive. Tinged with so much color that one's soul sang. Even souls trapped in immortal bodies.

As I drove north along the Pacific Coast Highway toward Malibu, I realized that today was the first day that Kingsley had not tried to call me or text me. I had always kept Kingsley at arm's length. I had done so for a number of reasons, and one of them was because I suspected he would do something like this. The man was an infamous womanizer.

Maybe I had been too cautious with him. Maybe I had shut him out of my heart for too long. Maybe I had made it easy for him to be with another woman.

*To fuck another woman.*

I was pressing hard on the gas again, too hard. I was whipping past other cars at an alarming rate. I eased up and unclenched my grip on the steering wheel.

According to Kingsley, he had been ready for a relationship. He had been ready to settle down, to explore something serious. I hadn't been. I was dealing with a lot of hurt and had no business starting anything new with Kingsley. But he had been persistent, and sexy as hell . . . and unlike anything I had seen before.

But a tiger didn't change his stripes.

Granted, this tiger—or wolf—had a little help from above. Namely from my guardian angel who had set Kingsley up. And Kingsley, being the dog that he was, fell for it hook, line, and sinker.

*Bastard.*

Maybe I should thank Ishmael for showing me Kingsley's true colors. Then again, maybe I should tell Ishmael to go to hell, since he'd caused this mess in the first place.

*But didn't he give you immortality?* a voice inside me asked. *And the gift of flight? And great strength?*

Had that been me asking those questions, or the thing inside me? I didn't know. Still, they were valid questions.

So I thought about them as I drove on. Ishmael had acted out of love and selfishness. Tainted love. Ishmael had put me in unparalleled danger. He had risked my life . . .

He had risked his own salvation for love. His love for me.

He had risked everything.

For me.

I thought about that . . . and I continued thinking about that even as I pulled up to Andre Fine's Malibu beach home.

# 40.

The house was gated and beautiful.

It was also difficult to find for anyone who wasn't an ace private investigator. Andre Fine wasn't showing up in my basic records searches. No surprise there. Many celebrity-types were hard to find. Often their properties and homes were in the names of their accountants or managers or other family members. In Andre Fine's case, the home was under a sister's name. It was a nice precaution to keep people like me from looking them up.

Except most private investigators didn't have the federal government's massive resources at their disposal. Or an ex-partner who owed his love life to them.

I wasn't here to interview Andre Fine. I wasn't here hoping he would see me. I suspected there was one way—and one way only—to get a confession from him.

For now, I waited down the street in my minivan, where I hoped to attract little or no attention. Generally, a woman sitting alone in a minivan on a quiet street attracted little attention. A man in a minivan would warrant a call to the police.

*Sometimes it's good to be me.*

*Or a woman.*

As I waited and watched, I reflected on the fact that tonight was a big night in the Moon household. After all, tonight was the first night that Tammy and Anthony would watch themselves. Without a babysitter.

Tammy was proving to be surprisingly mature, and Anthony was already stronger than most men. My sister, of course, was on high alert, with her phone nearby. Forty minutes into my surveillance, my text message alert chimed.

I glanced at the phone, my heart immediately racing. Was there something wrong at home? If so, why would they text and not call? I grabbed my cell and swiped it on.

A single message from Tammy: *Ant's being a jerk.*

I frowned and dashed off a text: *Don't call him Ant. You know he doesn't like that. And kindly turn your TV off for one hour.*

*But why?* she wrote back almost instantaneously.

*For calling your brother a jerk.*

*But Mom!!*

Another text came through, this one from Anthony's cell phone: *Fanny's being mean.*

*Don't call your sister Fanny. No TV for the two of you tonight.*

*Not fair!*

*You're mean.*

*This sucks.*

*Anthony's feet smell.*

*Tammy's breath smells. So do her armpits.*

*My armpits do not smell. I'm a girl!*

How I got into their loop of name calling, I didn't know. But they continued like this for the next few minutes . . . all while I shook my head sadly. Finally, I put a quick call in for my sister, who told me she was on her way over. I checked the time. My kids had watched themselves for all of two hours.

*Again, better than nothing.*

. . .

An hour later, a convertible BMW with its top down came up behind me. It was silver and sleek and probably more expensive than my house in Fullerton. Seated in the driver's seat was none other than Andre Fine. A beautiful blond was in the passenger's seat next to him. Both were laughing as they drove past me. Neither glanced at me. Just another perfect day in Malibu.

He turned into his driveway, waited a moment for his electric fence to swing open, then continued on, disappearing behind a long row of thick hedges.

I waited another half hour, then stepped out of my minivan.

# 41.

The gate was six feet high, made of wrought iron that was curled into vines that culminated into spikes.

As far as I was aware, there weren't any security cameras. And if there were, I wasn't worried. Since I wasn't wearing make-up tonight, anyone reviewing the footage would seriously question their sanity, or the equipment. They would see moving clothing, and not much else.

*Yup, I'm a weirdo.*

I glanced up and down the street, saw that I was alone, gripped one of the iron spikes, and jumped. I was up and over in a single leap, landing lightly on the other side.

There were no guard dogs, although a fat white cat skittered off past the BMW and clawed its way over a side fence. I decided to follow, this time hurdling the side gate in a single bound, no hands needed. I cleared it by a foot or two, and marveled again at my own athletic prowess. I wondered how I would fare in the Olympics.

Maybe Michael Phelps was really a vampire.

*Or a mer-man.*

Once in the backyard and away from prying eyes, I scanned the side of the house, looking for my opening. No, I wasn't against breaking a window or smashing through a door, but if there was another opening, I would take it.

The house was Spanish colonial and epic. The plastered walls were smooth and tan, and I was beginning to wonder just how much a karate champion made. There, on the third floor, was a wide veranda with an open French door.

I gauged the jump . . . and realized it might be too high for even me. Thirty feet was pushing the limits of what I could do until I spotted a drainage pipe snaking down near the balcony.

*Good enough.*

I gathered myself, took a breath or two, then leaped as high as I could. At just over twenty feet up, I grabbed the drainage pipe and used it to catapult myself the remaining ten feet, where I cleared the balcony railing and landed smoothly on the deck.

The balcony reminded me of a particular crime lord's balcony out in Orange County. Same beautiful construction. Stone columns. Marble railings. Epic view of the Pacific Ocean. At the time, the crime lord's night had not gone very well. In fact, he'd ended up dead. We'd see how Andre Fine would fare.

There was a sound behind me. A woman's voice. Humming.

I turned in time to see the same blond woman I had seen in the passenger seat emerge from the bathroom. She was fully naked and surgically enhanced. She was working a towel through her wet hair when she saw me. Her mouth opened to scream.

I was moving. Fast.

Just as a strangled cry escaped her lips, my hand clamped around her mouth. My other hand grabbed her around her waist and now, I was dragging her quickly across the polished wooden floor and into a walk-in closet. I threw her inside and shut the door, but before I did, I saw way too much jiggling.

Far, far too much.

There was a heavy, antique dresser along the nearby wall, and I wasted no time putting a shoulder into it. Heavy was right. It took me a few seconds to move it into place in front of the closet, cleanly knocking off the door handle in the process.

The woman inside found her lungs and let loose with the mother of all wails. Andre Fine, looking cut and chiseled and very fine himself, emerged out of the bathroom with a toothbrush dripping from his mouth.

"Jill?" he mumbled around the brush.

"She's presently indisposed," I said, "but still very jiggly, which, I'm sure, is how you like her."

He spun at the sound of my voice, the toothbrush flung out of his mouth, splattering foam across the wooden floor. He ignored the toothbrush. I figured I would, too. Instead, he stared at me and was no doubt doing his best to process what he was seeing. Instead of his bodacious and very naked girlfriend, he was looking at a spunky, dark-haired vampire with lots of attitude.

His eyes next went from me to his freshly relocated dresser now standing guard in front of his closet, a closet from which muffled cries and screams and banging could be heard. Andre Fine's face went through a number of emotions then, the most prevalent being disbelief and shock.

I get that a lot these days.

Andre was a tad under six feet but held himself well. Like a fighter. He balanced easily on the balls of his feet. His body was extremely muscular. His six-pack undulated with each breath. His aura was a vibrant green, flashing with wild energy around him. The faster the energy, the more likely he was to spring into action. More muffled shouts came from the closet.

"What's going on?" he said.

"We're going to talk," I said.

He scanned the room, tilting his head a little, listening hard. He was someone who trusted his senses, his instincts. I could see that. That was probably why he was such a good fighter. Except now the information that was being returned to him had to be a tad confusing. A woman alone. A house broken into. His jiggly girlfriend was imprisoned in a closet, a closet which was now barred by his heavy dresser.

"Who's here with you?" he asked.

"Just little ole me."

Without taking his eyes off me, he nodded toward the blocked closet. "Who moved that dresser?"

"That would be me."

He stared at me for another two seconds. "I'm calling the police," he decided.

"No, you're not."

"Do you have a gun?"

"No."

This time he actually shook his head, no doubt trying to clear it. "How did you get in?"

I grinned and pointed at the balcony. I grinned because his robe had fallen open and I could see his wahoo. Not very impressive. Then again, I had been dating the hulking Kingsley.

"Your weiner's showing," I said.

He ignored me. "Why are you here? What do you want?"

"We're going to talk about Caesar Marquez. And you're going to put your little wee-wee away."

He did so, absently, tying off his robe.

"You're here alone?" he said, clearly confused by this notion.

"Yes."

"Do you have any idea who I am?"

"Yes. You're Andre Fine. Five-time karate champion and, according to some, an expert at *dim mak*. Or the touch of death."

He shook his head some more and walked out into the middle of his room. He turned and faced me. "And you broke into my house?"

"Technically, I didn't break anything. Think of it more as *appeared*. I appeared in your house."

"You have a lot of balls."

"I have a lot of something."

He stared some more and the energy around him crackled, picking up. His bright green aura turned brighter. Added to the mix were some hot pinks and reds.

"Who do you work for?" he asked.

I shook my head and walked toward him. "New rule. I ask the questions from now on."

He watched me closely, eyes narrowing. He was also slowly getting into a fighter's stance, perhaps unconsciously. Jill screamed again from inside the closet, banging against the sturdy door.

I stopped a few feet from him. "You're confused as hell, aren't you? Poor guy. A woman comes here. Rearranges the place. Makes your big-boobed girlfriend disappear. Stands here alone, unarmed and unafraid. Confusing as hell, I imagine."

His eyes continued to narrow, even as he continued lowering into a fighting stance.

"Makes you want to do what you do best, huh?" I said. "To fight?"

He'd had enough. He lashed out with a straight punch that was much faster than I had anticipated.

# 42.

But he wasn't fast enough.

I tilted my head to the right just as his punch *whooshed* past my ear. His hand snapped back immediately and he looked at me comically, blinking rapidly. He hadn't expected to miss. He had expected, no doubt, to knock me out cold.

A woman. Nice guy.

He stepped back, cracked his neck a little and did a little dance to loosen up his limbs. His little pecker poked out again, curious.

I didn't move. I didn't answer. I didn't get into a fighter's stance. I said, "During an exhibition fight two weeks before Caesar Marquez's death in the ring, you delivered what many thought was a cheap shot."

Andre said nothing. With his aura crackling a neon green, he lashed out again. This time I didn't bother moving my head; instead, I brushed off the punch with a swipe of my hand. My counter-block had been fast. Supernaturally fast, and it sent Andre's forward momentum off to the side, where he stumbled a little, but quickly regained his balance.

"It was supposed to be an exhibition," I said, watching him. "I called the event organizers. No live punches. Just light stuff. Easy-to-block stuff. Entertain the crowd. Great photo ops. Three rounds of laughter and fun and good times."

Andre was bouncing on his feet now, bouncing and kind of circling me, too. There was no confusion on his face. Just grim determination. I had seen the same look in many of his YouTube videos. He was treating me like an opponent. I felt honored.

"But in the last twenty seconds of the third round, you punched Caesar Marquez. Hard. For no apparent reason, and against protocol. Some called it a cheap shot. I call it something else."

Andre Fine turned into a cornered wild cat, unleashing a ferocious onslaught of kicks and punches and spinning jumps, lashing out with elbows and knees and fists and feet. It was a pretty display. I had seen him unleash similar onslaughts against his opponents during his many filmed matches. During those matches, one or more of the punches or kicks would land home, sending his opponent to the mat, and making a winner out of Andre Fine. A five-time champion, in fact.

But here in the spacious area between the foot of his bed and his adjoining bathroom, the area where his big dresser had sat but was now conveniently moved across the room, I blocked punch after punch, kick after kick. Sometimes, I didn't block, but simply moved my head a fraction of an inch. At one point he tried a helluva fancy kick, jack-knifing his body splendidly, swinging his foot around so fast that, had I been mortal, I was certain my jaw would have been broken. I wasn't mortal though, so I saw the kick coming a mile away. Instead, I caught his ankle and spun him around like a ballerina.

We did this dance a few more minutes until I finally found the opening I was looking for, and delivered a straight punch. Nothing fancy. Just a straight shot delivered from shoulder height, and hard enough to send him stumbling backwards where he collided into his footboard, which he held onto briefly, before sinking down to the floor.

I walked over to him, knelt down, lifted his chin with my finger, and said, "Now, we're going to talk."

# 43.

We were sitting on his balcony.

Jiggly Jill was long gone. It turned out that Jill wasn't much of a girlfriend. She had been someone he'd picked up tonight at a party. I doubted she would go to the police. Truth was, she hadn't a clue what had happened to her or what was going on, and just before she left, just as she was pulling on her clothes, I gave her a very strong suggestion to *not* go to the police.

She merely nodded, grabbed her stuff, gave Andre one last, fearful look, and headed out front to wait for her taxi.

"Don't look so sad," I said. "There's more where she came from."

Andre was presently pressing a bag of frozen peas to his right eye and alternately smoking. It was multi-tasking at its best. I suspected the cigarette might be accelerating the rate at which the bag of peas was melting, but decided to keep my hypothesis to myself.

When we listened to a car door open and heard what we both assumed was the taxi speeding off, Andre ground out his cigarette and looked at me.

"Who the fuck are you?"

"A private investigator."

He blinked. "You're kidding."

"Nope."

"Where did you learn to fight like that?"

I shook my head and motioned to the pack of cigarettes. He reached down and shook one out for me. I plucked it out deftly. He next offered me a light and I leaned into it and inhaled. I exhaled a churning plume of blue-gray smoke, and said, "If I told you, I would have to kill you."

"Fine," he said. "I've never come across someone like you."

"And I doubt you ever will again."

He studied with his free eye; the other being, of course, hidden behind a melting bag of Green Giant peas. "I believe it."

I had a thought, and wondered just how far I could go with this mind-control business. I waited until he caught my eye with his one good eye, and said, "I will tell you what I am, but when I leave your house, you will forget it completely. Understood?"

He looked at me—and looked at me some more—and finally, his one good eye went blank. He nodded. My suggestion had sunk home. A moment later, the dazed look disappeared, and he looked at me again as he had a moment or two before: with confusion and maybe a little awe.

"I'm not human," I said. "Not really. I'm something else. Some call me a vampire."

He lowered the bag of peas. His other eye was nearly swollen shut. I saw it working behind all the puffy folds, trying to see through. "You're serious?"

"Deadly."

"And that explains why you're so fast?"

"Yes."

"And strong?"

"Yes."

He had witnessed my skills firsthand, had seen me doing things he had never seen another human do. It wasn't hard for him to accept that I was perhaps something different.

"But I thought vampires were, you know, only in books."

"A form of them are, yes."

He was about to ask me another question and I shook my head. "We're not here about me, Andre. Do you understand?"

He nodded again, resigned. He returned the peas to his swollen eye and sat back a little in his chair.

I said, "When did you learn the *dim mak?*"

"Years ago. From a master in Japan."

"Have you used it before?"

He brought his cigarette to his lips. "Can't vampires read minds or something?"

"Often."

"So it would do me little good to lie."

"Little good."

"And what will you do with this information?"

"I haven't decided yet."

"Will you go to the police?"

"Maybe. But I doubt they'll believe me."

He chuckled lightly. "True."

Andre Fine was thirty-six years old and well spoken, but I sensed an urban roll to his words. No surprise there, since he had grown up in New Jersey. I knew he had a long list of priors, some of them violent. He had spent six years of his life in various prisons. He was a street fighter—no doubt, a natural fighter—one who had honed his skill into something deadly.

As I sat there looking at him, I suddenly knew why he did what he did. And how he could afford such a lifestyle. Whether it was a psychic hit or not, I didn't know. But I suddenly knew the truth.

"You're a hired killer," I said.

He glanced at me and shook his head and smiled. "You're good, lady."

I waited. He waited. I knew his every instinct was rebelling against talking to me, but I knew he would, even without my prodding.

"Yes, I am. Of sorts."

"What does that mean?"

"It means I can't always guarantee death. Some survive the *dim mak*." He shrugged. "Others don't."

"Caesar Marquez was one of those who didn't."

He shrugged again. The sign of a true killer. Nonchalance about life and death. Would I ever be that way? God, I hoped not.

"So, people hire you to kill people?" I asked.

"That's how it works, lady."

"Only you can't guarantee death."

He nodded. "It's impossible to guarantee death."

"The victim dies two weeks later," I said, "so no one expects foul play."

He grinned at me, his cigarette dangling from his lower lip. "That's the beauty of it, lady."

"Your hands are registered as lethal weapons, are they not?"

"They are. So, you're really a vampire?"

"I really am."

"Jesus."

"He's not a vampire, as far as I'm aware. Give me your hands."

He did, hesitantly, setting aside the peas. I wasn't compelling him to do what I wanted, but I think he thought I was, and that was good enough. I took his hands and instantly had image after image of bar fights and street fights and back alley brawls. In all of them, Andre was wearing a hood and shades. In disguise.

"So, you often pick fights with your unsuspecting victims."

He shrugged. I'd seen the *dim mak* being delivered, a ferocious blow that left his opponents reeling and dazed.

"You've killed dozens of people," I said.

He shrugged again. "Who's keeping track?"

I stared at him, unblinking. He looked back at me, and promptly blinked and looked away. I sensed his fear, I also sensed he was about to do something stupid.

I said, "Who hired you to kill Caesar Marquez?"

He shook his head. "Sorry, babe. That's where my coopera-
tion ends, vampire or no vampire."

Except as he spoke the words, I saw a brief flash. An image.
It appeared briefly in his thoughts and was gone. I released his
hands and he sat back with the bag of peas.

"You can't prove any of this," he said. "No one would believe
you."

"True," I said. "They wouldn't believe me, but they would
believe you."

He sat there and thought about it and smoked, and high
above us, a low cloud briefly obscured the stars. The wind also
picked up. Somewhere in the Malibu Hills, a coyote howled.

"No one can know about what I've done," he said.

I said nothing and watched him closely. I was certain I hadn't
blinked in many, many minutes. He went on.

"My family is so proud. Everyone is so proud. That feels good.
It feels good knowing that I did my family proud. We were so
poor. The money was so easy." He was babbling now, and I saw
the tears. "Just one punch and I make thousands, tens of thousands. Sometimes, even more."

I watched and waited, catching a brief glimpse of what he
was planning on doing.

"I can't let my family down. I can't. They're so proud."

I said nothing, and watched as Andre Fine, a five-time
champion fighter, was reduced to tears and incomprehensible
mumbling.

I got up and left him there on the balcony.


# 44.


It was two days later, and I was back at the gym in downtown
Los Angeles.

I watched from the shadows as a cadre of boxers did their
best to punch the stuffing out of everything from punching bags
to speed bags to padded mitts.

Seated with me was Allison Lopez. I held her hand in a comforting, reassuring way. I didn't worry about my cold flesh, and,
indeed, she seemed to revel in it. She wanted to meet me here, a

place she always found comforting. Apparently, she loved hearing the sounds of boxing. The scuffing feet, the smell of sweat. It was here, after all, that she had watched Caesar Marquez blossom into a world-class fighter.

Now, we were watching a young flyweight, smaller than me, even, punching the unholy crap out of his trainer's mitts.

"His own brother," she said again, shaking her head.

"Yes," I said.

"But why?"

I looked at the posters that surrounded the gym. Most were of Caesar Marquez. None, as far as I could tell, were of Romero. "My best guess," I said, "was that he was jealous."

"Romero was an accomplished trainer. He was never a boxer."

"Never a boxer *of note*," I corrected. "His official record was nine wins and twenty-three losses."

She blinked and squeezed my hand. "I had no idea."

"Few did. A very unremarkable career."

"But he was so successful as a trainer."

I shook my head. "He was successful at training his successful brothers. Many of whom have had title shots. And Caesar, according to all reports, was the best of the lot."

"Still, why kill him?"

"Maybe he never expected him to die," I said. "Or he never believed he would die."

"He had to believe that some injury would occur."

I nodded. I assumed so, too.

"But how did he know to hire Andre Fine?"

A good question. Two days ago, after meeting with Andre Fine, I had spent the morning doing some investigating. A quick call to Caesar's promoter, Harry, confirmed that Romero had arranged for the exhibition against Andre Fine. This had surprised Harry, as Romero was rarely involved in fight promotions, or even publicity events. And what Harry told me next surprised me, although it shouldn't have: Andre Fine had once been an up-and-coming boxer, until he turned to martial arts.

"Let me guess," I had said to Harry over the phone. "Romero had been his trainer."

"Bingo," said Harry.

I had next called Allison Lopez and asked her the one question that I knew would break this case wide open. She confirmed my suspicions, and a few hours later, I was at the LAPD in downtown Los Angeles, meeting with a homicide investigator named Sanchez. Sanchez was a big guy with wide shoulders, who sported pictures of his UCLA football days on his desk. His desk also sported pictures of a very lovely wife.

Sanchez listened to my story, listened to the wild tales of *dim mak* and of hired killers and touches of death. To his credit, he didn't laugh or joke or even crack a smile. I told him of Romero's connection to Andre Fine, of Romero setting up the exhibition, and who had benefited the most from Caesar's death. Romero. Romero also happened to be the beneficiary of his brother's life insurance.

Detective Sanchez listened to all of this, then told me he would get back to me.

And he did, a few hours later. They had sent a squad car out to Andre Fine's residence in Malibu, where they had found his body swinging from a rope off his third-story balcony. All indications suggested a suicide. I tried to feign shock and horror at hearing this news, but in truth, I had seen it coming.

They next picked up Romero for questioning. To his credit, he admitted to almost everything. Apparently, Romero was looking to get out of the family business. And he also confessed that he planned to fly the coop, all the way to Bermuda.

Now, I caught Allison up on my investigation.

She said, "God, I remember now. Romero practically forced Caesar to do the fight. He claimed it was great exposure and publicity. Caesar didn't want to do it but his brother reminded him it was for charity and finally, Caesar gave in." She shook her head. "Jesus, set up by his own brother. What a bastard. I fucking hate him."

We were quiet. The gym wasn't. It was a cacophony of grunts and thumps and pounding. It sounded sexier than it was.

"Has the insurance money been awarded to Romero?" asked Allison.

I shook my head. "Not yet. These things take some time on the insurance company's part."

"And now?" she said.

"He paid to have his brother attacked. That will nullify the life insurance policy."

"So, what will happen to Romero now?" she asked.

"He'll be charged for soliciting Andre Fine to hurt his brother. There's no way a murder charge will stick, not with something like *dim mak*."

"Maybe he never meant for his brother to die," she said.

"Maybe," I said. "But he was willing to take that chance."

Allison nodded. "His brothers won't look kindly on what he did," she said.

"I don't expect they will," I said. "I have no doubt that Romero's life will be a living hell from this moment on."

She nodded and squeezed my hand and rested her head on my shoulder, and, as she wept silently, I watched two young fighters in the center practice ring exchange a flurry of punches. Both were wearing padded helmets. Both were sweating profusely. More importantly, one of them was bleeding from his lip.

I was dismayed to discover that it was the blood, above all else, that interested me the most.

# 45.

On Wednesday evening at 6:30, Russell Baker and I were jogging at Huntington Beach.

He was shirtless and jaw-droppingly sexy, and it was all I could do not to stare at him as we spoke. Staring at him while we spoke might have led to me running into a trash can. Still, I stole glances, every chance I had. I wondered if it was unethical to lust after my client.

"That's a wild story, Samantha Moon," he said. He always sounded so damn polite when he spoke to me. Too polite. I wanted him to sound . . . interested. This surprised the hell out of me. A few weeks ago, when he'd first appeared at my house, I had not thought of him as anything other than a client. But watching his fights, watching his skills, seeing the compassion in his heart, and his surprisingly peaceful aura for a fighter, well, something shifted.

That, and the fact that Kingsley had broken my heart all over again.

"It's more than a theory," I said.

"How can you be so sure, Samantha?" he said easily, smoothly, confidently.

"Call me Sam," I said.

"Sure thing, Sam," he said and looked at me and winked and something inside me did a sort of flip. My stomach? Or, perhaps, something further down?

I considered how much to tell Russell, and decided to keep things fairly sanitized for now. "Romero hired Andre Fine to deliver the *dim mak* to his brother."

"The *dim mak*," said Russell, shaking his head, "is only a myth."

"Myth or not, Caesar Marquez died two weeks later during your match, from no apparent punch or series of punches from you. Most people I've spoken to—from the referee to Jacky—don't think you hit him hard enough to do any real damage."

Russell shook his head. "I'm not sure if I should feel relieved or discouraged."

"It is what it is," I said, hating myself for using such a generic idiom, but I was finding being in Russell's presence, jogging together at the beach, so damn exciting that I wasn't thinking straight anyway.

"I suppose so," said Russell smoothly. "Caesar was a tough fighter. It was hard to land anything on the guy."

"Could he have been champ?" I asked.

"Maybe," said Russell, and he looked at me and winked again. "'Course, he woulda had to go through me first."

"Of course."

I smiled. He smiled. His stomach muscles undulated. I somehow just missed running into a blue trash can.

Russell said, "You believe there's something to the touch of death?"

"I do."

"Why?"

"The police have gone through Andre Fine's records. There's evidence that he'd been paid for many such hits. For someone who wanted to preserve his legacy in fighting, he sure kept a nice paper trail of his illegal dealings."

"What exactly do you mean by evidence?" asked Russell. He breathed easily, smoothly, his elbows relaxed at his sides.

"Investigators found evidence of nine paid hits, totaling hundreds of thousands of dollars. Seven of the targets are dead."

"Let me guess," said Russell. "They died of unknown brain trauma."

I nodded, although I don't think Russell saw me nod. "Good guess."

"Weird," said Russell.

"Weird is right," I said.

"So, maybe there's something to this *dim mak*."

"Maybe," I said.

Russell looked at me. "Weren't you afraid that he might hurt you?"

"Naw," I said.

"I would have protected you," he said.

And for some reason, that bravado seriously warmed my heart. "That might be the nicest thing anyone's said to me in a while."

He grinned and flashed his perfect teeth. "Except, why do I get the impression you don't need any protecting?"

"Oh, I need *some* protecting," I said.

He slowed down and so did I. He placed his hands on his hips and sucked in some wind, although I got the feeling he wasn't very tired. By my estimate, we had jogged five miles.

"You're not breathing hard," he said.

"Nope."

"You're an interesting chick, Ms. Moon," he said.

"Like I said, call me Sam."

"Would you like to get some dinner, Sam?"

"I thought you would never ask."

# 46.

The evening was warm and the front door was open.

Outside, children played in the cul-de-sac, laughing and sometimes shouting. I heard the rattle of bikes and skateboards and scooters. Not surprisingly, I didn't hear my own kids.

These days, they stayed in with me. Somehow, some way, we had grown closer, and for that, I was pleasantly surprised. My life had gotten easier, too. Feigning eating or stomach-aches and avoiding mirrors had been more stressful than I realized. Now, such worries—at least around my kids—were gone.

*Thank God.*

Yes, they still had many questions: What did I eat? How often did I eat? Did I kill people? How strong was I? Could I kick Daddy's ass? Could I fly? And so on.

I answered the ones that were age-appropriate, although I suspected my own daughter could look far deeper into me than anyone else ever could.

*Dammit.*

*No secrets,* I thought.

School was nearly out. The kids in the neighborhood were ready for summer. Everyone but my kids were ready. They were, at this very moment, playing a game of chess together since they had once again lost their TV, video games, computer games, iPod, iPad, Kindle, Nook, laptop, PS3, and phone privileges. Every now and then Anthony would yell that she was reading his mind and call out my name, in which case I would shout back for Tammy to quit reading her brother's mind.

Normal stuff.

Now, as I was folding laundry and watching the tail end of a new cable show called *Vampire Love Story* about, of all things, MMA fighters who happened to be vampires, a car pulled up in the cul-de-sac. I looked out the window. I didn't know the car, but I sure as hell knew the tall figure who emerged.

It was Fang.

# 47.

We were sitting on my porch, legs and shoulders touching.

I didn't mind touching Fang. I'd always liked Fang, and even now, I considered him one of my very best friends. What he thought about me, I didn't know. Especially not now, not with his mind closed to me.

He had asked if we could talk alone. And with both kids home, *alone* meant sitting outside.

"You're looking lovely as always, Moon Dance," he said.

"Why thank you, Fang," I said.

I couldn't say the same for him. Unsurprisingly, he looked gaunt and pale. Unhealthy, at best. It was unusual for him, as he had always appeared the picture of health and vitality. He'd always been a good-looking guy, even back when I knew him only as my bartender.

Now, I found him sickly-looking. His once-handsome face was now skull-like. His cheeks sunken. Eyes dark hollows. Skin waxy. He was, I suspected, a living corpse. No doubt he was very much in need of a feeding.

"You look, um, well," I said.

He chuckled. "Bullshit. I still haven't had my first feeding, and I've only now recovered enough to function."

I motioned to the Cadillac, where Detective Hanner sat quietly. "I assume she will provide you with your first feeding."

"You assume correctly. We're heading to her place now, and then . . . elsewhere."

I snapped my head around. "Where?"

"I don't know yet. But somewhere not close."

"Why?"

Fang looked down at his hands, which he was opening and closing as if he was getting used to his body all over again. Or perhaps the thing inside him was getting used to Fang's body.

I shuddered.

"She's going to teach me, Sam."

"Teach you what?"

"The one thing you were never taught, what you struggled with daily. What I did my best to help you understand." He looked at me. "She's going to teach me how to be a vampire. Her and others like her."

"What is this place?"

He shook his head. "She didn't tell me much. But it appears to be a sort of coven of vampires."

*Coven of vampires?* I reached out and took his cold hand. Jesus, is that what I felt like?

"She's going to teach you to kill, Fang."

He said nothing, although he did squeeze my hand back.

"She's going to teach you to kill innocent people. How to manipulate them, hurt them, take from them. She's going to teach you how to use them."

"I owe her everything, Moon Dance," he said, and now released my hand. "I owe her my life."

"No, you don't."

He moved away from me, just a few inches, but it might as well have been a few hundred feet. "She gave me the one thing that you wouldn't."

"I never denied you, Fang. I still needed to think about it. It wasn't an easy choice."

"For her, it was."

"Because she's using you, Fang. She's going to train you to be a killer. To kill for her. For them. Don't let them use you."

"They gave me everything I ever wanted—something you never would."

"But that doesn't mean you have to kill for them."

"They never said anything about killing, Moon Dance. They only want to help me, to teach me, to help me adjust."

"For what purpose, Fang?"

"I'll worry about that later, Moon Dance."

We were quiet. Sitting in the driver's seat was Detective Hanner. Her head was back. She appeared to be sleeping, but I suspected she was watching us. Indeed, every now and then I could detect a slight glow from her eyes. The flame within.

"I loved you, Moon Dance."

"Loved?" I said, wincing at the past tense.

"Yes, *loved*. But you didn't return my love. Not really. But most important, you didn't trust me. You feared me on some level. And you denied me the one thing I wanted most in this world."

"Exactly," I said. "So, how could I know if your love for me was real, or an infatuation?"

He turned his head and looked at me sharply. I saw the deep pain, but I also saw something else. Deep resentment. "You knew, Sam. You knew better than anyone how I felt about you."

And with that, he stood. He was about to walk away when he paused and, without looking at me, said, "Goodbye, Moon Dance."

He was about to leave when I reached out and grabbed his cold hand. "Wait."

He waited, still not looking at me.

I held his hand, which hung limp in my own. I debated on how much to say, what to say, and in the end, I could only say, "Goodbye, Fang."

He stood there for a second or two, then released my hand.

And left.

[THE END]

# BOOK 7

# Moon Island

*Vampire for Hire #7*

## DEDICATION

*Dedicated to all the loving parents.*

## ACKNOWLEDGMENTS

*A special thank-you to Sandy Johnston,
Eve Paludan, and Elaine Babich. My first readers
and editors who do such a bang-up job.*

There, on our favorite seat, the silver light of the moon struck a half-reclining figure, snowy white . . . something dark stood behind the seat where the white figure shone, and bent over it. What it was, whether man or beast, I could not tell.

—*Dracula*

# Moon Island

## 1.

"Someone killed my grandfather," said the young lady sitting in my office, "and Detective Sherbet thinks you can help me."

"I pay Detective Sherbet to say that. In donuts, of course. But not the pink ones. He has something against the pink ones."

The young girl, who was maybe twenty-five, grinned and almost clapped. "He was eating a donut when I met with him!"

"No surprise there. He's a good man."

She nodded, still grinning. A very big grin. "I got that impression, except he said there was nothing he could do for me, since my grandfather's death was ruled an accident."

"Nothing he could do," I said, "except recommend me."

"Yes. He said I could trust you and that you would probably help, depending on your caseload."

I looked down at my desktop calendar. There was an appointment in three days to meet with Tammy's teacher . . . and that was it. The 15th was circled, which indicated that I was due a child support payment from Danny. I wasn't holding my breath—and if I had, well, I could hold it for a very long time. So far, in seven months, Danny had given me precisely one payment, and that was because I had physically hauled his ass to the bank.

"I think I can fit you in," I said. "Tell me why you think some-one would want to kill your grandfather?"

"Well, I don't know."

"But you think his death is suspicious."

"Well, yes."

"When did he die?"

"A year ago."

"His death was ruled an accident?" I asked, making notes on a notepad in front of me.

"Yes."

"How did your grandfather pass away, if I may ask?"

"He was found dead in his pool."

"I'm sorry to hear that."

The young lady nodded. She reminded me of myself. Short, petite, curvy, dark hair. And unless she drank blood and hung out with other creatures of the night, that's where the resem-blance ended. Her name was Tara Thurman. I seemed to have heard her name from somewhere, although I couldn't place it now.

"Where did your grandfather live?" I asked.

"On an island."

"An island?"

"Yes."

"Catalina?" I asked, which was really the only habitable island off the coast of Southern California.

"No. It's in Washington State."

"I didn't know there were islands in Washington."

"There are dozens of them."

I nodded, and wondered if I had ever actually looked at a map of Washington. I didn't think so. Then again, geography was never my strong suit. Catching bad guys, now, that was a different story entirely.

"Lots of people live on the islands," she went on. "Except for my grandfather's island."

"What do you mean?"

"It's a private island. His is the only house, along with a few guest bungalows."

I thought it was time for that map. I asked her to step around my desk and show me on Google Earth where he lived. She did, leaning in next to me, smelling of perfume that I didn't recognize. She had me scroll above Seattle and—son-of-a-bitch—there were various chains of islands scattered up there. No doubt the last ice age had had something to do with that, but I knew as much about ice ages as I did about maps of Washington State.

Next, she took over control of the mouse and positioned it over a speck of land above an island called Whidbey, and near another island called Lopez Island.

"I don't see it," I said.

"Hang on." She magnified the page and soon, the very small speck of land became much bigger than a speck. As it took shape, the name of the island appeared on the screen.

I looked at Tara. "You're kidding."

"About the name? No, that's what it's called."

"Skull Island?"

"Yes. I kinda like it. I used to love going there as a kid, especially telling my friends that my grandfather lived on an island called 'Skull Island.'"

"Why is it called Skull Island?"

"There was a shipwreck there a hundred or so years ago. One person died, I think. Not to mention we've unearthed a Native American burial ground. The island, I think, must have been the scene of a horrendous battle. My family has found dozens of graves."

"Sounds . . . creepy."

"I guess so," said Tara. "But my grandfather's home is on the other side of the island."

"Not on an Indian burial ground, I hope."

"No," she said, smiling oddly. She seemed to smile at me oddly, and often. A big smile that seemed to painfully stretch her lips. "But we do have the family mausoleum nearby."

"Excuse me?" I asked.

"The family mausoleum. The island has been in my family for nearly a century, and, well, we're all buried in the mausoleum."

"I see," I said, although I wasn't certain I did. Private islands and family mausoleums reeked of a lot of money. If I wasn't so scrupulous, my daily rates might have just increased.

Damn morals.

Tara slipped back to her seat across from my desk. As she did so, I studied her aura. It had bright yellows and greens, mixed with a pulsating thread of darkness that could have been anything. I suspected that it indicated grief.

I said, "You loved your grandfather."

She nodded and looked away. She tried to speak but instead tears suddenly burst from her eyes. I snapped out a tissue from the box on my desk, and handed it to her. She dabbed her eyes and looked away. Finally, when she'd gotten control of herself, she said, "Yes. He was so much more than a grandfather, you know? My best friend. Always there for me."

As she spoke, the dark threads of vapor that wound through her aura bulged slightly, expanding, engorging. Her grief, I suspected, ran deep.

"Do you live in Southern California?" I asked.

"Yes."

"Have you spoken to the police in Washington State?"

"No. Not yet."

"Why not use a private eye in Washington State?"

"Because Detective Sherbet recommended you."

"How do you know Sherbet?"

"He's a friend of a friend. I was told he was someone who could help."

I nodded. Something about her story wasn't jiving. And perhaps more interesting, my inner alarm began to gently ring just inside my ear. I said, "Why do you think someone killed your grandfather?"

"Because he was very rich."

"That's a reason," I said. "But that's not enough for me to take this case and to take your money. Who was there when he died?"

"We were all there."

"Who's we?"

"The entire family. We use his house and island for our annual reunion."

"You said he died a year ago."

"Right," she said, nodding. "It's coming up again. The family reunion. This weekend, in fact. And I want you to come with me."

# 2.

My sister and I were jogging along the boardwalk at Huntington Beach. It was midday, Saturday. My kids and her kids were with her husband at Disneyland. I wondered what her husband did to deserve such cruel and unusual punishment. I said as much to Mary Lou.

"Oh, he loves it. He's a big kid himself, you know."

"Does your husband know about me?" I asked suddenly.

Mary Lou shot me a quick look. We were both dressed in workout pants and tank tops. We both *swished* as we ran. Mary Lou's expansive upper half bounced furiously, despite her tight sports bra. Her crazily bouncing chest reminded me of two cats trying to escape a paper bag.

"Of course not," she said. "I haven't told anyone."

I nodded and frowned. I had gotten a sudden hit of her husband isolating my kids to ask them questions about me. Then again, *you* try living with a secret that could ruin you and see how suspicious you might become. A husband taking not only his own kids—but mine as well—raised some questions.

"Does he suspect anything?" I asked.

"No."

"Has he ever mentioned me?"

"Mentioned you how?"

"In a way that might make it seem like he was digging for information."

"Nothing that I can remember. C'mon, Sam. He's just doing something nice for us so that we can spend the day together. It's been so long since we could just be sisters and nothing more. And now we can spend *days* together. Glorious days. Not just nights. Okay?"

I nodded. "Okay."

But there was something here. Unfortunately, I couldn't read family members, although I could read their auras. I felt guilty as hell searching my own sister's aura to see if she was telling me the truth, but that's exactly what I did as we spoke. The verdict: I *thought* she was telling me the truth. Something suspicious had passed through her aura as she answered my questions. A ripple of sorts. What that ripple meant, I didn't know. Reading auras was still new to me. Having psychic abilities was still new to me. Being a blood-sucking fiend . . . not so new to me.

I let it go. For now.

Mary Lou and I continued along the boardwalk at a steady clip. She was huffing and puffing. I don't huff or puff, although Kingsley might blow your house down. The big bad wolf that he was. Granted, I was much weaker during the day, but not so weak that I would need to stop jogging.

It was late spring and the days were growing warmer, but not so much by the beach. Mary Lou and I didn't live by the beach. We lived about ten miles inland. So a trip to the beach took planning and driving. Therefore, we planned and we drove. I probably would have preferred to sleep—okay, I most definitely would have preferred to sleep—but I could tell my sister needed some Sam time.

Hey, I was nothing if not an awesome sister.

Now Mary Lou's boobs seemed to be the main attraction on the beach. One guy stared at them for so long that he just missed running into a trash can. Mary Lou and I giggled.

These days, I could continue jogging into infinity. I was pretty sure my body didn't need to jog, that I didn't need exercise. I was pretty sure my body was a self-sustaining machine. But jogging felt . . . normal. It reminded me that I wasn't very far removed from the human species. I mean, I still looked human. I mostly acted human.

*Mostly.*

*I am human,* I thought. *Just . . . different.*

*Yeah, different.*

As we jogged, I told Mary Lou about my business trip this weekend, and that I would need her to watch the kids for a few days.

"They have islands in Washington?" she asked.

"That's the rumor."

"Sounds far," she said. "And cold."

"I think you and I need to buy an atlas. Or get out more."

She waved her hand at the sunny beaches. "And leave this? No thanks. Tell me about your case."

I did, easily and smoothly—and never sounded winded. Speaking as if I were sitting across from my sister at a Starbucks. Sipping water, of course. Always water.

When I finished, Mary Lou said, "Sounds dangerous. I mean, there might be a killer among them."

"Or not," I said. "My client could be delusional. The police already ruled it an accident."

"The island is isolated, right?"

I thought about that, nodding. "I think so, yeah. There's a ferry service to the island, I think."

"So, if it was isolated, perhaps the evidence had been well tampered with far before the police could come out."

"Good point," I said.

"And how long would it have taken the police to get there?"

"Another good point."

"So perhaps their assessment was wrong, or based on false information."

I looked at my sister. "You would make a good investigator."

"But a terrible vampire," she said.

I winced a little and looked around. We were alone on this segment of the boardwalk. Our shadows stretched before us. Mary Lou's shadow involved a lot of bouncing.

"Who says I'm a vampire?" I said.

She looked at me. "Still in denial, Sam? What else could you be?"

"I don't like that word, 'vampire.' I'm just . . . different."

She shook her head. "Whether you like that word or not, I'm pretty sure you're one, Sam. I mean, I never believed in them until you got attacked . . . but I sure as hell do now."

"Fine," I said. "So, why would you be a bad you-know-what?" I still couldn't say the word.

"Vampire?" she said again.

I cringed again.

She laughed and said, "Well, it's not that I would be a bad vampire. I would be a *bad* vampire, if you catch my drift."

Now I laughed. "Like an evil vampire?"

"Sure," said my sister. "I mean you can't go to hell, because you don't die. You can be as evil as you want. I think I would probably kill off most men."

"Most?"

"I would leave the pretty ones."

"Oh, brother," I said.

# 3.

We were on our third date.

Russell Baker was twenty-four and a professional boxer. I wasn't twenty-four. In fact, according to my driver's license, I was thirty-five. Thanks to the vampire in me, literally, I looked twenty-eight and possibly younger.

We were at Roy's Restaurant in Anaheim, a bustling place that consisted mostly of Disneyland tourist spillovers. Still, a nice restaurant with great ambiance and just enough background noise to make it seem like we were alone.

Russell Baker was dressed in tight gray jeans and wore a tight black Ralph Lauren shirt open wide at the collar, revealing some of his muscled upper chest. He wore his own type of medallion. It was a golden scorpion inside a golden disk, in homage to his birth sign. I'd heard about Scorpios. I've heard they could be the best lovers. The thought, perhaps not surprisingly, sent a shiver through me.

"You okay?" asked Russell.

"Just a little cold," I said, which was a half-truth. I was always cold. Always.

Russell seemed especially perceptive of me, and I was beginning to suspect the reason why. By our second date, I was certain he was picking up stray thoughts of mine here and there. Faster than what usually happens with most people who get close to me. After all, it had taken Detective Sherbet nearly a half a year to get to this point. Then again, Russell and I were getting close, fast.

Russell stood and plucked his light suede jacket from the back of his chair and came around the table and slipped it over my shoulders. He sat opposite me again, smooth as a jungle cat.

"Better?" he asked.

His jacket smelled of good cologne and of him, too. Essence of Russell. For me, it was a wonderfully exhilarating scent.

Despite the jacket doing nothing for me, I said, "Yes, much better." Which, again, was a half-truth. I loved his scent, and I loved his concern for me.

For me, dinner dates were a challenge. Salads were great to order for someone like me. They scattered nicely about the plate and gave the impression and appearance that I was eating my food. The wadded-up napkin in my hand contained half-masticated lettuce and carrots and beets. Anytime Russell headed for the bathroom, or checked his cell, or called over the waiter, that wadded-up napkin was gonna disappear into my purse. Lickety-split.

And so it went with me. A creature of the night—yes, a vampire, I supposed—attempting to date in the real world. Cold to the touch, unable to actually eat real food, and giving away her thoughts as if they were free.

"You're not like other girls I've dated, Sam," said Russell.

"Oh?" I wasn't exactly delighted to hear this. Lord knew I'd tried to be just like the other girls. Perhaps too hard.

And once again, I thought, *Geez, what am I doing?*

It was so much easier to be a single mom. Kingsley Fulcrum had quit calling—or trying to win me back—although I suspected I hadn't heard the last of him. Fang was gone, having disappeared with Detective Hanner, a fellow freak of the night herself. To where, I didn't know. According to Sherbet, Hanner had requested a three-month leave from the Fullerton Police Department.

Three months to turn Fang into a monster.

That thought alone turned my stomach. Then again, it could have been that stray bit of vinaigrette dressing escaping down the back of my throat. Yeah, that was gonna cause me some cramps later.

Russell was looking at me, frowning. "Who's Fang?"

My heart leaped. "Pardon?"

"You said something about a fang. I'm sorry, I'm lost."

"Oh, right," I said, thinking fast. I hadn't said anything about Fang, of course. Russell had officially picked up on my thoughts, unbeknownst to him. I said, "Oh no, I said 'dang.' As in dang this salad is good."

"You said dang and not fang?"

"Uh-huh," I said, looking away and shielding my thoughts. Too early to shield my thoughts from Russell. We were connecting—and deeply.

"Could have sworn you said something else."

"Well, it's kind of loud in here. So, you were saying I was different than the other girls?" I said, praying like hell we would change the subject.

That is, of course, if God heard my prayers.

"Right," he said, looking at me sideways a little. He then looked down at his food and played with his fork a little. Russell had very big hands, and heavily scarred knuckles. He had already told me he'd spent a childhood fighting on the streets of Long Beach. Finally, he said, "I guess it's because I feel like I can open up to you. Tell you anything."

"Is that a good thing?" I asked.

He reached across the table and took my hand. And to his credit, he didn't flinch at the cold. In fact, he never flinched at the cold. "A very good thing."

As he continued holding my hand and looking into my eyes, I think something inside me just might have melted.

I hated when that happened.

# 4.

The kids were at Mary Lou's and I was packing for my weekend trip when my cell rang.

"You're going on a trip," said the voice on the other end when I picked up.

I dropped my folded tank top in the suitcase. "How the devil did you know that?"

"I've been feeling it all day," said Allison. "A strong feeling that you were going away and that you needed me. I'm kinda psychic, you know. Not the full-blown type, but I think spending time with all of you vampires has sort of rubbed off on me."

I had met Allison on my last case, the girlfriend of another boxer. A murdered boxer. Allison and I had shared a . . . *moment.* A highly unusually moment.

*Two moments, in fact,* I thought.

She and I had connected, or bonded instantly. She had quickly seen through my façade, having dated a vampire herself. And the next thing I knew, she was allowing me to drink from a wound in her hand. A wound that had quickly healed once I was done drinking.

*My life is so weird.*

We'd talked often since, although we had yet to meet since that case had closed. She had quickly become like an old girlfriend to me. A sister.

A blood sister.

"Yes, I'm going on a trip," I said, now reaching for some jeans in my closet, cradling the phone against my shoulder and ear.

"See? I knew you were going on a trip. I'm coming with you."

"No, you're not."

"Yes, I am, Sam. You need me."

"Need you how?"

"This is a business trip, no?"

"Yes, but—"

"I sense very strongly that you are going to need my help, if you know what I mean."

Actually, I did know what she meant. I stopped reaching for my jeans as I stood there in front of my open closet. A closet, I might add, that was quickly filling up with clothes. Now that I could actually go into the light of day, I needed a whole new wardrobe, right? Like that tank top I had just dropped in the suitcase. Many cute tank tops, in fact. And shorts. And sandals.

Allison was, of course, referring to fresh human blood—fresh, as in, straight from the source. A living, human source. Such blood energized me unlike anything I'd ever had before. Yes, I'd had human blood—but never hemoglobin straight from a willing source.

And Allison had been very, very willing. Apparently, she loved the experience.

I said, "I don't think my client will allow you to come."

"Say I'm your assistant."

"I doubt she'll—"

"She will, Sam. Trust me. And trust me when I say you will need me. I'm here now at the airport."

I think my mouth dropped. Correction, I know my mouth dropped open. "What airport?"

"LAX. The 4:40 flight. Lucky for me they had one seat left."

"Let me guess . . ." I said.

"Row 17, Seat C."

I glanced down at my ticket next to my suitcase. Row 17, Seat B.

"You're freaking me out," I said.

"I get that a lot," she said. "Now, chop-chop."

And with that, she hung up.

# 5.

I was halfway to LAX, fighting traffic on the 105 Freeway, when a text message came through.

Oprah had a point about not texting and driving. Oprah, as far as I knew, wasn't a vampire with cat-like reflexes and an inner alarm system that alerted her to danger.

I glanced down at my iPhone, and was not very surprised to see that it was Kingsley. Secretly—or perhaps not so secretly—I had hoped it was Fang.

*Jesus, Fang . . . where are you?*

Still, seeing the text from Kingsley warmed my heart a little. The guy was trying soooo hard to be nice. He knew he'd screwed up and screwed up royally. He also knew there was probably a very good chance I would never even see him again.

Still, he kept at it. Kept being sweet. And the big oaf was worming his way back into my life. One sweet text at a time.

*Full moon tonight*, his text read. *Franklin and I are gonna get our freak on.*

I shook my head and texted back: *I don't even want to begin to know what that means, goofball.*

*Hey, I'll take goofball*, he wrote back a few minutes later. *Better than what you've called me in the past.*

*You're still a jerk.*

*I know. And soon I will be a hairy jerk.*

*Just try not to rob any graves tonight*, I wrote, texting rapidly. Supernaturally fast, I might add. *That's really, really gross, by the way.*

Kingsley, as a werewolf, had a taste for corpses. That is, when and if he ever escaped the safe-room his butler Franklin locked him into each full-moon night. A butler who was, of course, so much more than a butler.

*I know,* wrote Kingsley. *What's the deal with that anyway?*

In fact, I knew exactly what the *deal* with that was. Kingsley and I, although two very different creatures of the night, were not so different after all. Each of us harbored what I'd come to understand was a highly evolved dark master, an entity banned from this world, but returning through a loophole, so to speak.

*And we're the loopholes.*

These dark entities gave us our lives—our eternal lives, that is—and existed within us side by side, or, if not side by side, somewhere deep within us.

I shuddered again at the thought.

And so, it was the thing within Kingsley that hungered for the flesh of the dead. And it was the thing within me that hungered for blood.

After a moment, I texted back: *I think we both know what the deal is, Wolfman. Just be a good boy tonight.*

*Will do. :)*

I took in a lot of air, held it in my dead lungs, and released it back into my minivan. I gripped my steering wheel and thought of Kingsley and Russell and Fang . . . and shook my head.

And kept on shaking it nearly all the way to LAX.

# 6.

We were on the plane.

"Are you hungry?" asked Allison.

"Yes, and how did you . . . never mind," I said, recalling her penchant for being weirdly accurate. "Yes, I am."

"You can feed from me here, if you want."

"No, I can wait," I said, embarrassed. "And I don't like the word *feed*."

"Too ghoulish?"

"Too monstrous. Not to mention it sounds like something straight out of an Anne Rice novel."

"What do you prefer?"

"Drink," I said. "I drink. Nothing more, nothing less."

"Touchy subject?" asked Allison, patting my knee condescendingly.

"Touchy life," I said.

She laughed loudly, throwing back her head, drawing attention to us. I ducked my head lower.

"Oops, sorry," said Allison, elbowing me now in the shoulder. "Most of your kind like to keep a low profile."

"My 'kind'?" I said. "Please. And could you say that a little louder?"

"Oh, I definitely could."

I grabbed her and pulled her down to my level.

"You are out of control," I said, but now I was laughing, too.

"Only seemingly, Sammie," she said, giggling, and then growing serious. "Your secret is always safe with me. Always. Except, maybe, when I'm drunk. Kidding! Hey, ouch!"

I had squeezed her forearm perhaps a little harder than I had planned. "Sorry," I said.

"No, you're not," she said, rubbing her arm. "But seriously, Sammie. Your secret is always safe."

"Then quit using words like *feed* and *your kind*. I work . . ." I paused, my voice faltering. For some reason, I was feeling emotional about the subject. "I work . . ." But my voice faltered again.

"You work hard at being normal, Sammie. I know. And when I say these words, I remind you that you're not."

We were both hunched down in our seats. I turned and looked at her. She turned and looked at me. "That was surprisingly perceptive," I said.

"Well, you're not the first . . . *amazing person* I've been around."

I laughed. Allison had been the plaything for a playboy vampire who'd met his demise by the very hunter who had attacked me.

"So now I'm an amazing person?" I said.

She reached out and took my hand. Rather than flinch at the cold, she seemed to relish it, squeezing my hand even tighter and looking deeply into my eyes. "Sammie, I think you are, perhaps, the most amazing of them all."

I looked away and pulled my hand gently back. "You barely know me," I said.

"True, but I see things."

"So you say."

"And you see things, too—and you can do things others cannot."

"Other amazing people?" I said, glancing at her.

She gave me a half smile. A sad smile. "I was once connected to a very powerful vampire, Sam. Or who I had thought to be a powerful vampire. He was not as powerful as you, Sam. Not even close."

· "And you know this, how?"

"I know things, remember?"

I shook my head and we both grew silent as someone walked past us down the narrow aisle. When they were gone, Allison continued, "I've always been very psychic, Sammie. In fact, I used to work at one of those psychic hotlines."

I groaned. "Oh, brother."

"Groan all you want, but I was very good. Maybe some callers thought it was a joke, but when they got on the line with me, they got the real deal." She put her hand on my forearm. "And having spent months supplying myself—giving myself to another, if you know what I mean—only amplified my gift."

I thought about that. So much to learn about myself . . . about what I am, and about how all of this works.

"He turned you into a super psychic," I said.

"But not just him," she said.

I glanced at her. "What do you mean?"

She held my gaze. Allison had big brown eyes. So big that, had I been able to see my own reflection, I would, no doubt, be looking at myself right now. "You, too, Sammie."

"Me, too, what?"

"When you drank from me, Sammie, you sort of re-awakened the psychic in me. And then took it to a whole new level. Which is why I think you might just be more powerful than you-know-who."

I'd heard this before, from another vampire, in fact.

"Let's change the subject," I said. "Do you mind?"

"Anything you want, Sammie."

And we did, and how we got on the subject of the Kardashians, I'll never know. But it was better than talking about me, the world's biggest freak.

The Kardashians, of course, were a whole different level of freaky.

# 7.

Two and half hours later, we landed at Sea-Tac Airport which, apparently, was right dab smack in the middle between Seattle and Tacoma.

"Get it?" said Allison. "Sea-Tac. As in Seattle and Tacoma."

"I get it," I said.

"Am I being annoying?" she asked.

"Not yet," I said sweetly, as we stepped out into the chilled Pacific Northwest air. "But you're getting there."

"Most of my friends say I can be annoying."

"You have honest friends," I said, keeping a straight face.

"That was rude, Samantha Moon." But she laughed anyway.

Almost immediately, a shiny Lexus SUV whipped out of the pack of circling cars and pulled up next to us. I recognized the driver. My client, Tara Thurman.

"Wow," said Allison, peeking through the passenger side window. "She looks just like her mom."

"You know her mom?" I asked as Tara stepped out. I had researched the family and knew that Tara's mother had once been a fairly well-known model, and her father was currently the vice president of the family business. A business which just so happened to be one of the biggest hotel brands in the world. A business started by the great-grandfather nearly a hundred years ago.

"Of course," said Allison. "Everyone knows of her mom. At least, everyone down at the shop."

I wasn't sure which "shop" she was referring to, and before I could ask, Tara was already coming toward us. She certainly did not inherit her mother's stature nor build. Like I said, she was shaped more like me. Short and a little curvy.

Earlier, Tara had agreed to allow Allison to join me as my assistant. I was certain she wouldn't agree, but Allison had seemed confident that Tara would. To my surprise, my client had indeed agreed, telling me that, although these yearly reunions were generally for family, sometimes friends or significant others did join in.

I introduced the two, and we all climbed in. I took the front seat and Allison the back, and as the SUV pulled away, Allison leaned forward through the seats and said, "So, is the Space Needle really a needle?"

"Okay," I said. "*Now* you're being annoying."

. . .

As the 5 Freeway wended and twisted its way through the tree-lined suburbs outside of Seattle, Tara, Allison, and I had a crash course in friendship.

According to Tara, no one was to know that I was a private eye, or that Allison was my assistant. This wasn't a murder investigation. Not officially. This was a family reunion, on a remote island, during which I would pretend to be a friend, although I would be secretly snooping my ass off.

Luckily, I'm damn good at snooping my ass off.

We decided to give me a fake name, too. After all, it wouldn't do having a nosy family member Googling my name and finding my agency's website. So, we decided that being old college chums was best, chums who'd recently met again in Seattle and were only now catching up. Allison was my visiting friend, who got invited along for the weekend getaway.

So, we spent the remainder of the time in the SUV boning up on Tara's college. It turned out she'd gone to UCLA, and graduated with a degree in psychology. I was going to pretend to be a college dropout. Allison pointed out that someone with enough snooping skills could verify that I, in fact, never went to UCLA. So, we decided to give me a very generic name.

Samantha Smith.

In fact, being *Samantha Smith* for a three-day weekend might just be a welcome relief.

*And maybe a little fun.*

Especially as we approached the glittering emerald city, whose skyline matched the beauty of any skyline anywhere, and as we did, I received a text message from my son.

*Tammy's reading my mind again, Mom.*

I sighed and dashed off a quick text to my daughter: *Quit reading your brother's mind, booger butt. And make sure you do your homework.*

# 8.

The drive through Seattle was far too quick.

Admittedly, I wanted to stay and explore. The Space Needle, to Allison's dismay, was not a needle, but an orange-topped, UFO-shaped disk that looked less like a needle and more like a giant alien probe.

Still, the city was brilliantly lit, packed with nice cars, and restaurants seemingly everywhere. I could see why Frasier would want to live here. A light rain was falling, which, from what I understood, was as common as sunshine in Southern California.

*Vampire weather,* I thought.

Soon we were eating up the miles north of Seattle, while Tara and I continued to hash out our fake history together. We created parties we never went to, the names of boys we never met, and classes we never took together. A fake history. An iron-clad history. Allison quizzed us as we drove through a city called Mukilteo—a name I never did seem to pronounce correctly— and drove onto a ferry with service to an island called Whidbey.

"We're in the car," said Allison, sticking her head out the window, "but we're on a boat, too." She sounded perplexed.

"Yes," said Tara, looking at me and giving me a half smile. "A ferry, actually."

"A car on a boat," Allison said again, shaking her head. "What will they think of next?"

"You've never been on a ferry before?" asked Tara.

"I've never been on a *boat* before," said Allison. "Do these ferries ever sink?"

"Often," said Tara.

Allison pulled her head out of the window. Her reddish cheeks had quickly drained to white. "How often do they—wait, you're messing with me."

"Sorry," said Tara, giggling a little from behind the wheel. She winked at me. "I couldn't resist. My bad."

"No worries," said Allison. "I'm a kidder, too. Must run in our family."

"Excuse me?" asked Tara. "Family?"

Allison popped her gum. "Yup. We're like eleven cousins removed."

"Oh, really?" said Tara.

"Yup, I'm also distantly related to Bill Clinton and Barack Obama. Genealogy is a passion of mine."

I rolled my eyes. Tara smiled, uncomfortably.

Allison went back to sticking her head out the window, the way a dog might, as the ferry continued across the Puget Sound. The waves were choppy, but the ferry handled them with aplomb. We were in a long row of cars, many of which were filled with tired-looking men and women, all dressed nice, and all clearly returning home from work on the mainland.

When the ferry docked in a city called Clinton—and once Allison had taken her seat like a good girl—we followed the long line of cars off the ferry and onto the island.

A gorgeous island, no less.

"There's trees everywhere," said Allison. "And I mean some big-ass trees."

I was suitably impressed, as well, and after we stopped at a cute little coffee kiosk—at which I politely declined a cup—we continued north up the island, wending and winding our way through endless trees, stretches of beaches, and luscious farmlands.

The drizzle of rain followed us, but there was no traffic on this island. Just a few well-spaced homes, a few well-spaced cars, endless greenery . . . and a delightful lack of sun.

We passed cities called Freeland and Greenbank and a bigger town called Oak Harbor. Up we went over a majestic bridge called Deception Pass that made even my mouth drop. Allison *oh*ed and *ah*ed, and Tara seemed genuinely pleased to see our stunned responses. The bridge apparently connected one island to another, and arched high above roiling currents.

I felt almost as if I had taken flight, so high were we above the foaming waters below.

The bridge came and went much too quickly for my taste, as we wound our way ever north to another charming town called Anacortes where we parked the SUV and boarded a smaller boat.

Smaller, but not by much.

# 9.

I was standing near the prow, doing my best not to lift my arms and shout that I was the Queen of the World. Or, perhaps more accurately, Queen of the Underworld.

I stood there, holding onto a post, and stared out at the rolling sea. Heavy fog hung low over the water. The sea itself was slate gray and seemingly impenetrable. At the most, I could see down only a few feet. Nothing seemed to exist near the surface. No dolphins nor seals nor killer whales. The Puget Sound seemed devoid of life. Just a vast expanse of churning, dead, gray water, a barrier between islands. A great moat, perhaps.

Which didn't make it any less beautiful. On the contrary, I lived a dozen or so miles from the ocean, so it wasn't often that I found myself bouncing along a fast-moving boat, through a heavy fog, hundreds of feet above the ocean floor.

Tara was sitting with the captain, and Allison was below deck, battling seasickness and failing miserably. Last I heard, she was introducing herself to the tiny metal toilet attached to the main sleeping quarters below deck. The boat itself sported a bedroom, a living room, and a galley. The boat was cozy and was captained by a smallish man with a biggish beard. He could have been Ahab in another life. Or perhaps even the white whale.

With that thought, I thought of Ishmael. No, not the Ishmael from *Moby-Dick*. Ishmael who had been, at one time, my guardian angel. And who was now . . . I didn't know.

An interested suitor? Maybe, maybe not.

I didn't know much, but I did know one thing: *my life was weird*.

Sometimes too weird.

Sometimes I wanted to bury my head in the sand, or leap, say, from this boat, and drift to the ocean floor and exist in silence and peace, with the crabs and bottom feeders. Except I couldn't run away from what I was, or what my children had become. What they had become because of me.

Suddenly, panic and dread and a crushing fear filled me all over again.

*Breathe, Samantha.*

I did so now—slowly, deeply, filling my useless lungs to capacity with air that I didn't need—at least, not in the physical sense. Emotionally, maybe.

As I focused on my breathing, as the cold air flowed in and out of my lungs, in and out of my nostrils, I had the distinct sensation of being out of my body. I hadn't planned to be—who planned that sort of thing, anyway?—and hadn't even expected it. One moment, I was concentrating on keeping calm, focused almost entirely on the process of breathing, and the next . . .

The next, I was . . . elsewhere.

Not literally, for I could hear the roar of the boat's motors, the wind thundering over my ears, the water slapping against the hull. Yes, I could feel and hear and smell, but I was not there. Not in the boat.

Then again, maybe I really was nuts and was sitting in some insane asylum. Maybe the doctors had just given me my latest dose of zone-out meds.

*Do not be so hard on yourself, Samantha Moon.*

Was that my voice? Had I made it up? I wasn't certain. I did know that the sound of the ocean and the boat and the wind seemed to be fading even further away. Although I felt detached from my body—hell, from reality—the voice was, to say the least, a welcome sensation.

*Very good, Samantha Moon.*

The thought was not my own, I was certain of it.

No, not so much a thought as a *voice* whispered just inside my ear. I was very familiar with such telepathic communication . . . but this communication seemed different somehow. It almost seemed to come from inside of me—and around me and through me, all at the same time.

*A good way of looking at our communication, Sam.*

I was also certain I'd heard the voice before, as I'd sat upon a desert ledge, back when I'd let my mind drift and found myself in a deeply meditative state—and in the presence of something very loving.

And seemingly all-knowing.

*All-loving, Samantha Moon.*

I continued holding onto the post as my knees absorbed the rising and falling of the boat. But I wasn't on the ship. No, not really. I was elsewhere. Above my body. In a place nearby but not nearby. I struggled for words, searching for an explanation to where I was. To what was happening to me.

*Let's call it a frequency, Samantha. You are in a higher frequency.*

*I don't understand.*

*You will, someday.*

The boat dipped deeply, no doubt plunging into a trough, but I effortlessly kept my footing, my balance. Even in a deeply meditative state, my uncanny reflexes were working overtime.

In my mind's eye, I saw myself standing before something big. No, not just something big. The biggest. The biggest of all. The Universe, perhaps. There was movement, too. Planets were rotating. No, not just planets. Whole solar systems, galaxies, and universes were rotating. I saw stars being born and destroyed. I saw whole universes collapsing and birthing. The Universe was alive to my eyes, as surely as if I was watching a hive of bees at work.

I was certain that I was watching the Universe from the perspective of something much greater than me.

*You are seeing it through yourself, Samantha.*

*No,* I thought, and felt myself shaking my head back on the boat. *I am seeing it through God. The eyes of God.*

*Correct, Samantha.*

How I saw this, I didn't know, where I was, I didn't know. I seemed outside of space and time, all while standing here on the boat's prow, cutting through the fog and mist and now a light drizzle upon the Puget Sound.

*But you said I was seeing it through my eyes,* I asked the voice in my head. The voice that I was beginning to think was God.

*Correct again.*

*I don't understand.*

*Yes, you do, Samantha.*

Perhaps I did know. I'd heard the voice all my life but had never really understood it. Until now.

*It's because I'm a part of you, too,* I thought.

*Very good, Samantha.*

I was next given a glimpse of something that had never occurred to me before, not until now. *I'm not just a part of you,* I thought, *but you are me.*

*Very good, Sam.*

*I am you, experiencing life.*

*Very true, Samantha. As are all people, all things.*

*But, why?* I asked. *You are God, why experience life through me? I am nothing. I am a blip in the universe. All of us are blips.*

*And what if you had access to the sum total of all blips, Samantha? Billions and billions of blips?*

*I would have access to, well, everything.*

*Indeed, Samantha Moon.*

*Why are you talking to me now?* I asked.

*Because you are much more than a blip, Samantha.*

And now I saw, through another glimpse—or perhaps this was an epiphany—that I was no greater or smaller than others in our world. But because of who I am, or what I was, I had an open channel to God. To the Universe. To the spirit world in general.

*You're talking to me now because I can hear you,* I said.

*No, Sam. I'm talking to you now because you are listening.*

Footsteps slapped behind me, and I snapped back into my body and gasped when I saw the captain swing down below deck. He saw me and nodded and, although I tried to smile back, all I could see were worlds being destroyed.

And worlds being born.

# 10.

"You look like you've seen a ghost," said Allison. "And, for you, that's saying something."

"Gee, thanks," I said.

But the truth was, I had seen a ghost.

*Not a ghost,* I thought. *God.*

I shook my head again. The boat had docked along a float-ing pier. The three crew members were busy securing the vessel, using a system of ropes and, apparently, rubber tires that acted as buffers between the hull and the wooden pier. All of it seemed more complex than I could comprehend. Especially considering my mind—or soul—had been far elsewhere.

To the far edges of the universe, in fact.

*Lordy, my life is weird.*

Allison wasn't looking too swell herself. In fact, she looked, I suspected, as pale as myself. Why I still looked pale these days, I didn't know. After all, thanks to the medallion that seemed to be permanently embedded just beneath my skin, I'd been able to head out into the sun for the past few months now. Glorious months.

*You're pale,* I thought, as I reluctantly accepted the hand of one of the shipmates who helped me across the gangplank, *be-cause you're dead.*

I didn't feel dead, of course. I felt alive. And, when the sun went down, more alive than I'd ever felt in my life. Ever.

Once on the pier, as we followed Tara and a few other passengers—passengers that Tara knew and who were, I sus-pected, relatives—Allison caught up to me.

"Seriously, Sam, what's wrong?" she whispered in my ear. I couldn't help but notice her breath smelled of vomit. Blech. "You look . . . out of it."

"I'll tell you about it later," I said over my shoulder.

She was about to fall back behind me when her eyes suddenly widened. "God?" she said, obviously reading my thoughts—thoughts that I had left open to her. "You talked to God? Seriously?"

"If not, then a heck of an imposter."

"So weird."

"Tell me about it."

And with that, Allison turned her head and just made it to the edge of the pier before she heaved what little remained in her stomach.

• • •

"As you can see, this is a private island," explained Tara Thurman.

She was driving behind a motorcade of Range Rovers. There were three in total, including our own. The road wasn't paved, but it was the next best thing—smooth. Allison seemed to appreciate the smooth part, although she was still looking a little green.

"I feel green," she whispered to me, reading my thoughts.

Our strong connection was surprising even me. I suspected that, coupled with her own psychic intuition, our telepathic link was particularly sensitive, thanks to the exchange in blood.

"You bet your britches," she said.

"Will you quit doing that?" I whispered to her.

"Excuse me?" said Tara from behind the wheel.

"Oh, nothing," I said, mentally pushing Allison out of my thoughts. "You were saying about the island?"

Tara, who was focused on the dirt road and the caravan in front of us, hardly seemed to notice this particular conversation between Allison and me. Instead, she nodded, clearly proud of the island.

"Like I said, the island has been in my family for nearly one hundred years. It was first purchased by my great-grandfather, who built the home. My grandfather inherited it, and spent the last thirty years of his life here. The rest of us have used the island on and off for vacations and getaways and reunions."

I nodded. We were surrounded by massive evergreens, each rising high above the car windows, effectively blocking out the sun, which I was always thankful for. Yes, although I existed somewhat comfortably in the light of day, I always appreciated deep shade.

*Must be the ghoul in me.*

The island itself seemed to be primarily surrounded by cliffs and bluffs. So far, the only sandy beach had been where the boat had docked, where the row of Range Rovers had been waiting.

"Are there any bears on the island?" asked Allison from the back, poking her head between the front seats.

Tara laughed. "No bears or predators of any kind on the island. We have deer and raccoons and squirrels and a few resident seals that prefer the rocks along the north part of the island."

The road shifted inland, cutting through a narrow road that seemed to barely have enough room for the bigger vehicles. Tara drove comfortably, clearly used to this scenic drive. Branches occasionally slapped the fender and roof.

"We have food and supplies shipped daily from the mainland. There's a courier service we use. Not to mention any of us who come over from the mainland bring additional supplies."

"Sounds kinda . . . fun," said Allison.

"Heaven, if you ask me. My grandfather was always so open to all of us. What he had, we had. He held nothing back and always made everyone feel so welcome." As she spoke these words, her lips curled up into that curious smile again.

*So weird,* I thought.

I also couldn't help but notice the sadness in her voice. Her grandfather had been found, of course, face-down in a swimming pool. Allison seemed to detect Tara's tone as well and sat back in her seat. We were somber and quiet for the rest of the drive.

And what a drive it was. Winding roads, beautiful greenery, squirrels and rabbits . . . and then, finally, the road opened into a massive estate.

Where there had once been forest was now, perhaps, the most beautiful home I had ever seen.

"Sweet mama," said Allison.

# 11.

We pulled around a curved, brick, herringbone driveway.

The house, I think, was even bigger than Kingsley's monster of a house—Beast Manor, as I'd come to think of his home, complete with its safe-room.

This house was epic and rambling on a whole other level, and I was fairly certain there was even more of it in the back, too. Tara explained that the design was a Mediterranean-style Spanish Revival. Having minored in architecture in college—with a major in criminal justice—I knew the design well. But seeing it up close, and in such grandeur, was awe-inspiring.

*I could be very comfortable here,* I thought. *A home fit for a king. Even a vampire queen.*

Allison was still *oh*ing and *ah*ing as we stepped out of the Range Rover. I might have *oh*ed, but I certainly hadn't *ah*ed. The house itself was situated on lushly manicured grounds, complete with sumptuous gardens filled, in part, with fresh herbs. I saw everything from sage to rosemary, to mint and thyme. The home's courtyard had a distinctively European flair, with intricate brick and plasterwork. Trees were the overall theme of the home and sprouted from ornate planters situated everywhere. A five-car garage was off to one side. The garage and much of the home's façade was covered in thick ivy.

"I'm in heaven, Sammie," said Allison. "Remind me to thank you again for inviting me to join you."

"I didn't invite you. You insisted."

"And I'm so glad I did."

I shook my head as we each fetched our suitcases from the rear of the vehicle. As we headed up the wide flagstone stairs, I noticed Tara, our host, looking at me. Or, rather, at my suitcase.

"You don't roll your bag?" she asked.

Oops. My bag, I saw, was bigger than both Tara's and Allison's. And both of them were struggling a bit up the steps, rolling and lifting. I had mine in my hand, hefting it without thought or effort. "I like the exercise," I lied. "My trainer would be proud."

Tara smiled as if I had made some sense. Allison snickered behind me. And once we were inside the cavernous home, I acted normal and used my suitcase's own rollers.

The home opened onto two curving staircases with ornate, wrought-iron railings. Polished wood floors stretched seemingly everywhere. A beautiful, round marble table with fresh-cut flowers in a crystal vase greeted us immediately, along with the sound of laughter and voices and kids playing.

"Grandpa George—that's what everyone called him, even his wife—never made any of us feel unwelcome. The entire house was *on-limits*, as he would always say."

"On-limits?" asked Allison. She was scurrying to keep up behind us. Turned out my new friend had rather short legs.

*I heard that,* she thought, her words reaching me easily.

I giggled.

*I heard that, too. And yes, I have issues with my legs.*

I stopped giggling, or tried to.

"Well," said Tara, speaking over her shoulder as we headed into a gorgeous living room. "Grandpa George always told us the entire house was available to all of us kids. There was never a room we were not allowed in, except—"

She paused.

"Except what?" I asked.

"Well, the family mausoleum, of course."

"Er, of course," I said. "Grandpa George sounds like he was an amazing man."

Tara nodded and tensed her shoulders. "Yeah, the best."

We next passed through the kitchen, where three or four people were leaning against counters, drinking and talking. Tara said hi and introduced us as her friends. They all smiled and raised their drinks, but watched us closely. Very closely. It was the same for the other rooms and other people. Introductions, polite smiles, suspicious stares.

As we swept through the house and out through a pair of wide French doors, Allison caught up to me on her stubby legs and whispered in my ear, "What was that all about?"

"What do you mean?"

"The stares. Creepy."

"I don't know," I said.

"At least not yet," said Allison.

"Right," I said, as we now followed Tara along a curved, stone path that led through even more succulent gardens. There was a volleyball net set up out here, along with kayaks lined along an arbor with what was, perhaps, the biggest brick barbeque I'd ever seen. The home, I was beginning to realize, was designed for one thing and one thing only: pleasure, and lots of it. At least of the family kind. A sort of funhouse for adults and kids and everyone in between.

"But we're going to find out," said Allison.

"I'm going to find out," I corrected.

"Hey, I'm your assistant."

"Fictional assistant," I added.

And there it was, just around another turn in the path: the swimming pool where Tara's grandpa had been found last summer, face down and quite dead. I noticed Tara kept her eyes averted. I didn't blame her.

Next, was a row of guest homes in the back, which is where Allison and I would be staying. Bungalows, actually. Each was as big or bigger than my home in Fullerton. Tara showed us to one such structure, which proved to be a two-bedroom suite, with bedrooms on either end and a kitchen and living room in the middle. A fireplace was there, too. Firewood and kindling was stacked neatly nearby.

I made arrangements with Tara to come back and debrief us once we were unpacked and settled in. I also requested that she bring family photos. I needed to know everyone who was here. Intimately. She understood.

"Debrief?" asked Allison when Tara had left.

"That's detective talk," I said.

"You mean detective mumbo-jumbo."

"Remember why we're here," I said. "To catch a killer."

"Well, I'm here to keep you alive."

I snorted.

"Don't scoff," said Allison. "I saw it clearly."

"You saw what clearly?"

"Me saving your life."

"How?"

"I'm not sure yet."

"Convenient."

"Don't scoff at us mystics, Sammie. We work in mysterious ways."

I snorted again and picked the room on the left.

"Hey," said Allison. "Why do you get that room?"

"Because you work for me, remember?"

"Oh, damn," said Allison, plopping down on her own bed and then stretching out. "I forgot about that part."

But she was asleep before I could respond.

# 12.

Yes, I wanted to sleep, too.

And, yes, the medallion made it possible for me to withstand the sun, but the golden disk didn't take away the *burning desire* to lay down, close my eyes, and die all over again. Because that's how sleep often felt to me: a mini-death.

*I am so very, very weird.*

But I was also here only for the weekend. It was Friday afternoon, and coming on evening. I had tonight, tomorrow, and all of Sunday to solve this crime. Our flight back to civilization was Monday morning.

*Lots to do,* I thought. *Too much to be laying around and snoozing.*

I pulled out the one thing every good investigator needs: my clipboard with my case notes. Yes, I'd already been making notes on this one. Lots of them. Knowing I had only a few days to prep for this case meant that I needed names and pictures. I looked at my list now of the many names, some of which had thumbnail pictures next to them. I had drawn lines attaching the names to various family members.

For now, they were just names and pictures and slightly squiggly lines. The deceased in question was George Thurman, or Grandpa George. The name had a certain ring to it. Yes, he sounded important but—but from what I was gathering, he didn't act it. He was a recluse at heart who loved his family. Although he was known for his generosity to charities, he rarely, if ever, opened up his home to outsiders.

His home was his safe haven, his escape.

And now, his tomb.

George Thurman had had two sons and a daughter, all of whom now ran the family hotel empire. An empire that was very much kept in the family. Much like his home, where only family members were invited, the business was the same: only family members were appointed to important roles. For now, it was the eldest son, Junior Thurman, who was the president. The youngest son, August, was the vice-president. Other important roles went to brothers and sisters, uncles and aunts, nephews and nieces. George's wife, Ellery, had long since passed.

By all accounts, the family was über-rich. The two sons' own daughters were often found in tabloid magazines. One of them had even made a sex tape. I'd refused to watch the sex tape. For now. Yes, I knew I needed to be thorough . . . but *eww*.

From the next room, I heard Allison mumble something in her sleep. The mumbling then turned into loud snoring. I got up and shut her bedroom door, just as she let out a short, sharp snort.

*Nice.*

Back in the living room, I looked some more at my notes. The deceased in question, George Thurman, had long since retired, handing the corporation over to his oldest son. That had been, according to my research, nearly ten years ago. So, power couldn't have been a factor.

Money, maybe.

Undoubtedly, George had left untold millions behind, bequeathing them to who knows who. The potential to inherit millions of dollars might be a motivating factor.

But to sons who were already wealthy?

That didn't ring true.

I made a note to follow up on the disbursement of the inheritance, who got what and how much. But I suspected this was a dead end. Then again, what did I know? As for me, the most I could leave my own kids was a mortgage in which I was almost upside down. That and a minivan and, maybe, a few thousand dollars in petty cash.

*I need to get my shit together,* I thought.

I went back to what I knew of George Thurman's death. As I did so, I got up from the leather couch and moved over to the front door, where I stood in the doorway and looked out across the manicured grounds. There were four bungalows, and untold numbers of guest rooms in the mansion. Enough, surely, for twenty or thirty people to stay comfortably.

There was the pool behind the main house. There was a fence around the pool, which was a good idea with all the grandkids. There was also a balcony directly above the pool, a balcony that led off to one of the rooms.

Had he been pushed? Had he fallen in?

According to the autopsy, there had been no alcohol in the old man's system, nor any drugs. George hadn't had a heart attack, either, nor a stroke. In fact, there had been no evidence of foul play of any type. His death had been ruled an accidental drowning.

George Thurman had been seventy-nine at the time of his death. Too old to remember how to swim? Hell, how does one accidentally drown, anyway?

I didn't know as I gazed out over the sun-drenched backyard, as the shadows of evening encroached.

*Time to get to work.*

# 13.

Allison was still asleep.

I could smell the barbeque cooking. The smoking meat triggered a primal hunger in me, a hunger that I couldn't feed. I hadn't brought any of my own *nourishment* with me. Allison had volunteered for the job. Fresh blood. *Her* blood. Smelling the meat now triggered a hunger in me.

A hunger for *her*.

*Jesus.*

I found myself pacing inside the small bungalow. The floorboard creaked beneath me. I always paced at this time of the day, medallion or no medallion. When the sun was about to set, that thing which was inside me awakened.

Awakened to the night.

I paused at the open window. The sky beyond was purplish—and filling up with low-hanging clouds. So much for the sunny skies. This was, after all, the Pacific Northwest.

And just like that, the first drops appeared against the big window, splattering, collecting, sliding.

I continued pacing.

As I paced, both a sadness and an excitement filled me. Excitement for the coming night. Sadness for what I was. After all, just when I would think I was feeling normal, or feeling human, this would happen: the day would merge into night. And, when that happened, I would feel anything but normal. Anyone but myself.

I felt on edge, anxious, angry.

This would be when I would snap at Tammy and Anthony—and even more often at Danny—more than enough times for them to know to stay away from Mommy at this time of day. Of course, back in the day, my kids didn't know the reason why.

Now they did. Now they knew everything.

They knew Mommy was a freak. They also knew that they were pretty freaky themselves.

*Not my fault,* I thought, as I shook my hands and continued pacing. *I didn't ask for this. I was only out jogging. Jogging as I had done many times before. Hundreds of times before.*

Had the bastard been watching me seven years ago? Or had I simply crossed paths with him unexpectedly? An unfortunate crossing of paths?

I didn't know . . . and perhaps would never know, unless . . .

Unless I talked to the vampire hunter who'd killed my own attacker. The vampire hunter named Randolf.

Then again, wasn't there another who knew the answers? My guardian angel had been neither a guardian nor an angel.

Ishmael had, apparently, orchestrated my attack. How, I didn't know, but I was going to find out. What strings had he pulled? In the least, what did the son-of-a-bitch know?

I shook my hands again.

*Good God, when was the fucking sun going to set?*

Soon, I knew. Soon. I could feel it out there, beyond the forest of evergreens. Its rounded upper half was still above the distant horizon. I couldn't see it but I could *feel* it. Every ray. Every particle of light. Every fucking photon.

Screw Fang. He didn't have to push me so hard. I might have come around. I might have fallen in love with him, too. Screw Detective Hanner, too. Whatever her game was, I didn't know, but I did know one thing.

She wasn't going to win. Not if she came up against me.

And by stealing Fang from me—my very best friend—well, she made it personal. Very, very personal.

I accidentally elbowed the corner of the kitchen. Plaster exploded and the whole house shook.

*Easy,* I thought. *Calm down.*

I thought of Danny and Kingsley. Two cheaters. Two bastards, and I nearly drove my hand through the front door as I passed by it.

*That's not calming down,* I thought.

I thought of my kids and took a deep breath. I thought of Detective Sherbet and smiled. I thought of Allison snoring in the room next to me, and almost laughed.

I was calming down. Good. Willing myself to calm down. Yes, good. But there was another reason for why I was finally relaxing. Oh, yes, another reason, indeed.

The sun was slip, slip, slippin' away.

I paused by the big window and breathed in deeply, filling my worthless lungs to capacity with useless air. And by the time I had filled them completely, the anger and hostility had disappeared.

I felt like a new woman. Or a new vampire.

The sun, after all, had set.

And I was alive again.

Truly alive.

I turned around and saw Allison watching me from the shadows of her doorway, her hair mussed. "Feeling better?" she asked.

"Very," I said.

"Hungry?"

"Very, very hungry," I said.

# 14.

Dinner was served in the dining room.

And what a dining room it was. It had a vaulted ceiling complete with a hand-painted mural of a mountain that I suspected was the nearby Mount Rainier. Very Sistine Chapel-like, and it, no doubt, would have taken a skilled artisan months to complete. The dining table itself looked like it was out of a movie set. So long that it seemed comical, it was vaguely boat-shaped, as in, it tapered off near the end, wider in the middle. It had a beautiful golden floral inlay, with intricately carved pedestals holding the whole damn thing steady.

Italian, I figured, and worth more money than I would make in a month. *Two months.*

Steaming filet mignon and crusted chicken breasts and bar-bequed ribs filled many platters placed along the center of the table. All of which smelled heavenly. All of which were off-limits to me. Yes, I accepted a small serving of salad, claiming I was a vegetarian. Allison snickered at that, and I gave her a small elbow in the ribs.

Well, maybe, not that small. She *ooph*ed and nearly toppled over.

*My bad,* I thought.

*Meanie,* she thought back.

But she had played it off well, turning the explosion of air into a hacking cough that earned a few scowls from those around the table. When she was done hacking into her napkin, she glared at me. I shrugged and smiled sweetly.

I counted seventeen people in all. Thirteen adults and four kids. The kids ranged from tweens to toddlers. Tara sat on the other side of me. I recognized the man at the head of the table: George Thurman Junior. Or, as he preferred, Junior, according to Tara, who'd gotten Allison and I caught up, just before dinner. Patricia Thurman, Junior's beautiful wife—too beautiful and too perfect, if you asked me—sat to his right and didn't stop looking at me.

There was an older couple sitting together across from me. They both smiled warmly at me. There was a devilishly hand-some young man who hadn't stopped staring at Allison. To her credit, remarkably, she'd ignored him completely. I knew she was still grieving for her one-time boyfriend, the boxer, Caesar Marquez, and wasn't in the market for men. There were two men sitting together, rather closely. I caught them smiling warmly at each other. Next to Tara was a young man who looked oddly familiar. No, not familiar. I mean, yes, I'd seen his picture before, but there was something about him . . .

Then I figured it out. His smile. It was the same kind of big, expressive smile that I had seen on Tara, my client. Lips curled up. Almost clown-like.

His name was Edwin Thurman, and he was Junior's only son, the black sheep of the family with a history of drugs, public arrests, and jail time.

I scanned the entire lot. Yes, a psychic scan of sorts. I couldn't read everyone's mind, thank God. Yes, it turned out that I could actually influence thoughts. But I could also get impressions from people. I noted, in particular, that my inner alarm was ringing mildly. There was a potential threat here, somewhere at the table.

I hated when that happened.

Dinner was served. There was no wait staff, which I found slightly curious. A big house like this with no staff? Who cleaned and cooked and manicured the lawns?

So, we served ourselves, like commoners. Of course, I just picked at my salad and scattered it around and pretended to eat, all while I spat it back in my napkin. I drank the wine, which at least gave me some semblance of humanity.

The dinner was mostly subdued. No one asked any questions of Allison or me. No one really looked our way. No one, except for Junior's beautiful wife. The kids talked quietly among themselves, often laughing.

The many couples talked quietly, too. I scattered the salad sufficiently and Allison, bless her heart, reached over and picked at my salad as well. The end result was that I appeared to have eaten my light dinner, or at least some of it. I appeared, for all intents and purposes, to be one of the living.

As I pushed my salad away, feigning fullness, the young man sitting next to Allison looked at it, then at my nearly finished goblet of wine.

And smiled at me.

Knowingly.

# 15.

We retired to the great room.

Yes, *retired*. That's how Junior Thurman phrased it. I'm fairly certain I'd never retired to any room, let alone a great room. But, if sitting in comfy chairs and holding my wine and trying to pretend to be normal was retiring, then there was a first for everything.

As we sat, I sent a thought over to Allison for her to shield her own thoughts. She asked why and I told her to just do it, that I would explain later. She shrugged, and I sensed her mind closing to me, exactly the way I had taught her to do it.

*Good girl,* I thought, although she wouldn't be able to hear me.

The great room was, well, great. It had a soaring ceiling crisscrossed with thick beams. It had arches and a brick fireplace and oversized furniture. The room was something to behold. And, apparently, to retire in.

Outside, through the stacked windows framed with heavy curtains, the tall evergreens were now swaying violently, although I doubted the others could see them in the darkness. A storm was moving in. A big one, too.

"It's getting blustery out there," said Edwin, the young man who might have been handsome if not for the perpetual smile on his face. He could see the trees as well?

"Blustery?" said Allison next to me. She'd had two glasses of wine. She was also smaller than me and hadn't eaten much at dinner. I suspected the wine had gone straight to her head.

Junior Thurman, who'd been texting on his too-big cell phone, set it aside and looked up at her. He was holding a glass of sherry. I was fairly certain I'd never before seen anyone drink a glass of sherry in my life.

*Another first,* I thought.

"It's a word we like to use up here," he said jovially enough. He had a strong, resonant voice that seemed to fill the great room. His wife nodded. She had quit looking at me. Now she was staring down into her own glass of wine, legs tucked under her.

Junior went on: "Blustery is just our way of saying that we're getting some nasty weather out there, nasty even for the Northwest."

"We just call it a shit-storm where I'm from," said Allison, and immediately looked like she regretted it.

The kids who'd been playing cards nearby looked up. Junior frowned a little. Edwin, I saw, grinned even bigger.

"And where are you from, Allison?" Junior asked pleasantly.

"Texas."

"Ah," said Junior without elaborating, as if that answered everything. He turned his attention back to me. "Samantha, from where do you know my dear niece?"

"I've known Tari since we were in college," I said, reciting the script. Tara was "Tari" to friends and family.

Junior nodded. He held the glass of sherry loosely in his hands. The rich vermillion color caught some of the ambient light. From here, the liquid looked like blood. My stomach growled. My sick, ghoulish stomach.

He said, "Did you two have many classes together?"

"One or two," I said, "until I dropped out."

"And why would you do a thing like that?" asked Patricia, Junior's wife.

"I got pregnant," I lied.

"Twins," said Allison, jumping in.

Junior nodded, as if that made perfect sense. I nearly frowned at Allison. We hadn't discussed me having twins. She'd drunkenly embellished the story. Tara was looking concerned, too.

"Twins," said Mrs. Thurman. "How delightful. What are their names?"

"Tammy and Anthony."

"They're not, you know, identical," said Allison, slurring her words slightly.

Mrs. Thurman regarded Allison curiously. "I gathered that." She turned back to me. "And you've kept in touch with our Tari all this time?"

"On and off," I said, lying easily. It was, after all, what investigators did. We often lied to get our information.

"We reconnected through Facebook," blurted Allison.

"Oh, so you're friends on Facebook?" asked Edwin. He continued smiling. He seemed to be getting a kick out of all of this.

I saw where this was going, and saw where Allison had screwed up. I said, "I don't think so, not yet. We just emailed."

Edwin leaned forward and rested his elbows on his knees and looked directly at me. His face was angular, his cheekbones high. His lips were a little too full, even for me. He said, "Maybe we can be friends on Facebook."

"Maybe," I said. "Depends how friendly you are."

He laughed and sat back.

"I just love Facebook," said Allison. "Just last week a friend of mine sent me this cat video . . . I swear to God that little booger was clapping. Clapping! A kitten! Can you believe it?"

Apparently, no one could. Or they were too dumbfounded to speak. Junior shifted his considerable gaze from me to her. The president of Thurman Hotels was also, apparently, the leader of the family. "And how do you know our Tari?"

"Oh, I'm just here for the ride," said Allison, sitting back and kicking her Uggs comfortably. She snapped her gum. "I'm with Sammie here. Where she goes, I go."

"Cute," said Patricia.

Time to change the subject. "This is a beautiful home," I said.

The older couple sitting near the roaring fireplace sat forward. Elaine Thurman, sister of the deceased. She smiled brightly. Her aura, I saw, was bluish and yellow, which told me she was a woman very much at peace with herself. Her aura also had a black thread woven through it. Grieving, obviously. This was, after all, the one-year anniversary of her brother's drowning. She said, "The home has been in my family for generations. We've all been coming out to Skull Island for over seventy-five years."

"Why is it called Skull Island?" asked Allison.

Edwin leaned forward again. "There's a Native American burial ground on the other side of the island. It's supposedly cursed."

"Skull Island and curses," said Allison, elbowing him. "Where's Scooby-Doo and Shaggy, too?"

Which had been, of course, my exact thought.

"Well, the curses are just legends," said Calvin Thurman, or Cal, one of the uncles. He was, I suspected, dying of cancer. I knew this because of the dark spot of his kidney, a dark spot that was, literally, like a black hole, sucking in the color of his surrounding aura. Indeed, he leaned away from it, taking pressure off it.

*He doesn't even know,* I thought.

He held my gaze closely, and something seemed to pass between us. His eyes, I was certain, were trying to communicate something to me. He said, "Although there have been a few cases of unfortunate deaths."

"We don't talk about those," snapped Junior. "Not to strangers."

"Nonsense," said Cal, apparently not intimidated at all by his nephew, president of the company or not. He looked again at me. "It's in all the papers. Anyone can find that."

He continued looking at me. I looked at him. His eyes, I was certain, were pleading with me.

"Tell me about the deaths," I said uncomfortably. I had, of course, come across three such deaths in my own research of Skull Island. Were there some that I had missed?

But Junior's glowering stare finally cowered old Cal. He sighed deeply and winked at me. "Catch me later after I've had a few of these"—and he held up his Scotch—"and I'll tell you all."

He laughed. I laughed. No one else laughed.

Instead, Junior Thurman announced that tomorrow we would hold a memorial for his late father, George Thurman, whose death I had, unknown to the family, been hired to investigate. Junior went on: His late father had passed at this time last year, and he wanted to have a ceremony at the chapel located in the mausoleum.

Next, the conversation quickly turned to business. Tara turned and talked to me about my kids. All the while, I was aware of glances from various family members. Of course, some weren't glancing. Some were openly staring. Like Edwin Thurman. Edwin with his perpetual grin. Patricia, not so much.

Outside, the trees continued to sway and bend and appeared ready to snap, all while a sheet of rain swept over the grounds.

Welcome to Skull Island.


# 16.


We were back at the bungalow.

Just two college chums and their annoying new friend, all supposedly catching up—and most definitely not talking about murder.

Supposedly.

"You think they bought it?" asked Allison.

"Hard to say," said Tara. She'd brought a bottle of wine with her, of which we were all partaking. Some of us more vigorously than others.

"I think they bought it," said Allison, pouring herself yet another glass of wine.

"Tell me more about Edwin," I said to Tara.

"He's Junior's only son."

"Your cousin," I said.

"Right." Outside, rain slapped against the bungalow's windows. Tree branches groaned overhead, as the bungalows were closer to the surrounding forest. "He was never much interested in the family's business."

"But I bet he's interested in the family money," said Allison, laughing. "Oops, sorry. Was that inappropriate?"

"No," said Tara. "Of course not. You guys are here to find answers to my grandfather's death. I'm not sure, at this point, if anything could be inappropriate, or if I would even care. And to answer your question . . . I'm not so sure about his desire for money."

"What do you mean?" I asked.

"He lives fairly simply. In fact, he often lives here."

"Living here isn't living simply," said Allison.

"True, but even while he's here, he lives simply. In fact, he prefers sleeping in the basement. On a cot, of all things."

"He's here a lot?" I asked.

"Often. In fact, he's rarely not here."

"What does he do here?"

"Nothing, as far as anyone knows."

"How did he take your grandfather's death?" I asked.

"That's the strange part," said Tara, looking up from her glass. "He didn't seem to take it hard at all."

"What do you mean?" I asked.

"I mean just that. He didn't appear overly distraught."

"No tears?" asked Allison, piping in.

"None that I saw."

"Is there a room in the basement?" I asked.

"Of course, but it's so cold down there. Drafty. Miserable."

"Well, maybe he just wants to stay out of the way," said Allison. "You know, since he's here all the time."

"Maybe," said Tara.

*Or maybe the cold doesn't bother him,* I thought, sending it over to Allison.

*A vampire?* she thought back.

*Yes.* I thought. *I think. I can see his aura, so that's a problem.*

*Problem, why?*

*I can't see vampires' auras.*

*Gotcha. So, is that why you had me shield my thoughts back at dinner?*

I nodded and turned my attention back to Tara. "Were you here on the night of your grandfather's death?"

"Yes," she said. "We all were."

Tara next asked Allison for some more wine, who was only too willing to comply, and shortly, my friend and witness were both gone for the night.

I sighed, and made notes in my case file, all while the girls giggled and talked and got drunker and drunker. I made a mental note to fire Allison.

Rhetorically, of course.

# 17.

It was late.

Both Allison and Tara had drunk themselves into oblivion. Me, not so much. Other than a mild upset stomach, my two glasses of wine had had no effect.

I wasn't hungry yet, either. Earlier that night, I had drunk deeply from Allison's punctured wrist, as she'd looked away, winced, shuddered, and broken out into a sweat. The wound had healed instantly, and by the time I had finished, she was no longer sweating. She had been grinning ghoulishly to herself. The act of me drinking from her gave her some sort of high.

*Two sick puppies,* I thought, as I pulled on a light jacket and flipped up the hood. My tennis shoes were already on, along with my jeans. I stood at the open door. The rain and wind had let up a little.

It also gave her more than a high, I knew. It sharpened her psychic abilities, of which she was already quite proficient. The act of me drinking from her had now made her into a sort of super psychic.

It was in much the same way that my own daughter's telepathic powers had increased due to her connection and proximity to me. And, for that matter, perhaps anyone connected to me.

I exited the bungalow, and hung a left toward the big house. It was 3:00 a.m., and I was alone in the night.

I couldn't have been happier.

Today had been a bit overwhelming to me. Too many people, too many introductions, too many handshakes, too many times I had apologized for my cold hands, too many times I had pretended to be normal.

I continued along the stone path, through the manicured gardens, past the epic barbeque and headed toward the pool. I paused at the surrounding gate and took in the scene around me. Trees lined the far edge of the massive estate. The bungalows dotted the perimeter of the grass, near the trees. The massive edifice of the Thurman home rose high into the night sky, like something medieval and ominous. The pool fence itself was only about six feet high. Tall enough to keep the kids out. I unlatched the gate.

The pool itself wasn't overtly big, perhaps slightly bigger than the standard pools. In the winter, I suspected the pool was covered. It wasn't winter. It was the beginning of summer, so all the pool toys were near: floating inner tubes, floating killer whales, floating rubber deck chair. The water rippled with the light rain and wind.

*How could a grown man drown in his own pool?*

I studied the area, noting the layout. There was a balcony directly above the pool. A part of me had suspected that George Thurman might have accidentally fallen into the pool—or been pushed. The balcony suggested that the possibility was still there.

The autopsy had been thorough. No drugs or alcohol, no blunt force. Skin clear, no lesions or scrapes or bruises. Blood tests came back negative, too. No poisoning. No sign of foul play.

Just a dead man in the water.

As I slowly circled the oval-shaped pool, my inner alarm began ringing a little louder. The sound was followed by footsteps, and then the appearance of a man.

A smiling man.

# 18.

It was Edwin, of course.

"Good evening, Samantha," he said.

He came closer and I saw that his hands were covered in dirt. Dirt was also under his fingernails. And it wasn't just dirt, but something else. Clay?

"Pardon my appearance. I was on an emergency dig."

"Digging what?" I asked, and was all too aware that my inner alarm was ringing even louder.

He came closer, grinning macabrely. He looked, quite frankly, insane. "Tell you what, Samantha. I will show you someday. How does that sound?"

"Weird as hell," I said.

He laughed. "Yes, I suppose it does sound sort of odd."

His aura, like that of Tara and old Cal, rippled with a dark thread-like energy. Except in Edwin, the darkness was more evident. I had assumed the darkness was a result of grief . . . now, I wasn't sure what to think.

"Why do you keep smiling like that?" I asked.

"Oh, I'm just a happy-go-lucky kind of guy. Made even happier now that you're here."

My inner alarm blared loudly. "What the hell does that mean?"

"Oh, nothing. We just so rarely get visitors here on our little island."

"I'm beginning to see why," I said, and found myself inching away from him.

He laughed. "Yes, we are an odd lot. Not exactly your typical family. And like most families, we have our hidden demons."

His words hit home. "You're one of them."

The young man continued grinning bizarrely. "One of whom, Samantha Moon?" He used my full name.

"You're a dark master," I said, using the term for the thing that lived in me, the thing that had mastered immortality, the thing that lived on through me using the darkest of magicks.

"Dark master? I like that. I'm very flattered, Sam."

He flashed me another crazy smile, and now I saw something else within him. Something human. It was in his eyes, and it made a brief appearance. I saw the young man. The *real* Edwin Thurman. Hidden. Pushed aside. Suffocated. But as quickly as he appeared, he disappeared again, like flotsam rising briefly to the ocean surface, only to be sucked under the dark waters again.

Edwin—or whoever was before me—stepped around me, clasping his hands behind his back. I got a very powerful psychic hit, and one that I knew was true.

"You're not like the others," I said.

He glanced at me, arching an eyebrow. "Oh? Do tell?"

"You are, if I'm correct, *permanently* present. You're not hidden in the background, not like the others, not like the thing within me."

"Not a thing, Sam." His annoyance surprised me. He paused, held my gaze, and added, "My sister."

I gasped and backed away some more.

"And I'm not saying that metaphorically, Samantha Moon. Residing within you is my sister, and someday soon—very, very soon—she and I will be together again."

# 19.

A low fog hung over the dark ocean.

The particles of light that only I could see seemed to disappear into the fog, to be absorbed by the mist. I might have gained a lot of gifts since becoming the thing that I am, but one of them, apparently, was not the ability to see into fog.

I was sitting at the edge of a small cliff. Waves crashed thirty feet or so below. Some of the spray reached me, sprinkling my skin and lips. I didn't lick my lips. Even salt spray would upset my stomach.

The path from the house was a well-maintained one, as I suspected this cliff side retreat was a favorite hangout for the family. During the daytime, I was sure one could see for miles and miles. Now, not so much, even to my eyes.

To say that the conversation with Edwin had shaken me was an understatement.

His sister?

Obviously, not a Thurman sister, for I hadn't been talking to the real Edwin Thurman. No, I had been talking to something ancient and evil. Another dark master who sought entry back into our world.

And not just any dark master, I suspected.

No, he didn't have to hide in the shadows of the living, like that which had entered Kingsley and me . . . and now Fang. No, whoever he was, he had taken over the real Edwin Thurman—completely and totally.

Who he was, I didn't know. But he was powerful.

Perhaps even the most powerful of all.

And his sister was in me.

*Jesus.*

I suddenly wished I wasn't sitting on the cliff's edge, in the cold and rain and wind, but sleeping with my kids, one on either side of me, their warm bodies giving me warmth in return. I could almost smell Tammy's hair. I could almost even smell Anthony's stinky feet.

As the wind and rain picked up, drenching me to the bone, I did the only thing this middle-aged divorcée mother of two could do:

I took off my clothes.

And stepped to the edge of the cliff.

I summoned the single flame in my thoughts.

Held it.

Saw the image of the beast.

The beast I would become.

And then I leaped out as far and wide as I could, arching up and over the pounding surf.

The transformation was instant, taking hold of me before I plunged into the rocks below.

I was soon flying. High above the island. High above the fog. High above, even, the snoring Allison.

It was up here where I found my sanctuary, my peace, my escape. I was all too aware that it was the thing that lived within me that gave me this very ability. The thing I could never escape.

*We'll see,* I thought, and began flapping my wings.

# 20.

Allison and I were sitting together at breakfast.

I'd managed about three hours of sleep before Allison literally woke me from the dead. Now, we sat with the other Thurmans—or a few of them at least—on a wide balcony that overlooked the grounds. As Allison ate and I drank water, I caught her up to speed on the night's events. When I was finished, I said, "Your mouth's hanging open."

"It tends to do that when I'm shocked shitless."

I shushed her. Although we were alone at our little patio table, there were still other Thurmans eating nearby. The morning had been shockingly clear and warm, so much so that breakfast had been served outside. There was a nearby table filled with heaps of eggs and breakfast meats and pancakes. Someone had cooked up a storm. Many nodded at us as we sat and talked. Noticeably absent was Edwin Thurman and our hostess, Tara.

"And where is the man of the hour?" asked Allison. She was, of course, talking about Edwin.

"In his room," I said.

"You mean, the basement?"

"Right," I said.

"And you know this how?"

"I've got mad skills," I said. Although Allison was a close friend, she was still a new friend. She didn't know the extent of what I could do. Truth was, I didn't know the extent of what I could do either. So, for an explanation, I gave her a glimpse now into my memory, showing her what I'd done—and what I had seen.

She blinked after a moment. "You can remote sense?"

"I guess so, yes."

"Geez, the government's been training psychics for decades trying to get them to do what you can do."

"Well, I can't see very far, maybe only a few hundred feet or so."

"Far enough. I saw the image of him lying there on his little cot, sleeping. Very clear image. Very precise."

"Very weird," I said.

"Well, weird or not, it's helpful . . . and why the hell is he lying on a cot, in the basement, in this beautiful home?"

"Maybe they ran out of beds," I said.

"Or maybe it's because he's a vampire."

I shook my head and lowered my voice. "No. Not a vampire. He's something else. He's different."

"Different, how?"

"Greater. More powerful."

She caught the meaning of my words and also caught my own vaguely formulated thought. "Sam," she said. "Do you really think he might be the greatest of them all?"

Allison and I had previously discussed the thing that resides in me. She understood that it was this thing that fueled me and gave me eternal life. She understood that this thing needed to be fed, and blood was its choice. She understood that the powers within it emanated out to me, making me stronger and stronger.

I said, "I don't know yet. I don't know much about these entities. I don't know why they've been banished, and why they want back in. I don't understand the kind of magicks needed to give them access to me, and to live within me forever."

"But you think the thing that lives in Edwin Thurman might be the strongest of them all."

"That's what my gut is telling me."

She snorted. "Well, I can tell you one thing: I can tell you who's high on my suspect list of who killed George Thurman."

"We don't know if he killed him," I said.

"Well, he certainly sounds like he's got it in for you, Sam. Did he really say his sister is inside you?"

"Yes."

"God, you vampires are weird."

"Thanks."

"So, what's the game plan, Sammie? Other than me keeping you alive."

"You keeping me alive?"

"Someone's got to, kiddo. My sensitivities may not be as strong as yours, but I am getting a very, very strong feeling that not all is as it seems on Skull Island."

"Very melodramatic," I said.

"And very real."

My cell phone went off. I looked down at it: Danny. The ex. Allison saw it, too.

"You going to answer?" she asked.

"No."

It rang again. I drummed my fingers.

"Fine," I said irritably, and clicked on.

# 21.

"Sam, I want to see the kids more often."

"Why?"

"Because I love them."

"Why?"

"Because they're my kids, goddamn it."

"Sorry, but I'm going to need more than that."

"Sam, I'm warning you."

"Or what?"

"Jesus, Sam. All I'm asking is for you to let me see my kids—our kids—a little more. I only see them, what, every other week for a few hours. Supervised."

"You also happen to own a sleazy strip club and date even sleazier strippers."

"Hey," said Allison, looking up from her smart phone. "I used to be a stripper."

I covered the mouthpiece and lowered my voice. "Were you sleazy?"

"Sleazy, no. Good, yes."

I rolled my eyes and uncovered the phone. "So, you see my point, then," I said to Danny.

"I see that you're a controlling bitch."

"As always, nice talking to you, Danny."

"Wait, wait!" he screeched as I made a move to hang up. "Don't hang up. I'm sorry."

I didn't hang up, but I didn't say anything either. I looked out across the outdoor deck. So beautiful. This could have been a resort.

"You there, Sam?"

"I'm here."

"Sorry, I didn't mean that."

"Yes, you did."

"Okay, I did, but it's only because you're being a little unreasonable."

"Danny, I'm going to say this with all the sincerity I can. I really don't give a shit what you think about me, but I do know one thing, and one thing only: until you sell that sleazebag of a strip club you own and quit bringing your skank-whores home, you will never, ever be alone with my kids."

Someone from a nearby table looked over at me. Oops. I might have raised my voice a little.

"You can't tell me when I can or cannot see my kids."

"I can and I did."

"I'm giving up the law firm, Sam."

I snorted. "To run the strip club full time?"

"It's a lot of money, Sam. Easy money."

"You are choosing easy money over your kids. Strippers over your kids."

"You have it wrong, Sam. I don't date the girls."

Just hearing the word "girls" made my skin crawl. "No," I said, "you just fuck them."

"You can't tell me what to do, Sam. Who to see and who not to see. How to live my life. How to make money."

"No, but I can tell you this."

He sighed. "What?"

"You will never, ever be alone with my kids."

And I clicked off the phone.

Emphatically.

# 22.

"You've got that look in your eye," said Allison.

"What look?"

"That don't-mess-with-me-or-I'm-gonna-rip-out-your-throat look." As she spoke, she slowly reached over and gently pried my fingers from my iPhone. The bottom corner of the phone's screen was already cracked from my last conversation with Danny.

"Remember," she said. "He's a total pig."

"And that," I said, getting up, "is why I keep you around."

"You keep me around?" said Allison, grabbing her plate of unfinished eggs and hurrying after me. "Maybe it's the other way around. Maybe I keep *you* around."

"Sure," I said, and picked up my pace.

"Hey, where are we going?"

I opened the French door that led from the balcony into the magnificent kitchen. I looked back at her. "We're looking for a killer, remember?"

"Well, I think we found him."

"Maybe," I said. "Maybe not."

"So, where are we going?"

"I've got some investigator stuff to do."

"And what am I supposed to do?"

I motioned to the others who were still sitting outside on the deck, enjoying what was, I suspected, rare sunshine. Indeed, storm clouds were already gathering on the far horizon. And if I wasn't mistaken, they looked even nastier than the ones from yesterday.

"Do what you do best," I said. "Talk."

"Gee, thanks."

"Mingle. Get me the lowdown. Let me know who sets off your own inner alarm system."

She opened her mouth to say something else, but I shooed her back outside. She pouted a moment or two, then stuck out her tongue and headed back out onto the deck.

I paused in the kitchen, closed my eyes, and mentally searched the home again. I saw everyone, even Edwin asleep on his cot in the basement. One person was still noticeably absent: Tara. Perhaps she was out of my range.

So, I zeroed in on the one person I was looking for, and headed off.

Deeper into the massive home.

# 23.

I soon got lost.

I backtracked down a hallway or two, rounded a corner, passed an actual conservatory with its domed, glass ceiling, and found myself in the library.

No, I didn't see Professor Plum or Colonel Mustard. Definitely, I didn't see a candlestick, whatever that was. I did see, however, an older gentleman reading a book and drinking from a highball glass. The amber liquid in the glass wasn't, I suspected, lemonade.

Cal Thurman, George Thurman's brother, looked up from the latest James Patterson novel, this one called *Death, Sweet Death*, and smiled broadly when he saw me.

"Allison, right?"

"Close," I said. "Allison's my friend. I'm Samantha."

He chuckled. "Hey, at my age, anything close is a good sign. The other day I called my wife Rick."

"Who's Rick?"

"No clue. Have a seat."

I grinned and sat in the chair next to him. He asked if I wanted a drink, indicating a bar nearby. I mentioned that this was the first library I'd seen with a full service bar. He laughed and said he would drink to that, and did. Then he poured himself another and sat back down next to me. I noted the time: 11:45. Not even noon.

"So, what can I do you for?" he asked, and, with one gulp, nearly finished his fresh glass of the hard stuff.

"You suggested that I see you about some, ah, strange occurrences that have been happening on the island. I'm interested in hearing more about the curse."

"Did I?"

"Yes."

"Was I drunk?"

"You were drinking, yes."

He laughed. "That might explain it. Sure, yes. There's rumors this island is cursed. Dates all the way back to when, hell, I don't know, probably back to the Native Americans. Even before the white man came, the Native Americans were at war over this island. From what we gather, there was a lot of bloodshed here. Not to mention a shipwreck or two."

I'd read about the island having some history, and that it had been the location of a few tribal skirmishes, but I wasn't aware of a lot of bloodshed. I asked him to explain further.

"We've found two burial sites on the north side of the island. We're on the south side. And not just burial sites, but battle sites, too. Skulls cleaved nearly in half, severed arms and legs, and gashes to necks and ribs. Dozens and dozens of such bodies."

"Found where?" I asked.

"Mostly in the ground, but some were in a tunnel system that appears to run underneath the island. Edwin has taken an interest in the tunnels, and so has Tara, for that matter."

He eyed me earnestly. Granted, his eyes were bloodshot, but he was imploring me, I think, to read deeper into his words.

He continued, "Back in the day, my father was going to build on the north end, along the peninsula, where he would have panoramic views of the Sound and the city of Victoria. Instead, he built here, in the woods, which was really the only other viable spot."

"What made him change course?"

"The hauntings. The workers getting spooked. And, of course, the deaths. Which, of course, leads us back to the curse."

He explained further. "Two workers had been killed at the old site, both having fallen from ladders. Both deaths had been unexplained, as they had been alone. Another worker had heard one of the men scream. Sounded like he'd seen a ghost . . . and then plummeted to his death."

"Perhaps, he screamed on the way down," I suggested.

Cal shook his blocky head. "No. It was described as the most blood-curdling scream anyone had ever heard, followed by another scream. Which, I assume, was the poor bastard falling. Anyway, that's when the talk of curses began."

"So, what happened next?"

"My father decided to change course. And build the home on the south side, where we're at now."

"And no more instances of curses?"

"Samantha, there are always instances of curses."

"What do you mean?"

He opened his mouth, and suddenly shut it again. Tight. The smallest grin curled his lips. The same creepy grin I had seen on the faces of Edwin and Tara.

"I . . . I'm afraid I can't talk about the curse anymore, Samantha."

Cal seemed to be struggling with something, fighting something. My inner alarm began chiming softly. What the hell was going on?

I decided to change course. "Was your brother's death associated with the curse?"

"I . . ." he began and closed his mouth again. He was shaking now. And sweating. A reaction to being drunk? I didn't know.

I waited, silent, listening to my inner alarm growing steadily louder. Now I could see the same black ribbons circulating through his aura. The same ribbons I had seen in others. Ribbons I had rarely, if ever, seen before.

"What happened to your brother?" I pushed.

"I . . . can't . . . speak about it."

His voice sounded strangled, as if his throat had suddenly been restricted.

"Mr. Thurman, are you okay?"

He looked at me with pleading eyes. Then he gasped once, twice, and seemed to find his breath. "I'm . . . never okay, my dear."

"I don't understand—"

"The curse," he gasped, and his voice seemed to restrict again.

The ribbons of ethereal darkness swelled a little more, looking more like black snakes now, weaving through his aura, in and out, in and out.

"What about the curse, Mr. Thurman?"

He began shaking. He reminded me of my son when he was fighting off his sickness. Cal Thurman was fighting something. What it was, I didn't know.

He suddenly opened his eyes wide, gasping. "It has us all, Samantha. It controls us all. We are not free. We are never free. Please help, please—"

The black snake that had been circulating through his aura rose up suddenly. I saw its dark, diamond-shaped head moving rapidly through the man. It rose higher and higher—and plunged into his throat.

Cal gasped and grabbed his neck.

Now the snake coiled around and around his throat like a boa constrictor, squeezing tighter and tighter. Cal gasped and lurched to the side, screaming. In a blink of an eye, his aura went from pale blue, to deep black, and as I screamed for help, Cal Thurman looked at me with pleading eyes, and then quit breathing.

Forever.

# 24.

I immediately performed CPR.

All while I called out for help. Someone nearby heard me. A girl. I told her to get help. She stared at me for a moment, then took off running, her feet pounding along the polished tiles.

I went back to my CPR, doing all I could to get Cal's heart beating, to get him breathing again, and by the time the first adults arrived—Junior and his wife, followed shortly by Tara and Allison—I was certain that Cal was quite dead.

• • •

*Jesus, Sam, what happened?* asked Allison.

We were all sitting in the great room. All seventeen of us. Cal was still in the library, lying under a sheet. Further attempts to resuscitate him had gone for naught.

*Are your thoughts protected?* I asked.

*Yes, of course.*

*Something killed him. I watched it kill him. I'm seriously freaked out.*

Allison snapped her head around and stared at me. She wasn't the only one who stared at me. Most people in the room were looking at me. Also in the room was Tara. I'd been too busy and shaken to notice when she'd returned. Edwin hadn't stopped looking my direction. The sky beyond the big windows was a nasty gray. The first of the day's raindrops had begun to splatter against the glass. Jagged bolts of lightning occasionally lit up the underbelly of the heavy clouds. Junior, who had been on his cell phone in the hallway, came into the room.

"The Island County Sheriff can't make it out today," he reported. He looked ten years older than when I'd last seen him. He had, after all, just lost his uncle. "Nor can the paramedics, nor anyone else, for that matter."

"Why?" asked a little girl. She was, I knew, one of Junior's granddaughters.

"Because of the storm, honey."

I was holding my phone. I wanted to text Fang. To text Kingsley even. I didn't feel comfortable texting Russell yet. The poor guy was just beginning to know me. I couldn't lay something like this on him. What was I supposed to say? That I'd seen some dark entity strangle a man? For a new relationship, that might be a deal breaker.

Fang would have understood, and so would've Kingsley. Hell, so would have Detective Sherbet. For now, I was left with only Allison.

*Gee thanks, Sam.*

*Oops,* I thought. *You know what I mean. The others are, you know . . .*

*Freaky like you?*

*Right.*

Outside, the wind had clearly picked up. The tall evergreens were once again swaying and bending. Rain splattered harder, driven into the window. A lawn chair outside scuttled over the grounds, rolling like a tumbleweed.

*Did you really watch him die, Sam?*

*Yes, and I'm still shaking.*

I gave her a glimpse of my own memory of the event, reliving the moment the darkness appeared from his aura and reached up to his throat. I relived his last few words, too:

*"It has us all, Samantha. It controls us all. We are not free. We are never free . . ."*

*Jesus,* came Allison's reply. *Was he poisoned?*

*Maybe,* I thought. But I suspected it was something else, something that I didn't entirely understand, but it had to do with his last words to me: *It controls us all.*

Allison, who'd been following my train of thought as best she could, formulated the words that I had been searching for: *Sam, you think that, on some level, that whatever has control over Edwin, also had control over Cal?*

*But not just the two of them,* I thought grimly.

*All of them?* asked Allison.

*Maybe.*

Junior turned his attention to me. "Samantha, I can't express to you how thankful I am for your efforts on behalf of my uncle. I'm sure that you did all you could to save his life."

"I'm sorry I couldn't do more," I said.

"What, exactly, *did* you do?" asked Patricia, Junior's wife.

Her aura, I noted, was not rippled with the same black ribbon I had seen in some of the others. Her aura was a biting green. I opened my mouth to speak, but instead, looked around me. Junior, I noted, had a black ribbon woven through his aura. I looked again at Edwin: the same black ribbon. I looked at the kids. They all had black ribbons, some thicker than others. All of them. I'd never seen this before. Not like this, and not in the same pattern, and not with so many people.

*What the hell was going on?* I wondered.

"Standard CPR," I said, finally.

"Where did you learn this standard CPR?"

I glanced over at Tara. She was holding her breath. I glanced over at Edwin. He was grinning knowingly. The jig, I was quite certain, was up.

I said, "At the FBI Academy."

"Are you a federal agent, Samantha?"

"Not anymore."

Junior, who had been standing, stepped threateningly before me, arms crossed. "Then what the hell are you, Samantha?"

I looked over at Tara, who was standing near the arched opening into the great room. Her aura, I noted, was still rippled with the same black ribbon.

"I'm a private investigator," I said. "And my name's Samantha Moon."

# 25.

"What's going on, dear?" asked Patricia.

She got up and stood next to her husband. He slipped an arm around her waist and studied me, the picture of a loving couple. I noted again that she didn't have black ribbons coiling through her otherwise bright green aura. Green, the color of envy or distrust. In this situation, I didn't blame her.

"I'm not sure, honey," he said, and I believed him. I felt his confusion and hers, too.

I noted that the black ribbons that wound through his aura had picked up slightly. I looked over at Edwin. His ribbons were thicker, like mountaineering ropes, twisting through his aura.

Junior turned his attention to his niece, Tara. "I want to know what's going on, young lady, and I want to know now. Why did you bring a private investigator to the island?"

"And her assistant," Allison piped up.

Except no one was listening. All eyes turned to Tara, and as they did so, I noted something very, very curious. Her own black ribbons, which had been no thicker than a half inch, suddenly swelled—doubling, tripling their size. Now they veritably pulsated, swirling faster and faster around her.

*Curiouser and curiouser.*

I looked over at Edwin to compare his own dark aura . . . and was equally stunned to see that his once-thick ribbons had now shrunk to thinner ribbons . . . in fact, only small traces of black showed in him. He was shaking his head and blinking hard, as if coming out of a deep sleep.

All this happened while Tara Thurman stared at me. No, leered at me. Menacingly.

*What the hell?* I thought.

Edwin continued rubbing his face and appeared by all indications, to be waking.

*What the double hell?*

*What's wrong, Sam?* thought Allison, picking up on my thoughts. She and I still had our ultra-secret line of communication open. *What's going on?*

*I'll explain later,* I thought. *If I can.*

Tara leaned forward on the elegant, camel-back sofa. She crossed her legs slowly and wiped some lint off her knee. As she did so, one thing was certain . . . that damned creepy smile . . . the same one that seemed to be a permanent fixture on Edwin's face, was now obvious on her face. I'd seen it on her, too.

*The same smile,* I thought. *It's body-hopping.*

*Body-what, Sam? What's going on?*

*Not now,* I thought.

Tara continued wiping away at the speck. As she did so, she shuddered slightly, and I suspected I knew what was going on. It was getting used to her body.

"Tara?" prodded Junior impatiently. "What the devil is going on here?"

*Good choice of words,* I thought.

After a moment, with the same too-big smile plastered to her otherwise pretty face, Tara finally looked up at him, then over at me.

"Yes, I hired Samantha Moon, private investigator extraordinaire," said Tara. Except she didn't sound like Tara. Not really; at least not to my ears. The black ribbons that wound through her aura were thicker than ever, and pulsated like something radioactive.

"But why?" asked Junior. He didn't seem to notice the change in his niece. Nor did anyone else. No, not true. On second thought, Patricia was biting her lower lip and looking from Edwin—who was still blinking hard—to Tara, who was smiling psychotically.

*She knows,* I thought.

*Knows what?* asked Allison.

*Later!*

"I hired her to investigate Grandpa George's death," said Tara.

"But why? Why would you do that?"

Tara was looking at me, but it wasn't Tara. It was the thing that had been in Edwin—and was now in her. "I wasn't thinking straight, uncle. I was . . . I was confused. I thought maybe a private investigator could help us . . . perhaps shed light on what happened."

Junior crossed the room and sat next to his brother's daughter. "Grandpa George drowned, Tari."

"I know . . . but *why* did he drown?"

Junior gazed at her, then turned and looked at his wife. She shrugged. He sighed. I sensed no deception coming from them. I sensed no concealing of truth. They were legitimately at a loss for answers.

Finally, Junior said, "We don't know why he drowned, honey, but the medical report assured us there was no foul play."

Tara nodded, although the plastered smile remained on her face. She reminded me of the Joker from Batman. She started nodding, and now tears appeared on her high cheekbones. Tears and that big, disturbing smile.

"I just wanted help. I just wanted answers." She pointed at me. "And she was so willing to help, so willing to—no, I shouldn't say it."

"So willing to take your money?" finished Junior.

Tara looked at him, then at me, and nodded. Allison gasped next to me and made to stand up. I held her back. Junior turned and looked at me. "When the storm clears, you're on the next boat out of here."

"I don't think so," I said.

Something dark clouded over him. No, this wasn't a body-jumping dark entity. It was his own self-righteous anger. "You will leave, Samantha Moon, even if I have to make you."

"With all due respect, Mr. Thurman," I said. "I was hired to do a job, and I intend to finish it."

Someone in the room inhaled sharply. Tara, peeking out from behind her uncle, smiled even broader. Junior strode over and stood before me, threateningly. I didn't get threatened by angry men, even back before my immortal days. I was still sitting on the loveseat next to Allison—even though, I was fairly certain, we weren't in love. Junior stood over six feet tall and was used to getting his way. His uncle, Cal, was lying dead just down the hallway. This wasn't a time for him to make a scene or to make things even worse than they were.

I telepathically reached out to him. This was something I'd recently discovered I could do, something that, apparently, most vampires could do. For me, it was still new—and still something I wasn't comfortable doing.

*Calm,* I thought. *All is okay. I'm just here to help. I'm not the enemy.*

Junior blinked, and then unclenched his fists. He swayed slightly, looked at me confusedly, then turned and went back to his wife. He took her hand and she looked at him, also confused.

I stood, and so did Allison.

"I'm sorry for your loss," I said to the room in general. "Cal seemed like a good man. But I've also been hired to do a job—a job I intend to finish, one way or another. Each of you can expect a visit from me." I looked at Patricia Thurman, Junior's wife. "And I'll be seeing you first."

She blinked with the telepathic suggestion I'd also given her, and with that, Allison and I left the room.

# 26.

We were back at the bungalow.

Allison had poured us two glasses of wine and now, once we had dried off and were in some warm clothing, we sat around the small dinette table that also afforded a view of both the backyard and the brick mansion beyond. Rain slanted nearly sideways across the window, like so many silver daggers. We both kept our eyes mostly on the big house.

Allison was wearing a sweater and jeans and the thickest socks I'd ever seen. "What did you see, Sam?" she asked me.

Good question. I'd been asking myself the same thing since we'd left the house and dashed through the rain like two schoolgirls at recess.

"How good are you at seeing auras?" I asked her.

"Pretty good, but not as good as you. You see details that I can't—heck, that I don't think even the best psychics can see. You know, you could make a lot of money as a psychic, Sammie. Just saying."

"I'll pass. So you didn't see anything unusual about any of the Thurmans' auras?"

"Nothing that stood out, why?"

So, I told her about the shadowy ribbons, or ropes, that wove through all the Thurmans' auras like so many lassos.

"Through all of them?"

"All," I said, and she must have caught my next thought.

"You mean all the *blood* relatives," she said.

"Exactly." I gave her a glimpse of my own memory, so that she could see the shadows for herself.

"What is it?" she said after a moment, her mouth hanging open.

"I don't honestly know."

"The black ropes appear to be . . . binding them," said Allison.

"Good point," I said.

"Like it's holding them hostage."

I shuddered. Outside, a magnificent bolt of lightning appeared, rending the gray sky in two. The bolt could have come straight from Asgard, hurled from the mighty Thor himself. Or, if I was lucky, from Chris Hemsworth. The bolt was followed immediately by a clap of thunder so loud that Allison jumped.

After a moment, she said, "What the hell is going on, Sam?"

"I don't know, kiddo. But there's more."

Next, I told her about the change I'd seen in Tara, and, subsequently, the change I'd seen in Edwin. And not just changes of the physical kind, but within their auras. I showed her mental images as I spoke.

Allison nodded along, even as she was looking a little pale. When I was finished, she said, "Yeah, I thought our hostess was looking a little odd. All that freaky smiling. Thought maybe she'd hit the mimosas a little early."

"I don't think so," I said. "There's something else going on here."

"What? I'll admit, I'm lost."

I drummed my fingers on the table and watched as the back door to the big house opened and a woman emerged, a woman I wasn't surprised to see at all. She popped open an umbrella—which was promptly blown free from her hands, to tumble endlessly across the backyard. She seemed confused at first, then threw on her hood, and dashed across the big backyard.

"I think," I said, watching the sprinting figure, "that the entity is body-hopping."

"Body-hopping?"

"Or body-jumping, or whatever it's called."

"Do you have any idea how crazy that sounds, Sam?"

"No more crazy than everything else."

"Good point. And this entity isn't just any entity, is it?" she asked me.

"No," I said. "It might just be the strongest of them all."

"And you know that how?"

"Call it a hunch," I said. "And there's something else?"

"What?"

I nodded toward the window. "We have company."

# 27.

We moved to the bungalow's living room.

"These places aren't bugged, are they?" asked Allison.

"No," said Patricia Thurman, looking wet and miserable, and nothing like the socialite I knew she was. Her canvas shoes were soaked through and muddy. The hems of her white pants were muddy as well. Her jacket had kept most of the water off, but her face was still dripping wet. She dabbed it with a bath towel that Allison had given her.

"I don't know why I'm here," she said.

I knew why she was here, but didn't say anything. As I'd left the family, of course, I had given her a very strong telepathic suggestion to come see me.

*You devil,* thought Allison.

*Our secret,* I thought, and turned to Patricia. "Maybe you're here because there's something you want to tell us."

"You know, get off your chest," piped in Allison.

Patricia Thurman, who was probably forty-eight years old, but looked, after all her plastic surgery, forty-six years old, also appeared flummoxed. She really didn't know why she had decided to come out into the rain to speak with me. But now that she was here, I could see she was warming up to the idea.

"Well, I'm not in the habit of discussing my family to strangers, you see."

"I understand," I said. "Your niece hired me to help. She felt she had a good reason to."

"And, with Cal dying, maybe she does," said Mrs. Thurman. She tried on a weak smile for size, but it didn't last. It faltered and her lower lip quivered. "God, not Cal, too. Honestly, that's still sinking in."

"You liked Cal?" I asked, just to get the conversation moving. Sometimes the simplest questions led to a windfall of answers. We would see, especially since I just encouraged her telepathically to open up to me a little more.

"Cal was always kind to me, always full of laughter. Always drunk."

I smiled. "There's a lot of drinking with the Thurmans."

"Not that there's any problem with that," added Allison, which earned her a scowl from me.

"Aw, yes," said Patricia, ignoring Allison. "The drinking. The endless drinking. Well, maybe that's part of the curse, too. Had Cal told you about the curse?"

"He didn't have a chance," I said.

"I'm not surprised."

"What do you mean?"

"Never mind, I've said too much as it is."

She made a move to stand and I gently prodded her to relax, sending her a comforting thought that should have put her at ease: *You are among friends, it's warm in here, no one will hurt you, we're only trying to help.*

"Would you like some coffee, Mrs. Thurman?" I asked.

"Yes, please, that would be delightful." She smiled and blinked and then frowned a little, no doubt surprised to hear the words issue from her mouth.

"Allison?" I said.

"Yeah?" She'd been sitting at the edge of her seat.

"Could you make Mrs. Thurman some coffee?"

"Oh, yeah, right. I'm on it."

She got up and headed into the adjoining kitchen, working quickly, but listening, I knew, to the conversation going on in the living room.

"Tell me more about the curse, Mrs. Thurman."

"I don't want to."

"Why not?"

"Because the family isn't supposed to talk about it."

"What happens if someone talks about it?"

"They die."

"Because of the curse?"

"Because of . . . something," she said.

The smell of fresh coffee soon filled the small bungalow, awakening an old need in me, an old craving. I had once loved coffee more than life itself.

Mrs. Thurman was closed off to me again, and I prodded her further. But first, I wanted to make sure she was safe talking to me. Yes, I needed information, but, no, I didn't want to jeopardize her life in the process. After all, I had seen the dark snake rise up through Cal's solar plexus, to strangle the life from him . . . from the inside out.

*Which, of course, left no mark.*

*Just like with George Thurman in the pool.* Allison's thoughts appeared in my mind as she stepped out of the kitchen with two cups of steaming coffee. One for each of them . . . and none for me. I sighed.

I nodded. *Which could explain why there were no marks on George Thurman.*

*And why the coroner could only conclude he'd drowned accidentally.*

As Patricia Thurman accepted the coffee, looking a bit confused as to why she was still here, when, no doubt, her every instinct told her to leave, I gave her another gentle prodding, encouraging her further to tell me more of the family curse, but without divulging so much as to put herself at risk.

When she was done sipping her coffee, she smiled sweetly at me, crossed her legs, and said, "You were asking me about the family curse?"

"Yes," I said. "I was wondering if it's, well, real?"

She nodded and sipped more coffee and would have looked very elegant, if not for her muddy pants. "Oh, yes. It's very, very real."

"Does the curse extend to you?"

"No, not directly. Indirectly, maybe."

"What do you mean?"

"It means that if anyone in my family knows that I'm talking to you about the curse, I might not live to see tomorrow." She smiled at me again then added pleasantly: "And neither will either of you."

Allison put down her coffee. That was, apparently, enough for her to lose her desire for the good stuff.

"The curse is passed down through the blood," I said. "Which is why you're not directly affected by it."

"Why, that's very observant, Ms. Moon. I can see why Tara hired you. Yes, the curse has been passed down through the generations."

"Dating back to when?"

"Conner Thurman."

I knew the name. "George and Cal's father."

"Yes, the bastard who caused this mess," she said and turned to Allison. "Do you have any sugar, dear?"

"Um, I dunno. Let me check."

While Allison went searching for the sugar, I asked Patricia to elaborate on Conner's involvement with the curse. Which she did.

And what a curse it was.

# 28.

"It all began ninety years ago," Patricia revealed.

"Conner Thurman was an ambitious businessman. Perhaps too ambitious. He'd always looked for an edge over his competition. He'd come upon a secretive club of elite world leaders, corporate leaders, politicians, and celebrities. Not exactly the Masons or the Illuminati, per se, but certainly a group of rich and powerful people who enjoyed their elite status. They called themselves 'The Society.'"

Admittedly, I was riveted to Patricia's unfolding tale.

"Conner Thurman wasn't quite in their elite status yet. Yes, he'd had some success in the hotel industry, but certainly nothing that would have given him a golden ticket into The Society. After all, few ever got the golden ticket.

"Conner was enamored by them. He wanted to rub elbows with them. And he did, sometimes. Just enough to whet his appetite further. The occasional golfing trip. The occasional dinner with some of the others. Always occasionally. Never was he fully immersed. Never was he truly one of them."

This was getting good. I nodded at her to go on.

"And, yes, he very much wanted to be one of them. Joining The Society meant that nothing would stop him or his business. He would crush his competition. He would gain the only competitive edge he would ever need: he would have The Society on his side.

"That's all he would need. And so, he hung around. He accepted their meager offerings and not-so-secretly wished for more. He wished very hard for more."

"As we all do," I said.

"Be careful what you wish for," said Patricia, raising her empty cup, indicating that she wanted more coffee. I looked at Allison. Allison looked at me.

"Fine," said my friend grumpily. She snatched Mrs. Thurman's mug from her hand.

"Your assistant has a bit of an attitude," said Mrs. Thurman, and not too quietly.

A coffee cup banged. The coffee pot banged. The refrigerator slammed.

"Here, madam," said Allison a moment later—and a little bit too sweetly.

"Thank you, dear," said Mrs. Thurman, rolling her eyes.

"You were saying," I said, prodding her mentally. "Something about wishes . . ."

"Yes, Conner Thurman would get exactly what he wanted . . . and his family, even to this day—and perhaps forevermore—will continue to suffer because of it."

She went on. "Conner had been invited to a secret ritual. He had been told that it was an initiation ceremony. Conner was beside himself. Was he really, finally, truly going to be one of them? He hoped to God—and so he went with great expectations."

Initiation ceremony? Now it was starting to really sound like a creepy cult.

"And then?" I said expectantly.

"The ceremony was held outdoors at a private retreat. A gated, private retreat, complete with armed guards. It was the first time Conner had ever been to the Retreat. He would never divulge its location. But it was somewhere in upstate New York."

"Excuse me," said Allison, breaking in. "How do you know all this?"

"Because I'm one of them, dear. I may not be blood, no, but I am very much one of them."

She smiled sweetly and drank her coffee. Actually, not so sweetly. There was a darkness in her eyes. This woman, I suspected, had a cold-hearted streak in her.

She went on as I shuddered slightly.

"The ritual quickly got out of hand. There were dozens of men in various stages of dress. Naked prostitutes. An altar covered in blood. Fresh blood. Conner felt sick and turned to leave but was not permitted to. No, he had already seen too much. His choices were simple: become one of them, or join the fate of the others."

"He still wanted to be one of them?" I asked.

"Badly. After all, what were a few prostitutes?"

*Sick*, I thought.

Patricia Thurman continued, "One such prostitute was splayed out on the altar. Naked. Screaming. Begging for mercy. Conner was given a stone blade that he was told was imbued with supernatural power. He was told to use it to kill the screaming woman, to silence her, to sacrifice her."

I had a good idea what had happened from that point on. Patricia kept talking.

"He had looked at her only briefly, and then turned his face away as he drove the dagger deep into her chest while she shrieked and fought and finally died. His hands were soaked with her blood and he wanted to break down and weep. He wanted to plunge the dagger into his own heart, too. How could he do this to an innocent human being?"

Patricia was on a roll now. I don't think she could have shut up if she'd wanted to.

"Next, he was quickly pulled into a cabin, and over to another kind of altar. He had passed their test, apparently. They were well-pleased with him. They had him shower and dress in fine robes.

"He didn't feel like showering. He didn't care that they were pleased with him. He wanted to turn himself in to the police. He wanted to run away forever. He wanted to drop to his knees and weep.

"But everything was happening so fast. So very fast. The shower, the robe, and now kneeling before the new altar.

"Others were there, too. Others who seemed pleased with him. Others who were hooded and robed just like him."

Allison looked at me with chagrin. Patricia kept going.

"He was told it was time to become one of them. He shook his head and said no, that he no longer wanted to become one of them. He was told it was too late. The process had begun.

"They spoke of untold wealth and power. They reminded him what a privilege it was to be one of them, The Society. Still, he continued to shake his head, weeping into his hood. Listening again to the woman who had begged for her life."

*Why had he killed her?* I wondered.

"But the longer he was with them, and the longer he knelt before the strange altar, the further away the woman's cries became. He was told that she was nothing. A whore. A test. To forget about her. To think of himself and his family. His legacy. His empire that was to come.

"Yes, he wanted an empire. They would create it for him. They would help build it for him. They would pave the way for him. No one would stop his empire. No one. Not even God."

Patricia had pulled the God card.

She went on, "He was nodding now. Yes, he desperately wanted it. After all, he had proven himself, right? He had done all they asked, right? Surely he deserved the keys to the kingdom.

"Yes, it was time. It was time for him to claim his destiny. For himself, his family, and future generations.

"*Not yet,* they told him. There was still a final step. A final act of loyalty. A final price."

I was pretty sure I knew what it was.

• • •

Patricia paused in her retelling, looking haggard and drained, and far from the beauty queen she'd once been.

*Years of a family curse will do that to you,* came Allison's thoughts.

Patricia looked like she wouldn't go on—couldn't go on. I respected that. I knew this was hard on her, even with my gentle prodding.

So, I finished the tale for her, as I suspected I knew the ending. "He sold his soul," I said.

Patricia Thurman snapped her head around. Her mouth dropped open a little. The look of shock segued into grim defeat. She nodded. "Yes. And not just his soul. Everyone in the family's soul. Everyone. Every future generation." She paused, and seemed tempted to ask Allison for another cup of coffee, but set the mug on the table in front of her instead. She uncrossed her legs, and looked directly at me. "But your real concern, Ms. Moon, should be more obvious."

"And what would that be?"

"Why did they *really* invite you up here?"

I opened my mouth to answer. The answer, after all, should have been obvious. I had been hired to do a job. To find a killer. Instead, I thought about her question and closed my mouth.

She gave me a weak smile, got up, braced herself for rain to come, and then dashed out.

# 29.

I was on the phone with Kingsley.

"I assume you need something?" he asked pleasantly, rich humor in his deep voice.

"You assume correctly."

I was in my small bedroom. The door was closed. Allison was cleaning up in the kitchen. Occasionally, my small bedroom window rattled with the passing wind, which shrieked like a living thing. Or a dead thing.

I brought Kingsley up to speed, knowing I sounded insane as I did so, and knowing I sounded, perhaps, even a little hysterical. I was, after all, trapped on an island in the middle of a nasty storm—blustery, my ass—with what appeared to be one equally nasty dark entity. An entity that just might have lured me up here. Successfully, I might add.

Kingsley listened quietly, as he always did. A helluva trait in a man. He occasionally made small, noncommittal noises to let me know he was still there and hearing me—another great trait—and when I was done, he let out some air.

"Wow, Sam."

"Wow what?"

"That's quite a story."

"Thank you for that completely worthless assessment."

"Ouch."

"I'm freaking out over here. Tell me what the hell is going on, please."

"Calm down, Sam—"

"I've got Allison here with me . . . and I need to keep her safe, too, and I seriously have no clue what's going on."

"Sam, calm down. You didn't let me finish. Yes, that's a wild story, true, but I also think I know what you're up against."

"Oh, thank God."

"Don't thank God me yet, young lady. This thing is about as far away from God as you can imagine. And you and Allison are very much in danger. So much so that I'm heading up there now—"

"Wait, what?"

"I'm literally out the door, Sam."

"Wait, hold on, Kingsley! You can't be serious. Wait, are you in your car?"

"Yes." I heard the zip of a seatbelt being pulled out and a thrumming drone.

"Is that your engine starting?"

"Yes. Sam, this thing is old and evil and absolutely delights in destroying lives."

"Then what does it want with me?"

"I don't know, but it can't be good. Where are your kids?"

"With my sister."

"Good."

"You're scaring me, Kingsley."

"I don't mean to, but this thing is capable of anything . . . and it wants you for a reason."

"But why did you ask about my kids?"

"I don't know, Sam. But they came to mind."

"I ask because I've been getting a very bad feeling about them, too."

"Then do something about it, Sam. Have your kids and sister—and her whole damn family—stay at my house."

"I don't understand."

"They'll be safe there with Franklin."

"Your butler?"

"Oh, he's much more than a butler, Sam. And trust me, they will be very, very safe."

"So, how will you get here? The ferries are closed, due to the storm."

"I'll figure something out. See you soon, hopefully. Just be safe, Sam, and don't ever underestimate this thing."

"But, what is it?"

There was a small pause before he answered. "I think it just might be the Devil, Sam."

"The Devil?"

"Or something close to it."

# 30.

I clicked off with Kingsley, and just sat there on the corner of my bed.

The bedroom was small, with a single window to my right that looked out towards the woods beyond. The curtains were open and I watched the rain slanting sideways. They looked like blow-darts from an army of elves.

Or, much more likely, I was losing my friggin' mind.

Did he say the Devil?

As in Satan?

I got up and paced and thought about what I had to do, thought even longer about what I should say to my sister, and then made the call. She picked up on the third ring.

"How's the trip, Sam—"

"Something's wrong."

"What? Is everything okay?"

"I don't think so."

"Sam, what's going on?"

"That's the problem, Mary Lou, I don't know, but I think the kids might be in danger. And you, for that matter."

"You're joking."

"No joke, Mary Lou."

"You're being serious?"

"Sweetie, I am. More than I ever have before. There is something very weird going on, and I've been having a bad feeling about the kids for the past few hours now. I just spoke to Kingsley and he echoed the same feeling."

"Someone might hurt Tammy and Anthony?"

The gut-wrenching feeling gripped me again, tearing at me from the inside. I didn't know if this was a psychic hit or a mother's intuition. "I think so, yes."

"Jesus, Sam. Should I call the police?"

I thought about that, too, then told her to give Detective Sherbet a call at the Fullerton Police Department. To let him know my concerns and where she would be with the kids. She digested that last part.

"You want us to stay at Kingsley's house?"

"Yes."

"With his butler?"

"He's more than a butler."

"Sam, I'm scared."

"So am I."

"What will you do?"

I took in a lot of air and said, "I have no clue."

# 31.

I next spoke to each of my kids.

I let them know the game plan, let them know that they would be staying over at Uncle Kingsley's house. Tammy snorted. "Don't lie to us, Mom. I read Auntie Louie's mind. She's totally freaked out right now."

I rubbed my forehead and shook my head. It was, after all, impossible to keep anything away from my kids these days. The truth was, I didn't know what, exactly, I was keeping away from them. Only that I needed them somewhere safe. And fast.

I told Tammy to give the phone to her brother and she did. I told Anthony, who was now almost as tall as his sister—his recent growth spurt was alarming, to say the least—that it was his job to protect her.

"I'm on it, Mommy," he said. "If I have to."

"You have to."

"She's kind of a butthead, though."

"Butthead or not, she's still your sister."

"My *ugly* sister, you mean."

"I love you guys," I said, suddenly choked up. God, I even missed their bickering.

"We know, Mommy. You say it all the time. Sheesh."

"Because it's true," I said, drying my eyes.

"But it's *embarrrrrassing*."

"Maybe so, but you need to hear it."

He sighed loudly. "Fine."

"Well?" I asked.

"Well what?"

"You know what I need," I said.

He sighed again, and, ever so softly, whispered, "I guess I love you, too, Mommy."

I would have laughed if the tears didn't come to my eyes again.

He added, "Don't let the bad guys get you, Mommy."

"I won't, baby."

"Bye, Mommy."

And he hung up . . . and I wiped the tears from my cheeks, and took a deep breath and set my jaw. I had been clenching my hands so tight that my sharp nails had punctured my palms. I opened my hands and watched the small wounds heal before my eyes.

Whoever this motherfucker was, Devil or no Devil, he was not going to hurt my kids, and he sure as hell wasn't going to keep me from seeing them again.

Whoever the hell he was.

# 32.

"I need some air," I said to Allison when I stepped out of my bedroom.

"But it's pouring out there."

I glared at her as she leaped from the couch. "Let me get my jacket."

Soon we were heading away from the bungalows, along a dirt path that led deeper into the surrounding woods. The island itself was sort of long and narrow. The ocean would be only a half mile or so on either side. Although not huge, the island was choked with evergreens and ferns and something called stinging nettles, which Tara had warned us about.

I could give a damn about stinging nettles.

Even though it was only midday, the woods were dark. But here, under the canopy of evergreens, the storm was nearly non-existent, reduced to only a persistent, howling wind—and a few heavy drops.

The path before us was mostly dirt. I could see deer tracks in the mud, and what was surely a dog's tracks, although they could have been a coyote's. I frowned at that. I didn't think coyotes were on the island.

Allison looked miserable and cold. She buried her face in her oversized jacket. Myself, I was wearing only a light windbreaker. I was fairly certain my body temperature was even lower than the surrounding wind and rain.

I veered off on a smaller side-trail, and there we found a massive tree with the widest trunk I'd ever seen. I stopped and turned to Allison, who'd been following with her head mostly ducked, doing her best not to trip over the many exposed tree roots.

"We need to talk," I said.

"I figured that."

"We might be in some deep shit."

"I figured that, too."

"I just talked to Kingsley."

"The werewolf."

"Yes."

"Your ex-boyfriend."

"Yes."

"You do realize that a vampire dating a werewolf is a little too . . . clichéd?"

"Allison . . ."

"Sorry, sorry . . . you were saying?"

"There's some scary shit going on here. Kingsley's coming out."

"What? Why?"

"He thinks I'm in way over my head."

"Sam, from what you've told me, you've faced some crazy shit."

"Maybe none crazier than this."

"Even crazier than me?" asked Allison.

I laughed. I needed that. The tree branches high above us swished and swayed violently. Never had I seen trees like this. So tall, so beautiful. Now as I stood there in the forest, I noticed little balls of light moving about. These bright balls stopped often at plants and at the bases of trees. I watched one stop near a toadstool.

Allison caught my thoughts, and said, "I see those lights, too, sometimes. At parks, and sometimes on my balcony garden at home."

"What are they?"

"If I had to guess, I would say fairies."

I snorted.

"Scoffs the vampire," said Allison, shaking her head. "You, better than most, should know that there are some strange things under the sun . . . or under the moon."

"But fairies?" I asked. "With little wings? Like Tinker Bell?"

"Think of them as nature spirits, Sammie. And no little wings, as far as I can tell. Just peaceful, loving entities that tend to Mother Earth."

I watched the lights flit around the forest some more, dozens of them. Many dozens. They were often the same size, each no bigger than a tennis ball, and their colors ranged from light blue to burning white. One sidled up next to us, slipped between my legs and moved over to a dying fern. It moved carefully over the plant, touching down on each outstretched branch, and then moved on. I sensed, on some level, that it was comforting the dying plant. Weird, yes, but I found the gesture oddly touching.

"So, what do we do, Sam?" asked Allison after a moment or two.

"*We* don't do anything. *I* need to find out what the hell is going on here. You're going to stay in the bungalow—and stay out of trouble."

She was about to protest when she saw the look in my eye. "Fine, I'll stay out of trouble, but I want you to know that I'm lodging a formal complaint."

"Duly noted," I said.

"So, then, what are you going to do?" she asked, ducking as a particularly large glob of water splattered on her nose.

"I'm going to have a little talk with our client."

"Tara? But isn't she one of them?"

"Exactly," I said, and turned and headed back through the forest, with Allison stumbling and cursing behind me.

# 33.

As I left Allison in the bungalow, confident that she would be safe for the time being, trusting my inner alarm system—and my own gut feeling—I paused just outside the door.

As rain battered me, I decided to change plans, at least for the time being.

Instead of talking to Tara, I hung a right and headed back into the forest, and found a side trail that I had seen from high above the night before. The trail, wide at first, soon narrowed considerably. I didn't know much about forests or hiking or even trails, but I figured this to be a game trail.

I continued on, pushing through massive ferns that seemed almost prehistoric. Thorny raspberry bushes were in abundance as well, all filled with juicy berries that probably tasted heavenly. The trail angled up, as I knew it would.

Stinging nettles snagged my jeans as I carefully stepped over fat banana slugs—and even the occasional toadstool. I marveled at the mushrooms that clung to moist tree trunks. Nature at its weirdest. Water dripped seemingly everywhere. Lightning suddenly flashed above, zigzagging through the treetops, followed by an angry grumbling of thunder.

I continued on, slipping once or twice in the sloshing mud, winding my way up the trail that would lead to the highest point of the island.

Soon, as the trees opened and the wind and rain lashed me violently, I found myself on a steep switchback trail that afforded a majestic view of the manor far below. The trail soon led to a rounded rock dome high above the island. I didn't know if it had a name, but I called it Dome Rock.

Rain drove straight into my face, down inside my jacket collar. I didn't mind the rain at all. It made me feel alive. Human. Normal. Rain didn't judge or discriminate. Rain fell on everyone . . . mortal or immortal. Living or dead.

*Or some of us in between.*

I slipped and slid my way over the moss-covered rock and soon looked out over the Puget Sound, to distant islands and churning seas. It was so beautiful and epic and alive that it was nearly impossible to believe that a family was being terrorized by a body-jumping demon.

Nearly.

I knew one thing, though: I wanted answers.

And I knew just where to find them.

*God.*

# 34.

I sat cross-legged at the apex of the dome, completely exposed to the storm.

At times, the wind blew so hard that I thought it might lift me up and blow me off the rock mound. But it didn't, try as it might. Instead it tugged and pulled at me like an angry thing, as I remained seated and focused.

My eyes were closed tight; my hands rested on my knees.

The wind thundered over my exposed ears. Yes, my hood was down. I didn't want any barrier between me and God. I breathed in and out, slowly. Now, the wind blew even harder, rocking me further and, in the far distance, I heard the pounding of the surf against the rock cliffs.

I continued breathing, slowly, deliberately, deeply.

It took a minute or two of focused concentration, but soon enough, I felt a sensation of rising up, as if I'd entered a tube of some sort. A glass tube, because in my mind's eye I could see myself rising up. But, interestingly, not so much rising above the earth. No. Instead, I sensed myself rising up through what appeared to be levels.

*Dimensions.*

How I knew this, I didn't know. But the word felt right. Yes, I was rising up through the dimensions, even as the rain hit me full in the face. The sensation of being wet and cold seemed to be happening to someone else. Certainly not me . . . after all, I was rising, rising.

*Rising . . .*

The dimensions swept past me. On many of them I sensed entities, or beings, watching me, observing me while I came and went. Spiritual beings, I knew, highly evolved beings that existed in realms that we, as humans, could not comprehend . . . and yet, I sped past even them.

Higher and higher.

Until . . .

I was back. Not above the earth, or even above the Universe. I was *outside* of the Universe. Outside of space and time. I was observing creation as God would have. As God did so now.

*Welcome back, Samantha Moon,* came a thought deep inside my head. No, not exactly in my head. All around me, vibrating through me.

I sensed that I existed in the space between space, and it was a concept that was difficult for me to understand.

*You are doing fine, Samantha Moon.*

*Thank you. You are doing fine, too, from what I can gather.*

There was a gentle laugh inside me. *Kind of you to say, Sam. Do you mind if I call you Sam?*

*You're God, you can call me anything you want.*

More gentle laughter. God, I was discovering, had a nice sense of humor. *I understand that you think that, Sam. But I am, more accurately, the Source.*

*Source?*

*The Source of life in this Universe.*

*I see,* I thought. *I think. That's still pretty much God to me.*

*I will not argue the point, Sam. Either way, it's a pleasure to have your company.*

I sensed the vastness, the emptiness, the peace.

*Do you ever feel lonely out here?* I asked.

*Your question implies that I might find myself alone.*

*Well, yes, I guess. Are there many others like you? Other Sources?*

*There are a handful of us, yes.*

*How many?*

*Twelve, to be exact.*

*And from where do the twelve originate?*

*Exactly that, Sam. From the Origin.*

*And what, exactly, is the Origin?*

*My Creator.*

*I see,* I thought. *And you are my Creator?*

*You are my creation, yes.*

*And what do the other eleven Sources do?*

*They watch over their own multiverses, of course.*

*Of course. And why did the Origin create twelve of you?*

*To learn more about itself.*

*And why did you create me?*

*So that I can learn more about myself.*

*And thus, what? Report back to the Origin?* I asked.

*You are correct, Sam.*

I thought about this as the rain and wind pummeled my physical body a universe away, as I gazed out over the slowly-moving cosmos that rotated around a galactic center of some sort.

*That's pretty heavy,* I thought.

*It's as heavy or light as you want it to be. But, yes, I understand that these are new concepts for you in the physical world.*

*Is there evil?* I asked suddenly.

*There is the potential for others to show you the opposite of light, yes.*

I had a sudden insight, sudden clarity. I wondered if this insight came from the Source.

*The darkness is necessary to appreciate the light,* I said.

*Well said, Sam.*

*Can darkness ever destroy light?*

There was a slight pause before the voice vibrated through my being again: *Remember this always, Sam: A small match can illuminate the darkest room.*

I got the meaning and felt myself nod way, way back there on that rock dome, high above Skull Island.

*So, I should never fear darkness,* I thought.

*Live in light, Samantha, but acknowledge the darkness.*

*For without darkness, there cannot be light.*

*Very good, Sam.*

*Is there a Devil?* I asked suddenly.

There was a long pause. *You are asking if there is an entity that delights in causing mischief, who tortures souls for all eternity, who causes the good to falter, and the bad to be worse?*

*Well, yes.*

*No, Sam. No such entity exists.*

I nodded. Perhaps here in space, or perhaps back on the dome, I said, *I have a question about a group of beings I have come across; one such being is, in fact, residing within me, and undoubtedly hearing this very conversation.*

*Maybe she needs to hear this conversation, Samantha. Maybe you are her answer, too.*

*I don't understand.*

*Maybe you are her way back to the light.*

*I never thought of that.* I paused, formulating my thoughts. *I feel she is evil.*

*She—and others like her—have certainly made choices that might appear evil.*

*But they are not evil?* I asked.

*They operate out of fear, Sam. Fear of moving on, fear of giving up power, fear of retribution. They are, quite simply, misinformed.*

*Misinformed about what?*

*That life is eternal, that I am eternal. That they are eternal. That power is temporary, that love is everlasting.*

"Is there evil?"

"There is no evil, Samantha Moon."

Lightning flashed in the heavens above . . . until I realized that it had flashed directly above my body. I was about to ask another question, until I felt myself slipping back . . . or down through the dimensions. As I slipped down, down, God's words sang through me and around me.

*Love is everlasting.*

I opened my eyes and looked out over stormy seas and wondered again if I'd completely lost my mind.

# 35.

As I hiked back from the dome, still reeling from yet another encounter with God—or, perhaps more accurately, the Source—I sent a text message to Tara Thurman:

*We need to talk.*

Her reply came a few minutes later, as I slid and skated down the muddy trail.

*I know.*

*Meet me at my bungalow in twenty minutes.*

*Where are you?*

*Nature walk,* I texted and shoved my phone in my hip pocket before the rain could short-circuit something. I might be able to do a lot of things, but magically fix my iPhone wasn't one of them.

Back at the bungalow, I let Allison know we were expecting a guest. Allison read my mind, shook her head, and went immediately into the kitchen and took out a big carving knife.

"She's one of *them,* Sammie," she said, slipping it inside her waistband, and then yelping loudly when the point bit her.

I snickered and reminded her that the entity, as far as we knew, could only jump from one body at a time.

"Well, we don't know that for sure, Sam. In fact, we know very little about it."

"Which is why I want to talk to Tara."

Allison still didn't like it, except this time she gingerly slipped the knife inside her waistband. I chuckled and took a shower. Showers were still one of my few great pleasures in this new life of mine, and I reveled in the warmth it provided, always reluctant to leave. Even after the shower was long off, I stood there briefly in the stall, the heat and steam, and watched the water drip down my still-pale skin. Pale and flawless, granted.

*No,* I thought. *Pale and dead.*

I threw on my last pair of dry jeans, then tossed my sopping-wet clothes in the bungalow's washer. I'd just turned it on and was toweling my hair when a gentle rap came on the front door.

*As of someone gently rapping,* I thought, thinking of the Edgar Allan Poe poem, *rapping at my chamber door.*

. . .

As I reached for the door, I mentally reminded Allison to guard her thoughts. She understood . . . and reached down and adjusted the knife at her hip. I might have detected a small spot of blood appearing through her jeans where the point had poked her.

I next remembered the words of the Source: *They operate out of fear, Sam. Fear of moving on, fear of giving up power, fear of retribution. They are, quite simply, misinformed.*

Misinformed or not, the being that possessed the Thurmans was, I suspected, desperate and powerful. A hell of a dangerous combination. But I would not fear it, whatever it was.

*A small match can illuminate the darkest room.*

I opened the door, stepped aside, and let the Devil in.

# 36.

Tara, of course, didn't look like the Devil.

Or a highly evolved dark master, for that matter. In fact, other than looking wet and cold, she looked exactly as I'd remembered her: young, fresh-faced, alert, alive. Not pale and gaunt. Not vampiric.

*It's because he's not a vampire,* Allison said. *Not quite.*

I nodded minutely as I invited Tara to have a seat. She did so at the small kitchen table. I asked if she wanted Allison to make her some coffee. Tara shook her head—and just missed the nasty look Allison shot me.

I considered how to broach the subject of her family, and decided to dive right in. "I've heard about the family curse," I said.

Tara, who was wearing a cute pair of tight jeans and bright red rain boots lined with rabbit fur, snapped her head up. The black, vaporous thread that wound through her aura pulsated a little.

*He's listening,* I thought. How I knew this, I didn't know, but it seemed obvious now.

"Who told you?"

"That's not important now. What can you tell me about it?"

Her own once-vibrant aura seemed to shrink a little, a sign that she was going within, closing herself off to me. "Sam, it's really quite silly."

"From what I heard, it didn't sound silly," I said. "It sounded dangerous."

The black thread began rotating slowly through her aura now, weaving in and out. Tara held my gaze briefly, and then looked away. I felt her fear.

"It's really not something I want to talk about," she said. "Also, I don't see what this has to do with why I hired you."

"Why are you afraid?" I asked.

She looked at me, then at the door. I reached out and took her hand. As I did so, the black, ethereal snake swelled briefly and circled even faster, weaving in and out, watching me carefully. Yes, I sensed it watching me.

"You're not leaving," I said.

"Hey, let go."

"I know about the curse, Tara," I said, squeezing her even tighter, but not so tight as to hurt her. Tight enough for her to know she wasn't going anywhere. After all, I was going to have to get through decades of fear and confusion. "I know about your great-grandfather, and I know what he brought upon your family."

She fought me briefly, but to no avail. As I held her hand, I got psychic hit after psychic hit.

"No," she said. "It's just a silly superstition—"

"You and I both know it's not a superstition. You and I both know that something dark and angry and hungry has entered your lives. Something that will never leave."

"You're crazy, Sam—"

"You feel it in you, you feel it when it overcomes you. You feel it make you say things, do things, want things. You thought you were crazy. You thought all of you were crazy. But it's in you. You understand that now. It's in all of you. In your blood. Like a parasite. A leech. A disease."

"You're crazy, Sam."

"I'm not crazy. And neither are you."

Tears welled up in her eyes. She looked over at Allison, then back at me. "Why are you doing this? What's the matter with you? I hired you to find answers to my grandfather's death."

"And I am," I said. "But ask yourself: Why did you hire me? Why me, out of hundreds of other private investigators?"

"I live in Southern California. I . . . I liked your ad."

"You live in Los Angeles, nowhere near me."

"Your ad . . ." she mumbled.

"I see," I said. "And why were you looking for a private investigator in Orange County?"

"I don't—" She paused, fumbling for words. The black snake swirling faster and faster, weaving, in and out . . .

"You don't know why, do you?" I said.

"I don't—"

"You don't know why because *it* compelled you to call me, to hire me."

"Sam, please—"

"How did you know Detective Sherbet?"

"I didn't know him."

Something very much wanted me to have Sherbet's recommendation. I rarely, if ever, turned anyone away who had first come from Sherbet. Something wanted to guarantee that I would take the case.

"It compelled you to seek him out, didn't it?"

"Yes—"

My hands shot out and took both of hers this time. I dug my nail deep into her skin, making blood contact. She gasped, and in a flash, I saw it now, saw how it worked, saw how it used her and the others. The secret manipulation, down through the ages. I saw how it rarely, if ever, revealed its plans to them. It simply manipulated, used them. Like a sick puppet master. Mostly it left them alone. Mostly. That is, until it needed something from them—or wanted them to do something for it. In this case, it had compelled Tara to call me and hire me. But she did not know why. It had kept its reasons to itself.

I released her as she recoiled, rubbing her now-bleeding hands, shocked and clearly horrified. But I had seen what I needed to see. There had, of course, been something else I had seen. Something very, very strange.

"Tell me about the digging," I said.

The black snake had swollen to nearly twice its usual size. The entity was here, but hadn't quite taken over Tara fully. No, it was surveying the damage, assessing what needed to be done, if anything.

"It makes us dig," she said finally. "On the north end of the island."

"Dig for what?"

"I don't know."

"But it's searching for something?"

"Yes."

"Is that why you were gone yesterday?"

She looked at me with pleading eyes. I saw the torment in her soul, felt the anguish in her heart. I knew the source of her pain: the entity had taken so much from her and her family.

"Yes," she said. "It doesn't tell us what it's looking for."

"Us?"

"Yes. Mostly it uses Edwin and me. When he's resting, I take over."

"What part of the island, exactly?"

Tara shook her head. "I . . . I can't say."

"It won't let you say, you mean?"

She looked at me with pleading eyes. And nodded.

"Tara, would you like for me to remove this entity from your lives?"

Her mouth dropped open to speak, but she didn't, couldn't. The swirling black snake was so thick now, so dense, that it almost appeared real. The entity, I knew, had just taken her over.

*The son-of-a-bitch.*

Still, Tara nodded. A very small nod. It was all she could do against the will of the entity who, I knew, presently possessed her. Tara wanted help. Badly.

Now she stood slowly and smiled down at me. The same creepy smile I had seen on her before. "You cannot win, Samantha Moon," she said evenly, except it wasn't her. "Not against me. Not against us."

And she turned and left the bungalow.

# 37.

"That was so creepy," said Allison.

"As hell," I said.

"It allowed her to give you that information about the digging," said Allison.

"I know."

"It could have stopped her earlier, but didn't," said Allison. "Which means . . ."

"Which means it wanted me to know about the digging."

"But why?"

"I don't know," I said.

I nodded absently. I couldn't stop thinking about the desperate look in Tara's eyes, even as she was compelled to say the words that came out of her mouth at the end, even as she was compelled to get up and leave.

I shuddered as my cell phone rang.

Secure line. Detective Sherbet, no doubt. I picked up immediately.

"Sam, it's Sherbet."

"I would never have guessed."

"No jokes, Sam. Someone tried to break into your home last night."

"My kids—"

"Are safe with me. I'm here at Kingsley's home, if you want to call it that—"

"What happened, Detective?"

"A neighbor reported the break-in. Nothing was stolen, as far as we know." He paused. "But they really weren't looking to steal anything, were they, Sam?"

"I don't think so," I said.

"What were they looking for, Samantha? Be straight with me."

I thought of Kingsley's words, words that still made me feel sick to my stomach.

"My kids, I think," I said.

"Why?"

"I don't know yet."

"Christ, you get into some weird shit." He paused. "Sam, there's something else."

My heart thumped hard. "What?"

"Kingsley's rather, um, interesting manservant—"

"Butler," I said.

"Whatever. Frankie or whatever his name is, claimed to have seen someone lurking outside Kingsley's house this morning—"

"Shit."

"Sam, what the devil is going on?"

I gave him a glimpse of my thoughts, even long distance, and I sensed him shaking his head. "You have got to be kidding me," he said.

"No."

"That's some weird shit."

"Detective, I think it's important that you take my kids somewhere else."

"Where?"

I thought hard about that. "Somewhere I don't know. Somewhere safe."

"Somewhere you don't know? What the devil are you . . ." And then Sherbet, the only other human being besides Allison who was privy to my thoughts, finally caught on. "I understand. I mean, I really don't understand. In fact, I'm fairly certain I'm going batshit crazy. But, yeah, I think I understand."

"You do?" I said urgently.

"Yeah, you don't want me to tell you where I'm taking the kids because . . ." he paused, no doubt searching for words.

"Yes," I said, finishing for him, "because the thing inside me is listening."

# 38.

"We need to know why this entity brought me up here," I said when I'd hung up with Sherbet.

"And why it wants your kids," chimed in Allison.

Another very cold chill went through me. I began pacing in the bungalow. Who had come to my house? Who was outside of Kingsley's house? Why did they want my kids?

"I think we know who," said Allison, somehow following my frantic thoughts. "I'm certain the Thurman clan reaches far and wide."

I sat on the arm of the leather sofa, ran both hands through my hair. My too-thick hair. Never was my hair this thick when I was mortal.

"He controls them all," continued Allison, "anyone with a drop of Thurman blood."

"Jesus," I said. "So how do we stop him?"

"That," said Allison, "is why you make the big bucks."

"Great," I said, and thought again about the image I'd received from Tara: that of her and Edwin digging on the north side of the island.

"A good place to start," said Allison, following along. "Except if she doesn't even know what they're digging for, what makes you think we would know?"

"That," I said, "is why they invented the Internet."

"I thought they invented the Internet for porn?"

"That, too," I said. "Grab your laptop, and let's see what we can find."

"Yes, ma'am," said my new friend, and did just that.

$\bullet \ \bullet \ \bullet$

It didn't take us long to find something.

"A shipwreck," said Allison, pointing to the screen. "Over a hundred years ago, right off the north side of Skull Island. Okay, we are definitely venturing into Scooby-Doo territory here."

"Except Scooby-Doo and the gang didn't deal with a body-jumping demon who's after me and my kids. Read the article."

She did.

In 1896, a shipping vessel hit rough waters just north of Skull Island. Most of the crew of fifteen survived, except for the captain who went down, proverbially, with the ship. The remaining fourteen crew members, via life rafts, eventually washed up onto Skull Island, where they were soon rescued.

"Weird and cool all rolled into one," said Allison. "But I don't see how that helps us."

I didn't see it either. "What's the name of the historian quoted in the article?"

"Abraham Gunthrie, college professor from Western Washington University in a city called Bellingham."

"Where's Bellingham?"

She brought up the city and college on Google Maps. Bellingham was north of here, about an hour away as the eagle flies. Or, in my case, as the giant vampire bat flies. I bumped Allison rudely out of her seat and, while she protested and rubbed her bruised hip, I brought up one of my proprietary websites and entered in my username and password. A few clicks later and I had the information I needed. The professor's home address.

"That's kinda scary how fast you can do that."

"I use my powers for good," I said. "Mostly."

"You do realize that the storm is even worse. No one is leaving or coming to the island."

"Not everyone," I said. I logged off the site, got up and began packing myself a weatherproof bag.

# 39.

I was flying.

Through wind and rain and lightning. Kinda like the mailman, only scary as hell.

Below, the gray, churning sea spread far and wide. The vague shape of a distant land mass was my target. Lightning appeared around me, sometimes just barely missing me. I wondered what it would feel like to be struck by lightning. Probably hurt like hell. Would I plunge from the sky, to sink to the bottom of the ocean?

Maybe. Sinking to the bottom of the ocean didn't concern me much, since I had little use for my lungs. In fact, I quite enjoyed plunging into the water every now and then and gliding like a great manta ray.

Hanging from one of my scary-looking talons was my favorite Samsonite carry-on bag. I continued about a thousand feet over the churning ocean, buffeted by winds that threatened to knock me off course—threatened, but never succeeding. My wings were powerful in this form. I was powerful in this form. It would take a lot more than a gale-force wind to knock me down.

Shortly, I came upon a rocky shoreline and a few scattered homes. I followed a meandering road that wound along the edge of the land, affording, undoubtedly, wonderful views of the ocean.

More homes appeared as the road angled inland. And there, through the driving rain, was the sparkling city of Bellingham. I circled above it within the clouds, looking for a good spot to land, and found one in a park near the university.

I alighted smoothly upon a bench because, in this form, I seemed to prefer landing *on* something—rocks, tree limbs, park benches—which I could never quite figure out.

*Must be the bird of prey in me.*

I tucked my wings in, and once again saw the vision of the woman in the flame—and soon, a curvy but toned mother of two was squatting naked on the same park bench, a Samsonite carry-on bag looped around her ankle.

Sometimes it's fun to be me.

Weird, but fun.

# 40.

After dressing and hailing a cab, I was soon standing outside of Professor Abraham Gunthrie's quaint little home.

A typical Washington home, I discovered: clapboard siding, cute herbal garden, and a stone path through roses. There was a wooden wraparound porch with views of the university and his equally charming neighbors' homes. I wondered if he ever suspected a creature of the night would be descending upon his idyllic world.

Probably not. Then again, he probably never expected a private eye to come knocking, either.

Which is exactly what I did. Three times, loud enough to be heard throughout the small home. I watched a squirrel make a mad dash out into the storm and cross the manicured lawn. About halfway, it paused, no doubt regretting its decision to leave its cozy, acorn-filled nook somewhere high in the tree. Finally, it continued on, running and hopping alternately.

As it disappeared from view, I heard footsteps creak across a wooden floor and approach the front door. I already had my business card in hand as I waited.

The man who opened the door was older, as I knew he would be. Abraham Gunthrie sported a Van Dyke goatee, pointed at the end, and some errant ear hair. His eyebrows looked bushy enough for that squirrel I'd just seen to hide its acorns in.

"May I help you?" he asked. His voice was stronger than he looked. I briefly imagined him standing before his students, his deep voice easily reaching the back rows.

"Are you Professor Gunthrie?" I asked.

"For you, I'll be anyone you want."

Whoa. There was still some pep to his step. I smiled, perhaps bigger than I'd intended. He smiled, too, and showed me a lot of coffee-stained teeth.

"Professor Gunthrie, I'm a private investigator and I'd like to ask you a few questions about a shipwreck on Skull Island."

He blinked, absorbed what I said, then accepted my proffered business card, which he looked over carefully. He said, "You sound very official, Detective Moon." He winked. "I suppose I'd better invite you in, then."

"Thank you," I said.

And as I stepped past him, the old guy might have—*just might have*—checked out my ass.

The interior was as warm and cozy as the exterior promised. A fire burned energetically in the fireplace. Pictures of kids and grandkids adorned the wall. An elderly woman was in many of the pictures. The photos were of his deceased wife, I knew, because her spirit was presently standing in the room as well, watching us silently.

I'd gotten used to such spirits. Mostly, they didn't expect me to see them, and mostly, I pretended not to see them. In this case, I gave her a small nod and smile. The woman, who was composed of hundreds, if not thousands, of particles of white light, seemed to do a double take, then slowly nodded toward me.

"Beautiful home," I said, noting the maritime theme mixed with the family photos.

"Made more beautiful now," he said, winking at me. Slightly embarrassed, I looked over at his departed wife. She simply shook her head and appeared to chuckle, although it was hard to tell because her features weren't fully formed.

"Well, thank you," I said.

"Would you like some tea, Ms. Moon?"

"Water would be great."

"I can do water. Have a seat." He gestured toward a well-worn couch with a colorful afghan blanket thrown over the back.

Professor Gunthrie shuffled off into the kitchen, where I next heard water dispense from a cooler. Shortly, he returned with two glasses of water, which he set before us on little doily coasters at the coffee table. I sipped from my glass politely. He seemed pleased. In fact, he seemed pleased just to have any company at all. Even vampire company.

A model of a clipper ship stretched across the length of the coffee table. Tammy and Anthony would have broken that in two hours. Maybe one hour. Maybe instantly.

"So, what can I do for you, Ms. Moon?" he asked, glancing at my business card again. He seemed impressed. Or maybe that was wishful thinking on my part.

"I'm looking into a shipwreck that occurred on Skull Island in the late nineteenth century."

"The *Sea Merchant*," he said, nodding.

"What can you tell me about that shipwreck that, well, didn't make it to the papers?"

"Or onto the Internet?" he asked, winking.

"That, too," I said, grinning.

"Perhaps the most interesting would have been that the *Sea Merchant* was transporting a small amount of treasure."

"Treasure?"

"Of sorts," he said, and drank long and hard from his own glass of water. "A man by the name of Archibald Maximus lost his fortune. Lots of gold, and other valuables. Apparently, he was quite the collector. Are you okay, Ms. Moon?"

Had I any color in my cheeks, I'm sure it would have drained. As it was, I'm fairly certain my mouth might have dropped open. I tried to recover valiantly. "Any idea what this treasure might have contained?"

"Gold, from the reports. Not a king's ransom, granted, but certainly enough to keep the treasure hunters searching, which they continue to do to this day."

"I see," I said. "Thank you."

"Is there anything else I can do for you, Ms. Moon? Would you like something to eat? I just made a wonderful quiche—"

"No, thank you. I appreciate your help."

I stood to leave. He stood, too. "Do you have to leave so soon?" He was lonely and I knew it.

"I'm afraid so."

He looked briefly pained, and then nodded. As he walked me to the front door, I reached out to the female spirit watching us from the corner of the room.

"Your wife is here with you, Professor Gunthrie," I said.

"Excuse me?"

"I'm a sort of . . . medium. Your wife is here, in this room."

"Why would you say—"

"Her name is Helen, and she says she will always love you."

He blinked rapidly, and actually looked toward the area where the spirit of his deceased wife was presently watching us. "Well, you're a private eye, I'm sure you could have found that out—"

"She wants to thank you for planting the roses in her honor. She knows you think of her every time you see them."

His mouth opened, and then closed. He tried again, and then closed it again.

I continued. "She loves you now more than ever, and is with you always."

"Samantha . . . I don't understand."

"It's okay if you don't understand, Professor. She wants me to tell you that when you lie in bed and feel all alone that you are never alone. Not ever. She's lying right there with you, in spirit."

He rubbed his eyes. "I . . . I feel her, sometimes."

"When you see her in your dreams, she wants you to know that's her, coming to you."

"I dream of her all the time."

I smiled sweetly at him. "And there's something else she wants me to give you."

"What?"

I leaned in and kissed him ever-so-softly on the corner of his mouth. "That's from her."

He broke down for a minute or two and I waited, checking my watch. I nodded toward Helen, who had drifted over and was now standing nearby.

She thanked me, and I smiled at her, then squeezed Professor Gunthrie's hand, and left him weeping in the doorway.

Alone. In theory.

# 41.

I was back on Skull Island.

Total elapsed time was just over an hour. I found Allison where I'd left her: in her bedroom lying with the steak knife clutched in her hand. Her bone-white hand. Yes, I'd felt bad leaving her, but trusted our psychic connection to alert me should she be in any danger.

"What took you so long?" she asked, setting the knife aside after virtually prying her fingers open. "I thought super bats made great time."

I ignored her; instead, I filled her in on what I'd learned.

"And who's Archibald Maximus?" she asked.

"He's a librarian at Cal State Fullerton."

"The university?"

"Yes."

"What is he, like 215 years old?"

Her math, I suspected, was dubious. I said, "No. He looks younger than you, although that's not hard to do."

"Mean, Samantha Moon," she said. "Very mean. Is he a vampire, too?"

"No. Not quite. He's something else."

She read my thoughts. "An ascended master?"

"Or a warrior of the light," I said. "He's here to counterbalance the darkness."

"Is he single?"

"Allison . . ."

"Sorry, sorry. So, what does all this mean?"

"I don't know yet," I said.

"He obviously survived the shipwreck, since only the captain died."

"Right," I said.

"And he was transporting a treasure."

"Right again," I said.

"What kind of treasure would a warrior of the light have?" asked Allison. "I mean, isn't he supposed to be above material wealth and all that?"

"Maybe," I said, and thought of the simple young man I'd met a few times now working in the Occult Reading Room at Cal State Fullerton, a young man who wasn't so young after all. A young man who had, quite remarkably, reversed my son's vampirism, using the first of four powerful medallions.

Medallions he had shown me in a book. Medallions that were created, he'd said, to counter the effects of vampirism, although he had told me nothing more.

Allison had been following my train of thought, seeing my memory as I reviewed it.

"Four medallions," she said, commenting on the book Archibald had once shown me of the four golden disks.

"Yes," I said.

"And you have had two of them?"

"Yes."

"Aren't these, like, rare?"

"Well, there's only four of them."

"And one of them is presently on you—"

"*In* me," I corrected, and showed her the circular-shaped scar along my upper chest.

"Gotcha. And easy on the vampire cleavage, Sam. Kinda gross." She faked a shiver. "How did you get the first one?"

"It was sort of hand-delivered to me."

I gave her the image of the hunky, blond-haired vampire hunter who'd posed as a UPS deliveryman. She nodded. "And why did he deliver the medallion to you?"

"I'm not entirely sure."

"Sam, perhaps you are not seeing this, so let me spell it out for you: there are only four of these bad boys in the whole wide world."

I waited. She waited.

"Well?" she asked, exasperated.

"Well, what?"

She rolled her eyes and got up and stood in front of me. "Sam, somehow you are *attracting* these medallions."

"*Pshaw*," I said, blowing her off. "Only a coincidence."

"Is it, Sam? And now you are on an island where, quite possibly, one of the medallions is hidden."

"That's a leap," I said.

"Is it? The same entity, the same warrior of the light, lost his treasure over a hundred years ago, a treasure that has never been found—"

"Because it sank off the coast. It's buried in muck."

"Or is it?" asked Allison. She was on a roll. "There were fourteen survivors, Sam. They obviously had life rafts of some sort. How easily could our friend Archibald Maximus—the same guy, mind you, who first showed you the book containing the four medallions—how easily could he have hidden his treasure here on this island?"

"You're crazy," I said. "There's no evidence of the treasure being hidden on the island."

"And there's no evidence of it ever being found, either. Didn't the professor say that divers have been looking for it for decades? Well, maybe they're looking in the *wrong place*. Maybe they should be looking here, on this island—where, I might add, this entity friend of ours is compelling Tara and Edwin to dig endlessly."

I opened my mouth to speak. There was a sort of insane logic to what she was saying.

"Insane?" she echoed, reading my thoughts.

"Kinda crazy, kiddo," I said. "But what makes you think Archibald even had one of the medallions?"

"I don't know, but it makes sense. A treasure, Sam. A treasure. The medallion would be considered treasure, wouldn't it? Besides, what else would the entity have Edwin and Tara looking for? The family doesn't exactly need a few crappy gold coins."

"I could use a few crappy gold coins."

"Me, too," said Allison. "My point is this: there is a very good chance the third medallion is here, on this island."

"Then why lure me up here?"

"Isn't it obvious, Sam?"

"No."

"The entity—and now me—thinks that you can help it find it."

"Now *that's* crazy."

"Maybe, maybe not. Remember, Sam, you have possessed two prior medallions. By this point, it might be desperate."

"Fine. Then what does it want with my kids?"

And just as the question escaped my lips, I knew the answer. Allison, in tune with my own thoughts, gasped.

"One of the medallions is in you," she said. "And the other medallion . . ."

"Is in my son," I said grimly.

"Didn't Archibald break down the other medallion into some sort of potion?"

I nodded, feeling so sick that I could vomit. A potion that my son drank. "Yes."

"A medallion which reversed your son's vampirism?" said Allison.

"Mostly."

"So, in effect, one medallion is in you, and one is in him, and the third . . ."

"Might just be on this island," I said, and held my stomach, thinking of my son.

"But why does he want the medallions?"

"I don't know."

It was at that moment that a God-awful loud wolf-howl blasted through the blowing wind.

Allison jumped. "Jesus, was that a wolf?"

"Yes," I said, feeling some relief.

"Here on the island? I thought there were no predators."

"Not of the mortal kind," I said. "Get dressed."

# 42.

We found him in the back woods, dripping wet.

"Don't say it, Sam," said Kingsley.

"Say what?" I asked innocently enough.

"Anything about a wet dog."

"I would never say anything about you looking just like a wet dog caught out in the rain."

Kingsley shook his great, shaggy head and looked over at Allison. Only someone oblivious would miss the way his eyes reflected amber. Damn beautiful eyes.

Yes, I used to enjoy staring into those eyes, especially on nights when my sister had the kids. I had just been falling in love with the big oaf, when he decided to unzip his fly at the wrong time.

Bastard.

"Don't look at me that way, Sam," he said.

"What way?"

"Like you want to take a chainsaw to my balls."

Allison snorted. She was, I sensed, quite smitten with Kingsley Fulcrum. No surprise there. Hard to resist someone who stood six and a half feet tall, and had shoulders wide enough to see from outer space.

*Down girl*, I said to her telepathically.

*I think I'm in love.*

*No, you're not.*

To Kingsley, I said, "I'll add that to my to-do list. Might teach you a lesson."

"If it keeps you from hating me, then do it."

"You two are funny," said Allison.

"Who's the broad?" asked Kingsley, jabbing a thick thumb her direction.

"Broad?" she laughed. "Do people really talk that way?"

"They do when they're almost a hundred years old."

"Sam!" snapped Kingsley.

"She knows everything, you big ape."

"I've never met a werewolf before," said Allison, stepping around him. Kingsley, I noted, lifted his upper lip in what might have been an irritated snarl. "Are they always as big as you?" she asked.

"Sam . . ." growled Kingsley. His wet hair hung below the collar of his soaking-wet jacket and jeans. He was also—I could hardly believe it—barefoot.

"There are no secrets between Sam and I," said Allison. "At least not many. We're blood sisters, so to speak."

Kingsley growled again and shook his head, just like a wet dog. Allison and I squealed and took cover.

"Oops, sorry," he said, and I caught his impish grin.

"You can trust her," I said, wiping my face. "It's *you* who I can't trust."

"Low blow, Sam. I came all the way out here to help you, not take abuse."

"You deserve some abuse," I said.

"Fine," he said. "Then are we done?"

"Maybe," I said. "And that reminds me . . . how did you get out here? No ferries or boats are out in this weather."

"I can still swim, Sam."

"Dog paddle?"

"Ha-ha."

"Okay, I'm done," I said, until his words hit me full force. "Jesus, did you really swim?"

"Not all of us can fly, Sam."

I recalled the churning waves, the white caps. The sea was angry. Kingsley, I knew, was no ordinary man. Or even an ordinary werewolf. Mortal or immortal, few could have made that swim, especially in these conditions.

"We need to get you dry," I said.

"No," he said. "We need to keep you safe. What's going on? Bring me up to speed."

And so we did, there in the forest, while the big hulk of a man occasionally wrung out his hair, all while the treetops swayed violently. Finally, when we were done, he said, "I agree with Allison."

She beamed.

I said, "What part?"

"All of it. The medallion must be here. It's the only thing that makes sense. And I think we should beat the bastard to it."

"What do you mean?" I asked. I was pretty sure my eyes narrowed suspiciously.

"Let's find the medallion first."

"And then do what with it?" I asked.

"We'll cross that bridge when we get there."

I opened my mouth to protest. I wasn't as entirely convinced as my two friends—one of whom was, of course, an ex-boyfriend and just barely in the "friend" category. Still, I couldn't think of a reason to protest. Hell, maybe they were right. Maybe I was, somehow, attached to the medallions.

*If it's even here on the island,* I thought.

*It's here,* thought Allison. *I'm sure of it. I'm psychic, too, remember?*

I sighed and nodded, and was about to suggest that we go back for shovels when Allison pointed out that there was probably equipment on the other side of the island. I nodded again, recalling my flight over the north end of the land mass. Yes, I had seen what appeared to be sheds and outbuildings. All abandoned. No doubt, Edwin and Tara kept their equipment in there, or nearby.

As I worked through this, thinking, I caught Kingsley's amber stare. The brute wasn't even shivering, but his heart was hurting. I could see it in his anguished eyes. Yeah, he missed me. He also should have thought about that before breaking my heart.

Still, he had come all the way out here for me. So, I reached out and ran a hand over his beefy shoulder and said, "Thank you for coming."

"Anything for you, Samantha Moon," he said. "Anything."

I nodded sadly—perhaps for what could have been—and the three of us headed down the pine needle-covered dirt road that cut through the heart of the island, and headed north.

On a fool's run, no doubt.

# 43.

The storm seemed to be growing stronger.

Wind shrieked. Trees bent. Rain rattled leaves everywhere. As we trekked north, I couldn't help but think that Kingsley and Allison might be onto something. I was technically a carrier of one of the medallions, and my son . . . well, my son had *consumed* another medallion in a sort of potion concocted by one Archibald Maximus, who, as it turned out, was also quite the alchemist.

*The medallion is in my son, too,* I realized. *In his blood, perhaps.*

But what did the entity intend to do with my son? Was he going to drink from my boy? I shuddered and nearly worked myself into a panic. Jesus, and what did he intend to do with me? The medallion, as far as I was aware, was now eternally a part of me.

There were four such medallions, and if one of them was indeed hidden on the island, that would be three. The whereabouts of the fourth were unknown to me . . . and yet, even as I thought about that, the fleeting hint of a memory came to me. And then left just as quickly.

*Good God, did I actually know where the fourth medallion was?*

I didn't know, but I figured it was best to approach this one medallion at a time.

More importantly: what did the bastard want with all four medallions?

Allison, who'd been casting me sidelong glances in between cautiously stepping over exposed tree roots, also had been following my train of thought. Her words came clearly to me now as we stepped into an open area of the forest: *He mentioned releasing his sister, Sam.*

A sister who was presently trapped within me. A blessing and a curse, surely. A blessing because her dark power fueled my now-dead body, and, in turn, gave me superhuman abilities. A curse because I was now being used by her. I was, in effect, serving as her host.

I shuddered.

*But how could the medallions help his sister break free?* I asked.

*Lordy, Sam, how would I know? Heck, just a few days ago I was a hair stylist/personal trainer/photographer/actor in Los Angeles.*

*That's a lot of slashes,* I thought.

*It's called "multiple streams of income." Oh, and you can add another slash.*

*Oh, yeah?*

*Private investigator assistant.*

*We'll see,* I thought. *So, what good does it do us to find the medallion first?*

*I don't know, Sam, but it might give us some leverage. In the least, it could thwart his nefarious plan.*

I almost laughed at her word choice. Truth was, any plan that involved harming my son was nefarious. As we continued on, I wondered again how the medallions could be of use to the entity. After all, weren't the golden disks inherently good? They were, after all, created to counteract the effects of vampirism.

*Unless,* Allison said telepathically, *all four medallions come together. Perhaps then they can be used for evil. After all, a gun can be used to either defend or to murder.*

I looked at her. "That was shockingly erudite," I said.

"I have my moments," she beamed.

"What're you two talking about?" asked Kingsley, pausing and looking back. His long hair flung water everywhere, not that it mattered. We were in the open again and rain was literally driving directly into our faces.

"Girl talk," I said sweetly.

"Fine," he said irritably. "Looks like we're here."

Indeed, I could now hear the pounding of the surf, of water exploding against rocks. The hiss of retreating foam. We were at the north end of the island, near what appeared to be a straight drop down into the ocean below. Yes, the ocean was angry. The rain was angry.

Hell, even I was a little angry.

No, I was a *lot* angry.

"Okay," I said, "let's find this goddamned medallion."

# 44.

We stood at the cliffs.

My jacket flapped crazily. My jeans were soaked through. Yet, I never felt so alive. Wind and rain were elemental. I often felt elemental, too, deeply connected to the rhythms of night and day.

Allison, on the other hand, looked miserable. Her cheeks could have been two freshly-picked cherry tomatoes. She had also started sneezing. I needed to get my friend out of the storm—but to where, I didn't yet know.

"Where to, Sam?" Kingsley asked on cue. He seemed to be enjoying himself. This was the first time I'd seen the big gorilla since the "incident." If anything, he looked even sexier. Dammit. Apparently, wet clothing suited him well. I loved a man with meat on him, and Kingsley had just that. Thick and meaty equaled great cuddling.

"Don't know," I said, although my voice might have been lost on the howling wind.

The evening was coming on full dark—although never too dark for me. The ocean was alive to my eyes, foaming and frothing and churning. Salt spray exploded from below with each crashing wave. Some of that salt spray reached us. I tasted it on my lips, and then spat it out again.

I didn't know why I seemed to attract the medallions. Somehow, someway they seemed to find me.

He fearlessly stepped to the edge of the cliff and leaned out, looking down. Massive and immovable, he looked a bit like a cliff himself, only hairier.

"You said some others have been digging for it, too?" asked Kingsley.

I caught his meaning. "You think we should start where they've been looking?"

"It's not a bad idea. After all, they might have narrowed things down for us."

"Except I don't know where they've been digging—"

"I heard someone mention some caves that were near the beach," said Allison, cutting me off. "If I were shipwrecked and wanted to hide my gold, that's where I would pick."

From here, I could see a wide swath of sand not too far away, where the cliff dropped down to meet the beach. Which is where Allison suddenly set off for, sneezing as she went.

"I guess we follow her," said Kingsley, chuckling lightly. He bowed in my direction and waved his hand. "After you, madam."

We followed Allison down the grassy slope, slogging through puddles and ducking against the wind. My new friend seemed oddly determined. And her mind, perhaps even more oddly, was closed off to me.

I frowned at that as I followed her, as Kingsley's sasquatch-like footfalls crashed through the tall grass behind me.

# 45.

Miraculously, Allison led us directly to a cave.

The opening was just far enough back from the shoreline to not be flooded, and yet still deep enough to provide shelter from the pounding rain. Once inside, as our breaths echoed—well, Kingsley's and Allison's breaths echoed—I pulled down my hood and asked Allison if she was doing okay.

"Just cold," she said. She smiled at me faintly, her mind still closed off.

To me, she looked . . . distracted. And was blinking far too much. Perhaps she'd caught a cold.

Perhaps.

It was then that my inner alarm began sounding . . . as always a steady buzz just inside my ear. I looked again at Allison and she again smiled sweetly at me.

"Well, now what?" asked Kingsley, hands on his hips and dripping everywhere. His big cartoon feet were buried in the soft sand inside the tunnel.

"Here," said Allison, pointing. She'd brought her cell phone and was now using its flashlight app.

I didn't need a smart phone flashlight app to see in the dark, and neither did Kingsley, but we were polite enough. She aimed the light toward the back of the deep cave, and revealed something that none of us were too surprised to see: digging tools. Shovels and picks and strainers. It looked like a looter's hangout.

Rocks were piled up back there, too, many of which had been moved. Yes, someone was looking for something here, and, by all appearances, had been doing so for quite some time.

Kingsley inspected the area with Allison. I didn't. Instead, I closed my eyes and did my best to block out their voices, which seemed to echo everywhere at once. I kept my eyes closed and turned in a small circle. I lowered my hands and opened my palms. I breathed deeply, slowly, focusing.

Focusing . . .

Focusing on the medallion, as if it existed, as if it really could be here in the tunnel.

I didn't know how to find something that was hidden. After all, I'd only stumbled upon the second medallion in old Charlie's mobile home quite by accident. Back then, I had closed my eyes, like I was doing now, and the medallion just appeared to me, without effort—

I gasped.

There it was.

Burning in my mind's eye.

Clearly.

And it wasn't that far away.

Except, of course, it most certainly wasn't in the tunnel.

I opened my eyes and headed out of the cave . . . and toward the crashing surf.

# 46.

I looked out over the dark ocean.

Tiny filaments of light brought it all to life for me, illuminating what should have been complete blackness. I stood there at the edge of the foaming surf, which occasionally washed over my now-ruined sneakers. Since I was already soaked to the bone, I didn't bother removing my clothes, including my shoes.

Kingsley came up behind me. Amazingly, I could smell a combination of nice cologne and something musky. Something wolfish, no doubt. He placed a gentle hand on my shoulder.

"Is it out there?" he asked.

"Yes."

"How far?"

"Far enough that I need to swim."

"Where, exactly?"

"An underwater cave."

"Are you going to get it?"

"Yes."

"You need my help?"

"No."

"Do you love me?"

I opened my mouth, stunned by the question. Leave it to the expert litigator to drop a bomb on an unsuspecting witness up on a theoretical witness stand. "No," I said. "At least, not like I used to."

"You still love me, but differently?"

"Not now, Kingsley."

"Right, right. The medallion. So, what are you going to do?"

I looked back . . . and up at him. "I'm going for a swim."

Before I headed out into the water, I caught Allison watching me from the shadows of the cave. I was quite certain she was smiling. A big smile. A very big smile.

• • •

I stepped into the foaming surf, Asics and all.

I might be immortal. I might be cold to the touch. But that didn't mean I relished the idea of stepping into what appeared to be the coldest ocean ever.

"Think warm thoughts, Sam," called Kingsley behind me. For some reason, he seemed to be enjoying this. *Asshole.* Then again, the big yeti had recently made his own journey across this very body of water.

*If he can do it, I can do it.*

And so I started running, splashing through the ankle-high water. Shortly, the water rose to my knees, and when it got to my thighs, I took a massive, instinctive breath and dove forward, under a coming wave. I stayed under, kicking hard, using my strong arms to propel myself under the raging ocean.

I continued on, just a few feet under the surface. The occasional wave still rocked me, but shortly, I was ten feet or more underwater. Soon, I was deeper than that. Far deeper. I kicked hard, pulling myself forward with powerful strokes. The sound of the waves crashing above receded, and soon I found myself in a place of silence. Complete and utter silence.

I liked that.

I held the image of the cave system in my mind's eye. Luckily for me, the incandescent flashes of light that only I could see were just as prevalent down in the deep. That didn't mean I could see far, granted. No, in fact, I could barely see a dozen or so feet in front of me.

Good enough.

I wasn't worried about sharks or killer whales or even mermaids. A merman might be damn interesting, and I briefly found myself wondering again if such creatures really did exist.

Hell, why not? *I* existed.

Life down here was not abundant . . . at least, not this close to shore. I did see silver fish that scattered before me. Once, I sensed a darker shape above me, but nothing that triggered my inner alarm system, and so I continued on . . . down into the deep.

Down, down.

And there it was . . .

A dark opening emerging through the dark waters. It could have been the maw of a great beast, waiting for something cute and curvy and stupid.

Stupid was right . . .

I plunged straight into the tunnel.

Anything could have been waiting in there.

Anything.

# 47.

I trusted my inner warning system.

For now, all appeared safe, and so I swam down through the wide tunnel, past scurrying crabs and smaller fish. I tore through swaying seaweed, and startled something big that could have been a grouper; that is, if I knew anything about fish, which I didn't.

Either way, it flicked its thick tail and shot past me.

*Well, excuse me.*

I continued down. The walls seemed alive, as various plant life clung to it, all moving and swaying in the currents. Beautiful, I supposed. But I wasn't here to admire the ocean's beauty. I was here to recover something seemingly lost forever.

Seemingly.

My kids were a distant memory. Kingsley was a distant memory. Russell Baker and his beautiful biceps were a distant memory. All that I knew was right before me: a cave, the cold water, the ocean depths. I did not think of idle things. What Tammy and Anthony were doing right now didn't cross my thoughts.

I only knew the tunnel. I continued into it, swimming quickly, pulling at the water, kicking the water, moving faster than, no doubt, most experienced divers. I was a superhuman immortal on land or sea, apparently.

The tunnel twisted and turned. At times, it grew wider. At other times, I was forced to pull myself through small openings. I doubted scuba divers had ventured this far. Scuba equipment was limited . . . and wouldn't fit through the many crawl spaces I was presently pulling myself through.

And still I swam, keeping the image of the medallion firmly in my thoughts. It was my beacon . . . and I knew exactly where that sucker was.

I plunged into a small opening, not so small that I had to pull myself through this time, but small enough that I aimed my hands in front of me and brought my legs together. I was a mommy-shaped torpedo, plunging through the black water.

Black water that was alive to me.

Blazing with light.

I emerged into a massive underwater cavity. A cavern perhaps, but filled completely with water. That someone could have been here before me was an amazing concept. But someone had.

Another immortal.

The Librarian. The alchemist.

I swam down to a grouping of smaller rocks and saw the satchel there, swaying in the currents. How a satchel could have survived so long in salt water was beyond me. Then again, much of what the Librarian could do was beyond me.

I grabbed the bag, paused briefly, then turned, kicking hard, and shot up through the water, up through the tunnel, and then, after an indeterminate amount of time, surfaced far from shore.

I saw Kingsley waiting anxiously near the crashing surf.

Holding the satchel, I grinned and began swimming for the beach.

# 48.

We were back in the cave.

I wasn't shivering, although I should have been. Then again, I should have been dead somewhere deep inside that tunnel system, too. But I wasn't, of course.

*The freak lives on.*

Allison crowded me eagerly, her mind still closed off to me. Did she know her mind was closed off to me? I didn't know, but would talk to her about it later.

Kingsley, admittedly, took up most of the tunnel. A ceiling that I had thought was high actually got brushed by his big head.

The satchel sat dripping on a rock before us. The bag itself had been leather at some point, but was now black and seemed to be deteriorating with each passing minute.

Perhaps it had been held together by alchemical means.

Waiting just for me.

Perhaps.

I looked at my friends. Kingsley nodded. Allison's eyes were alight with an inner fire. Then I began opening the bag. And by the time I'd done so, the material irreparably fell away in tatters.

Revealing a single coin.

Not a coin, actually. A golden medallion inlaid with three opal roses. It caught the light of Allison's silly flashlight app, refracting it beautifully.

That such a medallion was presently in me was hard to fathom. That my son had consumed one in a potion was another hard reality to accept. That a demented entity was bent on releasing his trapped sister within me, was, of course, the hardest to believe of all.

But it was all true.

Every bit of it.

Further proof that I was undoubtedly in an insane asylum, far away from here, rambling to myself incoherently while nurses and staff stared at me sadly.

*Perhaps, perhaps not.*

For now, I was standing in a mostly-dry cave, staring down at the third of four priceless medallions. Priceless, that is, to me and my kind.

*The vampire kind.*

"Well, now we know why the others couldn't find the medallion," said Kingsley. "It was meant for you to find, Sam." He held my gaze. "You and only you."

I nodded. Of that I had no doubt. Except how and why Archibald Maximus knew I would be here 100 years later was, of course, the greater mystery.

"The first medallion reversed your son's vampirism," said Kingsley.

"Mostly," I said.

He nodded. He knew all about my son. No, we hadn't been romantic over these past few months, but we had kept in touch, and I had consulted with him on Anthony's growing powers.

"And the second one . . ." he began.

"The second helps me exist in daylight."

"So, one has to wonder," said Kingsley. "What will the third one do?"

"A good question," said Allison, who had remained silent up until now. "But one that must, sadly, go unanswered."

I turned to her, frowning. God, she'd been acting so weird . . .

And then I saw it . . . what had been a miniscule black thread, so tiny that it had gone unnoticed by me, quickly swelled before my eyes. I had a brief image of a garden hose coming to life, engorged with water, swelling, thickening.

The black, ethereal ropes encircled her aura, weaving in and out. Lariats of death. It was as if Satan himself had lassoed my friend.

Her dark eyes, once beautiful and full of sweet mischief, now shone with fear—even while her lips curled into a Cheshire Cat-like smile, the corners of her lips pushing up deeply into her rounded cheekbones.

"Is your, um, friend okay?" asked Kingsley.

"She's fine," answered Allison, in a voice I now recognized, its inflection similar to what had come from Edwin and Tara. And now from Allison. "She's just sort of taking, let's say, a temporary backseat."

"Sam . . ." said Kingsley, now facing Allison. "What the devil is going on?"

"He's here," I said. "In Allison, except I don't . . ."

"You don't understand how, Samantha Moon? Perhaps some things you aren't meant to understand, my dear. But let's just say this: your friend was right, she is indeed *distantly* related to the Thurman clan."

I grabbed the medallion and backed away. I had no idea what the entity within could do, what sort of powers it possessed. But if it was truly a highly evolved dark master then it might be capable of anything.

"There is no escape, Samantha Moon," said Allison. Or, rather, said the entity within her.

I looked at the hulking Kingsley next to me. "I like our chances," I said.

"Surely you wouldn't hurt your friend, Samantha Moon," it said. Tears appeared in Allison's horror-filled eyes, and poured down her cheeks.

"Just give me the medallion, Samantha Moon, and I will release your friend."

"Don't do it, Sam," said Kingsley.

"Or would you prefer to watch your friend drown herself in the ocean? Or, even better, bite off her own tongue and bleed to death in front of you?"

Allison's eyes widened, and I might have—*might have*—detected her shaking her head no. She was fighting the entity, I was sure of it, and one thing I was also sure of: she didn't want me to give it the medallion. I suspected I knew her reasoning: for now, the entity needed her alive. For now, she was safe.

"Why do you want my son?" I asked suddenly.

"I think you know why we want your son, Samantha Moon."

I took a threatening step toward Allison—my sweet and silly friend Allison. The entity only grinned broader, which seemed impossible to do, but it somehow managed to pull the corners of her lips even higher up. Tears continued pouring from Allison's pleading eyes.

"Would you like to strike me, Samantha? If so, I *strongly* encourage it." The entity turned Allison's face toward me and chuckled lightly. "As the good book says, turn thy other cheek and all that."

"You're evil."

"I am *motivated*, Samantha, by that which is important to me."

"You want to release your sister," I said. "From me."

"That, my dear, is a very, very strong motivation."

"And you need the four medallions to do it."

It nodded, raising Allison's eyebrows. "I see you have done your homework, Samantha Moon. You never cease to impress us."

"I have one such medallion in me, and my son has the other in him. I'm holding the third. Where is the fourth?"

Allison turned to face me. Kingsley, I noted, had moved close to my side. He was ready to pounce at a moment's notice. Kingsley might be a womanizing bastard, but he was certainly all hero.

The entity continued regarding me through Allison's eyes. "I see you do not remember, Samantha."

"I don't have any idea what you're talking about . . ."

"Sssister," hissed Allison. "Speak to her, remind her of what she has seen and forgotten."

I knew instantly of whom he spoke: the female entity within me. *His* sister. Even as I shuddered, a memory materialized within me, summoned, I suspected, by the dark entity who shared my body.

It was an image of Fang.

I gasped, and Allison grinned.

The image clarified, took on more shape. It was an image of Fang back before I knew he was Fang, back when he was just a flirty bartender. He always gave me and my sister so much attention—and now I knew why, of course. He'd stalked me, relentlessly. He'd also fallen in love with me. So many emotions with Fang: from anger to love to everything in between.

The image clarified further . . . the longish teeth that hung from his chain . . . teeth that I had once falsely assumed were shark teeth. They weren't, of course. They were *his* teeth, pulled cruelly in an insane asylum . . . pulled from his very mouth.

The image clarified further still. It was Fang smiling broadly at me and my sister, leaning an elbow on the scarred counter at Hero's in Fullerton.

There was something on his chest.

Just behind the fangs that hung from the leather strap.

Was it a tattoo?

No.

The image clarified further, coming into even sharper focus.

It was a circular-shaped pendant hanging from his neck. But I hadn't recognized it because it had been flipped over, revealing only its golden backside.

The fourth medallion?

"Fang," I whispered.

Allison grinned broadly, even as her eyes pleaded for me to help her. "Ah, sssister. I see she remembers now. The fourth medallion is, in fact, not very far at all."

"Sam . . ." said Kingsley next to me, pulling me out of my reverie. "Sam, you might want to see this . . ."

I blinked and looked to where he was pointing.

Through the cave opening, I saw people coming. Slowly, de-liberately, plodding through the sand along the beach. Toward the cave. Toward us.

I recognized them all.

The Thurmans. From the very old, to the very young, a dozen of them or more.

*Sweet Jesus.*

I snapped my head around and looked at Allison. The entity within her tilted her head slightly. "We are legion, Samantha Moon, and we will have the medallion—*all* of the medallions."

# 49.

"We can't hurt them," I said. "They're innocent."

"They might be innocent," said Kingsley grimly, "but they look like they mean business."

They also looked like zombies. Already many of them were appearing at the cave entrance, compelled by forces they might not have entirely understood.

Edwin was there, and so were his many cousins. There was Tara, too, just behind him. Old and young, all the Thurmans looked confused. Most were shivering from the cold, drenched, unprepared for the weather.

The dark cords that bound them—that cursed them—were all engorged, filled with hate, with venom. The cords pulsated and rotated and twisted through their otherwise beautiful auras.

Somehow, the entity had possessed them all, simultane-ously—and it was a heinous, horrible thing to see.

In that instant, Edwin charged, baring his teeth, dashing su-pernaturally fast through the short tunnel. Kingsley leaped in front of me and, with one mighty swipe of his meaty arm, sent Edwin flying hard into the stone wall to our side.

A dull thud . . . and now Edwin was slumping to the ground, bleeding from a head wound. He was alive, but unconscious.

Kingsley looked at him only briefly, and immediately turned his attention to an older gentleman, an uncle, who next made his own charge. The result was similar, although Kingsley, I noted, didn't hit the guy quite so hard.

"They're stronger than they look," said the werewolf.

"It's him," I said. "*He's* making them stronger."

Kingsley nodded as the older gentleman shook his head and picked himself up. I suspected that if all of the Thurmans attacked at once, things would get very ugly. "Are you sure we didn't step onto the set of a George Romero movie?" he asked.

"Sadly, no," I said.

"I think," said Kingsley, surveying the bizarre group before us, "something else is controlling them, from afar."

"Why do you say that?"

Kingsley reached back for me and took hold of my hand. "Who brought this curse upon the family?"

"Conner Thurman," I said. "Ninety years ago."

"We need to find him, Sam."

"He died," I said. "A long time ago."

Kingsley looked back at me and, amazingly, gave me a sardonic smile. "That," he said, "I seriously doubt. Trust me on this, Sam. I've seen some weird shit in my time. Granted, the walking dead is about as weird as it gets. But a curse like this needs a primary source. A head, so to speak. And that source—or head—would be Conner Thurman himself."

"He's entombed in the family mausoleum," I said. "Here on the island."

"Find him," said Kingsley, squeezing my hand. "And cut off the head of the snake. And I don't mean that figuratively."

"Jesus," I said.

"Pray all you want, but until Conner Thurman is found and destroyed, this curse will never, ever end—and they will never, ever stop coming for you and your son."

I thought about that as the Thurmans converged together. It was definitely about to get very ugly in the cave.

"I can hold them off, Sam," Kingsley said over his shoulder. "I can do so a lot easier and safer for them if I don't have to worry about you, too."

"But—"

"Go, Sam. Now!"

# 50.

As a male cousin dashed forward, sprinting supernaturally fast, Kingsley met him. This fight was more even, and Kingsley, I saw, had his hands full.

"Go, Sam!" growled Kingsley, finally heaving the young man off him, just as another sprinted forward. "Go now!"

I went, sprinting quickly through a gap between the Thurmans. Two peeled off and gave chase, while the others converged on Kingsley. Allison, to my dismay, was now running swiftly behind me.

*Unbelievable.*

But they weren't quite as fast as me. I suspected this was because the entity's own great strength was spread among many, rather than focused on one.

When I looked back again, I saw that I was alone in the forest.

The storm, amazingly, had subsided somewhat, although thick drops still splattered against my face. The medallion was also still clutched tightly in my hand.

I thought of Allison as I ran. The entity had threatened to kill her. Could he kill her? I recalled the shadow that had risen up in Cal, the shadow that had strangled the life out of him.

*Yeah,* I thought. *The entity could kill her.*

I picked up my speed.

Trees swept by in a blur. Once, I tripped over an exposed root and tumbled, my momentum carrying me many dozens of yards over the moist forest floor. I scrambled to my feet, aware that my right arm was broken at the wrist. A helluva tumble.

The pain was intense, but brief. I held my arm to my side and picked up my pace, and by the time I was at full speed again, I was certain my arm had healed completely.

*So weird.*

I flexed my hand as I ran, and the last of the pain subsided.

*So very weird.*

The dirt road soon opened into the Thurmans' backyard. The manor beyond was brilliantly lit—and noticeably empty. Patricia Thurman was in there somewhere . . . and anyone else not blood-related. Undoubtedly, she would be wondering what the hell was going on.

*And I thought my family was weird.*

Far behind me, I heard the sound of running footsteps. Allison and another person were still behind me, following.

I paused briefly, then hung a right and headed for the massive stone edifice that stood adjacent to the property, and was surrounded by a thin band of trees.

The Thurman Mausoleum.

# 51.

The mausoleum looked creepy, even to a vampire.

Admittedly, I didn't know what the hell I was doing, or what, exactly, I was looking for. Yet, Kingsley had made a good point: destroy the man responsible for all of this insanity.

That was, of course, if the man responsible was still alive.

Official death records had reported the man's death decades ago.

I tended to not question official death records.

That is, of course, until my attack seven years ago. Now, I supposed, anything was possible.

The mausoleum was situated about two hundred feet away from the main home, and was surrounded by a thin row of evergreens. Still, who would even want a mausoleum so close to a family vacation home?

I didn't know, but it was perhaps someone who needed to keep an eye on the mausoleum. Or, rather, someone in the mausoleum who needed to keep an eye on the family.

*Or both.*

I shook my head at the insanity of it all.

Insane or not, the threat to Anthony and myself was real. And any threat to my kids was going to get my full and unwavering attention.

The mausoleum was composed of cement and plaster, its portico supported by two intricately carved Corinthian columns. Three broad stairs led up to what I imagined was a heavy front door and was, once I checked, locked.

I briefly wondered how Kingsley was faring against the Thurman clan. I could only hope they'd lost interest in him once they saw that I was gone. Either way, I was certain the big fellow could take care of himself.

Somewhere out there, crashing through the forest, was my friend Allison. My new and very close friend, who was, amazingly, distantly related to the Thurmans.

*Go figure,* I thought, and raised my foot.

I wasn't sure how heavy or thick the metal door was, but decided to kick with all my strength.

Which I did now, slamming it as hard as I could just under the brass door handle. The door didn't swing wildly open, and the handle didn't explode off the hinges, either.

But something cracked and the door moved.

I kicked again, perhaps even harder, and this time, the door did swing open.

I stepped through the doorway.

# 52.

I was here on a hunch.

Kingsley's hunch, actually. He believed that the entity was primarily focused through Conner Thurman. His theory did make a kind of sense. After all, my body was immortal, impervious to death, pain, or decay. All thanks to the dark entity within me.

Thanks to *her.*

So why wouldn't Conner Thurman, who originally summoned the entity nearly a century ago, also benefit from the dark presence within him? Yes, the more I thought about it, the more I was certain that he hadn't died.

Conner Thurman had been, of course, in the public eye. Had he been alive today, he would have been, what—I did some quick math, which was, of course, never my strong suit—and figured him to be around 125 years old.

He'd faked his death.

I was suddenly sure of it.

Yes, it felt right. Kingsley's hunch felt right. Long ago, a channeled presence had told me to trust my gut instincts. Trust my feelings. I might be able to do many things, but I could not predict the future.

*Not yet, anyway.*

Yes, I'd had a few prophetic dreams of late. Dreams where I could, in fact, see the future.

But this wasn't a dream. At least, I didn't think it was.

These days, dreaming and reality often blurred. So much so that I continuously questioned my own reality. The only constant was my love for my kids. They were my rock. My safety net. My love for them was more real than anything. It transcended everything. All the craziness.

If not for them . . . I would have descended, I was certain, into complete madness.

I held it together for them.

But now, someone was threatening my son.

I clenched my fists and stepped deeper into what was, in fact, my first mausoleum. It was cold, yes. Dark, yes. No windows. Correction, two stained glass windows situated high above. The floor was a highly polished marble, now made slippery by my soaking-wet Asics.

Hunch or not, one thing was for certain: my inner alarm was ringing loud and clear.

*Here be danger.*

I was in a sort of long hallway with a high ceiling. On either side were shelves of some sort. The walls and shelves were composed of the same marble as the floor. Along some of the shelves were vases and flowers. Spaced along the walls were various plaques, all depicting names and dates of births and deaths.

My footsteps squished. Water dripped from me. I wasn't breathing, and so there was no echo of breath.

The tomb was silent.

Or should have been.

I cocked my head, listening in the dead of night.

Yes, there was a sound from somewhere.

Footsteps.

I paused, and verified the footsteps were not my own. Indeed, they continued on, echoing within what sounded like a stairwell. My hearing was good, granted, and the acoustics of the tomb enhanced the sound wonderfully.

Someone, somewhere, was coming up a flight of stairs. I was sure of it.

A flight of stairs that were directly ahead of me.

I remained motionless. I felt my normally sluggish heart pick up its pace.

Directly ahead of me, further down the narrow hall, a shaft of light suddenly appeared as a door opened.

Despite myself, I gasped.

A figure stepped out.

A figure I immediately recognized, at least from the pictures I'd seen. Conner Thurman. He looked remarkably good for being 125 years old.

I was careful to guard my thoughts.

"I see you found my home away from home, Samantha Moon," said a clipped and cultured voice. "Or, rather, my home *next* to my home." He chuckled lightly.

"You live here?" I asked, finally finding my voice.

"Often, although I get out as well, generally in disguise. But, yes, you could say that this is my sort of home base."

Was I talking to Conner Thurman or the entity within? I didn't know. Perhaps a little of both. Conner was a tall man who appeared to be in his mid-forties—likely the age when he had first been possessed by the entity within.

I noted he was not smiling, not like the others. Also, I couldn't see his aura, nor read his mind. He was completely closed off to me. Like Kingsley, or Detective Hanner, or the other immortals I'd encountered.

*Yes*, I thought. *He is the source.*

The source of the curse.

His family's curse.

Also, I was certain that Conner Thurman—the real Conner Thurman—had been overtaken completely by the entity within. Where the real Conner Thurman was, I didn't know, but I suspected he was trapped within, watching helpless within his own body.

Similar to the way the entity within me watched from within my body. Trapped within me—and wanting out. To possess me fully, similar to the way the entity now fully possessed Conner Thurman.

"Who are you?" I asked. I was aware of movement outside the mausoleum. I suspected Allison and perhaps some others had arrived. For now, they stayed outside. Undoubtedly, they were being controlled by the entity before me.

"I am a renegade of sorts, Samantha Moon."

"What do you mean?"

"You could say I don't play by the rules. I create my own rules."

"What rules?"

"The rules of life, death, and our immortal souls."

"I don't understand."

"I, and my sister within you, have challenged the powers that be, so to speak. Successfully, I might add. We have effectively removed ourselves from the soul's evolutionary process."

"I don't understand."

"Yes, I'm sure you don't. You see, there are universal laws in place that govern not only this world, but the worlds beyond. Others before you have created these laws, laws that govern your soul's journey through life and death. I happen to not agree with these laws, Sam. I happen to have a rather rebellious streak within me. You see, I like to do things my way. And so does my sister, and so do many others like me."

He began circling around me, hands clasped behind his back. He went on, "You see, we have figured a way out of this rat trap, Samantha Moon. And you can join us. Forever join us."

"What do you mean?"

"Give my sister the freedom she seeks, and you can share in our eternal journey."

"And if I refuse?"

"There is no refusing, my dear. You will become one of us or nothing."

I found myself backing away. There was the scent of something repugnant wafting off him. An actual smell of decay, perhaps. My inner alarm seemed to be blaring off the hook. Yes, I was in serious danger, I got it. I willed my own alarm to quiet down. Sometimes, the damn thing went off so loud that I couldn't hear myself think.

"You killed George Thurman and Cal Thurman."

"Yes, I kill when my hosts become problematic or useless."

"What will you do with my son?" I asked.

Conner Thurman stopped pacing and faced me. "Unfortunately, Samantha, your son consumed something very important to me. Something very important to the process of releasing my sister. But not all is lost."

"What do you mean?"

"I'm sure you have figured out by now that I will need all four of the medallions to release my sister."

I said nothing, already suspecting where this was leading. I clenched my fists.

"You see, I had a willing host. My host—Conner Thurman—permitted me to take possession of his body. And I gladly did so. Oh, yes. My sister's release requires aid, if you will. That's where the medallions come in."

"But why the medallions? I don't understand."

"The medallions were created to aid those like you, Samantha Moon. The combination of all four together was not foreseen, and not predicted. At least, not by those who created them."

He stepped closer, and I stepped back. I sensed great strength within him. I suddenly very much wished that Kingsley was by my side again.

"Fortunately, the magicks contained within the particular medallion that your son consumed are not lost."

"I don't understand—"

"Yes, you do, Samantha Moon. You understand all too well."

In a blink of an eye, he was behind me, reaching around my throat, one hand clawing up inside my sweater. I struggled but was shocked by his strength, his speed.

*So strong, so fast.*

His hand continued up over my stomach, over my breasts, up near my throat.

"You see, your son must now . . ." he began, whispering harshly in my ear, his fingertips now pressing into the flesh of my upper chest, "be consumed completely and totally. Every inch of him. Every drop of blood. Every hair on his head." He was breathing harder, faster. "And trust me, Samantha Moon—trust me when I tell you that I will enjoy him very, very much. But first—"

I screamed, and not necessarily out of fear or anger, but because his fingers had dug deep into me. He threw me away as an excruciating pain ripped through me.

Stumbling into the hallway wall, I gripped my chest as blood poured between my fingers.

I looked back in horror as Conner Thurman held in one of his hands the medallion that had recently been under my skin, a medallion that was, even now, draped in my own bloodied flesh.

"One medallion down," he said, turning to face me, "and three to go."

# 53.

"Lucky for you, Samantha Moon, that I need to keep you alive. You are, after all, graciously hosting my sister."

I braced myself against the polished wall, even while blood from my chest continued pouring free.

"This may sound, ah, rather ghoulish, my dear, but all that precious blood of yours will not go to waste. I will have one of my—for want of a better word—Thurman minions gather it up carefully for me later. Waste not, want not." He laughed.

The pumping blood quickly slowed to a dribble. I could literally feel the wound closing underneath my palm.

I gasped and stood straight.

He pointed to the disk-shaped bulge in my front pocket. "It would be so much easier, Samantha, if you would just give me medallion number two."

"Fuck you."

"For some reason, I thought you would say that." He cocked his head to one side. "Forgive me, sssister," he said, the word hissing from between his lips. "For what I am about to do."

He leaped forward so fast that I had only enough time to turn my head. Still, the blow sent me spinning, and rocked me unlike anything I'd felt before.

And it had only been a partial blow.

I searched for the wall, couldn't find it, stumbled and fell.

He ran up to me, and in one smooth and horrible motion, kicked me full force in the ribs, hard enough to lift me off the ground and hurl me deeper into the hallway, where I tumbled two or three more times.

I tried to gasp, but couldn't. Shards of rib bone had punctured my lungs. I was bleeding internally, and badly.

"My sister and I have decided that, perhaps, it would be best to keep you down here with me, Sammie. Oh, does it surprise you that I am still in communication with my sister? Oh, it's easy enough. She's accessible to me through your dream state. So, yes, we have prepared a special place for you down here, beneath my family's mausoleum. With the dead."

He came up to me and, if possible, kicked me even harder, a blow that sent me crashing into the far wall and succeeded, I was certain, in breaking all of my remaining ribs. Blood poured from my mouth, from internal injuries that no one had any right to survive from.

I couldn't think. I couldn't comprehend. I didn't know, entirely, what was happening anymore. The pain was so intense—and happening faster than my own body could repair itself.

"But you have proven to be particularly worrisome, Samantha Moon."

I tried absently to push him away but I was certain that my arm was broken as well. He grabbed me by my bloodied jacket and lifted me up to my feet.

"Let me explain the source of my worry," he said, and then threw me against the nearby hallway wall. My head hit hard enough for me to have briefly passed out. Just briefly. Already, I could feel him lifting me up again.

"I haven't quite figured out why you, of all people, seem stronger than all the others. Yes, my sister within is a particularly evolved dark master, but that doesn't explain it, either. Do you see my dilemma?"

He backhanded me so hard that I was certain my jaw broke.

"You seem to have developed talents that far outweigh the others. Why, Sam? Why?"

He dropped me to the ground, where I slumped into a bloody and broken heap.

"Yes, we need to keep you here where I can keep an eye on you, while we fetch your son. Or, as I refer to him, medallion number three."

He turned and faced me.

My thoughts were scattered, incoherent, shattered. I might have been having a form of a seizure. I couldn't think. I couldn't function. I could barely see.

And as he began walking toward me, to deliver a blow that I knew would either kill me or render me completely useless, something appeared in my thoughts.

A single flame.

# 54.

Within the flame was a creature that I knew all too well. A creature much bigger than me, and much more powerful. A creature who was, in fact, *also* me.

The creature seemed to be waiting impatiently, and as the blurred form of Conner Thurman prepared for his final blow, the creature in the flame rushed toward me.

Filling me. Taking over me.

*Becoming me.*

• • •

The transformation was nearly instant.

My clothes burst from my body as I rapidly grew and contorted. Soon, I was something that didn't belong in this world, nor any world, stronger and bigger than I had any right to be.

In a blink, my left hand reached out and grabbed Conner Thurman around the throat. He tried to speak, but only a strangled gasp emerged.

I lifted him off the ground, still holding him by the neck. I was tall enough now that my hunched shoulder just missed the stained glass windows high above. In fact, I very nearly filled the entire hallway. My leathery wings hung behind me.

I thought of the threats against my son.

I thought of what Kingsley had said to me:

*Cut off the head of the snake.*

And as I lifted him off the ground, as he kicked and gurgled and fought me, I continued squeezing.

And squeezing . . .

Something black and horrible appeared from his open mouth. A serpent, the same snake I had seen coiled around all of the Thurmans. It continued pouring out of Conner Thurman's mouth as if vomited by the Devil himself. Now it hung suspended in the air, twisting and coiling before me.

"*Sssister,*" it hissed, and slowly faded away.

I growled and threw Conner Thurman hard against the far wall, and as he slid down, I swiped a massive claw cleanly through his neck.

# 55.

There were four of us in the library.

Allison was holding Tara's hand. The two of them sat closely together, sharing, perhaps, the world's most unusual bond: both had been possessed simultaneously by a nasty son-of-a-bitch.

Kingsley occasionally patted my knee, and I let him. The gesture seemed to come from a source of support, not flirtation.

Earlier, I had called my sister and confirmed that they were all okay in a safe house. The safe house was, apparently, Kingsley's ski lodge in Arrowhead. I hadn't known Kingsley had a ski lodge in Arrowhead. Either way, all was well, and I breathed a sigh of relief and told them to sit tight for another day or so. I would explain it all later.

I had emerged from the mausoleum as naked as the day I was born and covered with blood—and completely healed. The headless body of Conner Thurman had done something extraordinary before my very eyes: it had literally gone up in smoke.

*So weird,* I thought now, as Kingsley patted my leg again. Tara cried softly as Allison hugged her close.

Allison had been outside the mausoleum, drenching wet and freezing and briefly confused. I helped her back to the bungalow where we changed into some dry clothes. Once done, she and I watched a very unusual procession: Thurman after Thurman emerged from the surrounding woods. All soaked to the bone. All lost. All confused. Some were even hurt. But none permanently so.

Kingsley emerged, too, carrying Edwin in his arms. The young Thurman had taken the worst of Kingsley's efforts to fend them off. Edwin, as far as I knew, was resting in his basement room now. Hurting, but okay.

Earlier, we had explained to Tara what had happened to her and her family. The news was, unsurprisingly, devastating. She looked at me now. "I hate him."

I waited. Outside, the storm had subsided. The trees were no longer threatening to break at their bases. A light rain drifted by the big windows.

"I hate him for what he did to my family. We couldn't fight him. We didn't know how. He manipulated our thoughts, our memories, our words, our actions. We were all his puppets."

I recalled the Source's words: *There is no evil, Samantha Moon.*

I wasn't sure I believed it. I had seen evil firsthand, and I believed it was real. I had seen the joy on the entity's face—or Conner Thurman's face—as it delivered blow after blow, breaking me and my body. A body that had, miraculously, been restored once I had transformed back into my human self.

*Not even a cracked rib.*

"You didn't know that Conner Thurman was still alive?" asked Kingsley.

She shook her head. "No, although the memories of serving him in the mausoleum are returning now . . ." She shuddered.

I didn't want to know what "serving him" entailed.

*Sweet Jesus.*

"He . . . he removed those memories from us."

Kingsley nodded. "He's gone now."

"I know," she said. "I felt him leave . . . and I felt him leave forever."

Allison was nodding. She looked at me and Kingsley. "I felt it, too. Granted, perhaps not as strongly as Tara, but suddenly, he was gone."

Tara nodded absently. I suspected she felt the same, except I knew the trauma of her ordeal ran so deep and for so long, that she would need many months or years to come to terms with what had happened to her and her family.

The Thurman family had a lot of healing to do. After all, did they really know each other? How much of their lives had been controlled by the entity?

I didn't know, but I did know that it was gone. I had seen it flee. To where, I didn't know. Perhaps another willing host. Perhaps even now it was cruising over the earthly plane like a diseased wind, looking for a willing partner . . . or perhaps even, an unwilling one.

*Yes,* I thought. *There is evil.*

The entity might be gone, but his sister was not. His sister was still within me, watching, waiting, existing. I shuddered all over again. Kingsley felt me shudder and patted me again. He added a small squeeze. Flirt.

Junior and Patricia Thurman next came into the room. Although Junior looked confused, he also looked vibrant. Noticeably absent—and perhaps most telling of all that the entity was indeed gone—was that his aura, along with Tara's and all the other Thurmans', was completely free of the black cord. The cursed black cord that had bound them all.

We left Tara with her uncle.

# 56.

I was back on Dome Rock.

The sun had not yet risen. Kingsley and Allison were asleep in the bungalow. It had been hours after the ordeal in the mausoleum.

God, had I really cut off his head?

I had. Or, rather, the thing that lived within me had.

No, it had been me. *I* had made a point to squeeze the life out of Conner Thurman—or the thing that animated Conner Thurman. I had made the decision to remove his head.

He'd *threatened* Anthony. He had been going to *kill* Anthony. *Consume* Anthony, in fact.

Yes, I had cut off his head, and I would do so a thousand more times if I had to.

The rain had finally dissipated. The ocean beyond seemed relatively calm. I could even see stars peeking through the thin cloud layer.

Before me were both medallions: the opal medallion that I had plucked from the ocean's depths, and the amethyst medallion that had once been embedded within my chest. Each glittered dully, catching whatever ambient light there was.

My chest had healed marvelously. Not even a scar.

"Penny for your thoughts," said a voice behind me.

I gasped, turning. I hadn't heard anyone approach, and my inner alarm had failed to notify me of danger. Standing behind me was, of course, the young Librarian. The alchemist. He was wearing jeans and a sweater and shoes that didn't seem appropriate for a hike up Dome Rock.

"I'm sorry to startle you, Samantha Moon."

"How did you get here?"

"The ferries are running again."

"How did you know I was here?"

He smiled and walked around me and stood over the two medallions. "I, too, am intricately linked to these guys."

"Because you created them."

"Yes. Do you mind if I sit?"

"It's a big rock," I said.

He chuckled and sat before me. A small wind blew steadily over us. His short hair didn't move. Neither did his clothing.

"There's some weird shit going on," I said.

"Yes, I imagine so."

"Why am I connected to the medallions?"

"I don't know, Sam, but I suspect it's a combination of many things."

"What things?"

"The vampire who first created you, for one. He was one of the oldest . . . and perhaps even one of the most powerful."

"I don't understand."

"Knowledge and power are always transferred through blood, Samantha. It is the carrier of all information, all knowledge. Have you not noticed that those around you, and those blood-related to you, are growing in power?"

"Yes."

"He infused you with his own knowledge, his own power. Sam, you have abilities you've not yet tapped into."

"I don't want them. I just want to be normal."

"That might still be possible."

I looked at him sharply. "What do you mean?"

He picked up the medallions. "I created these medallions, Samantha, to help someone like you find normalcy again."

"But they also do unspeakable harm," I said.

He nodded sadly. "There was an unforeseen consequence of the medallions, I'll admit."

"As long as they are in existence, my son will always be in danger."

"I cannot deny that, Sam. At least, if all four are in existence. However, they can also give back the normalcy you seek."

"So, my two choices are either normalcy for me or danger to my son."

He nodded once.

"That's not an acceptable option to me," I said.

"Then destroy one, Samantha Moon, and the medallions can never again be used for evil."

I nodded. I had been thinking the same thing. I touched the opal medallion. "What will this one do?" I asked.

"That one will remove your need to feast on blood."

"And the fourth medallion, the one that hangs from Fang's neck?"

Archibald Maximus, the young-looking guy with the old man's name, nodded. "Yes . . . the diamond medallion."

"What will it do?"

"A very interesting medallion, indeed."

I waited. Seagulls circled high above. Something small and undoubtedly furry scurried in the brush at the edge of the dome.

"If you'll recall, the ruby medallion reversed vampirism within your son."

I nodded. "Mostly."

He smiled. "The amethyst medallion gave you the ability to exist in the sun."

"Mostly."

"The opal medallion would remove your need for blood."

"We'll see."

"The diamond medallion grants the user, in effect, *all three*."

"What do you mean?"

"Once the diamond medallion is invoked, Samantha, one would have all the powers of the vampire, without the shortcomings. One would, in effect, have it all."

"Immortality, too?" I asked.

He nodded. "And great power, great strength, everything you currently enjoy. Without that which you don't. It is, in effect, the answer to your prayers."

"Why make only one?" I asked.

He smiled sadly at me. "I only brought forth the medallions into the world, Samantha. Think of me as the potter. I did not create the clay, only the shape within. The energy was always here, waiting. I only gave it shape and form."

"Can you create more?"

"So far, no. But with intent, all things are possible."

"Meaning?"

"When something is wanted bad enough, the Universe answers the call."

"So, for now, all that exists are the four medallions?"

"Yes, one of which is now infused within your son."

"That sounds so weird," I said.

"Life is a little weird, Sam. Beautiful but weird."

"I cannot risk that another will come for me and my son," I said.

"I understand." He looked at me for a long moment. "You do understand that you can wear only one medallion."

I hadn't known that, but I did now. I nodded.

"You must choose one medallion, Sam."

I thought of my options, and I thought of Fang. "I want these medallions destroyed," I said.

He raised an eyebrow. "Both of them?"

"Yes."

"You are giving up the ability to go into the sun? To bypass the need for blood?"

"Yes," I said. "For now. Besides, the sun is overrated. I'm really more of a night person. And, honestly, who really needs Chicken McNuggets, right?"

"You're going to go after the fourth medallion," said Archibald.

"You bet your ass," I said.

He nodded.

"So, what do we do with these?" I asked, indicating the two medallions.

"It saddens the heart, but I shall destroy them. Admittedly, the harm they could cause was unforeseen."

"How will you destroy them?"

"How strong are you, Sam?"

"Stronger than I look."

He chuckled. "Of that I have no doubt. Yes, they are composed of gold and other alchemical materials. And like all alchemical artifacts, the spells within can be severed."

"You want me to break the spell."

"It has to be you, Sam."

Still sitting on the smooth rock, as the sky slowly began lightening, I reached over and picked up the amethyst medallion.

"You're sure about this, Sam? As soon as that medallion is broken, you will have only minutes to get back indoors. Your body will return to the day and night circadian rhythms of the vampire."

"I understand," I said. "For my son, I understand. And it's far too late to use such big words."

He chuckled lightly as I gripped the medallion in both hands.

And applied pressure. A lot of pressure.

Nothing happened at first—but then, suddenly, the medallion snapped in half, followed by what I was certain was a supernatural popping sound. Maximus winced slightly.

I did the same with the opal medallion, and soon four halves lay on the rock before me.

"It is done, Samantha Moon," said Maximus. "Would you mind if I took these with me," he said, indicating the four broken halves. "The metal is of use for other alchemical potions."

"Knock yourself out," I said. "But I do have one question."

"Just one?" he asked.

"Okay, many. Why did you hide the medallion so deep in the cave?"

"It was meant to be a test."

"A test?"

"Yes. The shipwreck was fortuitous in the sense that it gave me an opportunity to hide the medallion somewhere I'd previously not foreseen. Well, not entirely foreseen."

"And to the world it appeared that a treasure had gone down with the ship?"

"Right," he said.

"How would Conner Thurman know about the opal medallion?"

"Conner Thurman didn't. The entity within him did."

"Is that why they built this home on this island? To search for the medallion?"

"Part of the reason, I'm sure. Undoubtedly, they saw the seclusion here as a good thing, too."

"How was I able to find the medallion and he didn't?"

He smiled. "Because it was meant for you."

"I don't understand."

"Or, rather, it was meant for someone like you. Someone worthy. Someone strong. Someone who would bring some light into all of this craziness. Soon, Sam, dawn will break, and you no longer have protection from sunlight."

"Are you coming with me?" I asked.

"No, Sam. I prefer to sit here and watch the sunrise."

"Don't rub it in," I said, slapping his knee.

He smiled sadly. "Go, Sam. You don't have much time."

Indeed, I could already feel my body shutting down with the coming of dawn. I got up and started moving across the domed rock. I looked back once and saw the Librarian now sitting cross-legged, his face lifted to the heavens.

Awaiting dawn.

For some reason, I found tears on my cheeks.

Not too long ago, I had seen my first dawn as a vampire. But now that ability was gone. It didn't have to be, of course. I could have chosen it. Or chosen the opal medallion—and never again have been forced to consume filthy blood.

Now, as I turned back to the trail that would lead down to the bungalows, to where Kingsley and Allison slept, I thought of Fang.

How he had found the fourth medallion, I didn't know.

Where he was, I didn't know.

But I was going to find him.

One way or another.

[THE END]

To be continued in:
*Moon River*
(Vampire for Hire #8)
Coming soon!

# Teeth

# Teeth

The defense attorney circled the witness box and studied the killer. The young man, with his head bowed and hands clasped loosely before him, looked as if he were in a confessional. The attorney nearly chuckled at the image.

*"Forgive me, Father, for I have sucked my girlfriend dry."*

He stopped circling and now stood directly in front of his client. As usual, the young man ignored him and stared down into his lap.

*Remember, Aaron,* thought the attorney. *Your fate rests with me. I'm your friend here, not the enemy.*

The crowd was silent; so silent, in fact, that the attorney actually heard a pen drop, clattering loudly on the polished tiles. The lawyer, however, was not so delusional as to believe that those in the courtroom were holding their collective breaths and waiting for him. Indeed, he knew they were spellbound by the young man. The killer. Hell, the whole damn world seemed spellbound by the young man, whom the press had dubbed the American Vampire.

The attorney removed his glasses dramatically—he always removed them dramatically—and spoke loudly enough for all to hear. After all, this was his big moment, too. This case would make his career.

"Aaron, you have been found guilty for the murder of Annie Hox. Now a new jury must decide your punishment.

In particular, they will decide if you are worth more alive than dead. The ball is in your court, Aaron."

The young man continued staring down at his hands, almost petulantly, like a scolded kid.

*A hell of a scolding,* thought the attorney.

Aaron Parker had always been a quiet young man, the very definition of introverted. Long ago he had learned never to trust anyone, especially not to open up to anyone. Now, sitting here for all the world to see in the witness box, he felt uneasy at best. The uncomfortable chair didn't help, either.

As Aaron shifted again, the lead defender paused in front of him, smelling of expensive cologne and looking, if anything, like he was enjoying himself. Aaron hated him. Aaron hated most people, but he especially hated his own attorney. The polished man looked like the older version of all the kids in school who had made fun of him. All the good-looking kids who had it good and easy.

Aaron never had it easy. Ever.

And so he hated the man, just like he hated all the others.

Despite himself, Aaron inhaled deeply, drawing in the man's cologne. Aaron always had a thing for scents and smells. In fact, he often thought of all his senses as being highly attuned. Especially his sense of taste.

He looked past his attorney, his small darting eyes finding the faces of those sitting in the courtroom beyond. Hundreds of faces, belonging to everyone from family members and friends, to the media and the damn curious. Expressions ranging from revulsion to amusement to horror. And all were staring at him. Every one of them.

*Just another freak show,* he thought.

As he gazed at the crowd, as he watched those watching him, he did what he always did, what many in the crowd had noticed throughout the course of this outrageous trial:

He opened his mouth, just a little, and the tip of his tongue poked out as he unconsciously ran it back and forth along his upper incisors. He did this for perhaps ten seconds—

And then he opened his mouth a little more, as he always did. Now his roaming tongue stopped at his massive canines—teeth that projected down from his upper jaw like mighty ivory stalagmites—

Wet, gleaming tongue sliding down one of the freakishly long stalagmites—the right one, in fact—down, down this massive fang, stopping finally at the tip. There it paused, and, like an elephant's curious trunk, gently tapped the tip of the tooth. Tapped it hesitantly, as if testing it. Tapped it carefully, as if fearful of it. Tapped it again and again and again . . .

"Aaron, can you please recount for the court the events that led to the killing of Annie Hox?"

The long tongue retracted like a frightened turtle and his lips slammed shut and the young man turned his attention away from a frowning older woman sitting in the second row—a woman who seemed to be staring at him almost sideways, as if afraid to look the Devil in the eye. Aaron Parker settled his gaze onto the smooth-shaven face of the defense attorney.

"Where would you like me to begin?" Aaron asked shyly, speaking in such a way that his lips barely moved, a way that completely concealed his teeth.

"At the beginning," said the attorney.

"The beginning . . . was a long time ago," said Aaron.

"Remember, Aaron, this is a new jury. They haven't heard your case."

The young man chuckled softly. "All they had to do was turn on the TV."

"Please, Aaron, just tell us your story."

The young man inhaled deeply and motioned vaguely to his mouth. He said, "I suppose it all started when they grew in."

"*They*, Aaron?"

"My teeth, of course."

"Thank you, Aaron, now will you please display your teeth to the jury?"

Aaron felt his pulse quicken. He was always aware of his own pulse. Vigilantly aware. And it quickened now because showing his teeth went against his every instinct. Showing his teeth inspired questions. Showing his teeth induced ridicule. Showing his teeth had often gotten him beat up, and worse.

"Please, Aaron, this is important."

*Dance for us, monkey boy,* thought Aaron.

Not wanting to see their reactions, he closed his eyes and turned his face toward the jury box. And opened his mouth. He might not have seen their faces, but he heard the gasps. And he heard their fervent whisperings.

*I am more than my teeth.*

"That's quite enough, Aaron," said his attorney. "Thank you."

*Now they know you're a freak,* thought Aaron.

*Yeah? So what else is new?*

He closed his mouth and slumped back in the chair, trying unsuccessfully to hide, and found himself staring up once again at the defense attorney. The man was indeed good-looking: muscular neck, strong jaw, square shoulders. Aaron went back to his clean-shaven neck, which was roped with thick muscle. And he kept on looking, searching really . . .

*Ah, there it is.*

The man's jugular vein, pulsing steadily, strongly. Aaron's stomach growled. Loudly.

The attorney heard the young man's stomach growl, saw the laser-focused intent in the young man's eyes. He paused in mid-pace.

*Jesus, he's staring at you again,* he thought. *No, he's staring at your neck.*

The attorney, despite himself, swallowed.

But Aaron was no longer thinking of the attorney. Indeed, as he gazed upon the man's neck he found himself thinking of Annie Hox. Specifically, her blood. Her sweet, salty, precious, delicious blood.

The young man felt an immediate swelling in his pants.

The attorney, who found the young man's gaze disconcerting at best, stammered slightly as he spoke again: "So your problems began, Aaron, when your teeth grew in?"

"Yes."

"In particular, the canines."

"Yes."

"The canines—often called cuspids, dog teeth, or fangs—are generally the longest of the mammalian teeth. Most species have four per individual, two in the upper jaw and two in the lower, all separated by the shorter and flatter incisors."

Aaron almost smiled. "If you say so."

"Would it be accurate to say that your adult canines grew in too long?" said the attorney.

This time Aaron did smile. "I would say so."

The attorney now moved over to the defense table, picked up an index card, and read from it: "Abnormal or excessive canine growth is a rare phenomenon, afflicting one in eleven million. It's considered an atavism, or a throwback gene, something that was necessary to our species hundreds of thousands of years ago, but not so much now."

"Lucky me," said Aaron.

"How old were you when your adult canines grew in, Aaron?"

"Seven."

"Did the other kids ever call you names?"

"Of course."

"Kids can be mean," said the attorney, frowning, nodding sympathetically. *Personalize the examination,* he thought. *Humanize the killer. Reach out to the jury.* "Cruel, even. What sort of names did they call you, Aaron?"

The young man had spent a lifetime trying to forget the names, trying to forget the nightmare that was his childhood. But here, in this courtroom, there was no forgetting.

*Not after what you've done.*

And so he dutifully answered the question: "*Aaroncula* was a favorite. So was *Scarin' Aaron.* But mostly they just called me *Fang.*"

"Did not the kids at your school come up with a song?" asked the attorney.

"Yes," said Aaron. *And thank you for reminding me of that, asshole.*

"Would you sing it for us, Aaron?"

As the young man cleared his throat, the crowd leaned forward. *This isn't* American Idol, *people,* he thought. *Now,* American Vampire *is a different story . . .*

He grinned inwardly and in a sort of sing-song voice, he sang: "*Vampire, Vampire with his teeth he popped a tire.*"

The attorney smirked, and some in the courtroom actually laughed.

*Yes, funny, isn't it?*

When the attorney seemed to remember that he was in a court of law, his expression returned to one of dour professionalism, and he asked, "How did you feel, Aaron, when the other kids made fun of you?"

"Like a mutant. I felt hideous. Kind of like I do now."

The attorney held his gaze. "Did you believe them, Aaron? Did you believe you were a vampire?"

"No, not at first. Hell, I didn't even know what a vampire was. I went home one day and asked my mom what the kids were talking about and she told me. As she did so, I remember seeing the hurt in her face, and the shame of being poor and not being able to fix my teeth."

"You had no dental insurance?"

"We did, yes. I think. But nothing cosmetic, from what I remember. The removal of the teeth was a personal choice and the insurance wouldn't cover it."

"So you had to live with them? Your teeth, that is."

"Yes."

Aaron spied a small woman sitting alone at the back of the courtroom, huddled to herself and weeping silently. His mother. She caught his eye and tried to smile bravely. He nodded to her reassuringly. His teeth weren't her fault, after all. One in eleven million. Dumb luck. But he knew she blamed herself for his deformity.

"And the kids continued to make fun of you throughout school?"

"Oh, yes."

"Would you say relentlessly?"

"Yes," said Aaron. "Every day. Dozens of times a day, if not hundreds."

"And," said the attorney carefully, turning to the jury, "like a child who's told he or she is stupid or wouldn't amount to anything—"

"I began to believe it," said Aaron.

"You began to believe what, exactly?"

Aaron knew the attorney knew the answer. This show was for the new jury. *Just play along,* thought Aaron. *The man's trying to save your life, after all.*

"I began to believe I was a vampire."

The lawyer let the words hang in the air. Aaron didn't move, didn't need to turn or look up to know that he had everyone's attention.

The lawyer, he knew, was building an insanity defense. *I'm not insane. I just love blood.*

Slowly, he licked his teeth . . .

"How old were you, Aaron, when you started to believe you were a vampire?"

"Fifteen."

"Was there one defining event?"

There was, of course, and the attorney knew it, and Aaron walked the courtroom through it, as well. It had happened one day when he cut his finger. Aaron was making dinner for his family. He liked to make dinner, liked to cook. Hell, he liked doing anything that kept him indoors and out of sight. He was chopping onions and wiping his eyes and not paying attention—when the blade went straight through the side of his index finger. It hurt like hell. The cut was to the bone. And there was blood. Lots of it. And as he bled, he just stood there at the kitchen sink, dripping, doing nothing to staunch the flow of blood.

"And what happened next, Aaron?" asked his attorney.

"I tasted it."

The attorney sucked in some air—and so did a lot of other people in the courtroom. One or two even turned their heads.

*Wimps . . .*

"You drank your own blood?"

"Yes."

"Did you enjoy it?"

"Oh, yes."

The lawyer paused and turned again to his notes, and Aaron's tongue darted out between his canines. Like a snake's tongue. In and out. In and out. Another bad habit, and one his tongue had seemingly evolved to accommodate, for it was itself now long and narrow. If Aaron wanted to lick the bottom of his chin he could.

"So what did you do next, Aaron?"

"I began cutting myself."

"And sucking your own blood?"

"Yes."

"Did you only cut yourself?"

"No, sometimes I used my teeth."

The attorney paused and looked pointedly at the jury box. Aaron knew what the look was meant to say. The look was meant to say that Aaron was clearly crazy, and how could they possibly condemn a crazy man to death?

*I'm not crazy,* thought Aaron. *I just want blood . . .*

"So you bit yourself?" asked the attorney.

"Yes."

"Where?"

"Mostly my wrists. But my whole arm was and is fair game."

The attorney looked slightly ill. "And then what would you do?"

"I would suck my blood, of course."

"Like a vampire."

Aaron nodded. "Like a vampire."

The attorney gave the jury another knowing look. "Aaron, could you please show the court your arm?"

Aaron fought his initial reaction to rebel, to hide, and instead sighed deeply and unbuttoned his cuff and pushed up his sleeve. He displayed his forearm for the jury to see. Nearly hairless, his pale arm was crisscrossed and dotted with puffy white scars, some fresher than others.

"Would you say, Aaron, that you finally found a use for your teeth?"

The young man grinned. "You could say that."

"Aaron, could you please describe for us the process of biting yourself and drinking your own blood."

And so he did. Once Aaron punctured his flesh with his own teeth, he would draw the blood straight from his veins and into his mouth. Often he would gargle the blood and swish it around like fine wine. When he was done sucking and drinking—or, *feeding,* as he referred to it—he was left with the most incredible hickeys, hickeys that would last sometimes for months.

"Of course," said Aaron, finishing his recounting, "I always kept my arms covered in public."

"To hide the scars and hickeys."

"Yes."

"Some of these wounds look fresh, Aaron."

The young man nodded and pointed to two scabby holes just inside his elbow. "Sure. I was sucking here just last night, in jail."

The attorney looked like he might have thrown up a little in the back of his mouth. The man, a true professional, obviously fought through his discomfort. "Do you ever get sick after sucking your own blood, Aaron? Surely, this can't be healthy."

"All the time. I was sick just last night. Puked blood everywhere. Looked like something from a Stephen King novel."

"But you continue doing it, even when you get sick?"

"It's not easy being me," said the young man, grinning.

"Aaron, did you ever seek any kind of professional help?"

"No."

"Why not?"

"Because there's nothing wrong with me."

"But you think you're a vampire."

Aaron grinned broadly, purposefully exposing the long, slightly curved sweep of his upper canines. "Maybe I am, Counsel."

The lawyer looked again at the jury box, his expression almost smug. *See,* it seemed to say, *is the kid loony or what?*

"Aaron, when did you first meet Annie Hox?"

"When I was seventeen."

"How old are you now?"

"Eighteen."

"And where did you meet her?"

"I met her at one of my jobs. I was working as a security guard for a warehouse. The graveyard shift, of course." Aaron smiled. "Annie worked there as well."

"What attracted you to her?"

"She was different, special. She was one of the few people who accepted me for who I am. She was what some people would call a *goth*."

"As in *gothic*," said the attorney, pacing slowly now in front of the jury box. "As in someone who dresses in black, paints their nails black, powders their face white, and reads Anne Rice novels. In short, someone obsessed with vampires."

"Yes," said Aaron, grinning at the stereotypical image the attorney drew. "She was that and more."

"Were you intimate with her?"

As soon as he finished asking the question, a woman in the courtroom began sobbing. A familiar sobbing. Aaron didn't have to look up to know who it was. Annie's mother. A big woman, she had sobbed throughout the entire court proceedings.

*So much for my private life . . .*

"Yes, we were intimate."

"Did you love her, Aaron?"

"With all my heart. Like I said, she accepted me for who I was. She loved my teeth. Hell, when we kissed, sometimes she would even lick them."

The attorney waited for the mother, who had burst into tears again, to settle down, and when she finally did, he asked, "Did you love Annie Hox, Aaron?"

The young man thought back to the pretty goth girl who accepted him for exactly who he was, the pretty goth girl with whom he had opened up to and shared so much, the pretty goth girl who listened to him attentively and treated him as if he mattered.

"Yes," he said. "I did. Annie was my savior."

"Then why did you kill her, Aaron?"

The young man seemed to shrink in upon himself, as if he were slowly imploding. The attorney had noticed this curious display from the young man before. *A defensive reaction, perhaps? As if the kid is trying to shrink away and disappear.*

The attorney didn't know, but the young man never failed to mystify him. And repulse him.

Aaron was indeed trying to shrink away; in particular, from the horrific image of Annie dying in his arms. Now, from the depths of the witness chair, he ran his fingers through his greasy black hair and looked out across the courtroom to Annie's mother. The woman was crying softly into her hands and rocking back and forth.

"It was an accident. I never meant to kill her."

"Tell us what happened on the night she died, Aaron."

"We'd gone to a party. One of her friend's goth parties."

"What did her friends think of you, Aaron?"

"They loved me. Sure, I was still a freak, but I was a superfreak." Aaron chuckled at his own play on words. "It was the first time that I could be me and not have to hide my teeth. It was the first time that I had friends."

"You were seventeen?"

"Yes."

"And it was the first time you had friends?"

"Yes."

The attorney nodded sadly. "Go on, Aaron. What happened after the party?"

After a night of partying and drinking and smoking, Aaron and Annie had left together. They stopped at a Taco Bell, then headed over to a park to eat.

"You both were drinking and smoking marijuana that night?"

"Yes, everyone was."

"What time did you arrive at the park?"

"Three, three-thirty in the morning."

"Thank you, go on."

"But we didn't get much eating done. As soon as I stopped the car Annie was all over me."

"Had she smoked or ingested anything other than alcohol or marijuana?"

"Yes. Ecstasy."

The attorney then reminded jurors of earlier evidence that verified Annie Hox had extremely high levels of MDMA, or Ecstasy, in her blood system. "Go on, Aaron."

Or, as one reporter would later put it: *what little of her blood remained.*

Aaron continued: "So we ditched the Taco Bell and moved into the backseat and started . . ." He shifted in his seat. "You know, doing it."

"Doing it? You mean having intercourse?"

"Yes."

"What happened next, Aaron?"

*Pervert . . .*

"About halfway into it, Annie had an idea. She thought it would be hot if I sucked her neck. That is, if a real-live vampire sucked on her neck."

"So she asked you to suck blood from her neck?"

Aaron nodded. "I told her no and that she was drunk and high, and she said fine and started getting up off my lap. But I didn't want her to get up from my lap. I wasn't, you know, finished yet . . ."

The young man actually blushed, and the attorney silently approved. *Blushing shows the jury you're still human, Aaron.* "So what did you do next?"

So Aaron told him. He told them all. And as he spoke, his voice grew stronger and he sat a little straighter. And as he spoke, his teeth showed more and more, flashing brilliantly in the muted lights of the courtroom . . .

He didn't want Annie to get up off his lap. He liked her just where she was, and so he told her, yes, he would suck from her neck. He would, in fact, drink her blood. She squealed and clapped and gave him a kiss so big that it had literally taken his breath away. And as he was left gasping for air, she lowered herself back down upon him, back down into his lap, and Aaron thought he had died and gone to heaven.

"Were you a virgin up to this point, Aaron?"

"Yes."

The attorney nodded. "Tell us what happened next."

So Aaron did. With Annie on his lap, rocking slowly and rhythmically, he had pulled aside her pitch-black hair, exposing the smooth sweep of her delicate neck, a neck that was now slick with sweat. Immediately, he found himself enchanted by the hypnotic throb of her carotid artery. Never before had he drank from another. Never before had he tasted another's blood.

This would be another first in a night of firsts, and his excitement was nearly overwhelming. Annie must have sensed his excitement, must have felt it deep inside her, for she gasped and moaned and rode him even harder.

The throbbing in her neck picked up in tempo. Her slick skin reflected some of the distant ambient street lights. The rapid pulsing in her neck glinted like a strobing light. Like a beacon. Beckoning him . . .

He lowered his mouth to that smooth, sweeping, gleaming neck, pulling back his lips and fully exposing his God-given fangs. Saliva formed under his tongue, threatening to spill out of his mouth, and as he drew closer to her neck, the beating vein disappeared from view and so he went solely on feel. On instinct.

First the tips of his teeth brushed her skin lightly. At the slight sensation, Annie trembled almost violently. Aaron could feel her excitement, literally washing over him.

"Do it," she whispered hoarsely in his ear. "Now."

He positioned his teeth over the pulsating vein and slowly applied pressure. Annie stiffened briefly, but continued thrusting against him. He applied more pressure. Now she gasped, paused briefly, but picked up speed again. He applied further pressure, biting hard into her soft neck, his own saliva spilling out and dribbling down her throat.

She ground her hips against his own. He heard her breathing through clenched teeth. She was in pain. And loving it.

Finally his teeth punched through, piercing her flesh and artery. Annie cried out. Blood filled his mouth, gushing in as if he had wrapped his mouth around a garden hose.

Annie didn't stop riding him; indeed, she heaved herself against him, faster and harder than ever. It was all he could do to keep her from bucking free, to keep his teeth from inadvertently tearing open her neck.

Aaron could barely keep up with the flow of blood. He swallowed great quantities of it, mouthful after sweet mouthful. Like a hungry babe drinking from his mother's teat. The warmth of her precious hemoglobin spread through him, coating his esophagus, his stomach. His lips. And now some of it began to spill free. Down her neck, down over her bare shoulders and breasts.

And still she continued to thrust. Her powerful movements rocked him, but not enough for him to lose his grip on her neck. Oh no. Like a pit bull, he held firm.

And still he drank.

Her blood was sweet and salty and coppery. It tasted far different than his own. He hadn't expected that. A pleasant surprise.

God, she tasted so damned good. So *perfect*.

Aaron couldn't imagine a more intimate encounter: two people connected in so many ways. His heart soared. His love for Annie soared. He loved her for letting him drink from her. He loved her for accepting him for who he was. He loved her in so many ways . . .

He sat back now in the witness chair, words escaping him. Tears flooded his eyes. He didn't bother to control them. He didn't care what others thought of him. Not anymore.

Aaron's attorney was standing before the witness box, hands folded loosely in front of him, handsome face somber and bone-pale.

"But you went too far, didn't you Aaron?" asked his attorney.

Aaron nodded. And he kept on nodding . . .

He had known he had to stop sucking her. He had never consumed this much blood before. Too much. And so much of it was spilling out now, flowing down her back and chest, puddling in his lap, soaking into his car seat.

But he couldn't stop.

Making love to her felt so good, so amazingly perfect— especially while simultaneously drinking her down—

That's when she started hitting him, beating his shoulders and back, scratching him, clawing him, begging him to stop. But he couldn't. *He wouldn't.*

Not now. *He was so close . . .*

He felt his own blood streaming down his back, pouring from the deep furrows dug from her black nails. And still he sucked. And still he drank. She had been fighting hard, but now she was losing her strength, her resistance weakening.

She fought him to the very end, beating weakly against his back, begging him to stop. But no amount of clawing or screaming or begging would stop him now. And now he was aware of her heartbeat growing fainter and fainter. Less and less blood was pumping into his mouth. His stomach was painfully full.

*She's dying,* he thought. *You have to stop.*

But he didn't. *Couldn't.* He was so close to climaxing. So tantalizingly close . . .

Finally she quit hitting his back, her hands falling limply to her side, and when her blood ceased to pump into his mouth, Aaron Parker the American Vampire climaxed mightily, powerfully, exploding into her.

He was certain she had died the instant he came.

His words hung in the courtroom, echoing faintly, like the sound of Annie's heartbeat just minutes before she had passed. Another woman was holding Annie's mother tightly, who now sobbed soundlessly into her shoulder.

The attorney crossed his arms in front of his chest and studied the young man in front of him. "You didn't mean to kill her, did you Aaron?"

"No."

"You loved her, didn't you?"

"With all my heart."

"And do you miss her?"

"Every minute," said Aaron. "Of every day."

"Aaron, do you believe you are a vampire?"

Aaron didn't move. Not at first. But then the left corner of his lip curled up, revealing a small section of the mammoth tusk that hung from his upper jaw. The young man nodded, and kept on nodding.

"Oh, yes," he said. "Very much so."

• • •

Aaron Parker was sentenced to life in a high-security mental institution. Having saved the young man's life, the attorney had done his job and was pleased, although he would forever be known as that *vampire's attorney*, something he would later regret.

A month after sentencing, a sedated Aaron Parker was hauled into the asylum's dental office, a creepy room located in the far corner of its vast basement. The single chair was commonly known as the "torture chair" by the asylum's residents. After all, any patient with a tendency of biting the staff was subjected to the removal of all of his or her teeth.

And Aaron had a hell of a tendency to bite.

After an hour of strenuous work, an exhausted dentist held up two extraordinarily long canines, both of which would later be purchased by a popular occult museum in Hollywood, where they were proudly displayed in a polyurethane case near the bones of the Elephant Man.

A month after the removal of Aaron's canine teeth, a guard at the asylum was found dead at his desk, his neck having been thoroughly chewed through, nearly decapitating the man. There was surprisingly little blood found at the scene.

Seven months later, the occult museum was robbed, too, its owner killed on-site in a similar fashion. The only items stolen were the vampire's two fangs.

The whereabouts of Aaron Parker, aka the American Vampire, aka Fang, are unknown to this day . . .

[THE END]

## [ OTHER BOOKS BY J.R. RAIN ]

STANDALONE NOVELS
*The Lost Ark*
*The Body Departed*
*Elvis Has Not Left the Building*
*Silent Echo*

COLLABORATIONS
*Cursed!* with Scott Nicholson
*The Vampire Club* with Scott Nicholson
*Dragon Assassin* with Piers Anthony

VAMPIRE FOR HIRE SERIES
*Moon Dance*
*Vampire Moon*
*American Vampire*
*Moon Child*
*Christmas Moon*
*Vampire Dawn*
*Vampire Games*
*Moon Island*
*Moon River*

SAMANTHA MOON SHORT STORIES
"Teeth"
"Vampire Nights"
"Vampires Blues"
"Vampire Dreams"
"Halloween Moon"
"Vampire Gold"

JIM KNIGHTHORSE TRILOGY
*Dark Horse*
*The Mummy Case*
*Hail Mary*

SPINOZA TRILOGY
*The Vampire With the Dragon Tattoo*
*The Vampire Who Played Dead*
*The Vampire in the Iron Mask*

GRAIL QUEST TRILOGY
*Arthur*
*Merlin*
*Lancelot*

ALADDIN TRILOGY
with Piers Anthony
*Aladdin Relighted*
*Aladdin Sins Bad*
*Aladdin and the Flying Dutchman*

WALKING PLAGUE TRILOGY
with Elizabeth Basque
*Zombie Patrol*
*Zombie Rage*
*Zombie Mountain*

SPIDER SERIES
with Scott Nicholson and H.T. Night
*Bad Blood*
*Spider Web*

NICK CAINE SERIES
with Aiden James
*Temple of the Jaguar*
*Treasure of the Deep*

GHOST FILES SERIES
edited with Scott Nicholson
*Ghost College*
*Ghost Fire*
*Ghost Soldier*
*Ghost Hall*

SHORT STORY
COLLECTIONS
*The Bleeder and Other Stories*
*Vampire Rain and Other Stories*
*The Santa Call: A Christmas
  Story*

# ABOUT THE AUTHOR

J.R. RAIN is an ex-private investigator who now writes
the Pacific Northwest. He lives in a small house on a
with his small dog, Sadie, who has more energy than Ro
Please visit him at www.jrrain.com.